SNOWBLOODED

Also by Emma Sterner-Radley

Whispering Wildwood

The Mapmaking Magicians Series
Silver Beasts
Golden Sea
Copper Throne

SNOWBLOODED

EMMA STERNER-RADLEY

SOLARIS

First published 2024 by Solaris
an imprint of Rebellion Publishing Ltd,
Riverside House, Osney Mead,
Oxford, OX2 0ES, UK
www.solarisbooks.com

ISBN: 978-1-83786-068-5
Copyright © 2024 Emma Sterner-Radley

10 9 8 7 6 5 4 3 2 1

A CIP catalogue record for this book is available from the
British Library.

Designed & typeset by Rebellion Publishing

Printed in the UK

THIS BOOK IS DEDICATED TO TWO WOMEN WHO
URGED ME TOWARD MY DREAMS

MY DEAREST WIFE AMANDA RADLEY

AND MY DEARLY MISSED SISTER, FRIEND, AND HERO,
MALIN STERNER (1973-2011)

Out of this flask your death by drops is flowing.
All unobserved, as laugh and song go by.
Trust me, a troop of maggots fiercely glowing,
Pours from yon glass that now you tilt on high.
You are consumed. Into tears you are turning.

— Carl Michael Bellman
"To Old Movitz, Ill with Consumption: An Elegy" (1790).
Translation by Charles Wharton Stork (1917),
The American Scandinavian Foundation.

I don't know what I'm saying or doing.
First, I'm freezing and then I am glowing,
every woman can set me a-flutter, every woman
can set met a-fire.

— Wolfgang Amadeus Mozart
"Non so più cosa son, cosa faccio" from *The Marriage of Figaro* (1786).
Translation by Henry Grafton Chapman (1911), G. Schirmer.

CHAPTER 1

VALOUR

VALOUR HEARD HOLLOW whispers within the dark. The voices of regular people, folklore creatures, and even the old gods. Heimdal, Freja, Oden, Tor, Sif, Loke, all of them. With the logic of dreams, Valour knew they walked the same grimy cobblestones and stood in the same shadowed alleyways as she did. She couldn't call out to them, though. Therefore, she was godsdamned trapped alone as her routine nightmare scenarios started playing out. Over and over.

She woke and grabbed the sweat-dampened covers, panting like a wounded animal, her heart racing and hurting. The images from the tunnels and the remembered smell of soured blood refused to fade. She sat up and snarled at herself. She had no patience for this. Valour had no patience at all. What she had was a job to do and nightmares to outrun. Not allowing herself breakfast, she washed, dressed, and still half-asleep stormed out while braiding her hair. She opened the door and... godsdamnit. She was staring right into a bloody broom closet! She shut it fast and looked around. No one was about. Thank Heimdal no one saw one of the highest-ranking assassins in the city fail at navigating a hotel hallway. She cursed fouler than a band of drunk sailors, opened the correct door, and left.

Rushing through Vinterstock's harbour, dodging between washerwomen and dock workers, Valour saw the last clippers to sail here before winter filled the sea with ice floes. The ships were lined up and ready to unload the tea, cocoa, coffee, spices, and other modern goods in their hold. Up top at least. Below the official cargo, there'd be crates of illegal magic tinctures. Shrewdness tonics, brawniness tonics, wellness tonics, and other 'ness tonics. Or simply 'ness. She wouldn't be partaking, despite the fact that that she could do with being smarter, faster, or stronger. While the drugs boosted your body to change certain things about itself, when one started using 'ness, it was almost impossible to stop. And, of course, there was a steep toll taken on the body each time. Not to mention your coin-purse.

She'd buy some fresh tea, though, and something to eat. Her favourite bakery was sure to have used some of the newly arrived ingredients to create tarts with sweetened cream, warm buns with exotic spices, and delicate creations crafted from sugar. However, she'd need coin for that. This brought her back to work, back to today's kill, which had to be accomplished before noon, when the gloriam prayer would be held at the Assassins of Axsten's sanctum.

She hurried to the address where the mark was lodging, passing rundown hovels that soon gave way to new-built townhouses, shops, and coffee-houses on cobbled streets. Her investigation had shown that there was an apothecary next to the address she'd been given. Now she lingered there, pretending to browse the apothecary window while putting her gloves on.

Gods in Asgård, how she hated waiting.

Chapter 2

PETRICHOR

PETRICHOR BURNED THE letter unread. Why shouldn't he toss it in the fireplace, watching it turn to cinders as he drank his morning coffee? The accursed thing wouldn't change anything and hope, as well as dreams, were a luxury and so not for him. He sat very still, watching the paper curl and burn. A solitary quiet enclosed the astronomy tower, all but him slumbering. Soon the university's students—about his age but without his life experience—would fill the halls, laughing and discussing the day's lectures. How he envied those rich brats, engaging in matters of the mind, keeping their hands clean, never having been broken.

Outside his window the stars died, blotted out with grey light by the dawn, as unable to stop their fate as he was.

The letter was nought but ash now.

Never mind. Another day had begun and he must get to work. At least he was exceptionally good at what he did. He tied his simple cravat, not meeting his own gaze in the looking-glass. He sipped the soot-black coffee, careful not to spill. This unembellished ensemble in grey broadcloth had cost him dearly. Tailors charged aristocratic fees and then always wanted to include deuced frills, lace, silk, or brash patterns. His tasteful clothes marked him out as an intellectual. Other than that, they might as well be a uniform and like his body—kept muscled but nimble—they were calculated to be perfectly suited for his work but not make him stand out.

He checked his knives were tucked neatly inside the specially sewn slots in his outercoat and that his new tricorne hat hid as much as possible of his face. Then he left to see to the day's kill.

CHAPTER 3

BLOOD IN THE SNOW

ACCORDING TO THE tolling of the tower bells it was an hour into Valour's watch and no sight of her mark yet. She was freezing her arse off. Maybe she should've spent her last pay packet on a new winter cloak instead of giving it to Widow Lindberg for firewood and supplies. No. She could warm herself by jumping on the spot, the old widow couldn't. There was a scent on the air, the blend of pine and iron that meant snowfall. Godsdamnit. She glared up at the bruised purple and grey sky, spotting clouds pregnant with snow that would fall within the hour. She recalled what her late mother always said: "Fresh snow is rotten news for us assassins, it shows up the blood."

Busy sulking about the weather, Valour nearly missed her mark arriving. Here the foreign aristocrat was, standing around boasting to an elderly local nobleman about his 'grand tour' and all the cities he'd seen and the operas he'd attended. No sooner had she gotten a good look at his rouged cheeks, powdered wig, and a ridiculous beauty mark painted at the corner of his mouth, than he had accepted an invitation from a shapely lady—in similar wig, rouge, and with a much larger beauty spot—into her posh townhouse, which of course Valour had done no research on. Shit.

Stomping her feet to keep from freezing her toes off, Valour waited. But there was absolutely no bloody point, as her mark didn't come back out. Instead, much later, she heard him some distance away, crowing about dancing something called 'La Crevette' at a court somewhere. The lady's house must've had a back door. Double shit!

She snuck around the row of houses until she got to where he stood, then ducked into the opening of a shadowed alleyway so she could hear but not be seen.

"I am glad you decided to visit our city." The local nobleman nervously smoothed his age-frosted ponytail. "We up here in Scandinavia are not spoiled with aristocratic guests, and I know Vinterstock's noble count, or greve as the title is here, was happy to see you and hopes you shall visit again tonight."

"Perhaps. I had not seen him since he was a young man visiting my country in the company of your king. And I must say, I found your greve eerily changed. It must be this wretched place. I did not expect Vinterstock to be so cold and small. Or so filthy."

His tone made it sound like he was a hair's breadth from calling their city, or perhaps their whole country, a backwater hole.

"Ah. Well, cities are dirty and the North is cold," said the other man apologetically.

Her mark didn't answer immediately, but she saw him turn to glance back into the townhouse. His make-up was smudged, that beauty spot now more like the imprint of a splatted spider.

"Mm-hmm. Tell me, Monsieur Ädelberg, the delicious sorceress you introduced me to in there. Would she perhaps entertain me tonight, instead of your taciturn greve?"

The Vinterstockian noble, apparently by the last name of Ädelberg, hesitated. No wonder. The greve had ordered the hit on this foreign fop because he was known to kill noblewomen and then escape justice by paying or blackmailing his way out. Obviously, her countryman did not want the lady killed. And the title of *sorceress* must be wrong; the magic of the old gods was meant to have vanished with the Vikings. Well, except for in the tonics. Right? She wasn't sure about any of this. She focused on her work.

Valour groaned under her breath. She could solve Ädelberg's problem if he just left. Sanctioned by authorities or not, assassinations were not to be carried out in front of witnesses. When Ädelberg was gone, Valour would sneak behind the fop and knock him out. After that, she only had to drag him the few steps down this alley into the opening to one of the city's underground tunnels. There she'd slit his throat and dispose of his body in the mass graves created for this very reason. Alas, the Vinterstockian bonehead didn't leave but stood there with the foreign killer, in the bloody cold, discussing masked balls. By the time Ädelberg *finally* said his goodbyes to head to a coffee-house, snow was falling.

At last, her mark was alone, leering up at the lady's townhouse.

Valour closed her eyes for a tick, bracing herself and breathing in the scent of snow. The deep breaths staved off the images from her nightmares creeping back into her mind. Almost.

She picked up a loose brick, slunk silently out of the shadows, and brought her makeshift weapon down upon his head. He fell backwards and she caught him, dragging him into the dark and his awaiting death. She tried very hard not to leave a trail of blood in the snow.

CHAPTER 4

GLORIAM

PETRICHOR HAD FINISHED his duty. He had chased his mark down into the tunnels, ensuring she halted by the mass graves so he wouldn't have to touch her bloodied corpse, then slit her throat while saying the sacred words.

"On the command of the Assassins of Axsten and the Greve of Vinterstock, you are hereby axed. May your offences be atoned for in the arms of death."

'Axed' was wrong, of course. A heritage from olden days when assassinations were displays performed with axes in the town's squares. Now, it was a concealed procedure, usually done with a razor-sharp blade. Still, he said the words that had been beaten into him. He probably said them in his dreams. Not that Petrichor dreamed much; most of his nights were sleepless and when he did sleep, it was only a bottomless, black void.

It wasn't his duty to stay while the mark died. Nevertheless, he always did. Despite the vile stench of the mass graves that had to be left open for identification of the marks. He didn't stay to pay his respects—that was soft-heartedness—but perhaps to show that he took responsibility for the death. To act as witness and sentinel as this woman passed on to whatever came next.

Before ascending to the streets, he wiped his blade on the handkerchief he carried for this purpose, and obviously washed meticulously each night, while trying to remember what crimes this woman had committed to merit execution without trial. Something about dead aristocratic children? It mattered not. Petrichor followed orders and didn't play god by choosing who got to live, unlike Valour. He couldn't afford scruples if he was to

15

carry out his plan. He stopped himself, remembering the burned letter and how impossible that path was. Hope was a weed. It grew without being planted and then refused to be fully eradicated.

Up on the streets, he checked his pocket watch. A quarter to twelve. Fifteen minutes until he had to be at the sanctum for gloriam. He would be there precisely on time. Valour, however, was sure to be late.

As Petrichor walked, snow fell. It landed like a fine dusting of sugar on the green-patinaed copper domes of the towers atop the greve's palace, which stood in the middle of this small but proud nation's second-largest city. Soon he spotted the dark, wooden pointed gables of the Assassins of Axsten's sanctum. He slipped between foul-smelling people like a shadow, never touching anyone despite the overcrowded streets. People should be *forced* to wash. Right when the tower bells began chiming midday, he knocked on the sanctum's doors, aiming for the engraving of the guild's crest—a capital *A* with a knife through it—burned into these doors just as it was branded into the skin of every assassin. Halcyon opened them. The current leader of the order was a competent, striking man of about thirty. Like Petrichor, he had become a member as an orphan. But unlike him, he was not a Vinterstock street urchin, having instead arrived on a trader's ship from the East. He spoke of his homeland of tall temples, never-ending sunshine, and dragon lizards. Petrichor took that with a fistful of salt; he'd been a toddler, how could he remember anything rational? Children's brains were swampy things, filled with too much imagination and emotion.

"Pre-eminent Brother Petrichor. Come on in!"

Halcyon ushered Petrichor in while blowing on his bruised, bleeding knuckles. He was the only person Petrichor liked, due to his intelligence, competence, refinement, and tolerance. Yet, those bloody knuckles reminded Petrichor of something he despised in their leader: Halcyon boxed. Sometimes Valour joined him. They could both be brutes and should've been given monikers that reflected their loutish natures. None of the order's designations fit their owners. Take 'Petrichor'—what did he have to do with the smell after rain? Why in the deuces could they not have been given names like Karl or Elsa?

The order had its eccentricities, he supposed. Sweden was now mainly Christian with a smattering of recent immigrants bringing their religions. The lion's share of Vinterstock, meanwhile, had split into two: one part following Christianity and the other secretly clinging to the old Norse religion. But in this sanctum and for the people within it, the Order of Axsten had become its own religion. Petrichor surveyed the copper etchings of past members on the walls, and the gloriam set of beverages and ritually prepared dried fish, everything orderly and familiar. Their lore and rites were connected to the first assassin, Axsten, who was stabbed thirteen times and miraculously lived due to his refusal to be weak. Petrichor realised that he enjoyed the steadfastness, asceticism, and structure this tint of religion gave the order. The city's other guilds were a barely controlled mess of debauchery, debates, and demands.

The other assassins filtered in, hanging up their hats and chatting, until nine were in attendance. Then they were waiting for Valour, precisely as he'd assumed.

They stood around the oblong table which held two large bowls of dried, salted white fish and ten steaming cups containing tea or coffee depending on the assassin's preference. As always, the cups were set out two in each row, and his was next to Valour's at the end. Not just because they were of a similar age but because they were seen as the order's luminaries, racking up the most and neatest kills in the past few years. He checked his pocket watch for the third time. They couldn't get down to the business of the day's roster of targets until the sacred words had been said, the beverages drunk, and the fish eaten.

Loud knocking echoed in the bare, high-ceilinged hall. Halcyon opened the doors and in stormed the churl of a woman Petrichor had been raised with. No, 'raised with' wasn't right. They had been yanked into adulthood while fighting each other for every scrap of food or attention.

She shook the snow off and strode into the room like she owned it. Her face had the undignified red cheeks of someone who had *run* here. What all those women she bedded saw in her, he had no idea. Everything about her was wrong. Her tall build was too brawny and her ash-blonde hair was falling out of a slipshod braid. Why was she wearing that ragged cloak and unfashionable boots? They made her look like the order did not pay her well enough to buy clothes. She had no respect for anything or anyone, including herself.

"Apologies, everyone," she panted. "Got held up behind a bloody cart. The donkey pulling it was as slow as snot trickling down a hill."

She clapped Halcyon on the back in greeting and smiled. Her friendliness dropped as she spotted Petrichor. "Hello, pompous wart. Did you manage to pull that stick out of your arse this morning?"

What he wouldn't give for a single day when she didn't greet him with that phrase.

He sniffed. "There is blood on the toe of your boot."

She pulled out a handkerchief from a pocket, spat on it—actually spat on it—and then wiped the droplet off her antiquated knee-high boot. "Oops. It must've been hidden by the snow."

The oldest member, Exalted Brother Encumbrance, approached. "So, the bastard daughter of the deadliest woman I ever met *finally* graces us with her presence." He watched Valour with the smirk of a tormentor enjoying the pain of his victim, which to be fair was his usual expression. "You are late, Venerated Sister Valour. Your mother was never tardy, you know. 'Tis a shame she is not here and has left us with nothing but you."

Valour—who only had two settings, silent or foul-mouthing—shut her mouth with a hard click of teeth.

Petrichor adjusted his cravat. At least Valour had memories of one of her parents, happy years together while her mother assassinated for the order. He had none of his family. He'd been nine when he was taken in by the order, starved and mangy after fending for himself on the streets. The first person he met was Valour, sulking after her mother's hanging, and she told him he smelled like piss and threw a rock at him that split his eyebrow. She must've been about seven or eight. He never asked. Why would he ask anything of such a rude mud-stained imp? He could recall Valour's most oft used insults as if she had said them today.

"Bet your parents died from the pox. Or were too boneheaded to find jobs, so they starved on the streets like newborn puppies."

"Gods, you're so weak, you weird little changeling. Are your muscles made of pus?"

"What did your parents die of anyway? Boredom from talking to you?"

That last one had made the adult assassins laugh every time she said it. Only Halcyon, a mere adolescent at the time, had suggested she stop. That had meant everything to Petrichor.

Now, Encumbrance spoke again. "Obviously, we shall finish the gloriam prayer before we divvy up today's marks. However..." His eyes glinted with malice. "I must mention that today shall be intriguing, as we have a task that is sure to test Sister Valour and Brother Petrichor like none has before."

CHAPTER 5

BRANDQUIST

AFTER THAT COMMENT about her mother, Valour refused to look at Encumbrance. He wouldn't see her grief. Instead, she shut him out and drummed her fingers against her thigh while letting her gaze travel the copper etchings of past members on the hall's dark wooden walls. The one of her mother was high up by the vaulted ceiling and so out of sight from here. The copperplate right in front of her, though, was of a woman with the name *Pound* imprinted below her portrait. It snagged Valour's attention as this Pound reminded her of Kajsa. They both had the same sort of dangerous look, with sharp features and an impressive shock of hair. If the wild watchmaker hadn't ended their relationship, Valour would've been married to Kajsa for... could it be two years by now? She winced at the thought.

Encumbrance's familiar voice droned on like a boring backdrop but then something caught and this time kept Valour's roaming concentration. A miracle had happened: the rotten codger had said something interesting. Regarding some sort of task that would challenge her and Petrichor?

Clearly not amused by Encumbrance's behaviour, Halcyon took his most authoritative stance with his hands clasped behind his broad back. "I care not how 'intrigued' you are, Brother Encumbrance. You know our ways and rituals, we perform the gloriam prayer first."

Most of the members looked disappointed but dutifully hummed their agreement. Valour was itching to know what the grim, old arsehole was talking about.

"Of course. My apologies," Encumbrance said. "I was merely whetting everyone's appetite. Do carry on."

"Take your positions," Halcyon said.

They all stood at their usual spot around the chair-less table.

Halcyon had taken the order's ceremonial axe out and held it in his open palms, ready to say the words. The assembled stilled, no more fidgeting or whispered chatter, even their breathing went into the assassin's quiet inhale and exhale.

"Humbly, we ask," Halcyon chanted, everyone filling in the rest of the prayer with him. "Our predecessors' spirits to guide our blades. Fate to help us on our path to obeying our orders. Luck to make us as hidden as our targets are unhidden. And death to take our marks, but never us."

Everyone reached for their individual cup. To an outsider, the cups surely looked the same. Squat, plain, and made of pewter covered in notches and scuffs. But Valour knew her cup as well as the back of her hand. She grabbed it before Petrichor had time to take his and made sure she nudged his cup in the process, simply because that sort of thing bothered him.

He winced, staring at the drops of grainy coffee that had spilled over the rim. A muscle kept twitching in his square jaw and he put his fingertips to it, trying to stop it by jabbing it.

A morsel of pity crept in as she watched him. Petrichor was so obsessive, stiff, and alone. Even Halcyon didn't like him, try as he might to hide it. She remembered when Petrichor had gone from being just a peculiar, annoying child to this unlikable creature, and shivered at what the order had done to him that year. Had it gone on for a full year? She didn't like to remember the details.

Then Petrichor glared at her and in his callous, deep voice said, "Clumsy swine."

Her empathy vanished, like it had so many times before. She lifted her cup and slurped, watching him grind his teeth at the noise.

They sipped their drinks. They were meant to be thinking of the assassins that came before them and meditating on death and duty. However, Valour daydreamed about marvellous women. She could stand her life if she just kept thinking about marvellous women. Especially a certain illustrious and charismatic black-haired hotel heiress who walked the halls of their shared home like she was conquering them. Or seducing them.

Valour's tea was, as always, too hot and brewed too long. She knew better than to say anything. Suffering was part of the lifestyle, hence the sanctum's great hall had no chairs, barely any light, and was perpetually cold. Bloody nonsense.

Finishing half of the cup meant they were allowed to eat some of the fish. Finally. She was starving! Chasing after that vapid nobleman and then dragging him down to the tunnels had been hard work on an empty stomach. They ate in silence, the bowls of dried, salted haddock soon emptied. They finished by draining their cups.

As soon as all were done, Encumbrance cleared his throat for attention. "As I mentioned before, my sources within the greve's inner circles made me privy to rumours about one of our targets today. 'Tis a challenge above all others and carries a peculiar instruction. It is…" He paused, for dramatic effect no doubt. "To be given to *two* assassins. Our yapping, show-off, little pups, to be exact."

Halcyon had picked up the target roster, thick paper carrying the seal of Vinterstock's greve, and was reading it with raised eyebrows. "Yes. It does indeed state that the hit should be shared between Petrichor and Valour."

"Shared?" Valour sputtered. "We're not expected to work together, are we?"

"It does not give any details," he replied. "Only that the job is to be given to both of you."

"Like a competition? To see who achieves the kill first?"

"I suppose you could see it like that, Valour," Halcyon said. "Or you could see it as the greve wanting to double his chances by putting his two most efficient assassins on the job."

Oh, she would see it exactly like a competition—one she'd win. That cold-hearted, pretentious bookworm didn't stand a chance.

The bookworm in question was adjusting his ponytail with an uninterested expression. "Who is this extraordinary target that I shall eliminate, then?"

"Brandquist," Encumbrance interjected with glee.

Valour did a double take. "Sorry, what now?"

"He is correct. It seems the target is Brandquist," Halcyon said, still reading.

She sought their leader's gaze. "As in the godsdamned, sly cutthroat who's been leader of the 'ness smugglers for decades?"

No first name. Just that surname, fearfully whispered by Vinterstockians, sounding like a knife being unsheathed.

Halcyon looked up. "Yes. I guess that is why the greve and his kammarherrar wanted our two best assassins on the job."

Valour could just imagine the leader of the city and his bootlicking inner circle wringing their hands and wanting to use their sharpest tools if they had to do this. Because that was the odd thing, wasn't it? That they felt they should do this. No one had ever tried to stop the mysterious Brandquist without being killed. Not to mention half the city being wrecked by the 'ness-dealing gangs as retribution afterwards.

"I thought," Petrichor started, appearing to weigh his words even more than usual, "that they had scant incentive to disturb the tonic trade?"

There were quiet snorts and muffled sniggers around the room. Everyone knew that the danger of going after Brandquist wasn't the only reason the people in power had not been more forceful in the fight against the 'ness trade. Most of the cabinet of kammarherrar guzzled 'ness tonics the way drunkards did booze.

Halcyon's mouth became a thin line. "It is not our place to question our orders, Petrichor. You and Valour have been told to assassinate Brandquist. You know the punishment for disobeying a direct order. Please tell me that is not what you're doing?"

Valour's back stung with phantom pains, reminding her of the times she'd rejected assassinations allotted to her. Every time she refused a hit on someone she believed not deserving of death, the four oldest members of the order took her down to the infirmary, made her take her shirt and stays off. After that, Sister Mire or Brother Encumbrance applied a scorching iron bearing the Assassins of Axsten crest to her back. All while some other assassin carried out the hit and got the accolade and payment for it. Valour looked at the crest burned into her hand and made a tight fist. That brand had been scorched there when she came of age and was a full assassin. All the members had that one. The others did not have a back full of the godsdamned things, though.

The only way you were allowed to say no here, without paying with burned-off skin and flesh, was if you left the order. And there were only two ways to leave the Order of Axsten…

One: run away, leading to being hunted by the other members. And, as the case had been with Sister Keeper and Brother Winnow when they were caught a few years ago, being tortured and then starved to death in a basement cell.

Two: hand over enough riksdaler to pay for a small house. She glanced around. Was that high sum the same one as everyone else had been given? Had they even asked? Or were they, to use her mother's expression for those who left, not as *traitorous* as her? Did they want to stay in the order that raised them, fed them, cared for them?

Petrichor's reply took her out of her thoughts. "As always, I shall do my job, accurately, quickly, and neatly." He cracked his knuckles, one by one.

"Excellent," Halcyon said, switching his attention to Valour.

She didn't have to mull it over. The remembered pains on her back and the fact that Brandquist was accountable for hundreds of deaths (due to 'ness side effects and overdoses) made up her mind. She nodded.

"Good." Halcyon returned to the missive. "No known addresses or places to start are provided, so this will require extensive investigative work."

No surprise there, considering no one knew who this Brandquist was. The two most prevalent tales were of a big, bald man wearing iron spikes on his knuckles and an aristocratic lad of nineteen with a fondness for burning his enemies alive.

"Halcyon," she began, forming the question in her mind as she spoke, "how will the greve's kammarherrar identify the corpse after I finish the hit, if no one knows what Brandquist looks like?"

He consulted the list. "The only provided identifiers of the mark are a rather ragged, large, black, woollen cloak with a deep hood, and a unique tattoo on the left lower arm. They do not divulge the tattoo's nature, probably for the risk of a fraudulent corpse being produced, but it says that when they inspect the body, they will know."

"I see." Valour chewed her lower lip. This would be a dung heap of a challenge. The one thing everyone knew about Brandquist was that he employed almost all the criminal elements in the city.

Halcyon read out the rest of the targets and they were divvied up among the other members. After that, the assassins said their farewells until they met up again for the evening meal and the following vesper prayer.

The tall doors creaked closed behind Valour and she strode away, thinking about where to start her hunt for Brandquist.

Normally, people shied away from watching assassins come and go from the sanctum, out of fear or superstition. No one looked at the building, no one threw more than a glance at the harbingers of death who walked out of it. Today, a trinket peddler turned out to be an exception. He raked his eyes over Valour like she was a dessert he'd purchased and then slapped her arse as she passed. Lightning fast, she grabbed his hand and twisted his fingers until she heard a series of crunches and his screams echoed off the cobbled street.

"Touch a woman without her permission again and I'll find you and saw your fingers off with a rusted bread knife," she said calmly.

He only wailed, staring at his hand.

She walked on, realising that she wasn't just hungry like a wolf, she was as hungry as the godsdamned Fenrir wolf. White fish might be good for you, but filling it was not. What was she in the mood for? Steak and potatoes? Blood sausage and root mash? She halted in front of the main square. Ahead of her, a crowd surrounded a raised dais on which a man and a woman read from a large piece of paper. There was no mistaking their posh outfits, overly powdered faces and wigs, or their imperial manner. They were kammarherrar, part of the greve's cabinet and inner circle. They took turns informing the Vinterstockians about the city's new rules against using 'ness tonics to gain employment or to win competitions. Behind them stood four beefy overseers, hands on the flintlock pistols at their hips.

A man, a butcher by the looks of him, shouted, "And what happens if we're found breaking the rules?"

The male kammarherre, so much the clichéd picture of a blue-eyed, blond, milky-skinned Vinterstockian that it stung her eyes, smiled. "Why, you will answer to the court of justice, of course."

The nerve. Even from over here, Valour could see that his eyes were gleaming with the intensity of someone who had taken a 'ness tonic. It was only a question of which one. It couldn't have been a brawniness tonic; he was as thin as the fashion for noblemen decreed. After all, it would be terrible to look like you'd actually done some work in your life.

His female counterpart began reading out new punishments for 'ness use with the air of someone who assumed all would hang on her every word. Didn't she, or her colleague, hear the sneers and complaints of the crowd?

This sort of thing baffled Valour. There were many ways she was uncommon in Vinterstock society:

She killed for a living.

She wore no rouge nor wigs.

She fucked only those of her own gender.

She preferred breeches to the more usual gowns.

She lived full time in a hotel without paying.

These things weren't seen as problems, merely quirky curiosities. But uncommon as they were, they didn't make her half as much of an outsider as these two. And yet, *they* controlled the city, a strange minority deciding for the majority, certain of their right to rule.

Perhaps not for long, though. Valour had heard things—whispers along darkened streets, rants in taverns and coffee-houses. People were asking what exactly their greve did for them, except sit holed up in his palace while raising taxes for the king's war and sending their children to die in the king's army. It didn't help that there had been gossip about the greve's personality having strangely altered. And rumours of people going to the palace and never returning. That last bit had to be a tall tale to frighten children or titillate adults, though. People died constantly everywhere in Vinterstock. So many starved or had to beg for scraps, selling everything and anything for a warm place to sleep. The suffering was gut-wrenching and made Valour give away any coin she made almost before it came in.

Yet, look at these two coin-hoarders, doling out orders and

restrictions with arrogant smiles. Not a clue. Not a care in the world.

She turned on her heel and chose another route. She might have to perform assassinations on their orders, but she didn't have to listen to them. Besides, she needed silence to think. The only people with nigh as much power over the city as these people were Brandquist and his underlings.

And she was about to make them want her dead.

CHAPTER 6
THREE EXCHANGES

PETRICHOR STAYED IN the sanctum after the others had left, reading the target list. Or rather re-reading the part where it said that both he and Valour were to assassinate the city's most dangerous person, but gave no help whatsoever in where to start. He knew from having done research in the past, in order to know every major figure in this city, that the sanctum's records had only the most basic information about Brandquist. Basic enough that every toddling street urchin would know as much.

"So," Halcyon said, clearing his throat. "Are you excited for the challenge?"

Petrichor considered saving face by saying yes. "I would have been when I was younger. Now, I find myself being... more cautious."

"When you were younger? You're only twenty-four. Although, I must admit that sometimes you appear fifty-four," Halcyon said with a tone that was probably jesting.

"I grew up alone on the streets and then under the roof of the Assassins of Axsten." Petrichor put the list back where he'd found it. "I have seen and done things most fifty-four-year-olds cannot fathom."

"I suppose you have." Halcyon looked around, as if searching for someone else to speak to. "So, um, is there really no part of you that relishes trying your mettle against an impressive foe like Brandquist?"

Petrichor didn't care who his target was. He was given a job; the pride came in doing it to the best of his ability and in pleasing the order. Still, he took a guess at what Halcyon wanted to hear. "Yes.

'Tis a chance to prove myself."

He touched his cravat, checking it was neat. Was it obvious that he wanted Halcyon to like him? Probably not. People often misunderstood his motives.

"Excellent," Halcyon said with a smile. It didn't reach his eyes. "Betwixt Valour's skill at predicting the behaviour of her marks and your methodical ways, you are bound to catch Brandquist in no time."

"*I* shall do so, yes."

"Also, there's sure to be a bonus at the end of this," Halcyon said. "The greve will no doubt give you so much coin you could buy yourself a flock of heimcrows to fly you up to the River Gjöll."

Petrichor considered the eerie crows the size of human babies and the river high up in the mountains that, according to old lore, was magic. "Why would I want that?"

"You wouldn't," Halcyon said as if that had been obvious. "It was... a sort of jest."

"Ah, of course."

Silence ticked on as Petrichor searched for something to say.

Once more Halcyon cleared his throat. "Perhaps you should get going? Do you have a place to start your search?"

"There are some students at the university I may speak to. I shall give it some thought. I would hate to be rash and forewarn my prey."

"Mm. Finding Brandquist will be quite hard. Killing him and getting him down into the tunnels? That will be harder than a bloody troll spine."

Petrichor lurched then collected himself. "Undeniably."

It was uncommon for their leader to curse, since the order decreed language should be clean. The last time Petrichor heard Halcyon swear was when he'd been outside the other man's room a fortnight ago and had heard moaning as if Halcyon was in pain. Petrichor had slid the door ajar, hand on his knife, and seen Halcyon prone on his back, as naked as the woman who was riding him rough and fast. Such ridiculous animal behaviour. Halcyon's eyes had been closed and he'd groaned and cursed loud enough to not have heard

Petrichor open the door.

At least Petrichor hoped that it was so.

Now, he said farewell to Halcyon, grabbed his hat, and entered a Vinterstock covered in untouched snow. Soon it would be trodden into browns and greys, but it was currently whiter than white and far too bright for his eyes. He retrieved his smoked-glass spectacles from their case in his pocket. When he put them on, he noticed an aged hawker who was glaring at the doors of the sanctum. The vendor was nursing his right hand while shouting to a woman and a younger man who stood opposite him about someone breaking his hand.

Petrichor would have walked on, if he hadn't heard the hawker say, "She was one of them eerie bastards. The *assassins*."

The woman gaped, clearly fearful. "Don't speak of those spectres aloud! You know we can't, lest we bring them to our midst." Her gaping morphed to a sneer. "Anyway, you're lucky she didn't call for the overseers, you foul git. The fine for molesting people went up last month."

Petrichor took longer than needed to pull his gloves on.

"I never molested her," the hawker screeched. "It was a bleedin' compliment!"

"I doubt that's the sort of compliment you'd like. Some big, leering bloke grabbing your intimate parts," the younger man said. "Anyway, considering she was an assassin, you're lucky she didn't snap your neck."

The woman shook her head. "She never would've snapped his neck. She would've dragged him into that guild house of theirs and plonked him in some torture thing. You know the ghoulish gear they keep in there."

None of them did in fact know what was kept in there. Superstition and fear built many rumours. Petrichor rolled his eyes, moving a little to stay blended into the crowd.

"All I'm saying is that I don't know if my hand will ever heal right," the hawker whinged. He turned to the younger man. "If you see a bird, pretty in a rough way, galloping about like her hair is on fire and wearing men's clothes with a scruffy cloak, stay far away."

Petrichor sniffed. There were three female members who wore what the traditionalists called 'men's clothes' but two of them walked with discreet and fluid elegance, like an assassin should, making sure no one would see or recognise them afterwards. They also wore proper outerwear. This varlet had met Valour.

The younger man snorted. "Like I'd be bloody pathetic enough to touch anyone against their will."

He and the woman went back to their own stalls, leaving the griping hawker alone.

Petrichor could have kept walking. The situation had been dealt with. Instead, he undid his coat and slid his hand into the inner pocket where a leather casing containing a long needle sat next to his assassin's blade. A few nights ago, Petrichor had stolen into the university's laboratory and coated the needle with a non-lethal but debilitating poison extracted from some exotic frog.

It was a fast and easy dance. Slide the needle out of its sheath, sidestep over to the hawker, stab him and hiss, "The Order of Axsten bids you to learn some respect." Then slip into a throng of people and vanish like a ghost. Now that was how an assassin should act. Valour never had learned the value of stealth and panache. Still, he had to admit that she had done an admirable job of wrecking that hand.

Petrichor was taking his preferred back-alley path and was about halfway to the university when the snow stopped falling. Thick, dark clouds blotted out the light, making the day seem later than it was and promising rain.

To his right, someone coughed wetly before saying, "Petrichor the assassin?"

Someone knew his name, knew *him*.

Petrichor spun to see a thin, ashen-faced man leaning against the frame of an open door. The man didn't register as a threat since he appeared mere days away from dying. Nevertheless, Petrichor made the usual assessments. Approximate height, weight, age, fighting power, and as much as he could see of the room behind the man. It was a well-lit dining establishment, full of people having their lunch. Wholesome and safe. Not a likely place for an attack.

"Well? Are you?" the coughing man said.

Petrichor sifted through his memory for anyone who might've seen him leave the sanctum and also overheard his name somewhere. Or did this man know of him from another assassin? "Who dares to ask?"

"I'll take that as a yes."

Petrichor thought out a reply but never had time to give it. With unnatural speed, the sick man grabbed his shoulders with shaking hands. Swiftness tonic. It was the only explanation for how the man could move that fast despite barely being able to catch his breath. Yes, there it was, that drugged light in the man's eyes. He had taken it for the fervour before death earlier. Now the cough and shakes were easily diagnosed as signs of severe 'ness overuse, coming right before the fainting and, finally, death. He cursed himself for making such a mistake.

Petrichor was about to implement one of the many fighting techniques the order taught, but realised there was no attack coming. All he saw in those 'ness-addled eyes was desperation as the sick man mumbled, "A message. I have a message to give you. Wait."

He released Petrichor's shoulders and leaned back against the doorframe. This would have been an excellent time to either drag the sick man away and end his suffering, or to simply leave. Except, Petrichor's curiosity and need for information kept him here. He did however reach for his knife, and held it hidden from any onlookers except the man.

The addict didn't seem to care about the weapon, too preoccupied with opening a hip flask and gulping down its contents. The sweet metallic scent wafting from the bottle proved it was 'ness. This one was probably a wellness tonic, since some colour returned to the man's face and a hint of energy slipped into his posture. A bandage on a giant gushing wound, since the effects wouldn't last long and the use of yet another 'ness tonic would likely halve what time he had left.

Still, the man seemed able to speak again, so Petrichor wasted no time. "What is this mystery message, then?"

"That if you try to kill Brandquist and fail, you and everyone you know will die. If you try to kill Brandquist and *succeed*, it will be the same outcome. But," he said with a half-baked, joyless smile, "since our research showed you only care about yourself, I'll add that your death will be long, slow, and most of all humiliating. We'll torture you in ways that'll make you soil yourself in public and spill your every secret, fear, and mortifying memory for the crowd."

Petrichor tensed. How did they know what form of threat would get to him?

"Ah. Well. That was… descriptive," Petrichor said. "I am assuming that the third option in Brandquist's mind would be that I do not try to kill him?"

"That would obviously be the best for everyone. Although, we're not fools. We know that if you don't manage the hit, someone else in your order will." He paused to lean even more on the doorframe and stifle a cough. "Therefore, since no one knows Brandquist's face, we suggest that a depraved criminal is killed and presented as him instead. You get the credit and carry on living while Brandquist keeps a low profile. Everyone will assume the hit was carried out."

"It will not be that easy. The order has been informed that Brandquist has a peculiar tattoo which we haven't been given the details of. The greve's people seem certain that this tattoo will eliminate the risk of a stand-in, so I assume it is something difficult to replicate?"

"Oh? Bloody hell! Aye, it is." The man now had a long coughing fit while the colour drained from his face. The wellness tonic must already have been wearing off. He tried to speak again but his wet cough got in the way, splattering mucus and blood onto Petrichor's chin and cravat.

Petrichor jerked back. Panic made his veins instantly run ice-cold. He yanked out his clean handkerchief and frantically scrubbed at his chin, neck, and cravat.

The man seemed to draw his last energy up before slurring, "The tattoo is a complicated thing, raised up in some way I don't understand. I have only seen it once. Aye, once, when I kissed it to pledge my loyalty to Brandquist."

Raised up? What did that mean? Petrichor kept scrubbing, trying to sound calm as he asked, "Surely that was enough to say what it looks like?"

"No, no. Dark. It was dark," he mumbled, more to himself than to Petrichor. "No one is allowed a good look at it, or it'd be duplicated by people trying to pretend to be Brandquist." He stopped, partly because his body had started convulsing and partly because he was coughing blood into his hand.

Vile as this fit was, it gave Petrichor a chance to rub harder at the dried stains, but also to think. This underling was definitely spilling more information than he should. This was why you didn't send dying addicts to do your errands: they could become distracted by pain, confusion, and the need for their next hit. Not to mention becoming confessional as death drew closer. In short, they talked too much. Petrichor could use that.

"I see. Well, is that not a risk worth taking in this situation?"

The man stifled his coughing. "Don't be daft. Brandquist doesn't see you as dangerous enough to risk his whole business by letting an imposter in. Also, there's something sacred about that tattoo. It has meaning, you see. A practical use." Gradually, he slumped into a sitting position. When he was down, he mumbled, "I've said too much. I'll take what you've said back to Brandquist and a new plan will be made. Until then, do nothing. And you must keep your co-assassin from acting as well."

Petrichor fretted that his scouring hadn't cleaned any of the foul fluids off him, but instead imprinted them into his clothes and skin, tarnishing him for life. He burned hot then shivered cold, his mind planning the dash home to a bath with drops of lye in it. "You mean you did not give Valour the delightful choice of torturous death or compliance?"

The man blinked, his eyes no longer eerily bright but dull and fading. "Our research told us that she wouldn't listen to reason."

Petrichor huffed at the understatement.

The man wheezed and his face twisted into a grimace, right before his breathing turned to rasping gasps. He tumbled back, halfway into the dining establishment, making a nearby waitress come rushing over.

Petrichor didn't know if the addict had fainted or died—hopefully not the latter, as the message would then not reach Brandquist—but he knew when it was time to take his leave.

He quit the scene as fast as possible without running, continuously rubbing his face as discreetly as he could without attracting attention from passers-by. The walk back to the university and the stairs up to the astronomy tower took an age. When he was finally home, he tore his clothes off, vowing to either scrub them for hours or to burn them.

He was quite certain that what the man had wasn't contagious; the symptoms were of classic 'ness overuse. But getting blood, pus, or dirt on himself? It still brought him back to that night when he was eleven. And those stains... No. He refused to remember. He leapt into the tub before it had even filled properly, scrubbing himself with a rough cloth while staring at the bare wall in front of him. Trying so hard not to let the memories in. Or the shame.

Chapter 7

KRONOVALL

VALOUR PICKED UP the pace; she was almost home. Living in a fancy hotel like the Kronovall was deliciously weird. Particularly for someone who had lived in the city's poorest area since she was old enough to move out of the sanctum.

A month ago, Halcyon had paused their boxing match to ask about her living arrangements. She had tried to get away with jokes about someone else doing the cleaning, but of course that hadn't worked. Neither had pointing out that her old cabin had wood rot. Halcyon had been there for most of Valour's life, helping her with her first monthly bleed and getting drunk with her after her first heartbreak.

He had studied her for a long time, then said, "Hm. 'Tis the need for noise, is it not? Considering your constant humming, whistling, and drumming your fingers on things, it is clear that you are more comfortable when it's not silent."

"Obviously," she'd said nonchalantly.

At the hotel there was always someone awake, making noise and showing that life carried on. Normal. Safe. Dependable. Noise was the easiest way to keep her mind from spiralling into places she didn't want it to go, but she wasn't going to tell anyone that. Not even Halcyon.

"However, you also loathe people, and hotels brim with those."

"Sure. But I don't have to socialise with them. I can hear them and see them, but from a distance."

He had sought her gaze then. "Sounds lonely."

"I like being alone."

"I didn't say 'being alone'. I said 'lonely', Valour."

36

She'd grunted and asked when they were going to actually box. Now she saw the Kronovall at the end of the street. The lavish spire-adorned building gleaming white as the snow. The current owner had renovated the place from a disreputable coaching inn to that most new-fangled luxury—a hotel. The building improved, but the clientele didn't. The smugglers and criminals simply put on silken suits and wigs before returning to make deals and drink 'ness or booze in nicer surroundings. The owner had needed what he called a 'deterrent' and Valour had volunteered, being rewarded with one of the smaller rooms. Hotel security guards couldn't be seen kicking criminals' arses in front of polite company. They were meant to stop any violence and then call for the overseers. Valour was just a guest at the hotel; she could threaten and pummel any rogues without the Kronovall being accountable.

Consequently, she now entered the hotel with the air of someone who belonged there, despite the glares from the—now respectable—other guests. They were probably counting the holes in her cloak.

Her mind busy with where she'd start looking for Brandquist, she forgot that she wanted something to eat, meaning she was halfway to the stairs before she stopped and let her hunger lead her back through the chandelier-lit lobby and into the formal dining room.

The first person she saw was the youngest waiter, Knut, smiling at her. They had often shared dirty jokes and late-night confessions while smoking a pipe out in the alley behind the hotel's kitchen. Well, Knut had smoked, joked, and shared confessions. That was the thing about being a quiet person, people loved to tell Valour things. So, out there she'd stand, leaning against the wall—warmed by all the burning stoves inside—and just listen. It wasn't all terrible. She enjoyed the evening air and hearing about what went on. Even if she had no advice, she'd nod, make sympathetic noises, or on occasion use the sharpest sword in her armoury: the vague hum. She bloody loved a vague hum.

Now she tipped her head in greeting. "Hello, Knut. Got a table for someone gasping for tea and a sweet treat?"

She hoped he wouldn't tease her for drinking tea with her fika and not coffee like most Swedes. It was getting old.

Knut's eyebrows rose. "Hello, Valo— I mean, greetings, Miss Valour. Is it time for fika already? 'Tis only a little after lunch. Do they not feed you over at the sanctum?"

"They sort of do, but I'm famished today and it is *always* time for fika. My usual, please?"

It wasn't really a question; she knew she'd get it as a perk for being the hotel's 'deterrent'. Nevertheless, she tried to be polite when she remembered.

"Of course, miss. Tea and cardamom sweet rolls coming up. Would you like them hot or cold today?"

"Cold. With whipped cream and set honey. Please."

"Of course. Please seat yourself, miss."

"I hate that you must call me 'miss' in public," she grumbled while, true to her assassin habits, she picked a table where she could see the whole room.

The tea arrived first. Knut began unburdening his large tray, starting with the hot water and then a cup and saucer, all in imported, painted porcelain. The remaining contents of his tray were a parade of delicate silver things: a strainer and tiny dish in which she'd place the strainer after use, a teaspoon, a tiny pitcher of cream, a single-serve-sized sugar bowl, and another dish containing thin lemon wedges. The silver assortment was finished with an ornate bread knife, a butter knife, and another teaspoon for her cream. It was all petite and elegant beyond what a low-born brute like her should have been allowed. She took a wicked pleasure in that, meeting the stares of the aristocrats at the tables around her and making sure she gave them her widest grin.

She thanked Knut, who gave her a conspiring smile and left.

She placed the strainer on her cup, marvelling at how this silly tea ritual with all its extravagances of condiments, delicate porcelain, and silverware had come to mean the world to her.

Her attention was grabbed by a man at the table opposite, who irately waved every server away. The rude man stood out like a sore thumb in his high continental hat and flimsy blue coat with powder-yellow lapels. Not to mention the vivid bruises on his craggy face. The man stared right at her, not even bothering to avert his gaze when she stared back. Odd.

Valour kept half an eye on him but was more interested in her tea. Time for the test. She decanted a few thimblefuls of steaming tea into her cup to check it was brewed to the right colour. Too pale. She waited to pour more. There was such a luxury in taking her time with this, in that it was allowed to take up time. No one would tell her to hurry up, not even her own impatience.

The ritual helped her to think. Perhaps the best place to start the hunt for Brandquist would be to find some of the gangs of 'ness addicts often loitering on Oden's Square? Maybe she could shake them down for information? They were usually nice people, only having had a bad run of it. Most of the time they'd only wanted a leg up in a tough-as-old-shit world. Just to be a little faster so they had time to finish that commission, a little cleverer so they could outwit their competition, a little stronger so they could stand up to their abuser. But then the 'ness made them feel so much better. After that, stopping was a goal far in the foggy distance. Or so she'd been told.

She peered at her tea. No. Not yet. She wouldn't wait too long, though. If it became over-brewed, she would have to bring in the last solution to save it—a few fat drops of cream.

The blue-coated man grabbed her attention again. He stood, showing that he was both tall and, more interestingly, that he was still staring at her. Her hands hovered over her concealed blades. Was he coming over? Was that a sabre strapped to his hip? He turned and left the room, rendering the questions moot. Maybe he had thought she was someone else or perhaps he was simply peculiar. Either way, she'd make use of her good memory for faces and keep an eye out for him.

She focused back on her tea. She poured a hearty amount into her cup, dropped a sliver of lemon in, and took her first taste. Perfect in flavour and temperature. In every way the opposite of the gunk the order served. She sipped while pondering if the addicts on Oden's Square might be too far gone to give clear answers.

Knut returned with a tray holding perfectly rounded rolls. They scented the air with buttery dough, sweetness, and the warming bite of cardamom. "Here we are, miss. I made sure to get you the biggest and freshest ones."

"Knut, it's official. You have become my favourite person."

New little silver things appeared too. A tiny bowl with a lid, which she knew would contain honey, and one without a lid, brimming with fresh, cloud-whipped cream.

Knut left again and Valour grabbed one of the buns, sliced it open, and applied the pale, thick-set honey. She finished it off by slathering on the cream and then took a bite that made her moan in a way that surely drew glares from the aristocrats, who sat there barely even sampling their liver pâté. She ate her cardamom roll with the reverence of someone having a religious experience. She lifted the teacup to take a sip, the porcelain just at her lip when she stopped, listening. Footfalls approached her table. Expensive boots and a gait less discreet than that of the wait staff. She turned her head fast enough to make her neck click, but found that it was only Kronovall's owner, Mr Rytterdahl. She exhaled, drank some tea, and watched his approach.

Mahadev Rytterdahl was an elegant businessman who owned most of the inns and hotels in Vinterstock. After many years of travelling, he had settled here in the cold and rough North and taken a local surname. With his amiable manner, sharp intelligence, and pleasing accent, he had soon become one of the city's leading and most loved figures.

Again, it was amazing what you could learn if you stood silently and listened to people.

Mr Rytterdahl stopped and leaned over as if he had something important to talk to her about in private. Wonderful. She hadn't even gotten to her second cup of tea. Or her second bun.

"Good day to you, Valour."

"Hello."

He gave a little cough. "Pardon the intrusion, but I fear I must ask a favour of you. One other than your normal duties as...

well, you know."

She toasted him with her teacup. "Deterrent."

"Hm. Yes, that. As I say, I need to request another favour."

Her flippancy notwithstanding, she cast a glance down at her luxurious fika. A shining, clean, quiet moment in all the dark, dirt, and din of her life. Something she could scarce afford or be allowed anywhere else.

She swallowed a sigh and put her cup down. "Take a seat and tell me what this favour is."

Mr Rytterdahl smiled apologetically and sat. "It concerns my daughter, Ingrid. Have you made her acquaintance?"

Valour schooled her features. She had thought about that charismatic black-haired beauty during gloriam. And yesterday too, after they had passed each other in the corridor and the mere presence of the dainty, perfumed woman had made Valour reel. Also the day before that, when she'd seen Ingrid guiding dignitaries around the hotel, spellbinding them with jokes and intelligent questions. And pretty much every day for the past few months, ever since her second day at Kronovall when Ingrid had spoken to her. The only time Valour had let that happen. She'd been in the lobby, staring at a painting of mighty Heimdal signalling the coming of Ragnarök. She'd been contemplating how she would feel if she was one of the gods and woke to a loud-arsed horn blaring out the end of the world, and then she had to fight before even getting breakfast. The answer was: bloody fuming. Ingrid had appeared at her elbow, beamed, and in her famous crystalline voice said, "Well now, if it isn't our Lady of Assassination and Intimidation. I have been hoping to speak with you. I trust you're well and hale on this fine morning?"

"Mm."

Ingrid had then clicked her tongue at the painting. "Did you know that Heimdal had nine mothers? Nine! Ye gads, some of us would be happy for one."

Valour had agreed, but not said as much. She nodded, then walked away. And she had kept her distance ever since. Because what else did you do with a woman who was forever talking to people, laughing, and looking them straight in the eye? All while having that… what would you call it? Presence? Magnetism? It all sounded pompous and didn't describe the overwhelming feeling one got when that woman was near. And Ingrid Rytterdahl hadn't stopped watching her from across the room and smiling at her.

Valour looked up at Mr Rytterdahl. "I've seen her about."

He chuckled. "Tight-lipped as always, I see. Well then, I shall get right to the point as well. Ingrid has been staying out late and spending increasing amounts of time away from me and the hotel. Which should not be any of my business. However…" Mahadev Rytterdahl scratched the back of his neck. "She is supposed to be apprenticing to take over my hotels one day, something made difficult when she misses meetings and is barely awake when she is here."

"I see."

"To make things worse, rumours have now reached me of her spending her evenings cavorting with soldiers and—oh, what is the word in your language?—ruffians."

"And you reckon you can force her to stop? With my aid?" Valour said, mainly because he was looking at her as if he expected her to interject something.

"Oh, do not misunderstand me. Ingrid is a sensible, grown woman of twenty-six. I am not looking to force her to do anything. I simply want to understand her and make sure she is safe." His eyebrows lowered, making Valour note dark circles under his eyes. "What is making her shirk her responsibilities to the hotels and the charities she heads? Is she truly out drinking the nights away with dangerous people?"

Unsure of what to say, Valour sipped her tea.

Rytterdahl wrung his hands with the sort of parental worry that Valour would have killed for. "All I am asking you to do is spend time with her. Find out if she is staying safe and perhaps remind her of the responsibilities she has taken on? I love her and want what is best for her, but she does not confide in me, nor heed my advice."

"Why would someone like her listen to me? I'm younger than her. Rude. A commoner. Uneducated. And, as you pointed out, not very talkative."

His face became a picture of pure surprise. "Obviously Ingrid does not care about those things! What she cares about is people who interest her, and you do."

Valour snorted.

"No,'tis true. I have asked my hotel security to watch over her, and she's given them the slip. I have asked the sons and daughters of my acquaintances to reason with her, and she has ignored them. You, however, she keeps speaking of with true admiration and interest. That is why I have asked you to..."

"Keep an eye on her?"

"Spend time with her," he corrected. "If you can keep her safe, then obviously I would be grateful for that, but I am not asking you to be her bodyguard or her minder."

Valour ran her finger around the edge of her cup. "You sure you want *me* around your precious daughter? I kill for a living."

"Yes, on official orders. My Ingrid would be safe with you, though. As safe as I have always been." His expression turned pleading. "What do you say?"

Valour wanted to say no so much it itched, but she could smell her tea, the cardamom bun, and the clean surroundings without any hint of wood rot, and so heard herself answer, "I'm in the middle of an unusually hazardous job, so I can't right now. I can spend some time with her when the hit is done, though."

Mr Rytterdahl grimaced. "I travel to the coast on the morrow and will remain there for a few days. It disquiets me to leave her alone all that time. Any chance you can accompany her for a day or two this week?"

Valour considered that. She wouldn't have to do much. She could simply check in with the other woman every other day and then go about her own business for the rest.

"Fine. But note, I am *not* responsible for her actions or her well-being. She is, as you said, an adult. And I'm busy." She paused to make sure he was marking her words. "I'll spend some time with her when I can, and if anyone bothers her, I'll obviously thrash them."

He sagged with relief and stood. "That is all I can ask for. Shall I send Ingrid up to your room when I next see her, so you can introduce yourself to her?"

Valour gave a vague hum.

He put one of his big hands on her shoulder. "Thank you, Valour. It means more to me than I can say. Right, I shall leave you to your tea and see you again in a few days."

"Sure. Safe travels."

She poured her second cup. It had steeped too long. Shit. She sighed, tipped some cream in, then glanced after the departing figure of Mr Rytterdahl. He had the same confident posture as his daughter, but none of her hip swaying.

Spending time with the daunting Ingrid Rytterdahl. While also trying to assassinate godsdamned *Brandquist*. On little sleep and ruined fika.

Well, wasn't this turning into a gut-sucker of a day?

CHAPTER 8
BURIED, PANICKED, REVULSED

PETRICHOR FORCED HIMSELF out of the bath-tub. He had scrubbed himself red and the lye still burned on his skin. Why didn't he feel better? The coughed-up blood and lung pus from that Brandquist henchman still seemed to be on him. *In him.* His pulse picked up. His vision blurred at the edges while an iron vice squeezed his heart and lungs.

Those words. They crawled out from the hole he had buried these recollections in and screamed in his mind.

"How dare you come in here looking like that, boy?"

"No," he moaned. "Please not that."

Naked, he stumbled from the bathroom to the bedchamber. In his mind's eye, he saw a space that made his tiny room and bath seem large. Had that basement cell been the sanctuary's smallest one? He'd certainly been the smallest assassin, a thimble taller than Valour but so much scrawnier, with hollow cheeks and a stomach that Halcyon said was concave. It hadn't been Halcyon who locked him in that cell, at least. Petrichor wasn't sure he would have survived that.

To think he had brimmed with pride earlier that day, when he'd managed his first execution on his own instead of performing it under the stern gaze of the late Sister Glass, the then leader of the order. He'd wanted to manage it on his own as a surprise. To show them that he could achieve things, that he wasn't useless and unlikely to amount to anything, as they often claimed. Even as the hit went so wrong and the screams of the dead man rung in his ears and the blood splatter tasted strange on his lips, his foolish self had been so proud.

Wait, that mark had coughed on him too, had he not? He'd spluttered blood even before Petrichor sliced him open. Had the mark been ill? That would explain why he had been easy to kill, even for a child.

Now Petrichor sat naked, trembling, and curled in on himself on the floor, hugging his knees to his chest. The cold of the room didn't chill him half as much as his shame at the memory of joyously running into the sanctum shouting about his kill. His outfit had been blood-drenched and faeces-spattered from when his knife had split the man's bowels.

All that would've been bad on a normal day—attracting attention with his appearance as he walked through town, and not even being discreet while bludgeoning and stabbing the mark—but on that particular day, it had been disastrous. He was so young. How could he have known that it was the order's anniversary? Or that this meant the greve and several dignitaries would be in the sanctum, drinking mead and glaring at the boy making a mockery of their directives to keep assassinations secret at all costs? How could he have known how he had disgraced the whole Order of Axsten, breaking the sacred rules and forcing the only people to ever care for him to make an example of him?

Still, no matter his age, he *had* ruined everything and deserved a much harsher punishment than they gave him. He put his hands on the cold floor and dry-retched. His heart punched in his chest and the room spun. He couldn't catch his breath. Was he dying? He screamed at himself for his weakness.

Little Petrichor had screamed in that cell too. How long had they left him down there? Eight months? The days had bled into each other. Either way, it was a lifetime for a boy who had just turned eleven. That was why he had forgotten about the order's anniversary; it had been his birthday and he could think of no better way to celebrate than to kill for his new family, showing that he belonged and could repay them for giving him food and shelter. What he usually recollected as the worst part wasn't the small space, nor the dark, the lice, the putrid hole in the floor for urine and faeces. Or even the endless time filled only with practising fighting techniques and trying to entice rats to keep him company. What broke him was that even the order members who brought him food didn't say a word to him. Probably out of revulsion for his actions.

He had cried, apologised, begged for them to tell him what he could do to make it all right. Explained that he'd only wanted to make them proud, to help, to show that he could be useful. "I'll be good. Please, I'll do anything." He had even hurt himself with a sharp piece of rock to show that he understood he must be punished.

All of it had been met with cold silence.

Silence and small spaces were common punishments the order doled out to its children. It was to harden them, to kill the pity of their heart to themselves and others. He remembered those words from the initiation ceremony and knew he had managed to deaden so much in himself since then. But not enough. Otherwise he wouldn't be in this wretched state now. He listened to the pulse pounding in his ears. Yes, the silence had been the worst thing, closely followed by the smallness of the cell. The dirty walls had seemed to close in a little each day, burying him under the sanctum, in his own shame, in his own filth, in his own loneliness.

Now and here, as a grown man in his own rooms, Petrichor uncurled himself and stumbled up with bones creaking from the cold. He paced, a cat in a cage, and only stopped to repeatedly thump his forehead against the slanted roof on one side of the bedchamber. His home's compactness had never bothered him before. Now, though, the threadbare brocade sofa, the hard bed, the spartan desk—they were all too close together and took up too much floor space. The unlit fireplace gaped like a black mouth about to swallow him. The astronomy tower's massive copper telescope, on the floor above his rooms, seemed to weigh down on his tiny space, crushing it. The uneven walls, which were covered with shelves filled with books and tallow candles made the room overfilled. The only bare wall— scribbled full of calculations for when he could enact his plan— was the slanted one, and it appeared to be lowering down on him.

He wasn't breathing correctly and his pulse drummed in his ears. How quick and hard could a heart pound without permanent damage? He had to breathe slower. Or quicker? How long was a normal breath? Panic made him hot, then cold, then somehow both. There was a weight on his chest, a block of ice he couldn't shift.

Why had he let that man cough on him, taint him, disgrace him! And why the deuce was this room so small and cramped? He shouldn't have covered every surface with books.

He stopped.

Books.

He should keep his attention on the books. Watching them helped him breathe, to focus on something other than the fact that he was dying and that he deserved to die.

On that shelf was his poetry collection, their faded gilded titles on cracked spines. Stacked next to his bed were his few prose books, bound in calf hide in greys and creams. The rest were volumes on the humanities and sciences, everything from alchemy to zoology. Some of them were university hand-me-downs, crying out to be rebound in something other than their cheap cloth. Some were bought with coin he should've saved for his plan. They were worth the cost, though. They took him away from the blood and filth of his work, away from himself and his memories. If he picked up a book now, he could escape for a few hours. Maybe then he could bury this weakness, become cold-blooded and deadened again.

However, he was as shaky as a leaf in a storm and his vision still blurred. He was in no state to read or even pick up a book. Instead, he put a hand against the nearest bookshelf to stabilise himself. His breathing was evening out. As the dizziness faded, fatigue replaced it. His mind was worn out from panic and the infected memories, while his limbs were heavy as marble. Looking down at said limbs, he realised he was still naked. With trembling hands, he pulled on stockings, breeches, shirt, and tried but failed to button the waistcoat. That, as well as the cravat and justacorps, would have to wait.

His gaze went to his bed. When did he last sleep through a full night? Exhaustion made him vulnerable to memories and emotions. He would allow himself a few moments' rest before he started the hunt for Brandquist. Still cursing himself, he lay corpse-still on the bed. He closed his eyes and fell head-first into his usual black void of sleep.

RINGING WOKE HIM. The church next to the university had a loud, doleful bell that kept resounding, telling him how late it must be. How long had he slept? Disorientated and disquieted, he opened his eyes to darkness. Shivering, he got up to light a fire to keep frostbite from rendering him useless as an assassin. He didn't light his tapers, though, not deserving such comforts.

He startled at a knock on the door, then calmed. It would no doubt be students here to mock the 'odd man in the tower' again. He slapped his cheeks until he was some semblance of his usual self and opened the door.

Outside stood an urchin with a snotty nose and an envelope dangling from one hand. "Got 'nother one, mister."

Petrichor tried to compose himself and process the boy's gibberish. "You mean you have a letter for me?"

"Not just any old boring letter. 'Nother of them with the gryphon on the seal. You know, in this browny-white paper."

Petrichor snatched the elegant envelope. "It's cream."

"No," the boy said gently, as if he thought Petrichor had lost his mind. "It's paper."

"The. Colour. Is. Called. Cream."

"Is it, sir? Why? This is a really, really, really, really light brown." He wiped snot from his nose. "Cream is just white. Like milk, but tastier."

Petrichor was about to explain about shades of white and the concept of beige when he remembered that this boy had delivered the letter that he'd burned. The child had asked if he could slide the wax seal off the envelope because he liked gryphons. Also if Petrichor was locked up in this tower because he'd stolen someone's food, but that was beside the point.

A second letter? Did that mean the contents of the first one had been positive? That shouldn't matter, of course. It wouldn't change anything, and yet... His gaze went to the envelope.

"You all right, mister? Your face turned all white. No, not white. Cream."

Fishing out a generous coin from a pocket and throwing it to the boy, Petrichor said, "Take this and get out of my sight, you snot-faced changeling."

"Mean language will make matron send you t'bed with an empty belly."

Matron. The boy lived at an orphanage or an almshouse, then?

He watched the urchin scamper down the spiral staircase. Then it was just him and the letter. Should he burn this one too? Having stood there gripping it for far too long, he finally shoved the missive into his pocket and heard it crinkle against his pocket watch. The time! He must get to vesper prayers and supper. The whole accursed day had been wasted. He checked his reflection in the bathroom looking-glass. He was as pallid as salt and there were red marks where he had struck his head. Never mind. He would have to be harder, *more disciplined*, than his weaker parts. He splashed cold water on his face before re-binding his ponytail painfully tight with a leather tie. He tied his cravat, put on his pristine hat and his stiffest justacorps, and with the solemnity of a knight putting on his armour, donned his outercoat and boots then left for the sanctum.

CHAPTER 9

INGRID RYTTERDAHL

WHILE THE SUN set and bathed Oden's Square in orange and blood-red light, Valour had asked three 'ness users about Brandquist. The first one was a woman who only convulsed and coughed before stumbling off. The second had clearly been deep in the cups of forgetfulness tonic, erasing most of his life to the point where he didn't know who he was. The third user had been able to tell her that his 'ness dealer had been forced to quit due to lack of product. Apparently, tonic supplies were growing scarce. His cloak had been in worse nick than even hers, so she gave him her woollen scarf and what coins she had on her and told him to seek warmth in the nearest hospice, almshouse, or even prison. The other 'ness users scattered when she approached. Shit. Such a heartbreaking waste of time. She started the walk home. Vesper prayers and the evening meal were only two hours away anyway.

Back in her hotel room, she did lunges while carrying a sack full of stones until her legs ached. She couldn't afford to lose muscle mass, not when she was taking on a mark like Brandquist. No matter how hard she worked, though, she couldn't stop thinking about the sufferers on Oden's Square.

Three unhurried raps on the door rang out, making her drop the sack, which barely missed her toes. Valour threw the door open, ready to shout at whoever had startled her, and… there *she* was.

The visitor flashed a smile and said, "Ingrid Rytterdahl," in place of a greeting.

Like everyone in Vinterstock didn't know who this woman was. And now she had stepped out of Valour's thoughts and fantasies, into her doorway. Valour was torn between wanting this wonderful creature's company and not wanting to talk to her. Still, at least it took her mind off the struggling souls on Oden's Square.

Ingrid stepped past Valour and into the room with some heady perfume wafting off her.

"Please, come on in," Valour said.

"Thank you," Ingrid said, unaffected by the sarcasm. She gracefully slipped her gold-buckled shoes off and placed them next to Valour's dirty boots. "I trust Papa told you he would send me up here to be introduced?"

"Mm."

Ingrid's long cloak—yellow silk with *actual sable lining*—slid off her shoulders as if on command and she tossed it on the bed, making the candles in the nearest sconce flutter. Then she faced Valour, who stood with arms crossed over her chest.

"I am sorry he roped you into this. Oh, and I'm also sorry for barging in like that. I find waiting to be let in nerve-wracking and so prefer to trespass. Then I can be thrown out if I'm not welcome."

"Huh. Unusual stance to take."

The word stance reminded Valour about her legs. She sat down next to the discarded coat on the bed and stretched the sore limbs out.

"Thank you for saying 'unusual' instead of something unkinder. I'll remember that," Ingrid said in a disarmingly warm tone.

Valour only nodded.

Taking a few steps further in, Ingrid glanced around the room. Valour followed her gaze from the knife left on the otherwise empty armoire to the sack of stones in the middle of the floor.

"I can arrange for some decorations to be sent up?"

"There were some," Valour replied. "I shoved them in a drawer."

"I see. You prefer to keep your surfaces clear?"

"I suppose. Or maybe I'm waiting for there to be something worth keeping on them."

"As the person who decorated these rooms, I shall try not to take offence," Ingrid said, laughter in her voice.

"Sorry."

Ingrid waved that away. "Think no more of it. So, how are you enjoying our hotel?"

Valour wasn't sure if there was anything worse than small talk. Perhaps having to do the dishes? Especially all the teaspoons. Still, it was a close thing.

"I like it."

Standing with her hands clasped before her, Ingrid gave off an air of expecting more, but then seemed to give up. "Excellent. I want you to be ever so comfortable here. I've been telling the maid to give you the fluffiest pillows and softest towels for months."

For months? Exactly as long as they had been dancing around one another.

Valour stopped stretching with a jerk. "No. Don't make anyone work harder on my account. Your staff has enough to do without having to ferret out the best towels for me."

"Such consideration," Ingrid said, her head pensively tilted. "Very gallant. Or perhaps I should say *valorous*. Your name is Valour, isn't it?"

Like she didn't know. "Yes."

"I like it. Rather amusing a name for a state-sanctioned murderer."

Valour ground her teeth. "The state-sanctioned bit of that sentence means I'm not a murderer." She bored her gaze into Ingrid's. "Assassin. Or executioner at a push. Not murderer."

"Oh, my apologies, I meant no offence! I know you have rid this city of many terrible people. Ones who, for one reason or another, cannot be tried for their crimes like regular thieves and brawlers." Ingrid tapped pensive fingers against her lips, which were the colour of rose water. "I suppose the overseers are the watchdogs, chasing after intruders and lowlifes. While your kind... you are the cats, killing off the disease-carrying pests in our midst."

"Thank you. I think? Although, I'm not sure 'pests' is the right word."

"You're welcome." Ingrid smoothed the pleats on her gown's pannier-widened hips adding, "I'll leave it to others to decide if our greve, like the rest of the country's aristocracy ruling over their lands, should be allowed to decide who lives or dies on his own whim, circumventing the court of justice." Any flippancy had left her voice now. "And why so many miscreants need to die that we require a whole order of assassins to carry out the sentences. Perhaps even why it is done in secret and without any input from Vinterstockians."

"Are you questioning the greve and the laws of Vinterstock?"

Ingrid smiled and quirked an eyebrow, intently moulding her face into a picture of light-hearted mischief again. "Of course not. If I did, he might send you after me, right? Tell me, lovely Lady of Assassination and Intimidation, is it true that you assassins carry long needles that you pierce people's hearts with?"

"Some do," Valour replied. "But it's old fashioned, like the axes we once used. Most of us prefer the surefire method of slitting a throat with a blade."

"Is a long needle into the heart not a surefire method?"

"It can be easy to miss a heart, especially if the mark puts up a fight. And a pierced lung takes too long to kill someone. You want to be sure you kill quickly, correctly, and without too much suffering."

"Are these delinquents not meant to suffer?"

"If the mark is meant to suffer, they usually end up in the court of justice and are sentenced to floggings or torture."

Ingrid whistled low. "Thank you for being honest. People so often shield me from anything grim, like I'm some sort of fragile flower who would wilt at the true nature of the world." She went to the bay window, pushing aside one of the thick velvet drapes to peer down at the street below.

Valour liked that big window and appreciated it even more now that it bathed Ingrid Rytterdahl in light from the nearest streetlamp while distracting her with the views of the city, giving Valour the thorough study of Ingrid that she had wanted for ages. The corners of Ingrid's mouth stayed arched up even when she wasn't smiling, as if she knew of some amusing secret. She wore rouge on cheeks that were a pale brown, a few shades lighter than her father's skin. Did she, like Valour, have one Vinterstockian parent and one foreign one? The only mention she'd ever heard of Ingrid's mother was the comment about settling for only one when speaking of the nine mothers of Heimdal. Valour wasn't about to ask for the details. What if Mrs Rytterdahl had passed away? Or cheated on Mr Rytterdahl and left with most of their fortune? Or ate the family dog and had to be locked up somewhere? Best not to ask.

"Busy out there," Ingrid mused before replacing the drapes. "I suppose people are making the most of the last imports." Her face drew into a deep frown. "That accursed ice keeping the clippers away. The hotel spends a fortune buying spices and such from continent salesmen when there is no sea trade."

Ingrid sat down in a gilded armchair and adjusted her towering, white wig. Valour had seen her in different wigs but preferred it when she simply piled her own black hair up high. Not that the wig made her look bad; Valour doubted anything could. It was simply that Valour had hunted lots of people with wigs and been amazed at how often they had to stop at a powder room to re-powder them. That would get dull if the two of them were to spend time together.

Valour hummed. "You do know what goes on in your father's hotels, then? He hinted that you were a rubbish apprentice."

"Rubbish? Papa did not say that."

"No. Hm. That was me. I can be… rude."

"Ah. Well, that accusation has been thrown at me too." Her gaze travelled over Valour's face. "Your expression makes me think you do not wish to be rude."

Valour gave a curt nod and busied herself checking a chafe mark on her palm from the stone sack.

Ingrid blew out a long, slow breath. "I do care about the hotels and I am more invested in one day running them than Papa knows." She closed her eyes for a moment. "I simply wish to have a life outside of work. Papa labours himself half to death. Human lives are painfully brief, so I'd rather work half as much and settle for half the income."

"Easy to say for someone who's grown up with plenty of coin in their purse."

Shit, why did she say that? This woman threw her far too much.

"True," Ingrid said, not seeming offended but instead… what? Sad? "Although, my family wasn't always rich. I know painfully well what it is to go to bed hungry and to be denied housing because someone dislikes the way you look or how you talk."

Ingrid blinked rapidly and then was all breezy curiosity again.

"Anyway, what does your family do?"

"Not much."

"What do you mean?"

"My father was a sailor and a drunkard. He drowned himself when I was four. Mother was an assassin but since being hanged for killing a nobleman who attacked her, all she does is fertilise the city's soil."

"Oh. I'm so very sorry to hear that."

"I'm sorrier." Valour scuffed her foot against the well-oiled pine floorboards. "Like you said, there's a lot of death around here. Maybe more than there should be." Valour bit the inside of her cheek. She'd said too much.

Ingrid regarded her for a long time. Valour tried not to meet her eye but also not to seem like she was avoiding eye contact. Instead, she evaluated her guest. Ingrid's nonchalance and breeziness was probably a wall to keep people from getting too close. The chattiness and curiosity were real, though. She wasn't sure about the coquette flirting; she'd need more time to gauge its genuineness. What was obvious was that Ingrid Rytterdahl was sharp as a knife, much smarter than people gave her credit for.

"If your mother was also an assassin, I gather she had one of those noun, verb, or adjective names too?"

"You ask a shit-heap of questions."

"True. Which is good because you do not strike me as the type who gives up a lot of information without being asked," Ingrid said with a cheeky smile. "Or the type who even answers direct questions, like ones about your mother's name."

"Raze," Valour mumbled.

"Sorry, what was that? Did you say 'race' as in racing around or 'raise' as in raising something up?"

"Neither. It was Raze with a 'z'. As in razing a city to the ground."

It had been years since she had said that name out loud. It made grief pinch at her heart with sharp, frozen nails.

"Her name was basically demolish or annihilate? Ye gads, that's marvellous!"

Valour shrugged. "It's an assassin designation. It served its purpose. What was your mother's name?"

"Was? Is it that obvious that my mother has passed?"

Valour froze. "N-no. Not obvious, I just assumed."

"Oh, it's not a problem. Motherless children often recognise each other, even when we're adults and know how to stash the loss behind our hearts. Her name was Embla."

"A local name? She was from here, then?"

"Yes. Papa's family travelled around, searching for work and finding little, and one day their journeys brought them to Vinterstock. He met mama and was spellbound." She paused to sigh. "One day, as an adult with enough coin for the journey, he came back. Together, they explored the world and had me. When I was nine, we moved to mama's beloved Vinterstock. She was warm, smart, and funny, none of which protected her from the black death."

"Shit. The plague?"

"Mm. I had just turned thirteen and couldn't comprehend how someone could go from perfect health to a wretch covered in buboes a mere six days later. I don't know if it was the fever or the constant vomiting that killed her in the end."

There were a billion things Valour wanted to say. About how that was a particularly terrible thing to watch someone die of. About how the loss of a parent hurt every day, even if you were barely aware of it. About how lost a child was after losing the one who was meant to be your guiding light, your comfort, your protector. How it taught you that you could never depend on anyone. How it created a hole you could never fill.

Instead, she said, "I wish that hadn't happened to you."

It was a ridiculous thing to say, but Ingrid gave a heartfelt smile. "So do I."

The grandfather clock in the corner chimed and Valour twitched. "Godsdamnit, I'm late."

"Oh my. Supping with some dapper gentleman, are we?"

Valour stopped halfway to her boots and slow-turned to look at Ingrid.

The hotel heiress held her hands up. "Yes, yes. All right. I *have* heard that you favour the fairer sex."

Valour pulled her boots on while trying to think of a polite way to throw someone out. "Sorry to ask you to leave, but it's time for vesper prayers at the sanctum."

"The mysteries of the religious zealots of death unravel! Is it true that you drink the blood from your marks out of gold cups under an equally gilded crucifix?"

Valour stopped lacing up her boots to once again give Ingrid an incredulous glare.

Ingrid laughed. "No, I didn't think so. How about the rumour about fasting until you see the dead and can beg their forgiveness?"

"Fasting until you hallucinate does sound like something the order might do, but not the apologising." Valour strapped her knives on. "Now, I don't mean to be rude, but I have to go. And while I suppose you do in a way own this room, I'd not like to leave you alone here." She put her cloak on. "There are sharp things stashed everywhere."

"Are we still talking about the room, or about you?" The words couldn't have been an insult—Ingrid's tone had been too kind for that.

Valour just said, "Put your clothes on." Then added, "Please."

The other woman obeyed, murmuring something that sounded like, "So much more exciting if you'd asked me to do the opposite."

Valour turned and busied herself with extinguishing the room's candles and oil lamps, refusing to blush in sight of Ingrid bloody Rytterdahl.

Robed in that sable cloak once more, Ingrid opened the door and said over her shoulder, "I like you precisely as much as I thought I would. I shall let you attempt to convince me to conform to what is expected of me. Good luck with that, though."

Then she left.

"Thanks," Valour muttered, and waited just long enough that they wouldn't have to share the stairs.

CHAPTER 10
THE VALOUR QUANDARY

PETRICHOR STOOD IN the sanctum's great hall. He clasped his hands behind his back—they still trembled otherwise. Could the others tell that he had suffered that unhinged fit of panic before coming here? He gripped his hands tighter.

Supper had, as usual, been served down in the refectory while the vesper prayer was held up here in the hall. They were in the final section of the forty-segment prayer now, Halcyon reciting Axsten's decrees in his pleasant voice. Everyone joined in for the last words of each passage, "May our blades be as sharp as his judgements."

In short, all was as it should be.

Except that there was a letter weighing far too heavy in Petrichor's pocket, that insistent trembling in his hands, and a remembered conversation with a dying minion of Brandquist's.

Should he tell Valour what the man had said? She wouldn't have shared the information with *him*—she had never shared anything with him. Why was he the only one who ever saw how vile Valour could be? Was that why she hated him? What would life have been like if she didn't hate him?

When the vesper service was over, and those whose kills had been identified down in the tunnels were notified, the assassins disbanded. Petrichor considered taking a carriage home as the weather was foul but walked all the same, thinking the cold might put him right. It didn't.

Back home, he paced, unable to calm down or to think of the next step to take in the hunt for Brandquist. The wind screeched past his windows, rattling them with an abhorrent noise. At least there was noise: the weather, students revelling in the rooms below, his fireplace crackling. It wasn't grave-silent like that basement cell. Now, though, it wasn't only the recollection of the shame, fear, and silence vexing him. There was that *other* memory too, of what Valour had done during his imprisonment. Would she even remember that?

Petrichor groaned before rubbing his sore, knotted shoulders. He was so tense that he worried his muscles would set this way, contracted and withering.

He went to his bookshelf, put his hand on the large volume bearing the title *Panaceas and Chrysopoeia* and pulled it out. Behind it, a rolled-up bundle lay tucked well out of sight. He took it out with reverent hands and brought it to his desk. From a drawer, he retrieved a large piece of wine-red calf-skin. Then he opened the kit and chose the sharpest scalpel from within. Even just gathering forth the materials and tools like this slowed his breathing.

He made the first cut in the leather as the decision crystallised in his mind—he would tell Valour what the coughing man had said. Not because he valued her opinion, wanted her to like him, or owed her any assistance. It was solely to see her face when he informed her of why Brandquist had decided against contacting her. Yes. Only that.

He folded the trimmed calf-skin, once, twice, thrice, submerging himself in the familiar task. Finally, some calm settled into his bones.

CHAPTER 11

VALOUR IS NOT PREPARED

THE NEXT MORNING Valour sat by the fire, barely awake and holding a teacup with both hands to warm them. She'd eaten her daily porridge and was about to wash it down with tea when there was a knock on the door.

Wearing only woollen stockings and an old nightshirt, and still holding her teacup, Valour opened it to the vision of Ingrid Rytterdahl, dressed and coiffured as if she'd recently come from the opera or some ball at the greve's palace.

"Hello again, our Lady of Assassination and Intimidation."

Before Valour had time to reply, Ingrid smirked and added, "Ready to pound it into me?"

The cup tipped in Valour's hand, spilling some tea as its holder tried very hard not to show any reaction.

Ingrid's flirtatious smirk grew. "By 'pounding it into me', I am obviously referring to drumming my duties and proper behaviour into me."

"Uh-huh. Sure." Valour snorted, then stood aside. "This time, I'll invite you before you storm in."

Like last time, Ingrid entered and shrugged off her shoes and sable-lined cloak with graceful movements. "Thank you. I'm sorry if this is a bad time and I am even more sorry about the ridiculous task you have been set. I mean, imagine cajoling an assassin into lecturing a grown woman."

"Your father more asked me," she said, and half-stifled a yawn, "to keep you company."

"That is a diplomatic way of saying that he wants you to spy on me, which is equally absurd and unacceptable of him."

If she found the idea so insulting, why was she here? Valour remembered the reason she had given last time they spoke, as well as the way Ingrid had been watching her for months. She 'liked' Valour. Well, that wouldn't last long.

"Before we get into all that," Valour said. "I need to perform my daily wash ritual."

An excellent excuse for more time to wake up and prepare her mind for another too fast-paced conversation with this overwhelming woman. Gods, that perfume of hers smelled wonderful.

Ingrid's gaze flicked to the bathroom door and then back. "I see. What I have heard about the Order of Axsten being fervent about hygiene is true, then. Shall I leave?"

"Up to you. You can wait here if you'd like. I never take long," Valour said, yawning again.

"You just woke up. May I ask why you seem so exhausted?"

Valour finished her tea in one too-hot gulp and slammed the cup down. "Didn't get much sleep. Nightmares."

"I suppose your job would give anyone nightmares."

"The other assassins don't have them." As far as she knew anyway, but she wouldn't admit to never asking.

Having coveted this woman from afar for so long was a problem. It made Valour say too much. Feel too much. She *had* to stay detached.

"Your occupation truly is fascinating." Ingrid moved nearer, so close that Valour felt the warmth of her, before adding, "Do you enjoy being an assassin?"

"We're back to your quick-fire questions, huh?"

"Yes. Bad habit," Ingrid admitted, humility creeping into her flirty expression. "I find them useful when it comes to my favourite hobby: learning everything and anything."

"Are they always this blunt and personal?"

"I was not aware that enquiring if you like your job would be personal. Or blunt, come to think of it. You need not answer if you don't want to."

"No."

"'No' as in you won't answer, or 'No' as in you do not enjoy your profession?"

Valour scrubbed her face with both hands. She had said too much already. "I don't want to talk about this."

"Then we shall leave it at me saying that I'm sorry you have nightmares and that I regret my prying." Ingrid stepped back with an air of respect. "Let me know if you want me to have some calming herbs placed under your pillow when the room is next cleaned."

Was it really going to be that easy to get out of that conversation? "Uh, sure. I will."

Ingrid gave every impression of having moved on. She took Valour in while raking her teeth over her painted lower lip. "I suppose you will take your hair out of that braid to wash. I must confess to wondering how you look with your hair down."

"Uh-huh."

Ingrid closed the distance between them again. "Will you… give me a little peek before you go in there?"

The way she said 'give me a little peek' didn't sound like she was merely talking about hair.

Thrilled by the flirtation, Valour studied her guest. By every account—and the rumour mill was overfilled with them—Ingrid Rytterdahl only enjoyed the company of men, so this flirting was unlikely to lead to anything. That wasn't unusual, of course. Every same-gender-lover had stories of opposite-gender-lovers enjoying living on the edge by trifling with them but shying away when things got real. The rich and bored were particularly known for this sort of tourism. Ingrid would be the exact type.

Valour didn't have the energy for games that led nowhere, though. She yawned. "I'm not giving you anything but some company and a bit of woman-to-woman advice about listening to your father."

"Oh, splendid," Ingrid drawled. "I certainly haven't heard that countless times before."

"I'm going to wash."

"Go ahead. I have a book to read." From a hidden pocket in the wide skirts of her dress, Ingrid produced a small volume. It had one of those furtive covers of censored books smuggled in from the continent. She gracefully placed herself in a chair and cracked the book open. Valour could see the words 'The Tzar's Solid Shaft' on the title page as she walked off.

When safe in the bathroom, she pulled off her nightshirt, stockings, and the hidden leather brace with four knife sheaths that she rarely went without, before pouring jugs of water into the basin. Shivering, she mixed some of the order's aniseed and lye soap with water in her hands until it was a grainy froth and rubbed it over herself. She stopped mid-movement at a knock on the outer door.

"I'll answer it," Ingrid called.

Before she could do anything, Valour heard the door creak open, and then a deep voice she knew all too well said, "You are not Valour."

Petrichor. What the troll-shit was he doing here? Valour scooped water onto herself to quickly get rid of the soap, not even flinching at the water's coldness in her hurry to finish.

"Very perceptive, sir. I'm not," Ingrid said. "In fact, I should say I'm about, oh, half the muscle power and twice the chattiness?"

"Who are you?"

Ingrid laughed and it sounded like bits of river ice landing in a glass of vodka. "Ye gads, is it not obvious? I'm her lover. Who might you be?"

Cheeks burning, Valour wanted to shout that Ingrid was nothing of the sort, but before she could, she heard Petrichor scoff, "You're not her type," and—uncharacteristically for such a soft-stepping man—stomp into the room.

Valour paused. She had a type? And Petrichor of all people knew what it was? He'd have to tell her at some point. She dried herself off with haste.

Petrichor's annoying trademark sniff could be heard even through the door. "I recognise you now. You're that carousing daughter of Mahadev Rytterdahl, are you not?"

"Carousing?" Ingrid said merrily. "I haven't heard that one before. But yes, I am indeed her. You know Papa?"

"I know of him. I make a point to learn about anyone important in this city."

"I see. Is that how you know Valour?"

"Valour?" he said in agitated tones. "She is less important than the mice in the eaves of this hotel."

"We do not have mice!"

"No, of course not. Valour is the only pet vermin you allow in your altar to overpriced opulence."

That was it. Valour wrapped the towel around herself and stormed out into Petrichor's personal space. "Why in Hel's realm are you here?" She remembered their all-important ritual and added, "Oh, and have you gotten that stick out of your a—"

"We do not have time for your usual nonsense, Valour. I must tell you something before I change my mind."

She stiffened, knowing that look on his face. "What's wrong?"

"I had an encounter," he said so only she could hear. "One connected to the hunt for Brandquist."

Over by the window, Ingrid sat down with her book again. In low tones, Petrichor quickly described a talk he'd had with a dying henchman.

"Huh," Valour said. "I wonder if Brandquist chose a useless messenger because it wouldn't matter if you killed him."

Ingrid drew in breath. "That is rather callous, don't you think?"

"The statement or the act?" Petrichor asked. Then he grimaced as if catching himself. "You overheard that? How sharp is your hearing? Are you not reading? Why are you still here? Valour, get rid of your landlady so we can speak."

"Landlady?" Ingrid rolled her eyes in Valour's direction. "I told him I was your lover, but he did not believe me. Apparently I'm not your type?"

"Hang on, we were discussing something important." Valour kicked the side of her bed. "Can you two stop distracting me? This is why I hate people!"

"I'll get back on topic when you oust the civilian," Petrichor said.

Ingrid opened her mouth to retort but Valour spoke first. "She's here because her father has asked me to accompany her for some of the week. And you"—she spun towards Ingrid—"can't go around lying to people in my life about who you are."

Ingrid shrugged. "I thought I was helping your reputation as a womaniser?"

"I have one of those?" That reminded her of another question, so she poked Petrichor's shoulder. "And what in the name of all bäckahäst-shit is my 'type'?"

Petrichor looked thoroughly uninvested. "Practical. Easy maintenance. More on the slattern end of the scale."

"Pardon me, are you questioning my promiscuousness?" Ingrid said. "I'll have you know I am much more of a stud than you shall ever be."

"Highly likely," Petrichor said. "I do not waste my time with messy, dull ventures like intercourse."

"We're not getting back on bloody topic here!" Valour bellowed.

At that point, Ingrid absolutely ruined her concentration by wiping some soap suds off her bare forearm and softly saying, "My sincere apologies."

Valour became acutely aware that she was only wearing a towel. It didn't matter that Petrichor saw her like this; in his eyes she was all but an inanimate object. Hel's realm, they'd been forced to take baths together to save time and water as children—right up until they'd tried to drown each other.

Ingrid Rytterdahl was another matter.

"Ingrid," Valour said while pulling her towel tighter. "Could you step outside while I talk to this nuisance?"

The hotel heiress touched her hair. "How about I give you some privacy by borrowing your powder room? This new wig is too tight and must come off."

"Fine," Valour said, locating some clean clothes.

When Ingrid had taken her first step into the bathroom, Petrichor picked back up as if he had never stopped speaking. "That addict was waiting for me on my preferred path back to the university. It's... not a place anyone would wait for me unless they knew my movements well."

The secretive arse-boil looked as uncomfortable as a hedgehog in a brush shop.

Ingrid, in the process of closing the door, quickly interjected, "Must be quite startling, finding out that they know where you live."

The door shut and the two assassins were left staring at each other.

Petrichor, pallid as a snow angel's tits at the best of times, paled even further. "They do not."

"Oh, come now, I thought you were meant to be the clever one," Valour said, pulling her clothes on. "Why else would they be waiting in that spot? If I were them, I'd go to your place to search it. Or wait there to give you another message. Either way, I'd thoroughly trash it, getting my dirty fingers on all your precious books."

She buttoned up her justacorps but stopped as she found the second button missing. When and where had she lost that? Godsdamnit, this was her least threadbare one. She looked up at the sound of Petrichor running out of the room as if his arse hairs were on fire.

Valour mumbled, "Goodbye to you, too."

Ingrid poked her now de-wigged head out from the bathroom. "Well?"

"Well what?"

"Are we following him?" She stepped back into the main room. "I mean, are you not curious to know if they've breached his home? If they have, they might come here next."

Valour tried not to stare as Ingrid struggled to pile up her thick, luscious hair before finally giving up and leaving it to hang unfashionably loose and draped over her shoulders. There were traces of wig powder left on the black tresses, like stars against the night sky.

Ingrid hummed pensively. "Although, I suppose the hotel does have security. We could stay here. Pick the *safe* option. If that's your preference."

Valour felt the corners of her mouth tug into a smile. What was it about this woman that made everything feel like an adventure?

She picked up a strip of leather and threw it to Ingrid. "Tie your hair up and get those posh shoes on. Let's go see if the prim worm has had his little haven disturbed. If he has, he'll cause shit, believe you me!"

They got their outerwear on and rushed after Petrichor. Valour had never visited him but knew very well where he lived. How he'd holed himself up in that astronomy tower like a heimcrow in a nest.

When they were at the university and running up the spiral staircase, she heard Ingrid huff and puff and called over her shoulder, "Are you all right?"

"Yes. Just... not in... assassin shape," Ingrid wheezed from a dozen steps down.

Finally up to Petrichor's floor, Valour rushed in through the open door.

He spun on his heels to glare at her. "What are you doing here?"

"We're part of a walking tour of the most boring places of Vinterstock," Valour muttered. "What do you think we're doing here, Prince of Prissiness?"

"We?"

There was wheezing and posh-sounding cursing from the staircase.

Petrichor scowled. "You brought the socialite?"

"Sure. She's interesting, attractive, and she annoys you. I might bring her everywhere."

He pursed his lips. "As you can see, she was wrong. No one has been here. I leave a strand of hair stuck in my door. If someone had disturbed the room, the hair would be on the floor. It was not."

Ingrid joined them, bent over with her hands on her thighs. "I... loathe... stairs."

She'd barely panted the words out when there were other footsteps coming up said stairs. *Running* footsteps.

Petrichor leapt over to a bookshelf, reaching for what Valour assumed was a weapon. Unless he was going to brain someone with a pile of books. Meanwhile, she snapped into her fighting stance, just before the doorway filled with four armed newcomers.

One of them, a white-haired woman with a cruel, pinched face, stepped forward. "Well now, you Axsten devils aren't usually this helpful. You both being in the same place—and picking this one, which unlike the hotel is unguarded—was decent of you."

Time for a bluff. Valour tried for a cocky grin and said, "Maybe we tired of you following us from a cowardly distance and decided to draw you out?"

"If that is so, I hope you accounted for what that would entail," the woman said, drawing the belt pistol that had glinted at her waistband.

Valour had, in fact, *not* accounted for what that would entail. Shit.

CHAPTER 12

BULLETS AND BLOWS

PETRICHOR DIDN'T HESITATE. The moment he saw the four attackers, he grabbed the made-ready pistol hidden behind his encyclopaedias of lethal plants.

"Tell me who sent you," he said, hoping they'd admit to the obvious answer so they could move on to more intricate and important questions.

There was no reply, though. Unless you counted the white-haired woman aiming her weapon squarely at him. It was a matchlock piece, a relic compared to his flintlock duelling pistol, but just as lethal.

"No talking and straight to the action? My sort of fight," Valour said.

From the corner of his eye, he could see her pulling out a knife from her boot and another from somewhere within her shirt.

"You may want to take refuge in the powder room," Petrichor said to Ingrid.

While speaking, he pointed his pistol at the older woman who was aiming one at him. They both had but one shot each before the lengthy and messy reloading process, but there was no escaping that one bullet at such close range could do extensive damage, especially if this woman was a good shot.

Ingrid did dive into the bathroom as requested, but not before sticking her head out into the hallway as she passed and shouting, "Help! Intruders!"

Petrichor grimaced. Calling for help was a sensible thing to do if you were Ingrid Rytterdahl, but not if you were seasoned Assassins of Axsten. Shouting for aid would only make a clueless

70

student or university steward wander into a rain of bullets and blows.

Swearing about possible interruptions, the white-haired woman bared teeth that were in as miserable a state as the bleeding gums around them. "Fine. To speed things up, I shall try a verbal warning after all. My colleague told you to stop hunting Brandquist and wait for further instructions, yes? Heed that advice."

Petrichor didn't bother schooling his face to not show the affront. "No."

"See now, I thought that would be your answer. Stubborn, bloody assassins," snarled another of the intruders. This one sounded younger, was of undetermined gender, and wore a hood pulled so low it covered most of their face.

One of the other thugs, a man the size of a small fortress, bounded towards Valour while howling, "No more talk."

At the same time, the white-haired woman lowered her weapon to aim at Petrichor's legs instead of his chest and put her finger to the trigger. Petrichor mimicked her movements, the difference being that with his quicker reflexes, he fired before she did and leapt aside. This meant his shot struck her thigh while hers only grazed his trouser leg, and the lead ball buried itself in the desk behind him. She keened and collapsed, hand against the wound and looking ready to pass out.

Petrichor surveyed their foes, wondering which one would be the best bet to give him information about Brandquist.

The older woman was out of the fray; next were her three associates. They didn't appear too used to combat but what they lacked in experience they made up for in determination, since they all looked like they wanted to rip his vocal cords out with pliers. They did not seem to have any firearms, but they were armed. The man trading blows with Valour had brass knuckles adorning both of his massive hands. The other two were the thin, androgynous hood-wearer, who brandished a cosh, and a curvy woman who held a long and menacing butcher's knife in each hand. They were both coming for him.

During his evaluation of their stances and builds, he said, "Valour, note that these varlets have decided that I am the biggest threat, since most of them are focusing on me."

He heard Valour pant and the sound of one of her knives go flying before she answered, "I'm fighting an honest to gods giant of a troll over here! He's five times the foe of your bloody rabble put together!"

"Hardly. As ever, you exaggerate," Petrichor said, subtly reaching into his coat for his knife with one hand and with the other taking a firmer grip of his pistol to use it to bludgeon.

The distraction was working. His enemies were watching Valour and him argue, and not noting what his hands were doing. Amateurs.

"Am not," Valour said before there was the thud of fist against flesh.

"I refuse to get caught up in a demeaning 'am not, am too' debate," Petrichor said calmly. His knife appeared stuck in its sheath. "Simply take my word for it when I say that you exaggerate. You have done so ever since you were a child."

"I'll exaggerate a fist into your face soon, snooty-arse!"

Then Valour jumped up to land a perfect punch on her troll's nose and the big man staggered back, screaming in surprise.

That fired the two smaller assailants out of their distraction and into action. They pounced on Petrichor before he had managed to fish out his blade. The knife-wielder led the charge. Petrichor ducked and swivelled as the curvaceous woman bore her blades down on him, resulting in her stabbing empty air. He straightened and spun his arm up, smacking her in the face with his pistol. Blood sprayed out of her nose, making Petrichor back away even faster than he had from the knives. He didn't have time to worry about getting blood on himself for long, though. The hooded assailant stepped past their colleague and raised the cosh to slam it onto Petrichor's head.

Quickly, he dove to the side, flattened his free hand, and chopped into the hood-wearer's knee, knocking his foe off balance. Then the knife-wielder was back and with her nose still bleeding, she stabbed at Petrichor's middle. He only had enough space to move away a little, so the weapon slashed his ribs. The pain wasn't too bad, but the fact that she had ruined his favourite waistcoat vexed him almost as much as the bullet piercing the leg of his breeches had. Brandquist owed him a new suit.

He and the knife-wielder both stared at his wound, but Petrichor focused back on the fight first, right in time to use the distraction to smack one of the bloodied knives out of her hand with his pistol. The blade slid across the floor of the small room and almost hit the white-haired woman, who was dragging herself out into the hallway. Fine, the old lady could escape. Petrichor would get his answers from the other three.

The knife-wielder stabbed at him with her remaining butcher's knife. He ducked, right as Valour—who was evading one of her troll's clumsy jabs—swept by and kicked the woman's hand so the knife fell.

She grinned at him. "You're welcome. Try to keep up, prissy pickler."

Petrichor sighed at Valour and her illogical insults but used the moment when the knife-wielder was searching for her dropped weapon to put all his force into kicking his leg up and smashing his boot into the side of her head. She sailed backwards and lay unmoving next to his bed.

Two down, one to go.

The remaining one, the hood-wearer, had recovered enough to attack again, but stopped to check on the curvy woman, caressing her hair and whispering something that sounded like, "Are you hurt, my love?"

Petrichor spent this pause checking his pocket for his trusty twine for tying up their foes for interrogation, all while throwing a glance over at a dishevelled Valour. She used her entire body and a bit of a run-up to slam the massive man against the shelves, causing a landslide of books to plummet down on him. The man screamed as a corner of the very well-written *Rockwork and Stonecraft of Vinterstock* hit him in the face.

"Do not let him damage my books," Petrichor called over to her. "Nor kill nor render him unconscious. We must have answers."

"I know," she barked, and lightning-fast kicked her assailant in the gut.

Anyone who had seen Valour fight knew her deadly mix of sophisticated Axsten fighting techniques, a disregard for pain, and pure brute force. The Brandquist underling was four moves behind in this chess game of violence and unaware that the match was already over. Petrichor tried hard, so accursed hard, not to be impressed.

Meanwhile his own foe, the hood-wearer, was standing again after checking on the butcher's knife woman. Petrichor didn't dally and instantly used the pistol as a blunt weapon once more to hit his enemy right in the crown of that ridiculous hood. Now he had time to put the pistol down nearer the gunpowder for future reloading and this time *successfully* retrieve his knife.

"Right," he said to the person in the hood. "Tell me where I can find Brandquist."

"I'll tell you nought. But I will break every bone in your body."

Petrichor said, "I doubt you have the skill or the anatomical knowledge." He stabbed the knife into his enemy's left shoulder, then swiftly snatched it out and plunged it into their left leg as well. The hood-wearer screamed and bent to hold their free hand over the gushing leg wound.

Petrichor stood straight and tightened his loosened ponytail, assuming all was done and that his answers would finally be coming. Instead, the hood-wearer swung their cosh in a forceful upwards thrust right at Petrichor's genitalia, followed by a hard punch with their free hand to the same spot. He heard himself gasp as he dropped to his knees. His eyes watered and shut as white-hot pain slammed through his middle in wave after wave, disabling him from action as well as coherent thought. He tried to get back his breath, and his focus. With a slow blink, he distantly saw the hood-wearer limp out of the room, only stopping to help the knife-wielding woman up so they could hobble away together.

Through the slowly subsiding agony, he told himself that it was acceptable that they left, that it was fine that he was in no state to chase them. They still had one Brandquist underling left to question.

That was when the henchman in question loomed in front of Petrichor. One of the giant man's eyes was swollen shut, he was bleeding from nose and mouth, and he stumbled with the stupor of someone who'd taken too many blows to the head. Fortunately, Valour had clearly disarmed him of those brass knuckles. Where was Valour? Petrichor looked around and found her lying on the ground, bent over and clutching her stomach, but alive and conscious.

"You should've agreed not to chase Brandquist," the large man whinged, spitting out a couple of teeth.

Petrichor was gathering himself to get back up, to ignore the pain that had gone from searing to an unignorable ache that spread from his groin through his body like ice crystals across a windowpane.

"Well, you see…" Petrichor managed to croak out. Then he used every ounce of willpower, of discipline, of pride, to stand and continued with, "Assassins from a distinguished order in the employ of the greve do not obey drug dealers." He looked around for his pistol. "That's not how the world works, you dullard. However, if you tell me what I wish to know, I may listen to what you have to say."

Valour appeared in his line of vision. She was wincing with pain and ashen-faced, but looked her usual bravado-filled self as she reached up to tap the big man on the shoulder and say, "Hey, troll-face."

The henchman spun his head around to her and, with the unmistakable glint of brass knuckles on her fist, she threw an uppercut at his nose. While he was stunned, she jumped on his back and hooked her arm around his neck. She hung there, strangling him. With his nose gushing blood into his mouth and his airways constricted, the giant man gargled and gasped, trying to get air and to get Valour off his back. He was too far gone to manage either.

"There," Petrichor said. "Now we have your undivided attention."

He afforded himself a moment to show domination, let his

pain lessen, and consider his questions for their foe. There was no hurry to tie him up. Say what you wanted about Valour, but at least she wasn't going to let their only remaining informant go.

CHAPTER 13

TROLLS, SPINES, AND UNSHAKEABLE FAITH

PETRICHOR WATCHED, FLABBERGASTED, as Valour let him go.

The gigantic man ran off and Petrichor tried to follow but stumbled due to the pain of moving. "Why in the name of all plague-ridden imps did you release him, Valour?"

"He was choking on his own blood and couldn't bloody well breathe!" she shouted back, cheeks embarrassment red. "He's not a mark. If he died, I'd stand before the court of justice for unlawful killing."

"Die? Did you see how fast he ran off? Did he seem about to perish to you? Don't stand there defending your folly. Retrieve him."

She was already chasing after the escapee though, and with her speed greater than the henchman's, she would no doubt have caught him… if a student hadn't stopped her by blocking the doorway and gripping her arm to ask, "Miss, are you all right? I heard shouts of requiring assistance and hurried to your aid."

"No! Yes! Argh!" Valour roared, eloquent as ever.

The henchman's thudding steps descended the hallway, and then the spiral staircase got quieter and quieter as Valour tried to get away from the knight in shining student robes, who was still holding on to her and in calming tones saying that she should let him help.

"Don't need help. I need to catch the troll!" she shouted.

The student frowned. "Troll? Please compose thyself, miss. You're delusional."

"Not delusional. Furious as shit. Move," Valour growled at him.

Petrichor strained to run after the escaping minion but—damn this pain that was worse than any stab wound or gunshot he had experienced—couldn't do more than limp a few steps before the pain made him nearly pass out. He had to watch Valour gently wrestle the student away and finally give chase. Petrichor scoffed. He would've struck the student or pushed him through the hallway and down the stairs in the hope that he would hit the fleeing henchman. One could get away with so much more when not burdened by a conscience.

When Petrichor had finally recovered enough to make his way to the stairs, Valour was coming back up and cut him off. "No point. He's godsdamned gone!" She smacked the doorframe in rage as she went back into his rooms. She mumbled something about her face bruising, then clutched her middle again and swore.

Petrichor was making every effort not to show his own pain. "Yes. But at least he can breathe freely, right?"

Valour crossed her arms over her chest. "Do you plan to spend the rest of the day bloody sniping and biting my head off?"

"Surely you will bite your own cursed head off? Even you must be overcome with boundless shame after letting our only source of information go like that." He hoped she was. Her red-cheeked scowling did seem to indicate as much.

"What I'm overcome with is the urge to pull your spine out through your nose!"

"Knowing you, you would foul up and grab my intestine instead of my spine."

They glared at each other in infected silence.

"I don't think we would have gotten anything out of him anyway," Valour said nonchalantly while pulling her many layers up over her stomach, assumedly to inspect the damage from those brass knuckles. "I'm not sure how much they would've known, anyway. They only seemed to have been sent here to scare us."

Ingrid strode out of the bathroom with casual poise. "Or kill you."

"They don't want us dead," Valour said, tucking her clothes back in place fast now that Ingrid had arrived.

"She's right," Petrichor reluctantly agreed. "The dying minion I met told me Brandquist knew that if they got rid of us, another assassin would be given the hit. Brandquist's organisation probably meant what they said: they want us to back off while they concoct another ridiculous plan that they expect us to enact."

"You can stay and ask them," Ingrid said, brushing something off Valour's sleeve. "I wager they will return to finish the job. With greater numbers and some rifles."

Valour groaned.

"Quite so," Ingrid said in reply. "So, you can stay and wait for that. Or…" She smiled. "You could ask me nicely and I could show you a place I hide out when Papa sends people to shadow or chaperone me."

Petrichor harrumphed. "No. We are the ninth and tenth assassins of the Order of Axsten." He made sure to put emphasis on every single word.

Ingrid merely raised her flawless eyebrows in query.

"The most feared, well-organised, and tightknit institute in not only Vinterstock but the entire country," he clarified. "Valour and I shall turn there."

With a measuring look, Ingrid said, "You have unshakeable faith in the order, don't you?"

"Refrain from analysing me," he snapped. "But yes, as a matter of fact, I do. I take it by your tone that you have none?"

"I know nothing of it and so will defer to your expertise, Master Assassin."

Valour snorted out a little laugh.

Petrichor adjusted his clothing and headed towards the door. To his annoyance, he heard the socialite murmur, "There is, however, an interesting question lingering. If justice has to be served surreptitiously, and without set and checkable parameters, is it still justice?"

He wanted to answer her, to rail against her ignorance and judgement. Except he had more important things to do. He would get to the sanctum and to the wise council of Halcyon. Then everything would be made clear.

CHAPTER 14

TO THE SANCTUM

WHEN OUTSIDE, VALOUR took relief in being out of the stuffy university. She sucked in a few deep breaths, rinsing out her system with icy, fresh air. She stopped when she noticed Ingrid watching the lifting and lowering of her chest. At least the wanton woman had the decency to then look away with an abashed expression.

A mix of being flattered and amused filled Valour, but only lasted until she remembered where they were heading and why. She fastened her cloak tight and followed Petrichor towards the sanctum. The mid-morning was draped in frigid mist, making it harder to see anyone lurking or following them. Valour squinted at every shadow and checked every passer-by, hoping some Brandquist followers would attack. She preferred a good fight to hiding. Not to mention how she longed for some clues so she could finish this cursed job and be out of Petrichor's company. He was still leading the way, head down but gaze visibly flitting from building to building, person to person, surveying all.

Valour, however, kept getting sidetracked by Ingrid nodding to nigh everyone well-dressed they met. They bowed or curtsied to her, often with a flirtatious smile.

"Would you stop drawing attention to us?" Valour whispered, not disguising her irritation.

"I am not doing it intentionally."

"Fine. From now on, just try to... not."

Valour concentrated on examining their surroundings again. She needed to keep her focus. For decades, Vinterstock had teemed with people working for Brandquist, either voluntarily or by coercion. She could be facing an army of a thousand 'ness fiends with spiked clubs if she wasn't careful. Or worse, with pistols.

Soon the high-gabled, blackened wood roof of the Sanctum of Axsten protruded out of the mist straight ahead. Petrichor picked up his pace. She wished she could be as confident as he was that they'd be granted sanctuary and help in there.

At the door, Ingrid put a hand on her arm. "May I come in with you?"

Petrichor was about to knock but jerked to a stop. "What? Of course not!"

"Just a quick look?" Ingrid said. "Everyone gossips about this place with such fright and superstition. I have been dying to see it. I wouldn't touch anything or say anything. And I certainly would never divulge what I had seen."

Valour chuckled. "If I let you come in, Petrichor and most of the other assassins would go berserk. So obviously I am all for it."

"So obviously you should have your head examined," Petrichor said. "You will not use the sanctum to show off to comely women."

"Oh, come now," Valour said, as tired of his predictability as his assumptions. "It's not like she'd roam the godsdamned halls freely. We wouldn't let her see anything sacred or secret."

His eyes narrowed. "She's an outsider. She stays outside."

Ingrid nonchalantly adjusted her gloves. "You know, you are being very confrontational and loud for a man trying to avoid detection." She nodded in greeting to a man who had just bowed to her with a deferential, "Good morrow, Miss Rytterdahl."

Petrichor's gaze travelled over the crowds around him. "You would not dare."

Ingrid faced him. "Wouldn't I?"

For a long while Petrichor stood glowering down at Ingrid and clenching his jaw, the muscles there working like his teeth were crunching down on this new affront he must swallow.

"You get one minute," he said. "Then you leave and wait out here for us. Or even better, you leave and never enter my sight again. Understood?"

Ingrid nodded, looking like a child on Midsummer's Eve who'd been promised to lead the dances.

As they approached the sanctum, Valour leaned close to her. "I'm assuming you weren't going to expose us."

"I would never do such a thing. *Some people* do not recognise a bluff when they see one."

Petrichor didn't follow their normal custom of knocking, probably so no one would see Ingrid. Instead, he quietly opened the door and walked in ahead of them. Over his shoulder, he said, "Valour, let's find Halcyon. As a courtesy, we ought to explain to him why we are here and how long we will require sanctuary. Ensure the socialite only stays here for her peek and then leaves forthwith."

"Socialite? I do have a name," Ingrid said with amusement. "Which is more than you can say, Mr The-Smell-After-It-Rained."

Valour said nothing, still mulling over her doubts about coming here.

No one was in the sanctum's great hall, but there were voices from the basement level. As Petrichor headed that way, Ingrid, who had been looking around wide-eyed, stopped. "This is where he expects me to leave, is it not?"

Valour soaked up Ingrid's awed observation of the hall. It was a welcome novelty to be able to show the worldly Ingrid something new, something unique. "It is."

"Should I?"

Valour stalled, well aware that she must say yes. And that she wouldn't. "I get the feeling you go where you wish, like a river."

"Rivers sometimes get dammed up or dried out."

"Ha, not the kind that has your level of income," Valour said with a chuckle. "Follow me."

"What about you? Will you not be in trouble?"

"I'm always in trouble. Come on."

She led Ingrid down the stairs, following voices and clamour past the dormitories and the infirmary until they reached the massive training room. In there, three sets of assassins sparred. Furthest to the left, Halcyon boxed with Sister Mire. Petrichor stood next to them, watching like a thunderstruck sheep. Valour halted by an alcove containing a statue of Axsten and placed Ingrid behind the sculpture so she could peek out from under Axsten's axe but not be seen. "Don't move until I say."

"All right," Ingrid whispered.

Valour went over to Petrichor, standing in between him and Ingrid's hiding place. She was starting to come down from the high of sneaking Ingrid in. How bad would her punishment be if Ingrid was caught? Never mind. Pain was temporary, and it wasn't like they could throw her out of the order. Regrettably.

Soon Halcyon spotted them and stopped the fight. "Brother Petrichor, Sister Valour. I'm glad to see you." He was drenched in sweat and spattered with blood, assumedly from where he'd gotten a good hit into Mire's face, judging by her gushing nose and furious expression. He held up his index finger. "Pardon me for a moment, I need to take this shirt off."

Petrichor clasped his hands behind his back, standing like a soldier. "Of course. It has blood stains on the collar and just below the breastbone, both on the right side," he stated.

"He meant because it's drenched in sweat, which is uncomfortable, you fussy fop," Valour said, earning her a classic Petrichor glare.

Halcyon unbuttoned the shirt. "What can I do for you?"

"In truth, 'tis a long story, which I will lay out for you later," Petrichor said. "The salient point is that Valour and I need sanctuary until we come up with a plan."

Halcyon gave a pensive hum while pulling the shirt off and throwing it over a target practice board.

To her annoyance, Valour thought she heard Ingrid gasp appreciatively. Valour, glad she was the only one within hearing distance of Ingrid, found herself evaluating Halcyon's torso for the first time. Sure, he was more muscled than her. But being older meant he'd had nigh an extra decade to build muscle and trim fat. Besides, women had to work harder to do both those things. Valour huffed. She had more interesting things decorating her chest than Halcyon had anyway. It was hard to refute the aesthetically pleasing nature of a pair of breasts, even if it did mean she had to wear stays to keep the godsdamned things fixed in place.

Halcyon picked up a towel to dry himself with. "Now, I fear I must insist on hearing some of this long story of yours before we discuss sanctuary."

Petrichor was quiet, too busy staring at the shirtless leader of the assassins. Probably for different reasons than Ingrid, but who knew with Petrichor? The shit-heel was about as readable as a book dipped in molten steel and then dropped to the bottom of the sea.

Either way, it was up to Valour to speak. She explained what had happened up to this point and finished with, "So, we wanted to come here to plan our next move in peace and quiet."

"And to inform the order of our progress and gauge your thoughts," Petrichor said.

"Sure, that too," Valour agreed with a half shrug. "Finding the next step is key. We can't do much if we're constantly under attack, though. I doubt we can get assistance from other members, but perhaps we can contact the overseers to act as backup?" She scratched her cheek, mainly thinking out loud now. "I mean, an attack on us is technically an attack on the city leadership, so the overseers should be deployed to help us. Hang on, maybe we should send a missive to the greve? He did give us the assignment personally."

"A definite nay to the last part. Keep the greve out of this or you'll only vex him. Give me a moment," Halcyon said, slowly re-tying his soot-black hair into a tidier ponytail.

Valour could only think of one reason for his stalling. She'd been right; they would get no help here.

The leader of their order sucked air in through his teeth. "I wish I could aid you two. I always do." He glanced behind him as Mire gave a mirthless cackle, then continued, "Nevertheless, I fear the rest of us discussed this when you were given the job. It was clear that going after the head of such a big organisation was going to cause waves and—"

"Of course it was," Mire interrupted with a sneer. "Unless you managed to find Brandquist fast, sneak in, and perform a clean, quick kill. Like actual assassins." She bore her gaze into Valour's. "I wagered this would be another of those hits you declined due to the target not 'deserving to die'. I was looking forward to punishing you. Tell me, how many brands have I burned into your back by now?"

Valour ground her teeth. She didn't want Ingrid to have heard that.

"If we had, unaided, already killed Brandquist," Valour said, focused on Halcyon, not Mire, "would you have helped us when Brandquist's army of underlings came searching for who killed their leader?"

She expected Petrichor to tell her to show some respect as he usually did when she questioned the order, but he merely stood there, as still as the statue Ingrid was hiding behind.

"We would," Halcyon finally said. "Although I do not think we would have to. When their leader has been slain, they will surely be frightened of the reprisals of the overseers and the rest of the assassins if they hurt you."

Valour clenched her hands at her sides. "What about now? Why do you think they're not worried about that currently?"

"I do not know." He blew out a long breath. "Look, I can only speak to what is happening within these walls. The king has declared another war, which means we have a long list of aristocratic deserters to execute without their soldiers knowing they forswore their duty. We do not have the people to spare for your hit." Mouth downturned, he added, "I would help you myself but between my work here and helping run the Canal Street almshouse, I haven't a minute to spare."

Good. Reasonable excuses. Valour had worried he wouldn't even try to find some, but simply throw the book of procedures at them.

"Then at least let us stay here at the sanctum to plan our next steps," Petrichor said, finally snapping out of his shock.

Halcyon glanced back at Mire again and she took that as an official invitation into the conversation. "You know our ways. While it lends credence to the rumour that the greve has changed and mayhap lost his wits, he gave *you two* this hit. And that was how it was meant," she said, her creaking voice giving Valour an earache. "The two of you are to be so talented, such perfect little assassins, such role models for the rest of us, despite barely being out of swaddling clothes. Well, show us what you can do then. Without the help of your elders or the protection of these walls."

"That's bäckahäst-shit and you know it," Valour said.

Halcyon held up a hand. "Show Sister Mire the proper deference. And you"—he faced Mire—"let me handle this."

Attention back to Valour and Petrichor, he said, "You do not require a safety net. You finally get to spread your wings to soar into battle like Valkyries. Also, you might see this as a chance for you two to bury your juvenile feud and work together."

"Work together *or* lean into working against each other," Mire said, her eyes gleaming. "We always found we got the best out of you when we pitted you against one another. Like little dogs that have been starved and ignored, fighting twice as hard. And being twice as entertaining."

Only the aversion to adding more burn marks to her back kept Valour from pouncing on the older woman.

"I cannot… fathom that you're actually not going to help us," Petrichor said to Halcyon.

Their leader winced. "As I said, I wish I could. However, I have strict reasons not to."

Valour had to admit that he did look earnest. The way he kept casting glances at Mire showed that he wanted to be more helpful but had his hands tied. When Halcyon had been chosen as leader by his predecessor, it had been controversial. He was only in his late twenties and thereby the youngest leader in the order's long history. Now, in his early thirties, he was younger than most of the members and had to fight to keep their respect, especially while he tampered down the more violent traditions of the order. He had even changed his accent to be posher and colder to sound more authoritative. Nevertheless, when Valour was alone with Halcyon, she'd tell him exactly how shitty it was to not even let them shelter here.

"I still say this is bäckahäst-shit," she muttered, turning to leave.

Behind her back, Halcyon said, "Valour, before you storm out of here all hard done by, remember that on this rare occasion there are two assassins on the task. Use that." He was close enough to place a hand on her shoulder and give it a comforting squeeze. She still didn't turn back. Quietly, probably so Mire couldn't hear him, he said, "Duck down and keep to the shadows and you'll be fine. From what you said, they know it would be folly to kill you."

She scoffed.

He lowered his voice further. "They mean to intimidate you into inaction. Do not let them. Find Brandquist, kill him, then come back whole and hale, and I shall buy you the fika of a lifetime."

She moved her head to the side so that he could see her nod; that was all she was going to give him.

Sister Mire sniggered and went to speak to the assassins engaged in a sparring duel with rapiers behind them.

Meanwhile, next to them, in an unusual display of emotion and brute force, Petrichor kicked a target dummy. One swift, high, hard kick that nearly took the head off the straw figure. Then he headed for the stairs. Halcyon stopped him too, reaching out a hand to touch his shoulder as well, but then snapping it back. Had she ever seen him touch Petrichor?

There it was again, that pang of pity.

"Wait." Halcyon took an overcoat off a hook on the wall. "Take this, Petrichor. It has a deep hood for hiding one's face and it is a coat your pursuers will not have seen you in before, making it easier for you to blend into crowds." Then he leaned in and whispered some quick words to the other man before stepping back and loudly saying, "I trust that you both will still adhere to prayer times."

"Of course," Petrichor said.

Valour stifled a sigh at his misplaced loyalty.

"If you can only attend one, prioritise gloriam. You have around an hour and a half before we set up the cups."

Petrichor gave a curt bow. "Understood."

Looking anxious, Halcyon bowed back. "May your blades be swift and your bodies impenetrable."

They gave the normal unison reply of, "And also you."

Valour waited for all the assassins to return to sparring before whispering, "No one's looking. Come on," to Ingrid, who immediately ducked out from the alcove. The two of them caught up with Petrichor, who was leaving the room at pace.

When they were out of sight, Petrichor hissed, "*She's* still here?"

"No," Valour said. "She's outside. This is an illusion I cast with olden magic to get your britches in a twist."

His lips pressed together as he picked up the pace. "Not now, Valour, I haven't the patience for your nonsense on top of what just happened."

With the sanctum doors shut behind them and the crowds outside avoided, Ingrid asked, "Was that not a bit harsh? Even for a coldblooded league of assassins?"

"The order has very particular and strict rules," Petrichor said.

Valour squinted skywards. The mist was giving way, revealing iron-grey clouds. "Mm. Those rules don't always make sense. Some of them were created so long ago they don't even apply to modern society."

Ingrid's eyebrows rose. "Do some of these rules mean you cannot get help or protection from your own kind?"

Busying himself with adjusting the coat Halcyon gave him, Petrichor kept silent in the loudest manner.

"Some of the guidelines can be interpreted as saying that the members shouldn't ask for help while on missions," Valour said. "That's why I didn't expect much from this visit. We're meant to be lone wolves, independent and able to avoid any enemy, even if we're fighting an army all by ourselves."

Ingrid frowned. "I read that wolves being lone is a myth. They live in packs for a reason."

"That's not the point," Valour said, hearing the weariness in her own voice. "This is meant to test our mettle. An assassin shouldn't want or need help. Or sanctuary. We are to be the scariest thing in this city, afraid of nought." She glared at the sanctum behind them. "Also, they clearly have no information to give us."

"That's not quite correct," Petrichor said. "Halcyon whispered a suggestion to me. A vague one, but 'tis better than nothing."

"All right," Valour said. "Are you going to share it with me?"

Petrichor put his shaded spectacles on and studied the sky. "I believe it's warming up. The mist is sure to turn to rain soon."

"Really? The godsdamned weather?" Valour snapped her fingers until he faced her. "Are you going to share the information, or do I have to go back in there and ask Halcyon what he said?"

"Fine, fine. He said that the most substantiated rumour he had heard was that Brandquist had taken over a large warehouse in an inhospitable part of the city. As well as several hideouts he operates from."

"Ye gads, that *is* vague," Ingrid said.

"Nevertheless," Petrichor said testily, "at this stage it is all we have."

He ran a hand over that ridiculous square jaw of his while his gaze kept flitting back to the sanctum. Valour noted that the hand wasn't steady. Was he this hurt because Halcyon hadn't helped or because they hadn't been allowed to shelter in their former home?

Ingrid pretend-coughed for attention. "Anyway, I assume you still require a place to hide and draw up a plan?"

Neither assassin answered.

"Don't fret, I will neither say I told you so nor make you ask for it," Ingrid said with a friendly laugh. "After all, I do owe you a favour for letting me see the sanctum. I suggest we take a carriage to my hideout since it's quite some distance. And as you noted, Petrichor, it's about to rain. Follow me."

She swanned towards the carriage stand without stepping in a single snow pile, gracefully flicking up her cloak's hood right as the first raindrops fell.

"Valour, *for now* this is our best solution, little as I like it. Thus, for Axsten's sake, close your mouth, stop staring, and do hurry up," Petrichor said before heading to the carriages as well.

She took a heartbeat to collect herself as the rain fell. She could hear the first rumblings of thunder heralding that Tor was riding across the sky with his hammer, Mjölner. Valour was as aware of the cold-shouldering sanctum looming behind her as she was of the bright, fascinating woman about to give them shelter walking ahead.

"Tor, help me," Valour whispered with a wry chuckle. "Life changes bloody fast for us mortals."

Still. She shouldn't, wouldn't, rely on anything. Not the sanctum, not Ingrid, not even the gods. Everyone let you down and everyone left you.

Once more composed, Valour strode to the carriage stand.

CHAPTER 15

THE HIDEOUT

DURING THE CARRIAGE ride, two things had happened. The thunder and rain stopped, and Petrichor wheedled out where they were going. So, the moment they were out and the cab was paid for, he took the lead. In his view, the other two were far too relaxed, too absorbed in early-stage courtship. He was not so blinkered. He would go along with this plan for now, but as soon as he could, he would do more research into the woman who was harbouring them. And he would find a way to not need her help.

After a while, they turned a corner and headed down a smaller street with old, dilapidated workmen's houses. The street couldn't have been used much, considering its snow had only been disturbed by the rain. The derelict houses displayed notices saying they were scheduled to be torn down to make way for rows of new townhouses. However, demolition always stopped during the sort of heavy snowfalls Vinterstock had suffered in the past couple of weeks.

He clicked his tongue. Not a bad place to hide.

The constant chatting from the women—mainly Ingrid—behind him stopped, replaced by munching.

He turned and found Valour eating. "How do you have food? Why do you have food?"

"Not that it's any of your business, but I was hungry." Valour picked up an amber object from her cupped palm. "Ingrid had some preserved berries. They were wrapped in waxed parchment, so don't give me a hard time about pocket lint."

Petrichor rubbed the bridge of his nose. "And you, an assassin, took food from a stranger without precaution."

"She's not a complete stranger and she's got no reason to want to poison me, barnacle-brain. If she did kill me, she'd be in even more trouble with her father."

"Moreover," Ingrid shot in, "I would upset the whole guild of assassins, with a witness like you no less."

Petrichor grunted in assent.

Sadly, Valour wasn't leaving it there. "I've had these before, too. On top of the hotel's famed sea buckthorn pancakes." She tossed the berry into her mouth and while chewing said, "I'm not a total feather-brain, Petrichor. You'll have to figure that out one day."

"They're cloudberries," Ingrid corrected her.

Valour furrowed her brow. "Not sea buckthorn?"

"No, those are yellow-orange too, but look like a cluster of tiny pearls along a branch. While these beauties"—Ingrid pointed to the berries in Valour's palm—"resemble raspberries, but instead of red they're a light golden colour. Hence the nickname 'mountain gold'."

Petrichor didn't have time for this nonsense. He walked on, trying to focus on his own thoughts. To little avail, as Valour— chewing loudly as ever to annoy him—asked, "How do you know so much about this?"

Ingrid shrugged. "I read."

"So do I on occasion. And dull mop charging away over there reads all the time. Neither of us spouts facts about Nordic berries, despite having grown up around them."

"I have a head for details and a good memory," Ingrid said. "I've needed it in my life."

Petrichor couldn't stand it any longer. "Can we stop talking about *berries* and get to this hiding place before every 'ness dealer in Vinterstock attacks us?"

"Sure," Ingrid said. "I'm not afeared or in a hurry, but if you're quaking in your shiny little boots, I shall speed this up." She marched forward with her head held high.

Valour sidled up to Petrichor and smirked. "Your boots really are absurdly shiny."

"That is not an insult. Furthermore, they're not little. They are the average size for men's feet."

The exasperating hotel heiress stopped at a traditional wooden house that must've once been bright red but since then had faded to a pinkish-grey. Its roof was half caved in.

"My hideout is in the basement. One can enter through the house by use of the front door, which you see there," Ingrid said, pointing it out. This woman shared Valour's taste for stating the obvious. "Or one can use the backdoor, like we shall."

She guided them down by the house and through a broken fence into a snowed over, unkempt garden covered in raindrops and icicles. They waded past a rickety outhouse and over to a basement door.

Ingrid opened it and they all stepped into dank darkness. The place didn't appear furnished at first, only a cellar that had once been used to store jars of preserves and bottles of cider, but she slipped in between two shelves and was gone from view. Petrichor and Valour followed, both keeping an eye on every corner while treading with care.

Behind the shelves, Petrichor spotted a utilitarian fireplace and a table with two chairs. The table held two candlesticks with the Hotel Kronovall logo on them, a tinderbox with the same insignia, a bowl of what looked like candied ginger, a bottle of either red wine or port, and a stack of books bound in the brown paper of forbidden imports. Petrichor's gaze went, as usual, to the books. What had caused them to be censored? Sex, blasphemy, or violence? Considering Vinterstock's love for those things, it was hypocrisy either way. He noted Ingrid talking to Valour about the room with her gaze flicking between Valour's eyes and down over her body. He made his guess: sex.

With a sigh he focused back on the basement, which was illuminated by small windows with thick, warped glass up at ground level. He could smell dust, dirt, and the many dried sprigs of bitter wormwood that hung on the walls, ready to be mixed with alcohol by owners who had long ago left. In the corner was a stack of blankets and a mattress. Just the one. Petrichor would rather sleep on a bag of potatoes than share with Valour. She must've been thinking the same thing as she mumbled, "Looks like there's enough blankets to create a makeshift mattress out of."

"Oh?" Ingrid smiled at her playfully. "You mean to say you would not snuggle up together on the actual mattress like two abandoned puppies?"

"We are adults, humans, and certainly *not* abandoned," Petrichor snapped. Halcyon would not abandon them. He'd only had to pretend to while Mire and the others were there.

Quickly grave, Ingrid met his eye. "No. You're not. You have my assistance. I know that's not much, *Master Assassin*, but I can at least offer you this hiding place and buy you all the food and firewood you require."

"And for that, we're grateful beyond words," Valour said.

Ingrid's scowl melted at Valour's earnest tone.

Petrichor tried not to roll his eyes. He gave it a day, two at most, before these women mounted one another. He had to ensure he was far away then.

Ingrid opened an ornate gold locket around her neck to reveal a small timepiece. "Oh. I made an appointment with a friend at Anckarström's coffee-house later, I must make haste."

With hesitance, Valour moved closer to her. "I don't like the idea of you walking around the city alone."

Ingrid gave her an incredulous look. "That is sweet of you, but I have lived a few years longer than you." She smiled a little. "And during those years, I've come across kidnappers, 'gentleman' suitors who didn't like being turned down, and Papa's ruthless business rivals. To name only a few factions that have hunted me. And as you see, I'm still here and in rude health."

"I'm sure you can handle yourself. I just meant that you've been seen with us. Some arseholes are following us and wanting to hurt us. They might do the same to you."

"They pursue you. Not me. I will be fine."

Valour went to the table and grabbed a fistful of candied ginger. "If you say so. Just be careful."

It interested Petrichor to watch this interaction. He could not have cared less about this Ingrid Rytterdahl, but Valour's reactions were another matter since he believed in studying one's competitor. Valour cared what happened to this woman but was not invested enough to argue or take action. Was this not the start of something amorous after all? Was Valour's interest purely sexual? Or duty to the woman's father?

The door shut behind their erstwhile hostess.

Petrichor glanced about their hiding space. He assumed Ingrid wished to shelter them out of carnal desire for Valour, and perhaps for the bored socialite to garner a bit of excitement by partaking in something risqué and dangerous. However, Petrichor did not live a life where he simply assumed things and then did not dig further. He may not be granted help from the order, but he could still seek information from the Assassins of Axsten's records. That well-ordered archive contained not only the annals and sacred texts of the order but also indexes of the noteworthy citizens of Vinterstock. Should he venture back to the sanctum, though? It was a grave risk. Not as risky for him as for others, of course, since he could make himself as imperceptible as a shadow and as quick as a wolverine. Yes, he would go. He didn't like how things had been left with Halcyon. Petrichor was still furious with him and wanted to see him to… what? Get an apology? A further explanation? To steal a moment in his presence?

He shook that last thought out of his mind and headed for the door. As he adjusted his outerwear, he casually told Valour, "I shall inspect the neighbourhood. I might be a while as I like to be thorough. No need to accompany me."

She snorted. "I wasn't going to. Just don't draw anyone back here."

He glowered at her. "Obviously not, you dullard. I will knock three times as I return so you know it's me. Do not cause a mess while I'm gone, I must live here too and shall not abide any of your clutter or filth."

She made a rude noise, so he left without any further comment.

CHAPTER 16
DIGGING EVER DEEPER

As BEST HE could, Petrichor masked his features by pulling his scarf high as he hailed a passing carriage, pretending to be merely avoiding the cold air on his face. Shame he hadn't brought his hat, and that he couldn't walk back to the sanctum. But he couldn't tarry. Every moment out here could draw his attackers and, on his return to the hideout, make Valour question where he'd been and the risk he had taken. Granted, she might find out later from one of the other assassins. He wouldn't be the one to give her information unbidden, though.

At the end of the journey, he paid the carriage driver and stole back into the sanctum. There, instead of skulking like a wraith, he strode as a proud assassin, first down the stairs, past the refectory, the infirmary, and the training room—where most of the assassins still seemed to be—and finally into the archive. It was the most secluded room of the sanctum and as so often these days, it stood empty. The small space had its familiar smell of dust, ink, paper, and leather bookbindings. Petrichor filled his lungs, allowing himself a moment to enjoy it. His eyes adjusted to the muted light of the room's many nearly burned-down candles behind thick glass shades. There were no windows here, of course. Sunlight could not be allowed to damage the frailest and oldest of the objects. The stone walls were lined with shelves that were stacked with order annals, sacred texts, and record books. In the room's middle squatted a few desks with inbuilt seats, reportedly inspired by those found in Christian monasteries.

Petrichor found a recent volume and with the help of the index came across the name Ingrid Rytterdahl. Her entry was short, detailing only her familial connections and her *very public* private life. Which was made up of her cavorting with everyone from the country's most esteemed nobility to the city's poorest criminals— the latter being explained by the writer as being due to 'a sense of connection to the lower class, owing to her upbringing as a child of impoverished parents' and her spending time with the aristocrats as 'a wish for this merchant-class girl with a foreign father to become a legitimate part of upper-class Vinterstock society.' When this was all over, Petrichor would ask Halcyon if he could pen an addendum. He was quite sure that Ingrid's frolicking with the more dangerous of the city's lower classes wasn't due to a kinship with the poor, no matter how impoverished her childhood had been, but rather that the under-stimulated woman wanted a thrill, as well as the opportunity to brag and tell scandalous stories to her rich friends. No doubt Halcyon would say Petrichor was being too harsh on the socialite, but no, people were terrible creatures, himself included. He saw nary a bit of good in them, in himself, or in the future. He thought of the still-unburned letter. No, the future was as cold, dark, and immovable as the stone walls of this room. He would amount to nothing more than what he was now. Well, then so be it. Petrichor would continue to be the best assassin this city had ever seen.

He read on, moving over to the entry on Ingrid's father. Nothing criminal or out of the ordinary there either, other than some questionable business dealings in his early years. However, that described most people who succeeded in Vinterstock.

The room's only aperture, the pine door, snicked open. A woman came in. In fact, she was gently pushed in by a man hissing, "Stay in here until I can get rid of Sister Mire."

Petrichor froze. He knew that man's voice. Halcyon.

The leader of the assassins shut the door and hurried away, closing the woman in there with Petrichor. He knew her too, albeit not her name. It was the woman he'd seen in Halcyon's room that fateful day. The one who had been naked on top of Halcyon and riding him to distraction. Now she stood, as proud and unflinching as a goddess, smiling indulgently at the door and shaking her head as if the head of their fearsome order was some little boy who wanted her to play a silly game. She did look older than Halcyon, but perhaps not by more than ten or fifteen years. It was hard to tell with her sharp features in shadow where she stood, facing away from the candles. She had ruined the room's familiar smell, scenting it with juniper and something animal, making the room stuffy as if her mere presence sucked the air out of it. He shuddered when he realised he had the same juniper cologne, but the added musk? It no doubt came from sex. The woman's shock of hair was arranged high on her head but the extravagant up-do had lost its solidity and most of its powdering. She was also adjusting her white robe à l'anglaise's deep neckline, showing that it had been tugged down for access. Just dipping into her slightly wrinkled cleavage was a pendant of a golden horse that he recognised as a symbol of one of the old Norse deities. Not Oden, since he remembered that Oden's horse—the one born to Loke after Loke had turned himself into a female horse—had eight legs. But it did belong to a male god, he thought. Höder? Brage? Valour would know.

The daunting woman caught him looking, and she searched his face for a moment, clearly seeking something that she didn't find.

"Admiring this?" She tapped the pendant, seeming as untroubled by his gaze as she was at having skipped greetings or explanations of her presence. "It's Gulltoppr, the golden-maned horse belonging to Heimdal. Did you know some say he invented our social classes?" She didn't wait for his answer. "Granted, our system of commoners, merchant class, priesthood, and nobility is obviously more advanced than what they had back then." While clearly enjoying the sound of her own voice—plum and with an aristocratic speech pattern—she faced the shelves, like they were more worthy of hearing her speech than he. "I thought that a droll thing to wear to this place since the leader of the assassins acts like a mere thrall, guiltily sneaking his lover in and out, not daring to put his inferiors in their rightful place, letting them question him and steer him."

"You dare criticise Halcyon to me? Here of all places? What are you doing in our sanctum?"

He recalled Valour sneaking Ingrid in and knew the answer. Of course he knew. Lovers were not to be brought into the sanctum, but some members still did it. Granted, it was usually ones less responsible and respectful than Halcyon. Yes, Petrichor knew why she was here. And yet, he was glad he had demanded this woman answer for her presence.

"What do you think, you prying tot?" she snarled in a distinctly non-aristocratic tone, screwing up her face and baring her teeth. "That I am here for a godsdamned cup of coffee? Or your oh-so-winsome company?"

Her anger had come like lightning from a clear sky. Why was she suddenly furious with him? *She* was the one trespassing and slating Halcyon.

Petrichor put a hand to one of his concealed knives. It was a move as swift as it was subtle, yet this woman's gaze snapped right to it.

"I do hope you are not about to draw a weapon, you assassin ovum." Her burning rage was gone as fast as it had arrived. Now, she wore an expression of disdainful amusement. She stalked towards him, power and strength wafting off her like her juniper perfume. "That would have frightful consequences." Suddenly, something in her hand glinted in the candlelight—a short-handled razor. She saw him eyeing it. "You noticed that, hm? Did you see me draw it? I'd wager not. I must say, both the assassins and this archive have gone to seed. This room used to be filled with order members studying and preparing. Now, they do little but fight each other and call it sparring. Or sit and bicker like old grandparents."

He stood so he could look down on her, glad she was a finger's length shorter. "Only the fact that Halcyon placed you in here keeps me from bodily evicting you. Or cutting your tongue out for what you say of our order."

She laughed, an ugly and harsh sound that echoed off the walls. "The way you say his name is sweet." She leaned nearer, as if about to impart a secret. "I can hear the affection, my sad, sweet urchin."

His nostrils widened at her approach. There was a scent under the perfume and female musk. Something metallic, like the iron in blood or from rusting spikes. It made his head hurt in a strange new way, like it was trying to remember something long buried. Or to not remember. Petrichor took shallow breaths to avoid the odour and hissed, "Cease calling me a child."

Coolly, she waved that away. "I shan't be calling you anything. I hear my darling Halcyon's steps. Or should that be *our* darling Halcyon? Either way, I shall soon be out of your presence."

He pulled out his blade, the whisper of the metal leaving its sheath just barely audible. "Good."

At that, she laughed again. Then she cupped a hand to her ear. "Do you hear that?"

There was no sound in this windowless, thick-walled room but their breathing and Halcyon's approaching steps. "Hear what?"

"I do believe it is raining." She drilled her gaze into his, her eyes burning with some inner fervour. "I despise the smell after it has rained. I wager you do too. That heavy, sodden, dirt smell crowding the air. Everything buried suddenly fills the nostrils, as the rain brings out its forgotten stenches. Oh yes, I wager you hate petrichor violently."

She gave a feral grin, one that vanished like smoke the moment the door opened. Only Halcyon's muscled arm and shoulder entered as he grasped the woman's waist and quickly drew her back out. He didn't even notice Petrichor. The door closed and their footfalls retreated.

Alone once more, Petrichor stood bolted to the spot. Did her comments about the smell after it had rained mean she knew his name? Was it even raining out there? Then there were her remarks about how the sanctum and its assassins had been before. Mere fabrications to rattle him? Or did she have real knowledge of this place? More knowledge than someone brought in only to satisfy the carnal lusts of its current leader? Petrichor's hand gripped the knife harder, then yet painfully harder, matching his thinking. No, that woman hadn't had the air of some courtesan; she had given off the feeling that Halcyon was *her* courtesan. Who was she? And what would Halcyon see in a woman like that? She was not what he needed at all. How could he let her wander about in *their* sanctum? He must have his reasons, must know something that Petrichor didn't.

Several emotions surged in him. He loathed every single one. He crushed them into powder and focused on what was important: returning to the hideout. And not telling Valour any of this. Not only because he had ventured back here, but also because she would no doubt be gleeful at Halcyon's debauched *vixen* being snuck into the sanctuary and brandishing a razor at him. Petrichor sheathed his blade, returned the book that had lain abandoned on the desk, and left. He saw no sign of Halcyon or his strange paramour. What was worse, when Petrichor got outside... there wasn't a single drop of rain.

Chapter 17

Animal Behaviour

Back in the hideout, Petrichor sat down at the table and planned their next steps. He was trying not to think of the woman in the archive, since doing so made him to want to crawl out of his skin. He needed to focus on his life and keeping it, not on what Halcyon did with his body and his heart. Cogitating on the hunt for Brandquist and on the attack back in his rooms was ample distraction, and he let it fill his mind. After a while rain started hammering against the small windows. On top of that was the crackling of the fire Valour had lit. And, almost drowning both those noises out, was the clamour Valour was making. Currently shirtless down to her stays, she was shadowboxing vigorously in a corner. Like as not, she'd been doing that since he left for the sanctum, and she was now wheezing like a broken bellows between punches.

"Could you stop that?" he snapped. "I cannot think due to your din."

"I could." Wheeze. Jab. Wheeze. Uppercut. Wheeze. "But I won't."

He kept his voice calm, aware she was trying to vex him. "I see. May I enquire as to why?"

"I think better when I'm moving."

"In that case, you must have come up with some sparkling gem of a plan by now. Pray tell."

Valour stopped. "Sure. I plan to pull your innards out through your ears with a crocheting needle."

"I liked it better when you were grunting." Petrichor stood to stretch his legs while thinking out loud. "That attack back in my rooms. It wasn't quite… right. For example, why did only one of them have a proper weapon?"

"Well," Valour said, for some reason wiping herself down with a

102

handkerchief doused in wine. "Perhaps they worried that if they were better armed, they might accidentally kill or maim us and anger the order or the greve. Meaning more people would be put on the hit?"

He paced around her with his hands clasped behind his back, trying not to think about her strange excuse for washing. "I hate to admit it, but that has merit. The whole attempt was clumsily done, though."

"It was piss-poor," Valour said, pulling her rough sailor's shirt back on, ill-dressed as ever. "Brandquist should stop hiring 'ness-addicted thugs. They don't make good henchmen."

Petrichor found himself agreeing while trying not to dwell on the fact that it was nice to have someone to discuss with. Something bigger was amiss with this whole thing, though. Why could he not figure out what? There were so many things that he needed to figure out, so many things just beyond the grasp of his fingertips.

VALOUR WATCHED AS Petrichor paced faster and something fell out of his pocket. He didn't notice, only hummed pensively before saying, "For decades, Brandquist has been the most powerful criminal in Vinterstock, employing sleek mercenaries and stalwart career criminals. Why would he send such useless intimidators?"

She stared at what had fallen to the floor. It was an envelope, which looked like it had ripped in his pocket.

Petrichor still hadn't noticed.

She hummed her agreement. "The giant I fought reeked of horses, hay, and sweat. A groom or perhaps a stable hand, certainly not a full-time criminal. And his breath stunk of 'ness."

"I shall make a point of telling Brandquist not to employ useless, tonic-addicted henchmen. Right before I assassinate him." He sneered at her. "Note that I said 'I'. Not 'we' or, god forbid, 'you'. Note that and leave the real work to me as the superior assassin."

Valour took calming breaths. Of course he had more kills to his name. It was easy to get high numbers when you didn't have any qualms about who you killed. Still, only one of them could slay Brandquist, and knowing the order, only one of them would get the reward. She couldn't let this arrogant arsehole get the coin. She'd spend it on charitable stuff while he'd spend it on… What did he spend coin on?

"No reply to that, I see," he said with a glib wave of his hand. "No wonder. I assume you struggle daily to string your sentences together, uncultured brute that you are."

That was it. Childish as the gesture felt, she grabbed his torn envelope and fished the paper out. "I suggest you start being nicer. Otherwise, I might throw this into the fire."

His face reddened and he lunged forward to grab the letter. "Vile creature! How dare you read my private correspondence?"

That muscle in his jaw jumped like never before. It felt so good to see him shaken that she didn't want to admit to not having read it. He snatched for the letter again, so she held it higher. When he caught hold of a corner and pulled, she held fast. The paper ripped with a sound loud enough to be heard all the way into Valhalla.

Petrichor looked as stricken as if it was he who had been torn in two. Their gazes locked, guilt creeping into Valour's edges.

"It should still be readable," she tried.

He glared daggers but said nothing.

She handed him her part of the letter and watched him shove the two paper slips into his coat pocket.

"Look," she said, "as much as it bothers me to say this, perhaps Halcyon was right. Maybe we need to give up any idea of killing Brandquist alone and work together?"

"Me and you?" He eyed her like she was something unfortunate he'd stepped in. "I'd rather die."

She ground her teeth. "Gods, you're right. What kind of bäckahäst-dick of a bad idea was that?"

"Are you physically capable of refraining from that sort of language, Valour?"

"Why? Do you find the idea of folkloric horse dicks distracting?"

He blanched, as she'd known he would, and snapped, "You know very well that I was referring to the order's teachings. Keep our speech *clean* and precise, remember? Besides, did you not fight Sister Sequential because she used genitals in an insult last month?"

Damn. That ruined her one-upmanship. "Mm, our private parts shouldn't be used as something bad. It creates too much shame around our bodies and sex. I mean, there is nothing more wonderful than a cun—"

"Cease. Using unclean language shows a lack of discipline."

"That's not it. You scowl when I say 'shit', but you don't stop me. This is about you and sex."

He was growing vexed. Why did that make her feel so good?

"Everything with you comes down to base things like intercourse, Valour. You do not seem to realise that some of us merely find it..." He frowned. "This is none of your business. Change the topic or be quiet."

"Shan't. Answer the question or I'll start singing dirty shanties at the top of my voice. You find intercourse what?"

"Fine." He ran a hand over his raw-boned face. "I find it messy but most of all exceptionally *dull*."

"Huh. Are you sure you were doing it right? And with the right person?"

"In the name of science, I have tried every type of sex with every type of individual," he said with a dismissive wave. "Granted, it was messy at times and I didn't like that, but most of all, it was just such a waste of time."

"Waste of time? Did you try it with someone you loved?"

"Love lives in fairytales."

"How would you godsdamned know? You'd never dare to unclasp your heart enough for love to get in."

His stormy expression intensified. "I am only allowing this discussion because you must learn to control *your* heart and your urges. That way I shan't have to hear about your shouting matches with the city's watchmakers."

Her good mood was bludgeoned. He'd never mentioned Kajsa before.

"One," she said, barely controlling herself, "it was *one* watchmaker, you wart-eater. And she was the one shouting because I didn't want to get bloody married and pregnant."

He raised his eyebrows. "I heard it was about certain rumours of infidelity."

"That was gossip and lies! I'm faithful to the core."

Steps and someone stomping snow off their boots sounded from outside the door. They both reached for their knives.

"Only me," Ingrid called through the door.

She came in with the colour high in her cheeks from the cold. Her hair was now teased and clipped up in a high coiffure, prettier than a wig.

Valour immediately stepped forward with a "Oh. Hi. Welcome back."

"Try for some dignity," Petrichor said at her side.

"Dignity?" Valour couldn't believe his audacity. "What, like the way you become a simpering mess whenever Halcyon enters the room?"

He stiffened. "Leave Halcyon out of this."

A nerve. A big, exposed nerve.

"I can speak of Halcyon if I like," she said. "He's my friend. Not yours, though. You know why, right?"

"What I know is that I am privy to details about him and his lov… Never mind." His voice was armoured. "Simply shut that uncouth, foul mouth of yours."

"You unnerve him. And bore him."

Petrichor stepped closer to her than he had been in years. His eyes were blown wide and his lips pinched tightly together until he parted them to snarl, "Do not touch my letters or anything of mine again, and *never ever* speak of me and Halcyon."

His sudden desperation and pointless hatred towards her made her own anger dim. She was hungry and tired, mainly of him.

"Whatever," she said. "Let's just hunt Brandquist separately in the daytime and then come back here each night to share what we've found. That way the case will be over sooner and we can go back to avoiding each other."

"Fine." Petrichor moved away, correcting his clothing and his composure. "However, we cannot share information without first garnering some. We need leads. Preferably, we must speak to someone who has contact with Brandquist, first or second hand."

"I tried to speak to the one group of open 'ness addicts I know of," Valour said. "The ones on Oden's Square. But the poor wretches were too far gone to get much sense out of. All I got was that the 'ness imports have decreased."

Ingrid, who had been standing some way back from the two quarrelling assassins, approached with a hesitant air. "Would you judge me if I said I could perhaps help you with such a lead?"

Petrichor looked like he'd forgotten that she was present, but the expression soon changed to one of interest. "What do you know? Or rather, who do you know?"

"Well, as Valour is aware, I spend my time with some people who are… not the most virtuous citizens of the city."

"Ruffians," Valour said with a grin. "That was the word your 'dear papa' used."

Ingrid rolled her eyes. "Most of them are regular people who don't like being tied down by norms. Or who don't appreciate the way our city operates. Anyway, a couple of them deal 'ness."

Seeming unsurprised, Petrichor said, "Are any of them sufficiently high up in the hierarchy to have contact with Brandquist?"

"One of them. Johan. He's worked for Brandquist for years and has his own workforce of dealers, so I should say he's rather high-ranking."

"Excellent," Petrichor said. "Can you take us to him?"

"I think he would be wary if I came in with both of you. However, I may be able to sneak Valour along. Johan has a beloved sister who resembles her quite a bit—it might make him more relaxed."

Petrichor made a displeased sound.

"You'll just have to trust that I'll ask the questions you want answered. And that I'll report all the details back to you," Valour said.

She made no effort to hide her glee.

CHAPTER 18

USEFUL LEADS

PETRICHOR TOOK HIS time pondering the meddlesome socialite. As much as he hated it, he needed her connections and this hideout. Valour cleared her throat, reminding him of something worse: he could use another assassin on this case. Especially one who could get into places he couldn't and make people open up to her.

In his mind, he circled through every curse word he knew.

"Well, what do you think?" Valour asked, smirking.

After one measured roll of his neck, he said, "I suppose I have little choice. You two go and report back every detail."

"And what will you do?" Valour asked. "Sit here and talk to the stick up your arse?"

"There is a group of students at the university," he admitted reluctantly. "Top of their classes. Rich parents. They're tonic fiends and oft brag that their dealer is Brandquist's second in command."

Valour put her hands on her hips. "And when were you going to tell me about that?"

"I wasn't. However, now it seems necessary if I'm to win this race."

Valour had bent to readjust the knife sheath on her leg but glared up at him through her lashes. "You, win?" She pulled the leather strap tight and stood back up. "Trust me, I'll win. It's just unfortunate that when I do, you can claim to have helped by sharing some of your measly information."

Ingrid drew back. "Race? Win? You do know you are talking about someone's death, right?"

They both looked at her without replying.

"I mean," Ingrid said with an air of self-consciousness, "I am aware that death is your profession. And that Brandquist sells drugs which make people addicted, sick, and sometimes kill them, and so he deserves little pity. Nevertheless, this is a human life, and we don't know if Brandquist has family or loved ones."

Valour winced. "Sorry. We have to grow numb to these things."

"We're wasting time," Petrichor said, not willing to indulge in qualms. "You two speak to that high-ranking dealer, I shall go to the university."

"Are you sure about talking to 'ness addicts?" Valour asked. "As I said, most of the ones on Oden's Square were not in any shape to answer questions."

"These brats are high-functioning addicts with contacts everywhere. Also, they have parents who spend mounds of coin having them healed up and dried out betwixt semesters," Petrichor said, checking that no hair had fallen out of his ponytail. "I shall procure the answers."

Valour gave a sceptical snort. "If you say so."

"How dare—"

"Pardon me," Ingrid interrupted. "If you're going to engage in another juvenile quibble, I shall go get something to eat. I haven't eaten since last night."

Petrichor lost interest and began checking his weapons and clothing while mentally mapping out the most covert route to the university from here. Absently, he heard Valour say, "Since last night? Woman, you must be famished!"

"Not really," Ingrid said. "I enjoy occasional sweet treats but full meals make me nauseous, especially if they have certain textures. Papa actually took me to a physician about that."

"And?"

"The physician claimed I was a hysterical girl who wasted food and should be force-fed," Ingrid said with scorn. "At which point we left and have since told all our acquaintances to avoid said physician."

"Good," Valour said. "I'd like to teach that quack a thing or two about name-calling and force."

Petrichor stopped his preparations. Valour looked every bit

the valorous hero, ready to speak up for anyone wronged. The sanctimonious brute hadn't been so good-hearted when she stabbed him with that comment about Halcyon. He straightened. "No skipped meals will go to waste in Valour's presence. She eats like a starved piglet."

Valour's head snapped towards him. "Just because you're a boring old git who only sits in a dark corner eating stale porridge while punishing yourself for breathing, it doesn't mean the rest of us are animals. Or shouldn't be allowed to enjoy life."

Enjoying life. Such a silly myth. Petrichor clasped his hands behind his back, staying calm since that annoyed her the most. "And by 'life' you mean cardamom sweet rolls?"

"Sure. Why not? I love eating all manner of things and there's nought wrong with that, you dull pisspot," she snapped. "You know, right now I'd kill for some warm, honeyed cardamom buns and a few civilised cups of tea."

"That does sound divine," Ingrid pitched in.

"See," Valour said, pointing to the other woman like she was evidence.

"Civilised cups of tea?" he said. "First of all, cups cannot be civilised. And secondly, you wouldn't know *civilised* if it struck you on the mouth."

"Ah, striking my mouth. Yet another bloody thing you fail at. Remember last time you threw a punch at me? I ducked and you ended up breaking your knuckles against the stone wall."

Her snigger grated on him like sandpaper on teeth.

"A stone wall is softer than your head, Valour. I wager it would be a wittier conversational partner as well."

After a long time of silent glaring, she picked up a tinderbox and threw it at him.

He moved so it missed. "Do not start that, you overgrown child."

"Give me one reason not to, *unwanted troll changeling*."

Petrichor staggered, trying to hide how hard those words had struck. "Are you truly going to play the orphan card? Last time you did that and threw something at me, it did not end so well." He was unsure of how old they had been. Fourteen? Fifteen? He knew they had fought so viciously they had both ended up in the infirmary.

"I remember tossing Sister Mire's old, discarded stays at you, sure. But after that you threw like four slices of rulltårta at me, so don't be all superior."

"Yes, and then you gobbled up every bit, even gathering the spilled jam off your shirt with your fingers and eating that! As I said, you are a pig."

"Gods in Asgård! This proves my bloody point. You really do think anyone who enjoys whatever little pleasure they can dig out in this grim, shitty world is an animal," she said, gesticulating wildly. "While it's actually a human experience that's completely passed you by." She tugged her shirt sleeves up and he saw the tensing muscles there. "I was only thirteen and had been denied supper for days, you miserable toe-face."

Ingrid waved her hand between them. "If you must quibble like children, may I request that you pick a theme that isn't judgemental about eating habits? Go back to Cousin Miriam's stays or something."

"Sister Mire," they corrected her in unison.

"Pray, excuse my fatal error," Ingrid said with a hint of hurt in her sarcasm.

Valour inclined her head towards her. "You're right. Eating issues are not something we should be using as weapons against each other."

Eating issues? What about her using the one thing that could break him?

"Stop pretending to be the bigger person and genuflecting to her. Face me," Petrichor hissed, his pulse far too high.

Valour ignored him, still looking at Ingrid. "Nor do I need to bring up food habits when there are so many things to criticise about *Parentless Petrichor*, starting with the massive stick up his arse."

Again. She did it again. Well, he had forbidden ammunition too. "Tell me, Valour. Do you still fear falling asleep? And when you do sleep, are you shuddering and whimpering for your mother?

How are those crippling nightmares of yours, you soft-hearted weakling?"

Valour bared her teeth, veins showing at her temples and on the bulging muscles of her forearms. He stood his ground, chin up and shoulders back. Valour placed her hands—stronger than their size conveyed—on his chest. She gave him one forceful shove, nearly toppling him.

He regained his balance and took a fighting stance. "Touch me again and this will turn into a brawl that will incapacitate both of us, starting with you."

"Eat me, you stinking corpse-maggot."

Petrichor had always been the only one that didn't get alarmed when Valour was this angry. Did she on some level appreciate that? Or did she wish she could scare him?

He sneered. "Eat you? Not only would you be disgusting but I wager you would be downright poisonous."

Valour raised her fists. He braced for the pain, hoping there wouldn't be permanent damage.

"Maybe we should break this up?" Ingrid said, one slender hand on Valour's forearm. "We have information to gather, do we not? Petrichor interrogates the university students and you and I go to my 'ness-selling contact. Right?"

Nothing happened for a beat. Finally, the churl slowly lowered her fists, her face and body still exuding a raw hunger for violence. Petrichor noted a throb of power at having caused that. Then repulsion filled him. Perhaps they were both animals?

Ingrid kept her hand on Valour's arm and was soothingly caressing the bare skin.

He adjusted his cravat and said, "I shall see you both back here later for a debrief. Other than that, keep out of my way."

As he departed, he saw Ingrid from the corner of his eye. She was giving Valour's arm one last stroke and crooning, "For the record, if I were to eat you, I bet I would find you neither poisonous nor disgusting, but quite delicious."

Such filth. Petrichor slammed the door shut.

The grey light outside was piercing and there was a wet, icy wind. He wrapped his arms around himself, trying to remember what it felt like when someone else did that. Or when someone put a hand on your arm to steady you, comfort you, side with you.

He slapped himself hard on each cheek, and then walked right into that bitter wind, heading for the university.

CHAPTER 19

JEWELS AND DRUGS

IT WAS GOOD to walk to where Ingrid's contact sold 'ness. Valour was doing something when she walked, not merely sitting on her arse while someone else controlled the journey, as would've been the case if they took a carriage. Today's damp and freezing wind was a downside, though. She did up the extra clasps on her tattered cloak, but it didn't help much. "So, where do we find this Johan?"

"This week he is in a jewellery shop. I've been told Brandquist has a moving schedule, since selling from the same place would mean the overseers would soon come knocking."

"Makes sense."

Ingrid shivered as a raw gust hit them. "Johan says Brandquist has roped in some of the city's shops, workshops, and even small factories to be fronts for the 'ness trade."

"Do these places volunteer?"

"I believe so. They get payment or protection for their trouble. Sometimes even a helping hand with repairs and such, which comes in handy since everyone lacks staff."

Valour thought of all the Vinterstock sons and daughters that the greve had sent abroad to fight the king's battles, and the whispered complaints about it down every snowy street. Whispers that could become shouts at any time. The greve and his cabinet of kammarherrar couldn't kill, imprison, or send them *all* out to war.

She peered at a wheezing, hunched old woman pushing a cart. "The greve is bleeding his city dry and letting its citizens keel over in droves. Seems sort of short-sighted. If your population dies then your city dies, right?"

"Indeed," Ingrid said. "Vinterstock is run appallingly compared to other cities I have seen. I started a petition to the king, telling him exactly that, but it was intercepted by a kammarherre who blackmailed my father into making sure it was never sent." She shook her head. "The inequalities of Vinterstock grow day by day, the lower classes suffering in multitudes of ways. It's not quite as bad in the rest of the country, but injustice still reigns there as well. I collect friends who are as outraged about this as I. Someone in power needs to do something."

Valour agreed with that last point. And Ingrid 'collecting' such friends was interesting. Were they all merchant class or were some of them nobles? What did rich people outraged about the poor's suffering do when they gathered? Cry a tear of sympathy into their champagne and patisseries?

Right now, Valour had more urgent issues to worry about, though. "Yes." She cleared her throat. "Next question. How well do you know this Johan? Should I have my knives at hand?"

"You ask a lot of questions for a quiet person," Ingrid said with laughter in her voice. "Are you practising for your interrogation?"

"Part of being an assassin is not going into situations until you've done reconnaissance and gathered vital information." She quieted until they had passed a hawker selling cheap cravats and bonnets. "Particularly on the important decision of whether to storm in with drawn blades or enter with a charming smile."

"Ah, I see. The charming smile will do here. At least as long as you don't blurt out that you want to find Brandquist to kill him."

"No. I've been thinking on that matter. I think I'll say that I want to find Brandquist to get a job with him." Valour quieted again as they passed another hawker, this one selling alum and shouting about how it kept your armpits fresh. "Perhaps adding that I was a second in command in the 'ness trade in, I don't know… say, Kallborg. Then moved here because of a lover's quarrel, and now I'm looking for a new job."

"Why not simply say that you are in search of a position?"

"Because if I do, it's likely that your drug-peddling friend might want to hire me himself. I need to convince him that I'm experienced and should speak to the big boss about taking on my own patch of the city with my own group of sellers."

"I suppose there is logic in that."

They walked on, Valour listening to the bustle of the city and the squelching of their feet in that distinctive slush made by rain on heavy amounts of well-trodden snow, with liquified horse shit to give it occasional interesting brown patches. She should say something. Try to impress Ingrid, maybe even charm her if she could? No. Ingrid was different than her usual objects of desire and she would not, could not, allow herself to develop feelings.

"Valour?"

"Mm-hmm."

"Can I confess something?"

"Is it that you've drunk your fair share of 'ness tonics? Because I sort of assumed that."

Ingrid bristled. "No. It was not that. But I'll have you know that I only tried shrewdness tonics and I did so merely to live up to Papa's expectations. Nothing else."

"Shit." Valour banged her fist against her thigh. "Right. Sorry. That was none of my business. I'm terrible at guessing. What was it you actually wanted to say?"

Ingrid fidgeted with the hood of her cloak and then pulled it up, far over her face. Valour didn't blame her. The warming weather that the rain brought hadn't lasted for long.

"What I was about to confess to," Ingrid replied, "was that I have no idea if Johan has a sister. I said that as an excuse to spend time alone with you."

"Me?"

"No, the snail frozen to that fence over there. Yes, you."

"Oh. Right. I see. Well, thank you, I guess." She clicked her teeth against each other in an uneasy drum beat, then the perfect reply came to her. "I totally understand why you wouldn't want Petrichor along. He's worse than a toothache and the monthly bleed pain put together."

"While we are on the topic of him…" Ingrid said. "At the risk of being rude, may I ask what your brother's problem is? Well, except that someone soaked his clothes in lye."

"My brother? I don't—can't—have one." It struck her what might've confused Ingrid. "The Order of Axsten's use of 'Sister' and 'Brother' are just titles, you know. It's meant to make us feel like we're part of an institution rather than individuals. Not to make us think we're a family."

Axsten had decreed that they were to be honed, emotionless, perfect weapons in the city's armoury. Not a family, but a collection of knives and axes to be wielded by the greve. Outsiders never got that.

"I see. I thought you were allowed to have a family, though?"

"They allow having children and getting married. To keep us from being preoccupied by repeatedly wooing lovers or getting the pox, or anything else you get from bedding strangers." Valour watched her worn boots as they just barely kept from slipping in the slush. "However, we're meant to put the order and our kills above the needs of any spouse or children."

"I see. Well, my apologies for the misunderstanding. Papa mentioned that you had a brother in the order and when I saw how you quarrel with Monsieur Surly-Breeches, I assumed it was him."

"Even if we were allowed to be, he and I sure as shit aren't siblings," Valour said. "I'd rather be the sister of a moulding turnip."

Ingrid laughed and Valour couldn't help but feel proud at having caused it.

When the laughter died away, Ingrid said, "Brother or not, he cuts an odd figure. I find him hard to categorise."

Valour snorted. "He's a pain in the arse. There, done."

"Ha, I suppose that would be your description."

"What would yours be?"

"As a stranger to him…" Ingrid looked skyward as she pondered. "I suppose I'd say: melancholy and disdain moulded into a figure of marble muscle and sharp angles, making the end result an arresting statue dressed like a bank clerk with a voice deep as a fortress well."

That sounded almost admiring. Yuck. "Statue is about right. 'Marble muscle' is overselling it, though. He has only as much musculature as our fighting training requires. In contrast to me."

"Oh. Boasting, are we?"

Valour didn't know what to do with the playful lilt in Ingrid's voice or the quirking of that left eyebrow. Every gesture this woman made was measured just right, and yet, it never seemed practised.

"Just stating facts." Valour pulled her cloak tighter.

"I see," Ingrid said, watching Valour tug at her outerwear. "I've heard strong people are more hot-blooded than the rest of us. Nevertheless, it strikes me that no one can handle a Nordic winter without whole outerwear, or a scarf, or something to cover your head. Your cloak does not even have a hood."

"The cloak's hood had moth holes, so I got a seamstress to remove it. I gave my scarf away. Halcyon bought me a cap as a joke, made of pink silk and lace. I gave that away as well, since I'd rather eat glass than wear it."

Ingrid snickered. "Perhaps a frock with a hood would suit you better?"

"A frock?" Valour tried not to smile. "We mere peasants call those coats."

"Whatever you call it, you should have one. Preferably with fewer holes than your cloak, and not stitched together with spider thread sometime during the twelfth century?"

"That's rude. It's not that old," Valour grumbled, growing more impatient to get to their destination by the moment.

"Perhaps not, but it is that torn and threadbare. You need new outerwear."

"Can't afford it. Are we almost there?"

"Soon. Back to the topic of your outerwear. Would you let me purchase a coat for you, my semi-frozen Lady of Assassination and Intimidation?"

"I'd rather wear that godsdamned lacy cap."

Ingrid laughed again. There was a possibility that Valour would one day get used to the clear tinkling of that laugh, but that day was sure as shit not today.

They spoke about the weather and how the winters had seemed less cold when they were younger, until Ingrid stopped outside a sweet little storefront and said, "Here we are."

The shop had ornate but dusty windows, powder-blue paint peeling off the woodwork, and a faded sign with beautiful script on it.

Valour touched the daintily carved doorframe. This wasn't what she expected a drug-peddling location to look like. "This is where they sell 'ness tonics?"

"Yes. A darling little place that doesn't stand out to overseers." Ingrid regarded it with a melancholy smile. "Apparently the owner used to be a serious jeweller but had too much competition from imports and needed to get the riksdaler coming in from another source. Everyone must pay their bills."

"You do know a lot about all of this. That's just because Johan told you, is it?"

Ingrid pursed her lips. "You mean do I also know about this because I took shrewdness tonics?"

Valour shrugged.

"I'm not an addict," Ingrid said finally. "I didn't drink them for very long or very often."

"Good. I'd hate to see you with the shakes, rotting teeth, and weird sleep habits. Or later when your heart starts giving out and your lungs turn into bags of bloodied pus."

Shit, she sounded like someone's mother. Or an overseer.

"It takes a long time before you get any of those symptoms. Most people never get to that point, as I'm sure you know," Ingrid said with a strange expression. Her hands were trembling as they grabbed the jewellery shop's door-handle. Valour was about to ask if she was all right, but Ingrid pushed the handle and entered.

The little shop had seen better days but was clearly well loved. There were polished glass cases containing rings, necklaces, and bracelets in silver and gold. Ingrid headed for the largest case, though, which was filled with gemstones. They didn't look ready to be placed in jewellery but were rough stones in pale blues, dusky blood reds, bottle greens, and every hue of yellow.

Ingrid ran her hand over the glass case and reverently whispered, "To think that such natural, pure beauty exists. Sapphire, ruby, emerald, and... citrine, I think?" The words didn't mean a snail's shit to Valour, but she wasn't about to divulge her ignorance.

An old man wearing small spectacles and a large cross around his neck came in and bowed. "Welcome. May I help you young ladies with anything?"

Ingrid drew herself up and Valour saw her awed expression morph into a charming, elegant mask. It reminded Valour of actresses she'd seen in plays. With the difference that Ingrid did it much better and, sadly, there was no ale being served as she did.

"Good day to you, sir," Ingrid trilled. "Since the beautiful beast behind me is refusing to buy me a wedding band and make an honest woman out of me, I shall have to settle for a quick chat with Johan."

Valour fought off an urge to leave. Why did Ingrid persist in joking that they were a couple? Also, 'beautiful beast'?

The jeweller's happy expression faded. "Johan? Oh. I thought I had customers..." He pulled his banyan across his narrow chest and took a feeble grip of his cross. "I shall fetch him."

Valour's heart stung.

"Wait a moment, please," Ingrid called, and now the trill had been replaced with her real voice.

The elderly man stopped mid-shuffle.

Ingrid examined the glass case. "I'd also like to buy, um, that citrine there."

She was pointing to one of the yellow stones about the size of a strawberry.

He perked up and quickly retrieved the fancy rock out of the case. "Excellent choice. Good hardness and homogenous colour. Some might say it's smoky quartz and not a citrine. Nonetheless, 'tis a beauty, is it not?"

Ingrid held it up to the light. "It is. I like that it is smokier than the others. It makes it the same shade of blonde as my friend's hair."

The jeweller winked. "Friend, eh? I thought she was your fiancée?"

Ingrid leaned in with a conspiratorial smile. "No. She waited too long and so the moment passed. She is but a friend now." She tossed the gem to Valour and added, "A friend with a citrine. Or a smoky quartz. Depending on how you see things."

"Friendship is the foundation upon which you build a happy marriage," the jeweller said. "I should know, I have been married to my best friend for sixty-four years."

"How lovely! Congratulations," Ingrid replied. "I wish you many more happy years together. Does she, or he, work here with you?"

The old man brightened. "My treasured wife only works here occasionally. She's usually down at our church. She's just started a holy crusade against these new, dangerous experiments taking place."

"Dangerous experiments?" Ingrid queried.

"Mm, you know, the ones being set up around the country to find other sources of magic than the one used for 'ness making." He furrowed his wrinkled face even further. "It worries me. Magic is an affront to God. The old Norse religion, or rather *superstition*, still lingers in too many people's minds, however. That makes them unafraid of magic and the dark mysteries that hide in our world."

Valour felt her eyebrows shoot up her forehead. Not only because this man was tangentially involved in the magic tonic trade himself, even if it was out of necessity. But also because of her respect for the old gods—who had influenced and shaped this land's people— and the magic that they had allowed their worshippers to borrow. After all, 'ness tonics were created by humans, not the old gods, who surely would've wanted their gift used for something more helpful or inventive. She was glad that academics across the land were searching for more sources of whatever magic still lingered and studying what little they had already found. This world needed to change for the better; perhaps the magic could help with that. Heal the sick. Feed the poor. Somehow stop citizens from becoming cannon fodder in the king's war. At least, if the magic was in the right hands.

"Hm. Perhaps if the experiments are allowed to continue, we might find some magic that can be used for good?" Ingrid said tactfully, clearly on the same page as Valour. "However, it does your wife credit to be fighting against the tonic trade. Say what you wish about the use of 'ness but it can have... a terrible cost."

She looked pained. However, she shook herself a little and her face returned to normal. Changing the topic, Ingrid asked follow-up questions about the man's wife and their happy marriage, seeming genuinely interested. Her tone was warm and kind and there was no hint of the artifice that she so often cloaked herself in.

The jeweller stopped in the middle of a new sentence about his wife. "Oh, listen to an old man prattling on. You are here for the citrine, not tales of my wife and I and our battle against the old magic." He named the price of the gem and offered to cut and set it.

Ingrid fished out a moleskin purse from within her wide skirts and handed over far too many riksdaler. "No need to cut it. Rough and natural can sometimes be far more beautiful."

He gaped at the coinage in his hands. "This is too much."

"No. I believe it is just right. However, I do still need to speak with Johan," Ingrid said apologetically.

The old man nodded with an air of dejection and shuffled off to get the drug peddler.

Valour noticed that she'd closed her fingers around the stone as if it was something precious that might escape. When she looked up, she found Ingrid watching her.

With effort, she managed to twiddle the gem past her layers and into her waistcoat pocket. "Did you actually call me a beautiful beast back there?"

"I did. Would you have preferred I said a 'beastly beauty'? Something which I was once labelled, by the way."

"Of course I wouldn't."

"There you go, then," Ingrid said, running her hand over the glass case again and observing the stones within. "Beautiful beast, a term signifying the best of both worlds—a beautiful heart with the strength of a mighty beast."

"Do you mean my heart has the strength of a beast or that my body does?"

Ingrid looked back at her, a smirk tugging at her lips. "Darling, you simply must stop talking about your muscles. They are big. You are strong. I get it."

Valour huffed and focused on her shoes.

"Well now," Ingrid said, sounding serious again. "You look the picture of someone who has something to say but is keeping it back. Can I convince you to share?"

Valour hesitated long enough for a decrepit grandfather clock next to them to tick a full minute away. "The beast thing. Petrichor compares me to an animal all the time. And I've heard it from others too. I suppose I was wondering, that's all."

"Wondering what?"

Valour groaned. Putting words on uncomfortable things was pure bloody torture. "I wondered if it's because I'm not the type of woman that some people expect."

"You mean physically? By being taller and brawnier?"

"Sure, that too," Valour said, tugging on her earlobe. "But I meant by cursing like a sailor and drinking and womanising. By not wearing dresses and face paint to make me look delicate and pretty. By grunting rather than, um…"

"Pouring silvered words?"

"Exactly. Does that make sense?"

It took a while for Ingrid to reply. Valour was glad. She didn't know what she would've done if Ingrid had laughed and dismissed it. Or answered without consideration.

To fill the pause, Valour craned her head to see into the back room where the jeweller had gone. Was he having to convince Johan to speak with them? Was Johan not on his way out but instead making a run for it?

"There might be something to what you say," Ingrid finally agreed. "Perhaps that is why society terms you a beast, at least. In Petrichor's case, I wager it is because to him, it is the gravest insult."

"Mm, he'd be scared and repulsed by anything so disordered as nature," Valour said.

"That covers society and Petrichor. In my case, well… I've always been attracted to the animalistic nature in people and I'm attracted to you, so that probably accounts for my use of that term." Ingrid toyed with the lace at the hem of her gloves, seeming lost in thought. "Moreover, I wish I had the freedom to be wilder and more feral. It suffocates me to have to be so 'femininely' civilised all the time."

Valour hummed vaguely.

Ingrid gave her a lengthy, searching look. "However, I see how it would be more appropriate for you to call me a beast than for me to call you one. If I slip up and do it again, remind me and I will apologise. Meanwhile, feel free to call me any sort of beast you like."

"Right. Um, sure."

Ingrid stepped closer. "Also, for what it is worth, animals are thought to have no soul while you… well, I wonder if you do not have more soul and humanity than most of us."

Right as Valour was about to ask what she meant, the jeweller returned. Behind him trod a handsome, hulking Viking of a man, with a bushy beard and loose-hanging hair in a reddish blond. There was even a mass of chest hair peeking out through the thick-set man's open shirt. This bloke looked like some sort of pale-furred bear.

Ingrid and the man regarded each other intently and for far too long. Then they shared a smile, full of meaning. Valour harked back to Ingrid talking about wanting more feral, animalistic things in her life. Did this bear man scratch that itch?

Valour coughed for attention and Johan stopped making eyes at Ingrid long enough to give Valour a glare. "Who's this?"

"This?" Ingrid said, putting a hand on Valour's arm. "Oh, this is our Lady of Assassination and Intimidation. She's my new bodyguard."

He visibly relaxed. "Your 'dear papa' pushed another watchdog on you?"

"Afraid so. At least this one isn't as virtuous as the other ones, which is why I brought her here."

"That and I asked her to," Valour said in her most take-charge tone of voice. "I'm looking for work. The kind that pays well and that is no business of the greve or the overseers."

"You're looking to work for…" Johan stopped himself and squinted at her for a moment. "…the person I work for?"

"I am. I had a high-ranking position in the organisation in Kallborg, with two dozen sellers under my command. Then I seduced the boss's niece and when he found out, I had to make a quick departure. You know how it goes."

He gave an unconvinced nod.

"Long story short," Valour said, "I'm a hard worker with a clear head but in debt and needing coin fast. Selling 'ness for Brandquist seems to be the solution."

He shook his head. "You won't get very far if you talk about it that openly."

"I'll be subtle when I know if it's worth it," Valour said, leaning one shoulder against the wall. "I don't even know if I want to work for Brandquist. What's he like?"

Johan gave a booming laugh. "Brandquist is one of the biggest secrets in Vinterstock. You really think I'll stand around here gossiping about him?"

Valour clicked her tongue. "So, it is a 'he' then. I mean, I know everyone says Brandquist is a man but there are so many rumours, and I'd like to know something about the person I'm considering swearing my allegiance to. Is he good at what he does?"

"Good enough to be able to do the job and stay hidden while doing so," Johan said, crossing his arms over his chest. "Most people who work for him never see him or even come near him."

"Someone as important as you does, though. Right? Ingrid says that you're in the top ranks, so I'm assuming you spend a lot of time with Brandquist?"

"Look, the organisation does need new blood. Hence why I've indulged you, but I don't see the point in anymore questions. You either trust in Brandquist or you don't." He leaned over the glass case until his face was near enough to hers that she could smell beer on his breath. "If you want, I can set you up with a small stash of 'ness and a part of town where we don't have a seller. But only because you're here with Ingrid and I trust her. As far as I know you might go blabbing to the overseers, so I'm not answering more questions until you've proved your loyalty."

Dead end. Part of being a successful assassin was knowing when it was time to change tactics.

Valour poked a finger at the fat and muscle of his chest. "Listen, mate. I'm not going to work for someone I don't know. Tell me where to find Brandquist so I can go ask for a job in person or maybe I *will* go talk to the overseers."

His nostrils flared and his beard moved as he ground his jaws. "Are you actually standing here bloody threatening me?"

"It seems I am. If you can't give me a location, at least give me some more information. Appearance, habits, anything that can help me find him."

Johan looked to Ingrid, who—with her voice sweet and smooth as honey—said, "No need for threats and heated tempers, is there?"

"It seems there is," Valour hissed, not hiding her hostility.

"I've had enough of your attitude." Johan pulled out a cleaver and laid it on the glass case, his hand resting on the weapon's hilt. "Leave before I split you in two, from your head down to your arse."

Valour sighed. Why was nothing ever easy?

"No, you furball. You're going to give me a lead or at least tell me what I'm looking for. If not, you're going to have to use that clumsy hatchet of yours while I use these." She pulled the knife from her boot sheath and one from her belt. Their perfectly sharpened blades and worn handles didn't seem to scare Johan nearly as much as they should.

"Ye gads, Johan. Offer her something," Ingrid said, voice lacking her usual confidence.

Valour took a moment to wonder if Ingrid was afraid of what she might do, or what he might do. Either way, Johan was clearly not listening as he grabbed the cleaver tighter and began vaulting over the glass case. The big man did not have years of assassin training though and he seemed treacle-slow to Valour. She stopped him before his feet had left the ground. He looked down at one knife prodding his chest right over where his heart was and the other against his throat.

"Perhaps I should come clean and introduce myself," Valour said. "I'm not someone trying to sell 'ness. I'm one of the Assassins of Axsten. And if you do not give me what I want, I will gladly cut you up like a ham and watch you scream, beg, and bleed for hours."

"You're only allowed to kill when ordered to," he said, sounding about as certain as if he was betting on a limping horse at the races.

"Who said I'd allow you to die?" Valour asked.

Trembling, Ingrid put a hand on his. "Have a care and do what she says so no one gets hurt. Please."

It was hard not to be impressed by how Ingrid made those big brown eyes plead in a way that would make anyone want to give her the world.

Johan was no exception, or maybe it was the fear that made him speak. Either way, he said, "I don't know where Brandquist is or how you find him."

"Lies!" Valour roared, pushing the knife at his neck until droplets of blood bubbled up.

He moaned with pain before blurting out, "It's not. He arranges where and how we meet. I can only get hold of him by sending a message up through the ranks of the organisation and then waiting. Even then, he'd decide whether or not he wanted to actually speak with me."

"You have met him, though. At least tell her what Brandquist looks like," Ingrid countered.

"Most of us only meet him when he has that large black hood on, and that covers most of his features."

"Most people, yes," Ingrid said, her voice now cajoling. "You are different. You know him well enough to have seen his face at least once. Come now, tell her. I promise it's all right."

He glanced down at Valour's knives. "Why? So this witch can go around harassing every Vinterstockian who looks like the description?"

"I'm sure no one will be harassed and no one needs to be hurt," Ingrid said. "You will merely mumble a few quick words, ones that no one shall trace back to you. Then we shall leave you to get on with your work."

At that, Johan's massive frame relaxed a little.

Inwardly, Valour did the same. She was grateful not to have to do the lion's share of the talking, nor having to push her blade further into this man's throat. She'd have to thank Ingrid for curbing the amount of bloodshed.

They made a good team.

The thought hit her like a punch to the gut.

No. She could've done this on her own. She did not need Ingrid's help, didn't need Ingrid in general. In fact, it was quite likely that if she had come in here violent from the start, she might've gotten the results faster. Yes, that was it. Valour always got results faster on her own. Relying on others only slowed things down.

She pressed the knife harder, making blood trickle down his neck and into his open shirt to land in his chest hair.

His face contorted. "Fine! I'll tell you! Just get that damned knife away from me."

"I'll withdraw both my blades when you've told me something useful," Valour said through gritted teeth.

"Fine. Brandquist is short and wiry. He has trimmed, dirt-blond hair with sideburns but wears a white, overly powdered wig over it. Pockmarked cheeks and deep-set eyes. There's a tattoo on his wrist."

"What else can you tell me?" Valour removed the knife at his throat, holding it up so he could see the blood on it. The one against his chest she poked deeper, ensuring the tip pierced the shirt. "I said, what else?"

"There's nought else," he said in a choked voice. "Shit, the only other thing I can do for you is pass on a message and if I do, I'll be missing before the sun sets and I have no bloody clue what happens to those Brandquist makes disappear."

"There must be more," Valour said, letting the knife bite further into his chest.

He blinked several times. "Um, I'd say he's middle-aged, but I cannot be sure. As I say, most of the time he wears that big hood and I've seen him so rarely. You'd have more luck finding a shadow than Brandquist—he's everywhere and nowhere in this city. There's nothing else I can tell you."

He looked so sorry that there was no other information he dared spill without spilling his own blood, and so Valour believed him. She considered making him pass on a message to arrange a meeting with Brandquist but didn't want his heart's blood on her hands. Nor did she want to risk Brandquist finding out about the ruse and fleeing or burrowing deeper into the city's dark crevices.

"All right," Valour said on an outbreath. "If you think of anything else that can help us, without getting you instantly killed, then tell Ingrid and she'll pass it on to me."

He wouldn't of course, but it never hurt to try.

Johan nodded with the vigour of a man who had just understood that his size and confidence didn't mean he was immortal. "Aye, I'll do that."

"Ingrid, take that cleaver and slide it along the floor out of his reach."

The other woman obeyed.

"Good. Go ahead and leave. I'll follow you soon," Valour said.

When she heard Ingrid's footsteps receding, Valour took the knife away from Johan's chest and backed out of the room without taking her eyes off him. She thought she had cowed him, but you never knew with blokes who saw themselves as the hunter and one day found themselves the prey. All of a sudden, they lost all sense in a burst of having to prove their dominance—something that often came with brandishing a hidden weapon or pouncing like a wounded bear.

Johan, however, looked as defeated as he probably felt. Good. His shame would mean he did not want to think about this or talk about it. That would be the best solution for everyone.

When they were back out on the street, Valour tucked her knives back in their sheaths but stopped as something familiar caught her eye. A tall man stood across the street and watched them. His unpleasant face was bruised, his posture rigid as a soldier's, and there was an air of menace about him. All this in contrast to the foppish blue silk coat, groomed sideburns, and inane hat that he wore.

Her brain itched. She had seen him before and he had put her hackles up. Why? When?

"May I enquire as to why you're staring at that man?" Ingrid whispered, sounding embarrassed at the rudeness.

Valour kept straining her mind until it came to her. This was the bloke in the Kronovall dining room who had gawped at her while she had her fika.

She explained to Ingrid.

Subtly, Ingrid slid her gaze towards him. "Hm. Could it be a coincidence? Or were you followed?"

Her pride flared. "I'd know if someone was tracking me."

"Of course. Happenstance, then. Or perhaps he's a secret admirer?

You are a very attractive woman."

A carriage for hire rattled along the cobbled street and the blue-coated man quickly hailed it. She swore as the carriage disappeared into the city. Could she have been followed without knowing? He might have been stalking Ingrid, but then why stare at her in the dining room? She wasn't even acquainted with Ingrid then.

That was a problem for another time.

Right now, Valour was glad to have a description of Brandquist, even if it wasn't much to go on. Interrupting her thoughts was the loud rumble of her stomach. Her breath hitched. She'd missed gloriam prayers. Should she go straight to the sanctum and take her punishment?

She felt watched. Ingrid was raking her eyes over her body and then, with an adorable blush, looked away when caught. That made her mind up. She'd go find lunch somewhere with this woman. Gloriam prayers and the Order of Axsten could bloody well go hang.

CHAPTER 20

THE OBSERVATORY

WHEN PETRICHOR WENT to ask the students about Brandquist, the early afternoon had rid the sky of any remaining clouds. The winter sun was low as ever, covering the city with eye-piercing light reflecting off the snow. In short, it was a terrible setting to try to sneak into a place that might be watched. Petrichor would've sold his best knife for some dark clouds or fog. He adjusted his smoky spectacles, pulled the hood of Halcyon's old coat down over his face, and kept to the least frequented alleys and streets.

When he was close to his goal, someone walked a little too near and so he moved behind a wide spruce until the person had passed. It was only a child. He squinted. Not just any child. Of all the people in Vinterstock, he had run into that infernal letter-delivering boy that he had taught about shades of white. He took another look. Was that the same urchin or merely one with similar clothes that hung off a reedy frame and the same sort of drawn face? Either way, the child ran into a derelict cottage with a sign reading: *Mrs Mariedal's Orphanage*.

Petrichor eyed the cottage roof, which stooped under snow that no one had cleared, and the cracks in the windows that had been covered with tattered cloth on the inside to keep out the worst of the cold and damp. What would his life have been like if he had grown up in a place like this instead of as a street urchin taken in by the Order of Axsten? Better or worse? At least the sanctum was well maintained, dry, and without draughts. There had been food and drink, and the assassins had afforded him an occupation and a regime to which he could adhere his life. An orphanage like this threw children out when they turned thirteen—earlier if they did not get enough alms from the greve and the city's rich to keep their far too many urchins in food and basic clothes. And that was for those who even got a place in an orphanage to begin with. He never had such luck. Vinterstock's streets were much worse than orphanages and the sanctum combined. There was no forgetting the demeaning and dangerous things he had needed to do to survive before the order took him in. Nor how many of his friends had died around him.

He reburied those memories and entered the university.

The moment he stepped into the vestibule his nostrils complained at the stench of sulphur, suggesting that the alchemy students had ruined some experiment again. He rushed away from it, up the spiral staircase. At the top, he stopped and regarded the door to the observatory.

The three students he was seeking would surely be lounging in that room as usual. They were the university's—no, the *city's*—brightest and most confident young people, not to mention the most entitled. He had studied this group and all they had: years of education under their belts, enough coin for the best books, social skills, and an understanding of society's games passed down by their rich and devoted parents. All leading to a gleaming future at the top of the city's hierarchy. Did they worry about the side effects of their 'ness addictions? Did they ever have to worry about anything whatsoever?

He took the last steps to the black door marked: *OBSERVATORY*.

Petrichor flexed his muscles and shifted to feel his hidden knives, reminding himself that he had things these elitists did not. He squared his shoulders, arranged his features into a condescending sneer, and knocked. Footsteps sounded from the room on the other side and he fought the desire to leave.

The door opened a sliver, just enough that he could see strands of honey-blonde hair and a bright blue eye. Even with that tiny glimpse, he recognised the blonde as one of the three and regretted that he had never bothered to learn the students' names. He could've used that to unsettle her.

"Occupied," she said.

Petrichor lowered the hood and took his tinted spectacles off, trying not to fidget with them as he did so. "I am not here to make use of the observatory. I've come to converse with you and your companions."

"Why?"

From inside the room, other voices asked who it was. The blonde turned her head and loudly said, "It's that peculiar assassin that rents rooms here. He wants to speak to us."

There was snickering and some mumbling Petrichor couldn't make out.

They knew who he was? How? Had the university rector warned them all against fraternising with him or something? He gritted his teeth. How many people in the city knew of him?

Once more the eye, strands of honey-blonde hair, and some pasty skin became visible. "Go on. Speak."

Petrichor fought the urge to stab a finger into that blue eye. "This conversation is not one suited to a hallway. Let me in and I shall explain."

The student gave an incredulous giggle. "In here with us? Why would I?"

"As I said, the topic is delicate. I only have a few questions for you, though. It will not take long."

"It would still use up precious time we could spend reposing and planning future experiments before our next lecture." She stifled a yawn. "Our time is more precious than you can ever understand. 'Tis not to be wasted on the likes of you."

The door was closing. Petrichor weighed his options and then blurted, "Don't you think it might be perilous to your health to deny the request of an assassin?"

The door opened again, a bigger slit this time. The blonde giggled, and there were laughs from within the room too, sounding closer. The other two must've drawn nearer the door to hear better.

"Are you threatening to kill us? We are not some frightened, superstitious townsfolk, you know." Even with only half her face showing, the bored disdain on it was obvious. "You cannot execute us unless the greve has put out a warrant for our death. If you hurt any of us, the overseers will find you and drag you into the court of justice."

Petrichor clenched his hands into fists, digging his nails into his palms. It stung like a candle burn, someone knowing the rules as well as he did. Perhaps even better than he did.

He peered into that one unnaturally gleaming blue eye. Wait. That gleam...

His fists loosened. "You know what, privileged little coin-bag? You will let me in and you shall answer my questions."

"Will I? Do enlighten me as to why."

"Simple. I just caught you using 'ness tonics and, even worse, doing so on university property." He placed a hand on the door. "The fact that I stopped by the rector's office and asked him to ensure you answered my questions means that as soon as he has finished his tea, he'll be here. Thus leaving you with nowhere to run and nowhere to hide your drugs."

"Dirt-poor little pile of manure!"

Petrichor continued as if she hadn't spoken. "Now, I *could* head off the rector, who is probably starting up the stairs as we speak. Then all will be well, with no one being thrown out of the university."

"I wish you'd go sit on something sharp."

Petrichor tutted. "Now, is that any way to speak to someone who holds your glittering futures in their hand and could drop them and squash them under a boot, just like so much broken glass, hm?"

There was a long spell of nought happening, then that bright blue eye blinked. "You are lying. The rector isn't coming."

"Really? Earlier you called me peculiar. Are you certain you can predict my behaviour?"

Hurried, murmuring voices came from inside the room.

"More importantly," Petrichor drawled, "is that a risk you're willing to take when all you have to do to be safe is give me a few answers to some quick questions?"

From behind the honey-blonde student, a snobbish, masculine voice boomed, "I suppose we must let him in."

The black door opened wide.

Petrichor made a show of going to the staircase and shouting down it, "No need to come up, Rector. You wait there while I get my answers and then I shall buy you some sugar and cinnamon for your husband's baking as a thank you."

Then he turned back to the honey blonde, who now held the door open for him.

He had been a fool to start off with the threat of injury; violence only got you a small distance with people like these. Threatening to take away their power. Their superiority. Their privileges. That was what you used with people like them.

Head held high, he strode in and leisurely took in the incredible room.

Not being a student, he had only been allowed glimpses of it. Sunlight broke in through gaps between the ceiling's shutters to display a dome-shaped space with walls painted midnight blue. The dark blue was dotted with stars aligned around it in intricate constellations, making what he recognised from his books as a precise star map. The only furnishings were standing copper candelabras placed around the circle of the walls. And, of course, at the centre of the room was the large brass telescope on its spinning table. For a heartbeat, he wished he could be alone to study the artistically painted night sky he had stepped into. Imagine being allowed to make something so beautiful, so elegantly decorated and yet so practical... However, his profession concerned death, not beauty, and so he shifted his focus to the students.

The man with the voice almost as deep as his own was closest and beside him stood the honey-blonde woman. Further back, leaning against the telescope, was the more aesthetically pleasing, androgynous one. They regarded him, bold as brass and just as polished, with not a hair out of place. They were as daunting as gods, and that was clearly how they saw themselves.

The androgynous student pointed up to the windows. "Pray tell, do you know how to open those shutters? I wish to see if we can spot any heimcrows flying over."

The other two half-stifled sniggers.

Petrichor sighed. "Alluding to your drug abuse when you think no one will comprehend it. Very droll. Sadly for you, I know the role the heimcrows play in the creation of 'ness tonics. I also know the stench of 'ness, and you three are awash with it. What I need to learn is from whom you buy it?"

The deep-voiced student stood straighter. "You have come to blackmail us, then?"

"I shan't need to if you're polite and answer my questions."

The three looked at each other, some form of silent communication taking place.

The androgynous one finally huffed out a sigh. "I suppose we might as well. *She's* moved anyway."

"Don't tell him that," the honey blonde snapped.

Deep voice put a hand on her waist. "Do you want him to blather to your family? No? Then shush and let me take the easy way out of this." He turned to Petrichor. "If I divulge where we buy our tonics, you'll leave and not tell anyone what you know about us?"

"Unequivocally."

"I have your word as a member of the league of assassins on that?"

"Order of assassins," Petrichor corrected him. "But yes, you have my word."

"Fine. We used to buy them from a bell-ringer's apprentice." He pointed in the direction of the church.

Petrichor crossed his arms over his chest. "Used to?"

"Yes, the bell-ringer's assistant moved. I don't know where to."

"I see. Then you haven't given me any useful information. Perhaps I ought to tell your families about your habits after all." Petrichor feigned leaving.

"Wait," the aesthetically pleasing one said, flashing a conciliary smile. "We can divulge the information she gave us about her job?"

"Go on."

"She was a favourite of Brandquist's but was coming to the end of her service. Apparently, he switches his sellers around a lot so that no one will get caught. Old sellers get either moved or—"

"Vanished," honey blonde interjected. "Right into a countryside ditch, they say."

Deep voice rubbed his eye, the one Petrichor had heard was glass. "Tell him about that place the bell-ringer mentioned."

"A place?" Petrichor prompted.

The genderless student nodded. "It was apparently where she and Brandquist used to go to drink."

"Tell me where that is, and you will have fulfilled your part of the bargain."

After some hesitation, the honey blonde gave a street address in the northern end of the city.

Busy with the relief of having somewhere to start, Petrichor didn't stop to think about how to take his leave. These brats seemed so unimportant now.

As he left, he stopped outside his rooms. Should he retrieve his pistol? Perhaps also that rolled-up toolkit hidden behind *Panaceas and Chrysopoeia*? His pulse picked up as he thought about something else he could fetch: the riding boots Halcyon gave him for his twentieth birthday.

He could still see Halcyon's hesitant expression as he said, "Not for you to ride in, of course. Who has that sort of coin? I picked them because they are hard-wearing, good in snow, and you will look most handsome in them."

It was the only birthday gift he could remember getting. Moreover, it was the only time someone had given him a compliment on his looks. Unless you counted catcalls from strangers about how he could be handsome if he wore a wig or showed off his calves, which Petrichor emphatically did not count.

He heard voices in the hallway and decided dallying wasn't worth the risk. He had been lucky so far not to have come across any Brandquist minions, or someone who would report to them. He put his spectacles back on and pulled the hood over his face. He would return to retrieve his favourite belongings later. Now, he had a lead to follow.

Chapter 21

THE IMPORTANCE OF COATS

VALOUR WAS WALKING back to the hideout on her own. Ingrid had claimed to have a quick errand to run and taken a carriage. Either some trouble at the hotel or a wig emergency, Valour assumed, trying not to dwell too much on the other woman.

She slowed, focusing on what she now had to go on in the hunt for Brandquist. A description, that was all. What if Petrichor had found better leads when interrogating those students? That would be a good thing, right? Now that they were sharing information? Except, in her mind, they were still competing. Always had been, sad as that was. She directed her mind to the mystery blue-coated man instead. If he was working for Brandquist, why hadn't he spoken to her? Or bashed her head in?

All this thinking made her ever hungrier. She stopped right by the canal bridge and was considering getting some food when a carriage stopped next to her. Ingrid stepped out with an armful of something brown.

"What's that?" Valour said.

"Something I acquired for you."

Valour crossed her arms over her chest, pointedly saying nothing.

"Please hear me out. I know a shop that makes outercoats that I thought would be perfect for you. So, I hurried over there, picked one out that I think would be *just right*, and bought it," Ingrid said, clasping the coat with pleading body language. "If you accept it, I will ask the shop owner to arrange for some coats of various sizes to be sent to an almshouse or a workhouse? Say, twenty of them?"

"Isn't that one of those charity things you do all the time? Why do I have to accept a coat from you for you to do it now?"

"Ah, but the only alms aid our company offers right now is the barest minimum for food and shelter. This is the off-season, and even our belts need to be tightened," Ingrid said as a worry line carved its way between her brows. "However, I will spend the riksdaler on the coats and face Papa's wrath at doing so, if you accept this one."

"Wrath? Mahadev Rytterdahl dotes on you."

"By having me followed and spying on me? By trying to get everyone to convince me to fall in line with how he wants me to live my life?"

"It's a shit way to go about things, sure, but he only wants you to be able to take over when he kicks the bucket."

Ingrid stared at her for a long time. "Do you truly believe that is what his controlling behaviour is about?"

"Um… Well, yes? That and he worries about you not being safe in this knife-pit of a city."

"It's not just that. He does it because he—" Ingrid stopped, then gave an annoyed grunt. "You're changing the subject! We were discussing your new coat. Which you desperately need, Valour."

"Thanks and all, but when I get that fat bonus for catching Brandquist I can buy myself, and the almshouses, heaps of clothes."

"That will be a long time from now. Until then, please accept my offer," Ingrid said wearily. "Look, I really want to buy you and some of the city's poor some coats."

"Why?"

Ingrid did look guilty about something. Her wealth?

"The poor always deserve and need outerwear. And buying one for you? Ever since I saw your wretched old cloak, I have been thinking hard about what to buy you. What you'd need. What you would like." She took on a jovial air. "Furthermore, I should hate for my new, fascinating companion to freeze to death before I've had time to ask her all about an assassin's life."

"You can ask, but you won't get answers."

"Right." Ingrid looked down at the coat she was clutching, joviality vanishing like a blown-out candle.

Valour rubbed her half-frozen earlobe. She did want a coat. And she wanted to give others free coats. Also, for some silly reason this clearly meant a lot to Ingrid. "Fine. Show me the coat. If it fits my needs, I'll accept it and pay you back when I get the reward for catching Brandquist."

"Agreed!"

Ingrid handed over the coat and their gloved fingers brushed.

"You know, I almost picked up a delectable piece in violet," Ingrid said. "Large pleats, golden brocade, the finest imported silk lining, and cinched tight at the waist. It comes with a plumed hat, apparently. It would suit you even better than that lace cap."

"Very funny," Valour said, trying not to chuckle.

Not expecting much, she held up what Ingrid had chosen for her. It was a heavy coat made of high-quality leather in the shade of coffee, lined with thick wool. Solid but not rigid. Unobtrusive pewter buttons. Hard-wearing stitching. Looked like her size too.

"It should last a lifetime. It's thick leather so it can withstand rain and scrapes, but is still pliable and will shape to your body with use," Ingrid said, caressing the coat's sleeve like the arm of a lover. "With that wool lining, it's warm for when you wait on marks too. I thought you might like the colour and its no-nonsense look. I believe it will fit, but if not, I can have a seamstress alter it."

Valour hefted it, trying to not show how impressed she was. "Might work. As long as it doesn't get in the way when I move."

"Try it on and we'll see."

"I'm still not sure about this. I don't like being beholden to people."

Ingrid groaned like the creaking of an old door. "Egad Valour, just try on the deuced coat!"

She had to smile to herself, sort of liking it when Ingrid got filthy-mouthed and domineering. "Fine, fine, don't have a conniption fit. Hold the coat for a tick."

As Ingrid did that, Valour tugged her cloak off and hung it over the bridge railing for someone else to adopt.

Instead of handing the leather coat back, Ingrid reached up and draped it over Valour's shoulders. Their proximity meant Valour finally figured out what Ingrid's perfume reminded her of: fika. She took a few deep sniffs. Vanilla, cinnamon, and something fresher… Lemon?

Unusual, rich, overwhelming, and sweet but with a tart bite. Just like Ingrid.

Valour put the coat on properly, doing up the buttons. It followed the shape of her body, from her hip into the waist and then plenty of room for her chest and shoulders. She shifted about a little and found she had a good range of movement in the buttery leather.

"It's long," she said, searching for faults. "Kicking will be hard."

"Unless you only use the top buttons or you keep it open," Ingrid said, deftly unbuttoning it in a far too distracting way. "It appears warm enough for you to keep it unbuttoned when you're moving."

"True, I suppose."

Valour rolled her shoulders and then puffed her chest out. Ingrid had been right. This thing would be both warm and flexible enough. It also offered some camouflage in the city's dirty darkness, while the leather would give protection from blows and cuts.

Shit. It was perfect.

She couldn't fall in love with this coat. Not only because she didn't want to be indebted. Nor because it was ridiculous to be so enamoured with godsdamned clothing. The main issue was that Ingrid, this relative stranger, had gotten to know her well enough to know exactly what she wanted and needed.

Now, Ingrid slowly raked her gaze over her. "Ye gads, woman, that thing fits like it was sewn together while you were wearing it. And it looks stunning on you. Practical but handsome with an air of... rough menace."

"Oh?" She made sure not to show the effect Ingrid's words had. "Glad to hear it looks as good as it feels."

"Good is an understatement. I have turned remarkably warm all of a sudden." Ingrid's voice had dropped to a sensual purr. "So," she said, locking her gaze on Valour's, "will you let me give it to you? I mean... do you want it?"

There was no missing the double meaning. Back to undiluted flirting, then? Finally some good news.

Valour made sure to aim her tone of voice at 'rough menace' as she replied. "Hel's realm, yes, I bloody well want it."

"Then it is all yours, beautiful."

Valour tried to not smile. She was no longer sure if Ingrid's flirting was down to being a tourist in same-gender lands, some sort of rebellion against her father, or a genuine wish for sex. Either way, her mind worried less about any budding emotions and her belly had forgotten about its hunger. All focus was on a new, hot pulsing between her thighs.

They held eye contact for a moment, Valour captivated by those bedroom eyes. Not the greyish brown of her own, but a warm, clear, liquid brown.

Then Ingrid smiled and said, "So, um, when I next have a chance, I will request twenty coats to be sent to the neediest almshouse."

"Great. Let's get going," Valour said, shaking off her arousal.

She rebuttoned her new prize, enjoying the comforting smell of leather and the thought of how Petrichor would envy the quality and practicality of this coat. Coats... That reminded her of what she should be thinking about. She had to focus!

As they ventured onto the canal bridge, Ingrid said, "What are you so lost in thought about?"

"Huh? Oh, the bloke in the blue coat."

"The one we saw outside the jeweller's shop?"

"Mm. He must be following me. I didn't notice because he only popped up at certain times and because he made no effort to sneak." She scratched her ear. "What's that about?"

"Don't ask me. This is your area of expertise. Mine is charming hotel guests into upgrading their rooms and going to exclusive masked balls to make the right contacts."

"Sounds about as fun as adders spitting poison in your eyes," Valour said distractedly.

Ingrid laughed. "That depends on who the guests are. In both scenarios."

"For you maybe."

"I suppose so. The masquerades are diverting. They afford people a unique chance to let go of their inhibitions by covering their faces and drinking too much champagne."

They had to slow down on the bridge. The godsdamned thing was constantly slippery in winter. "I bet."

"It means anything goes. There really is an inordinate amount of sex, merriment, and lustre at those occasions. The last one that the greve held had royal visitors, the king and queen. And most of the country's aristocracy."

"Uh-huh." Valour tapped her fingers against the bridge's handrail and walked as fast as she dared. This was taking ages, and she couldn't concentrate on Brandquist nor the blue-coated man.

"There were foreign dignitaries too. I met two baronesses and one dauphin."

"Really?" Valour mumbled, not having a clue what a 'dow-fan' was. Probably some sort of exotic pet. Maybe a fish.

"Yes. And three viscounts, no less. I danced with one of them for most of the night."

"Mm-hmm." Valour tapped faster against the handrail.

"The evening ended as usual with the entire gathering buggering each other silly in a fountain."

Valour nearly tripped. "You what?"

"Oh, so you *are* listening?" Ingrid said. "Are you all right?"

"I'm frustrated."

"Sexually?"

"What? No! At being followed. And that we didn't get a location to start searching for Brandquist. Or some names. He must have a family, must come from somewhere, must have a place to live."

Half-smiling, Ingrid gave a theatrically disappointed sigh. "Ah, work-related frustration. The dullest type. I wish you could focus less on your hunt and more on more diverting things." She grew serious. "My months of admiring you from afar have, however, shown me that your work comes before everything else."

"Mm. It does. At least I have a description now. There's still so much I don't know, though." Valour stopped walking and slapped the handrail. "Perhaps I've started at the wrong end when it comes to getting to Brandquist? Maybe I need to start with the 'ness trade itself."

Ingrid stopped too, leaning daintily over the railing. "I don't know everything about 'ness tonics. However, my curiosity has provided me with some information over the years. Why not ask me?"

"Really? Great. Are they mixed here? What's even in them? If I can get to where the ingredients come from, I might be able to trace that back to Brandquist."

Ingrid had been gazing out over the frozen Vinterstock canal, but now her head whirled towards Valour. "You don't know what 'ness is made of?"

"I know what I need to know: its benefits and its shit-awful side effects. I never bothered with the details."

"I see. Luckily, bothering with details is my forte. 'Ness tonics are made from a trifecta of ingredients." Ingrid held up three fingers and ticked them off as she said, "A type of leaves, magic water, and particular kinds of blood. The leaves are the one part we must import from warmer climes: 'ness leaves. I'm afraid I know little of them. The importers hold their secrets close."

Some answers at last. And magic... She'd known magic was involved in making the tonics, of course. Still, the subject made her heart hurt, reminding her of the tales of Norse gods, magic, and sacrifices that her mother had told her. "All right. What about the magic water and the blood?"

"The water is to soak the leaves in. However, it must come from Gjöll or it does nothing but create wet leaves."

Finally, something Valour knew. "That's the river at the top of the Fjäll Mountains."

"Mm-hmm. It's so high up that humans cannot venture there."

"How do we get the water, then?"

"The 'ness makers have trained corvids to fly up there with containers. Then to fill them with either river water or ice and return. They normally get it right, clever things." She paused to tie her scarf tighter. "Obviously, the crows drink from the water up there and so come back as heimcrows."

"That's where heimcrows come from? Huh." Valour noted the sneaking feeling of sounding uneducated creep in. She had to counteract that. "Did you know that the name Gjöll comes from the tales of our old gods?"

"No?" Ingrid subtly brushed a handkerchief under her red-tipped nose.

"Let's keep moving," Valour said, freezing as well. "Gjöll was believed to be the river separating the living and the dead in Norse mythology. Maybe it actually is. That might explain its magic."

"A fascinating thought, to be sure. I wonder if all the magic in this world can be traced back to the time of the Vikings." She hummed pensively. "And where the line is between magic and modern discoveries. I mean, the principle of lightning rods does rather sound like magic to me. Anything that one cannot explain may seem like magic, might it not?" Ingrid said, walking close to Valour and watching her raptly.

"I guess so."

"Do you believe in the Norse gods?"

"I don't fully believe in anything but a sharp knife and a good meal," Valour answered. "I do like them, though. The creatures from Nordic folktales the most, then the old gods."

That was a vast understatement, of course, but Valour was starting to irk a little at this chummy conversation and didn't want to sound too invested.

They carried on down the bridge, Ingrid walking so close to her that their shoulders touched. "May I ask why you like them?"

"Our gods?" Valour gave it some thought. "Because they're not like some ideals of what a god should be, but more human. They're often too busy with their own lives to care about us. They can die. They're flawed. They lose their temper. They kill. They cheat. They make mistakes. And that explains the world around us, in my opinion."

"They do not only have negative traits, surely?"

"No," Valour said. "They can show mercy, protect us against evil creatures, craft magical things, and manage feats of wonder."

"This may be a foreigner's ignorance, in which case pray excuse me, but from what I've read, some of them didn't seem to treat women very well?"

Valour stomped harder on the bridge than needed. "There are many tales, and prejudiced people only tell the ones they like. The ones that make those different to themselves seem inferior."

"How many tales are there?"

"I don't know," Valour admitted. "Many got lost as Christianity swept the North. Quite a few stayed in circulation here in this city, though. I don't know why. I guess the old gods just suited the spirit of Vinterstock."

"And the tales are rarely written down as far as I understand?"

"Mm. They're usually told. Often passed from woman to woman. Make no mistake, some of the really excellent gods are women. And some are of different races. Freja being an example of both. Our gods can be arseholes, but they are a diverse group of arseholes."

"Thank you for sharing." Ingrid brushed something off Valour's sleeve. "I do not think I've seen you speak so animatedly about anything. Not now, nor back at the hotel. Not that I ever saw you talking much back then."

Too much. Flirting was fine, but this was starting to feel like Ingrid was trying to get to know her. Valour stepped to the side so their shoulders were no longer touching. "Maybe. Anyway, can we get back to 'ness tonics?"

"Certainly." Ingrid dropped the hand that had been brushing the sleeve. "Where were we? Ah, yes. The leaves are soaked in the water for weeks and then crushed into the blood of a person with lots of the quality you wish the tonic to have. For example, naturally intelligent people for shrewdness tonics."

"So drinking 'ness is guzzling a load of smashed leaves, mystic river water, and blood?"

This was at least putting a stopper in her hunger.

"Yes. Although, now that importing sugar is cheaper, many pour some in to make the tonics more palatable."

"I see. Thanks. For explaining, I mean."

Valour was about to add that they should head back to the hideout when she was stopped by the sight of the cold afternoon clouding Ingrid's breath, vapour sliding over those rosewater lips. That mouth looked *so godsdamned good* and a throb emanated from between Valour's thighs. This waxing and waning of horniness was making her dizzy. Still, she clung to the familiar arousal. So much better than when Ingrid looked at her with those astute eyes and that warm smile and showed every sign of wanting to insert herself into Valour's life. Ingrid Rytterdahl was too quick, too much, too close, too confusing, too magnificent for Valour.

But gods, she was irresistible.

"Brr. 'Tis turning colder," Ingrid said. "We'll pass some coffee-houses and tea parlours on the way back to the hideout. Can we stop for a hot drink?"

Valour didn't have time for socialising and hot drinks. She'd wasted too much of her hunting time already. Furthermore, assassins were to be hardy enough not to give in to bodily needs like cold, hunger, thirst, or... anything else.

Therefore it made absolutely *no bloody sense* that she now grasped Ingrid's gloved hands to rub and blow on them before softly saying, "Of course we'll stop for a drink."

CHAPTER 22

THE PANIC, THE LORD, AND THE MEMORY OF VALOUR

PANIC CRAWLED DOWN Petrichor's spine like a thousand icy spiders. His ribcage constricted, squashing everything hidden inside it. Did he need a physician? No. His heart had always been strong and his lungs clear. This was mere panic, only in his mind. He could overcome it. He crouched on his haunches and tried to fend off this new fit by focusing on his surroundings, glaring at the tunnel's dirty stones, used in lieu of bricks. This section's emptiness made it his favourite. Most Vinterstockians didn't frequent any part of the city tunnels out of fear or superstition. This part, however, wasn't even used for the mass graves, sewage, nor as useful shortcuts for the city's shadier population. After a collapse a decade ago, it now led to a dead end and so was only used by Petrichor and hosts of charcoal rats, most of which currently sat half-hidden in the darkness around him. He felt a sort of kinship to these misunderstood creatures that lived unwanted and sequestered in shadow. They sat far away, clearly fearing him.

Right now, he feared himself too.

He watched the flame of his candle flicker with his frantic breaths.

Why in the ever-loving fires had this happened now? He had been so confident when he left the observatory. Sneaking through the city, though, he found himself riddled with unease once more. Why? Whatever it was, it drove him to distraction and brought back that feeling of not being free. Of being isolated. Of having no control.

He kicked one of the tunnel's support arches, making the rats scatter, as the memories seeped back in. Would he never be done with those cursed months in that cell?

Sweat prickled his palms. He couldn't return to the basement, not like this. Valour would be there. Not to mention that socialite of hers, who at the next ball would no doubt clutch onto some baronet's arm and gossip about mingling with the city's baser elements. He could see Ingrid in his mind's eye.

"La, sire, but you would not believe what I have been about. Hiding assassins from tonic peddlers!" Here she would no doubt pause to titter and flutter a peacock fan over her painted face. "One of them was in a terrible state. A shell of a man, utterly unable to be even the slightest bit coldblooded. Weak as a reed, I tell you."

Yes, that would be a good way for a nouveau-riche hotel heiress to impress the blue-blooded aristocrats. He shook his head. Valour might be willing to take such a woman along on her mission and let her in, but he was not such a fool.

There was a thought. Was it wise to divulge what he had learned at the observatory? He could maintain his advantage and protect the information by keeping it to himself. To share anything with Valour now would also be sharing something with the socialite, and whoever she told. Could he trust Valour's judgement when she was thinking with her genitals? Had he ever been able to trust Valour with *anything*?

That question mingled with his panic and brought up a suppressed memory. Valour had been delivering his meals for the last months in that cell. It was clear that she'd been instructed to not speak to him. Her silence had been worse than that of the adults, simply because—despite her natural quietness—he could always force her to speak to him by mocking her or challenging her until she started a quarrel. Their childish fights, verbal or physical, had been a nice break from the strict training to erase their humanity or studying how to kill. He had preferred arguing about who ran the fastest to learning what it felt like to drive a knife into flesh, or how not to care when someone begged for their life.

Nevertheless, during those months it did not matter what he screamed at her; Valour kept quiet as the grave. During one particularly weak moment he had wailed, begging her for any noise, even her annoying humming. She had stood outside the door for a while. He had heard her breathing, but she said not a word. He had shouted profanities at her, claiming that he hadn't wanted her to speak anyway, that he had merely tested her resolve.

Was it the next day when she halted after shoving in his daily tray containing bread and watered-down beetroot juice? Her small hand, and a thick but equally small book, had come through the hatch. She threw it deliberately at him. He screamed with rage, rubbing at his collarbone where the book had struck. When he'd calmed, he realised that she had given him something to cure his boredom and, in a way, keep him company.

After all these years, they had never spoken about it. Why had she followed the rules of not speaking but broken them to give the boy she hated a book? And why had she picked that one? Petrichor pictured the kit in the leather pouch hidden behind his books. None of *that* would've been in his life if it hadn't been for the volume she chose to throw at him. He was a tad calmer now, yet his breaths still came in painful heaves and cold sweat covered him.

Meanwhile, the rats had snuck back. He could see one standing on its hind legs and watching him with unblinking eyes. How many illnesses did creatures that lived off human corpses carry?

There was a strange sound. Petrichor stilled.

Something larger loomed behind the rat. With steps thumping and claws scraping against the stone floor of the tunnel, the larger thing entered the light. It was a rat too, but one of abnormal proportions, as big as the city's stray hounds but so much more compact with thick-set muscle. This lord of rats bared its teeth, large and needle-sharp.

So, the stories were true. Petrichor had discounted the tall tales of a rat enlarged by magic living down here, having grown to this size by drinking sewage from 'ness users or by eating the heimcrows returning from the mountains, their bellies full of the magic water. Either way, here the beast was. Its teeth were still on show and so were its curving knife-like claws, protruding from paws that more closely resembled hands.

Petrichor made his calculations. The beast blocked his path out.

Like its smaller cousins, this lord of rats must have feasted on the corpses down here too. Therefore, he could not let it bite or claw him, lest he get an illness there was no cure for. Not to mention that this thing was large enough to take his arms off with one bite. Taking the proper stance, Petrichor unsheathed his two largest knives. Why did this have to happen when he was debilitated, partly from the fight back in his rooms but mainly after soul-sapping panic? What a pathetic way to die this would be, killed and eaten by an overgrown rat simply because he had become weak.

The rat leapt, aiming to wrench a piece of flesh off Petrichor's thigh. Lightning-swift, he dodged left just as the animal's jaws loudly snapped shut in the air where his leg had been. Around the monster's feet, normal rats scurried past in fright. The rat lord caught two in its teeth, devouring them with violent vehemence, as if taking out its frustration at missing Petrichor on its smaller siblings.

Then, the monster pivoted back to him. It screeched, showing bloodied teeth gory with the smaller rats' fur, and stalked nearer. It was now set on him like a hunter on its most wanted prey. Its grey fur was matted in places with something reddish-brown that Petrichor did not want to ponder. The beast had a sick and rotting stench. It watched him, black eyes only visible because they glinted like metal in the firelight. Filth, disease, and an animal who had eaten of Petrichor's victims, thus becoming a reminder of all Petrichor could ever be... What worse death could he meet?

It pounced again. This time it aimed for the middle of his torso and not a limb, making it harder for him to merely dance out of the way. So, it was quite clever, then. Petrichor waited until it was almost close enough to bite, then acted with whip speed. He stabbed his two knives into its back, then jumped to grab the protruding stone above him that he knew was in this part of the tunnel. This meant the rat lord, stabbed and screeching, ran right into the stones of the wall behind where Petrichor had stood. Dizzy and enraged, it spun in circles under him, swiping its rending claws up at Petrichor's legs and scratching deep grooves into one of his boot soles. Quite clever, yes, but not clever enough.

He dropped down on top of the monster, letting his boots land with his full weight square on its back. The thud came with a cracking of bone. He yanked out his buried knives, avoiding any blood spray by ducking back, and drove the knives the entire way into the beast's back again. This time he must've hit something vital, as the monster instantly stopped thrashing. Its head still snapped back, though, trying to bury those long, urine-yellow, diseased teeth into Petrichor's flesh. Heart beating out of his chest, Petrichor gave the twisting head a sturdy kick. The rat lord gave one last ear-piercing screech and fell into a boneless heap.

Dazed, Petrichor stepped off and back a few steps. When his gloves were on, he used his handkerchief to clean his knives. He dropped the ruined handkerchief on the rat lord's face, thereby covering its unseeing eyes as the beast settled into death. He'd managed it. Without being wounded or contaminated. He had, in fact, done it without much effort. Even in his debilitated state. Petrichor took a deep breath and checked himself for signs of the earlier bout of panic. There were none. He had gotten through that without the panic incapacitating him or the lord of the rats killing him. Perhaps he wasn't always fated for the worst outcomes? The bout of optimism passed as the rush of the fight left him. It had only been killing a rat, and killing was all he was meant for.

He sighed at the sight of the corpse. He would not tell Valour of this. She liked rats and would never cease badgering him about slaying what she would no doubt have wanted for a pet or attack dog, even though it would have bitten her arms and face off and diseased her. The stench was both sour and bitter in his nostrils. Considering his earlier conclusions about Valour, Petrichor decided to return to the basement. When it came to the problem of the loose-tongued heiress, he would simply have to take the chance. This time. He could always keep other, more useful information back later.

He strode away, watched by rows of rats. His steps were soundless and his heartbeat calm. Still, he intentionally didn't look as he passed some of the graves where his victims rotted.

CHAPTER 23
SCREAMING HER NAME

HALFWAY TO THE hideout, Valour and Ingrid passed a squat building with a pitched roof. "Anckarström's. My favourite coffee-house," Ingrid said, nodding towards it. "It is one of the few places in Vinterstock that sells my specific hot beverage."

"Good," Valour said, stopping and rubbing her grumbling belly. "I could eat and drink my body weight by now."

Ingrid consulted the tiny timepiece in her locket. "Well, it's nigh two in the afternoon, so you have missed the midday meal."

"What I missed was the gloriam service."

"Oooh. More information about the secretive assassins. What is gloriam?"

"A prayer ceremony. It's sacred. I can't give you details."

"I see. Such a pity that you missed it. You shall have to attend it extra diligently tomorrow instead. For now, we should get some sustenance. Are you coming in with me?"

Valour didn't say that this wasn't something one could make up for the next day. Gloriam was the order's most important event and she'd never missed it. Until today. "I should stay here and keep an eye out for Brandquist's dogsbodies or that bloody bloke in the blue coat."

"As you wish. Any requests?"

"Black tea. And something to eat." She caught herself. "Please."

"Your desires are my command," Ingrid said, and went in.

Valour leaned against a street lamp, which reeked of oil so probably had a leak, and studied the area. She didn't move a muscle as she waited, but her mind raced, travelling from her task to the missed gloriam service to Ingrid. Something dug into her rib. She took out the gemstone tucked into her waistcoat. The same shade as her hair, huh? What an odd thing it was to have someone pay attention, especially for someone who was ever the one to pay other women attention. She shoved the stone in her coat pocket when a waft of perfume signalled Ingrid's return.

"Here we are, my Lady of Assassination and Intimidation. I got my drink and a meatball sandwich with a black tea for you. I asked them to add a slice of lemon to the cup."

Despite Ingrid's protests, Valour exchanged some coins for the pewter mug and paper-wrapped sandwich. "You know how I take my tea?"

"You think I would admire you from afar for this long and never ask my staff about you and your preferences?"

"Admired me or were just curious about the oddity living in your hotel?"

Ingrid blew on the contents of her cup. The scent of it wafted over to Valour, milky and sweet. "I have never seen you as an oddity, Valour. More like a wonderous rarity." She cupped the mug with her gloved hands, lavish black velvet against the rough pewter. "The first time I saw you, I wanted to know you. *Everything* about you. Yet, try as I might, I was unable to catch your attention."

"Oh, you caught my bloody attention."

"But, as Petrichor said, I wasn't your type?"

Valour had to buy time. She made for a low brick wall next to them. She couldn't tell Ingrid that she'd been intimidated, worried that Ingrid would pull her into conversations that were too much. Make her be sociable. Captivate her. Get under her armour. Like she had now.

"The sewage that comes out of Petrichor's mouth shouldn't be listened to," she murmured as she sat on the wall and put her cup and sandwich down.

"I am glad to hear it," Ingrid said, her voice as joyful as it was flirtatious.

While unwrapping the sandwich, Valour threw the question out. "Did you somehow coerce your father into asking me to spend time with you?"

154

Ingrid sipped from her cup. Over the rim of it, her eyes glittered.

"Mm. Thought so." Valour chuckled before taking her first bite.

Ingrid joined her on the wall, both of them sitting sideways so they could face one another. Ingrid let her knees lean against Valour's. They ate and drank in silence, not taking their eyes off each other. Valour tried not to focus on that tempting mouth enveloping the rim of the cup. She searched for something to say to break the taut, heated tension instead.

"So, um, what's that you're drinking?"

Ingrid held the cup closer to Valour, showing its pinkish-white contents. "Rose petal–infused milk with a dash of cream to thicken it."

Valour sniffed the concoction. "What sort of weirdness is that?"

"My kind of weirdness, darling," said Ingrid in an amused tone. "It serves as a drink and a snack in one. Keeps me from making myself ill with too many sugared treats."

Valour gave a vague hum, trying not to think about the warmth where her legs touched Ingrid's.

"I actually invented this drink," Ingrid said. "On a cold, late night when I had spent hours poring over the accounts in Papa's office. Having a pot of hot, sweet milk by my side when doing that is far more useful than a plate of steak, cabbage, and potatoes."

She wanted to disagree with this far-too-enchanting know-it-all, but couldn't. Valour went through life hungry but often didn't have time or patience to eat. This was something warming on a cold day but also something to feed the muscles, without giving her a full belly so she couldn't chase down her marks.

She swallowed a bite of her sandwich. "Fine. I'll admit it, that sounds useful."

"Thank you. I knew one day I should come upon someone who understood."

"Surprised that it's someone like me?"

Ingrid licked milk off her lower lip. "Not really. As I watched you around the hotel, I often daydreamed that you would understand quite a lot about me."

Too close again. Valour had to make some distance. And not think about how her own daydreaming had been reciprocated. "I bet that has changed now that I've opened my mouth. If not, give it time."

Ingrid's face took on a look of utter earnestness. "The more time I spend with you, the more you speak, the more I like you."

"You don't even know me."

"I don't take long to decide whom I like or dislike." She smirked. "Perhaps I only like you because you're attractive, though?"

"Don't play the shallow socialite with me, I know it's fake. Besides, I'm not half as attractive as the men that beg at your feet." Valour drank some tea. "Nor the women, who no doubt gossip about how much they hate you but would open their hearts and spread their legs if you asked. It'd take more to intrigue you."

"Fine. It was because you're different," Ingrid said, voice clear with sincerity. "The fact that you're an assassin but refuse to kill those you deem undeserving of it shows a strong moral code. More importantly, you are prepared to take the punishments for said code. To bleed to keep others from bleeding, which is rare in Vinterstock."

Valour became very interested in her sandwich.

Ingrid sought her gaze. "Also, you're clearly funny, determined, smarter than you give yourself credit for and—how to put this—sort of tinged with destiny."

"Destiny?" Valour said around a big bite of sandwich. "What in Oden's gouged eye are you on about?"

"I believe you're the sort of person that interesting and important things happen to."

Valour stopped mid-chew. Someone had said something like that before... Right. Her mother had stopped her from diving into the Vinterstock canal for a swim, telling her she had to be careful because the gods had gifted her a special future.

But that would require three impossible things: that the gods were real, that destiny existed, and that she was special.

She swallowed her mouthful. "Troll-shit."

"You do have the filthiest language, though," Ingrid said with a laugh. "Luckily for you, I like my women filthy."

"You do *like* women, then?"

"Naturally. Do you think I have been flirting with you under the misapprehension that you were a man?"

"No. I thought you were trifling with me. That the second the clothes started coming off you'd bolt, like man-loving women usually do."

"Ah, but I'm talented at doing several things at once, like being attracted to men and women simultaneously." She sipped at her milk. "Also, of course, those who fall somewhere in the middle, who are often the most interesting."

"Oh."

"Do you mind that I flirt with you?" Ingrid asked.

"No." Valour drank some tea in the hope that the cup would hide any embarrassment on her face. "Especially not if you mean it."

"Good. Because you are not only fascinating and *inconceivably gorgeous*"—Ingrid leaned closer—"you also have the most magnetic effect on my body. I constantly want to give into the pull and simply... slam right into you, my delectable Lady of Assassination and Intimidation."

The way she said 'slam' was undiluted, delicious filth and almost made Valour choke on her tea.

Valour put her mug down, feeling a smile pull at her cheeks. "That nickname. It's weird, you know. Far too long too."

Ingrid took her gloves off, slow and deliberate, letting Valour see each long, slender finger sliding out. "You may have a point. Shall I call you Val?"

"Only if you want me to start throwing things." She trusted her expression was conveying that the only thing she wanted to throw right now was Ingrid, onto a bed.

"Faith, m'dear." Ingrid batted her eyelashes. "Sounds exceedingly dangerous. How do you feel about 'beautiful' or 'darling'? You didn't complain when I used them."

Valour was watching those naked hands. They were mesmerizingly elegant and expressive. And in this light, their shade of brown reminded Valour of gold, of the golden locket that was no doubt buried in the lace at Ingrid's cleavage right now. Gold. Mountain gold. Where had she heard that? Oh, right, when Ingrid had told her about cloudberries. This woman was just as much of a rare treat as those berries, and gods, how Valour wanted to devour her.

She deliberately licked her lips. Being subtle was dull. "Here's an idea, why don't you call me by my name?"

"I suppose I could. However..." Ingrid sat closer, so that their legs intwined as much as her dress allowed. "I was rather saving that for when I screamed it during my climax."

Brazen. Direct. *Perfect.*

"Did I shock you?" Ingrid studied her. "Please do not tell me that your womanising reputation was wrong and that you only bed women you're in a relationship with."

"The other way around. My life doesn't suit love and relationships."

With a sceptical hum Ingrid said, "Sounds like an excuse, but hey..." She placed one of those magnificent hands on Valour's chest, right above her left breast. "As long as it gets me into these clothes and then into you."

Valour didn't have a godsdamned thing to say to that.

Ingrid's lips parted and the mist from between them showed that her breaths were coming hard and fast. So did the rise and fall of her chest.

A heartbeat. Two. Three. Then Valour asked, "How long do you think the walk back to the hideout is?"

"Too long," Ingrid breathed. She stood and leaned out onto the street to hail a carriage.

BACK AT THE hideout, they clumsily pulled each other's clothes off and kissed like their lives depended on it. Ingrid kept moaning into her mouth and it was driving Valour mad. She slammed Ingrid against the wall, worrying she had been too rough, but Ingrid just moaned dirtier and kissed her deeper.

Was this real? All those months of admiring and desiring Ingrid and now she was here, in Valour's arms, returning that desire in full.

They were almost naked when Valour had the presence of mind to mumble, "Did you lock the door?"

"I did. If Petrichor returns, he shall be livid that he cannot get in."

"Tough. Now can you help me get this thing off you?" Valour said, pawing at Ingrid's chemise, which was far too tight. And she had thought the dress, the panniers, and the over-elaborate stays were hard to get off. Undressing rich women was like opening a present wrapped in five sorts of paper and then padlocked.

Ingrid deftly pulled the chemise over her head, ripping it a little but not seeming to care.

Finally, the alarmingly exquisite gift that was Ingrid Rytterdahl was fully unwrapped and taking Valour's breath away. Frantically, she kissed the other woman's neck and shoulders. She had to move fast. If she stopped for even a heartbeat, she might start thinking and feeling.

Meanwhile, Ingrid's hands were eager and everywhere, and Valour didn't complain. She moved to give the black-haired beauty's wandering hands access to anything they wanted, growling like a wolf when Ingrid's fingers entered her. She caressed Ingrid's body distractedly. The thrusting of those deft fingers was deliciously hard but everything about Ingrid's body was soft, from her skin to her curves to the soaked silk between her thighs that Valour, wanting to tease, only grazed. She couldn't remember her own body ever being that soft. She'd gone from a bony girl to a muscular woman. There were some soft places on her, though, and Ingrid's free hand found them all. She kneaded Valour's breasts, her buttocks, and then kneeled to replace her fingers with her tongue in the softest, and wettest, part of Valour's body.

Valour heard herself moan at a far higher pitch than she was used to as Ingrid licked her into climax. Ingrid knew just what to do, what speed to go at, what motions to use. Either this woman was an expert at this, or they were tailor-made to be lovers.

When Valour's orgasm ebbed out, the kneeling Ingrid looked up at her. Those dark eyes held far too much tenderness for someone just having fun. Valour sobered. She had to keep her head. Ingrid could get under her skin, change her, break her, see who she really was. Besides, it was only a matter of time before Ingrid realised how far below her Valour was and moved on to the next diversion. Everyone left Valour in the end. She had to protect herself; gods knew that no one else would. This was just fucking, nothing more.

As soon as the haze of orgasm had cleared enough that Valour could move, she pulled Ingrid up to her feet and pushed her against the wall again. Her fingers found their way between Ingrid's legs and attended to the hard little pearl there until Ingrid—true to her word—screamed Valour's name.

As Ingrid shuddered with the aftershocks, Valour looked down at the hand holding on to her arm. On the wrist was a mass of scars, which before had been hidden by the sleeves of Ingrid's dresses and coats. Ingrid pulled her arm away and wrapped it around Valour's waist, clinging onto her.

"Are you all right?" Valour whispered.

"I am utterly blissful."

Ingrid hummed in sated pleasure and rested against Valour's shoulder, floppy as a rag doll with her face nuzzling into Valour's neck.

Valour was aware that her resolve to keep her head was fading.

She picked Ingrid up and carried her to the mattress.

CHAPTER 24

ORDERS FROM B

PETRICHOR WAS WALKING out of the tunnels on his way back to the hideout, daydreaming about strong, hot, night-black coffee. It might help clear the peculiar, headachy fuzziness he was experiencing.

Scraping noises ahead made him stop. That wasn't the scurrying of rats. He pushed on, one hand holding his candle high while the other hovered over the blade inside his coat. He spotted two unkempt children by the wall. A lad held a dingy lantern and a scrap of paper, while a lass was reaching up to draw, copying what was on the note.

Petrichor smiled to himself. When he lived on the streets, he would rejoice at finding a piece of chalk or coal and coming here to scribble on these same stone walls. He made to pass by without disturbing them but heard, "He's coming. Run!"

The children darted off. Good. Hiding from adults was wise when you were a street urchin. Something did irk him, though. 'He's coming.' The girl hadn't said, 'Someone's coming,' but '*He's* coming.'

He made for the wall they had been drawing on. Right under a patch of lichen was not a drawing at all, but a message. For him.

~~Petrik~~ *Petrichor the* ~~Assess Assai~~ *Assassin. Last warning from B.*
Pretend to hunt for B when you talk to the other assassins but actually do nought until B gives you new orders.
If you don't, you know what will hap

The message cut off where the urchins must've spotted him. His blood turned cold, but not because of the words. Those children were in the employ of a drug-smuggling gang. He could imagine far too well what that could mean for them and their lives.

Rage blew away every bit of his earlier self-pity. His plans, his worries, his futile feud with Valour, his own life... They could wait. At this point, all he could think of was punishing Brandquist and then everyone else in society who made children suffer. Even if it meant killing every adult in Vinterstock.

Chapter 25

Afterglow and Aftershocks

Valour lay on her back on the mattress with Ingrid splayed half on top of her. Every part of her was languid and she sighed contentedly as she caressed circles over Ingrid's shoulders.

After a while, Ingrid kissed her collarbone and craned her neck up to look at her. "Hello, mysterious lady."

Valour snorted. "Is that meant to be me?"

Ingrid placed another kiss on Valour's chest. "It is indeed."

"I see. Hello to you too, then."

"Would it ruin the post-coital bliss if I asked you some questions?"

Valour wasn't sure but even she wasn't rude enough to say yes after what they'd just done. "Ask."

"We need not talk if it bothers you?" Ingrid surveyed her. "Tell you what, why don't you ask me some questions first? It may make us more comfortable talking to each other."

"All right. There was something I meant to ask before we fucked. Is my breath all right? If not, do you have some tooth powder and a brush?"

"Your breath is fine." Ingrid play-slapped her. "Ask a real question."

"Fine. Hang on, I need to think of something."

Ingrid laid her head back on Valour's chest and all was quiet as Valour pondered.

"All right, I've got one. When we talked about your father, did you say something about his reasons being more than the obvious ones?"

"I did. Yes, Papa does worry about me and wants me to take

over after him. However, I grew up in those hotels and I do a lot of the work already. Furthermore, I have a head for learning as I go. If he stepped back today, he knows I would clean up my act and take his place without issue."

"All right." Valour played with Ingrid's hair. "What's his main motive, then?"

"I think it's about keeping me close. Since we lost Mama, he wants us to be each other's confidants and best friends. Having control over me lessens his fretfulness. Then there's the marriage thing, of course."

"The marriage thing?"

"Valour. I'm twenty-six years old. I know you assassins can choose if you settle down or not, but the rest of us are expected to get married and have children, preferably before we're twenty-five." She blew out a long breath that tickled across Valour's chest. "Why do you think Papa sends me to all those balls?"

"He sends you? I thought you went because you like to dance and drink?"

"Well, yes, that is my reason for agreeing to attend. His reason for pushing me to go is to stop me from being an old spinster. He wants a ring on my finger and grandchildren in my belly."

"Oh. And I'm guessing you don't want that?"

"Not children, no. Perhaps a spouse."

Valour shuddered. "Rather you than me."

Ingrid craned her neck up again. "Don't you think it would be nice to have a person to connect to? Someone who would be on your side and choose you over all the other people in the world?"

"Human relationships come with steep costs. Besides, I'm bloody rubbish at them." Valour squirmed, suddenly not as comfortable with Ingrid's weight on top of her. "Are you asking those questions or not? If not, I should get back to work."

Ingrid's face lit up. "That brings us perfectly into my first question. You seem to dislike your profession. Why?"

"I don't dislike all of it," Valour muttered.

"No? Which portion is the problem? Obeying orders? Having to sneak around? The strict regime? Hunting people?"

Valour swallowed. She shouldn't answer that honestly. So why was the truth right there at the front of her mouth? Ingrid's expression was sympathetic, even non-judgemental. The answer broke out. "The killing part. If I had to chase down pus-sucking crooks to bring them to the overseers or something, I'd be fine with it."

Ingrid reached out to brush a stray lock of hair away from Valour's face. Her fingers were warm in the chilly room, and Valour had a strange desire for Ingrid to cup her face and say something kind.

"I see," Ingrid said, tucking that lock behind Valour's ear. "Why exactly do you hate killing?"

"Why wouldn't I hate killing? You're the one who called me valorous. A valorous person doesn't bloody well skulk around slitting throats in the dark now, do they?"

"I was only asking, no need to become so vexed."

The afternoon sun slipped through the grasp of the clouds and its rays hit Valour right in the eyes. She groaned. "I'm not getting vexed. I just… Why do we have to talk about this?"

"Because it would unburden you. And I'd get to know you better."

"Unburden? Why would I deserve to be unburdened? And for all the pig shit in Alfhem, I don't see why anyone would want to get to know me better."

"I can give you countless reasons. In the end though, you should want to unburden yourself for your own sake. Talking about this might clear things up for you."

Valour shielded her eyes. "Can we cover those windows or something?"

With a frown of pity, Ingrid said, "You are changing the topic, beautiful."

"No. It's just that I don't need to clear things up. I'm clear as glass."

"All right, then I fail to see why you cannot tell me the full truth. No need to make a speech, simply give me a quick answer. It'll be good for you."

Should she reply and get this over with? "If I answer, can we go back to kissing?"

"Gladly."

"Fine." Valour rubbed her forehead. "So, I guess I… I mean, this will sound selfish, but whenever I kill someone, I feel like they didn't just lose their life. I lost something."

"What did you lose?"

"I don't know! Ugh. It sounds all Christian to say I lose a bit of my soul. But maybe they're right? All I know is that whenever I kill, it's like I kill a part of what makes me feel human. What makes me feel good about myself. Every time the deed is done I..."

"Go on."

"Shit, you say 'go on' like it's that easy. Give me a moment!"

"Take your time." Ingrid kissed the spot where Valour's collarbones met. "We are in no rush."

More sharp sunrays pierced the basement's windows, refracting through the warped glass.

"I suppose I can't reckon with myself why I should be allowed to end lives." Valour closed her eyes and made herself say the rest. "I know what it's like to grieve until it breaks you, until you spew your guts out and then cry your heart out until you're godsdamned hollow." Her voice wavered and she had to fight to keep it steady as she added, "And the person I just killed? They have a family that grieves like that."

"Oh. Of course. God. I'm so sorry." She wrapped her arms around Valour as best she could. "I must point out that you don't decide to kill people. You only follow orders, like a soldier."

"It doesn't matter if I'm following bloody orders. It matters that this person was breathing a moment ago, and then I took that away. What does that make me, Ingrid?"

Ingrid was quiet for a moment. "Someone who does the only thing they feel they can. Trust me, most people do things they will later regret, often to survive or to stay sane, and then struggle to face themselves in the mirror."

"It's not looking at my reflection that bothers me. It's looking into the eyes of the person I'm about to kill. Despite only killing those I think deserve it, the murderers, the abusers. Even then, taking a life feels like... You know what, I don't want to talk about this anymore."

"All right," Ingrid said softly. "May I ask about your nightmares instead?"

Valour's breath caught. Flashes of the dark and damp tore into her mind. The feeling of her mother's knife, so big and heavy in her tiny hand. The questions, gods the questions that she couldn't answer.

"That counts as talking about my job," she snapped. "Anyway, I don't think about them. The shit I have to deal with when I'm awake is bad enough."

"Perhaps you need to stop being an assassin?"

"Oh, I need to stop? I hadn't thought of that. Hel's realm, now it's all so bloody clear. I'll just say goodbye to the other assassins, saunter out of the sanctum, and snag another job in a heartbeat. Easy."

"I know it is not simple. If it was, you would have done it already." Ingrid sounded so patient and gentle, despite the fact that Valour was all but screaming at her.

She tried to collect herself. "Sorry. You're right. I just... Well, leaving is complicated and nigh impossible. Not only because assassinating is all I know how to do. But..." Valour shielded her eyes. "We have to cover those godsdamned windows. Or move the mattress."

"We'll get back to the windows and that being an assassin is certainly not all you can do. Right now, though, I'd like to hear where that last sentence was going. But what?"

Valour let her hand drop over her eyes. "But because... I owe the Order of Axsten everything. It raised me, fed me, and gave me a solid profession in a city where there are few of them."

"And have you not repaid them with years of loyal work?"

"It's not just that. My mother worked for the order, loved it, worshipped it. She wanted me to be an assassin. Somehow, it feels like the only thing she left me."

"Ah. I see," Ingrid said, her compassionate tone overwhelming.

"Then there's the steep leaving fee. I think they set the sum so high that no one can afford it." Valour took the hand away from her eyes. "You know what, though? If there is as high a reward for Brandquist's assassination as Halcyon thinks, that might be at least half of the amount."

"That would be incredible."

"Mm."

Ingrid reached out a hand and caressed Valour's cheek. "You know that it's all right, don't you?"

"What is?"

"What you do. What you are. You're so hard on yourself and there is no need. You are trying your best and that is more than enough, Valour."

At the same exact time, Valour's stomach lurched and her breath hitched, causing the strange sensation of the floor falling away and sending her plummeting. Had anyone ever told her something like that? No. Not even her mother.

Valour noticed a subtle clinking from the door. It was one she knew well. Someone was picking the godsdamned locks! She shot up to sitting, reaching for her knives, when Petrichor strode in.

Relaxing, Valour pulled the covers up to ensure Ingrid was covered and glared at him. "Oi, arse-mouth, you didn't knock. And I didn't say come in."

"For now, this is my home," Petrichor said with bored dismay. "I should not require an invite simply because you have decided to mount each other. Nor to have to lockpick. Anyway, I have matters to discuss with you."

Valour faced Ingrid. "Sorry about him. Especially about the 'mounting' thing."

"Don't be," Ingrid said. She gave that beaming, flirtatious smile of hers and it blew away most of the tension from their earlier conversation. "In the spirit of my attempts to be more feral, 'mounting' sounds like a perfect term."

"Could you afford me the courtesy of discussing this later?" Petrichor said in clipped tones. "I shall turn my back to rekindle the fire, thus you'll have privacy to get dressed. Then you will hear my report."

Valour shuffled out from beneath Ingrid. "I'll wait for no man and only listen if you've got something useful to say."

She got up and rifled around in the abandoned clothes, trying not to snigger when Petrichor grumbled about her uncouth habit of showing off her naked body.

Ingrid didn't seem to mind, though, smiling and watching where she lay with the covers barely draped over her. Such ease was a feat whenever Petrichor was around. Valour had to admit to enjoying how little Ingrid was bothered by him, and how very bothered he was by her.

The man, or annoyance, in question had finished putting more logs on the fire. She glanced over at him as she dressed. He stood statue-still, his gaze set on the middle distance and his face blank, bloodless, and chiselled. Ingrid had been right; marble was a good word for him. Was he even breathing? Halcyon was right too when he said that Petrichor was eerie. Shut-off somehow. Only half-alive?

He made her skin crawl and so she broke the silence. "What did you have to tell me?"

Petrichor clasped his hands behind his back. "I was naturally referring to our agreement to share information."

"Yes, obviously. So share, snooty-arse," Valour said, stumbling about as she tried to put on her breeches while standing and looking at him.

"You know, it cannot be overstated how some basic manners and even a modicum of decency would benefit you."

"Go impale yourself on a pike," she said, finally doing up the buttons.

He pointed a bony finger at her. "For that, you will go first."

She wanted to bite his head off but decided to speed things along instead. The sooner she got rid of him, the better. "I didn't get any leads as to where Brandquist is," she said, carrying on dressing. "It seems he communicates via passed-on missives these days, so Johan couldn't lead us to him."

"Are you telling me you found nought useful? Nothing at all?"

"I got a description, wart-head. Apparently Brandquist is wiry, short, and middle-aged. According to Johan he also has deep-set eyes, pockmarked cheeks, and the tattoo that we already knew about. Hm, what else?" She searched her mind, but it was oddly muddled. It wasn't like her to not recall a mark's full description. She startled at that, unavoidably worried. Moments passed before it finally came back to her. "Oh, right. Sideburns and short blond hair that's usually covered with a white wig and his big, black hood that hides much of the face."

Speaking of hair reminded her of the mess on her head. She undid her braid, semi-successfully used her fingers as a comb, and rebraided it.

Petrichor looked at her tresses as if they had insulted his cravat.

"I know, I know," Valour muttered. "You think I look like a peasant."

"No. Peasant women have the decency to pin their hair up. You look like a five-year-old."

"I do not!"

"True. I misspoke and should be more exact." He smoothed the hair at his temples. "You resemble a five-year-old peasant who has never heard of a looking-glass."

"Oh? Pray tell, oh wise authority on appearances, what should I look like then?" Valour said, trying to mimic his pompous tone.

Petrichor inclined his head to where Ingrid lounged on the mattress. "Akin to her usual appearance, but in more practical clothing and keeping some of your useful musculature."

"Wow. You didn't need to think about that at all. Have you been spending time planning that answer?"

"I have been spending time planning your funeral."

"Aw, how sweet," she said with as much sarcasm as she could. "Do I get pretty lilies?"

"Weeds. Ones speckled with mud. Like you are most of the time."

Ingrid stood, wrapping herself in the covers. "If you two are going to carry on quarrelling and not say anything of consequence, I shall go get dressed behind the shelves. Valour, feel free to peek."

Petrichor watched her leave with an expression that Valour

had seen on him many times before: mistrust.

"Good riddance," he murmured, rubbing his temples as if he had a headache. "I had serious misgivings about sharing our information on Brandquist with someone we do not know."

"Not to worry, snot-nose. I've gotten to know her inside out in the last few hours."

"These are serious matters. Do not be vile and do not be glib."

"You bring it out in me. So, easier said than done and all that. Anyway, she's over there now. Tell me what you found out."

Valour kept her features carefree. She wouldn't show that she too had considered how much she was sharing with Ingrid. It was fine, though. Ingrid was trustworthy and was spending all her time with them, so no gossip could leak out. Besides, Brandquist would be hunted down soon and then, thank the gods, all of this would be over.

CHAPTER 26
WHERE BRANDQUIST DRINKS

PETRICHOR GLANCED OVER at the shelves. Ingrid seemed busy with her ridiculous amounts of clothing and was an adequate distance away. That was good. Sadly, she hadn't taken this headache of his with her.

"My interrogation bore fruit," he said, again massaging his temples. "The students used to buy their tonics directly from a bell-ringer's apprentice who was Brandquist's right-hand woman."

Valour scrunched up her nose. "A bit like Johan was meant to be so high-ranking? I'm starting to think they all claim to be in Brandquist's inner circle without being able to talk to the shit-heel even if their life depended on it."

"I do not know precisely how close this woman was to Brandquist, but according to the students she would go drinking with him."

"All right. Where's this bell-ringer now?"

"Bell-ringer's *apprentice*. She moved abroad. It appears Brandquist switches his personnel around and when someone has been ousted, he provides them with either a better life elsewhere or makes them disappear in other ways."

"As in, kills them off?"

"Actually, 'vanish' was the word the students used. Although, one mentioned burials in countryside ditches," Petrichor answered. "Anyhow, this bell-ringer-in-training told them of some sort of tavern that she and Brandquist frequented. If she was telling them the truth, and they in turn were truthful with me, that would be a place to start."

"Agreed."

"Very big of you to say so."

172

"Don't start. Let's just go investigate this tavern," Valour said, looking around, no doubt for her boots and coat.

He made himself swallow a frustrated sigh. "Do allow me to finish for once."

She grimaced but stayed in place.

"There was something else. I took a shortcut through the tunnels to get here and caught two urchins scribbling a message on the wall for me."

"For you? Saying what?"

Petrichor recited the message, down to the 'hap' which must be a cut-off 'happen'.

Pensively, Valour tapped her fingers against the chair's back. "That was it? You should've chased after them."

"Yes. The overseers love it when cloaked assassins hunt children around Vinterstock."

Valour drummed her fingers louder, not helping his headache one whit. "So they knew you were there and would see it. You were followed, then?"

"No, you oaf. More likely they knew that assassins use those tunnels daily and that I was either bound to see it or have one of the other assassins report it to me."

"Whatever." Valour slapped her hands on her thighs and stood. "Unless you have any other news, we should head for this drinking hole of Brandquist's."

Ingrid returned, dressed in her robe à la whatsit in muted red and with her hair surprisingly neat and stylish. "We're going to a drinking establishment? This day keeps showering me with roses. Speaking of which, is it currently raining or snowing? Shall I need to cover my hair?"

Petrichor glared at her. "You are not coming along."

"She can if she wants to," Valour said.

He used all of his extensive discipline to keep calm. "You're only allowing that because you know it irks me."

"You bet your clenched-tight arse I am."

"Well, I feel exceedingly wanted," Ingrid muttered while checking her reflection in a pocket mirror.

"Indeed, you are being treated beastily by us rough and dull assassins," Petrichor said. "Perhaps you should go do something more entertaining?"

"Nice try, Master Assassin. Sadly for you, being told I am not allowed to do something makes me want to do it all the more. That was ever my way."

"I see," Petrichor huffed. "Well, if we must all go, let's at least make haste. We are taking a carriage."

Valour seemed about to argue but Ingrid snaked an arm around her waist and said, "In a carriage, we can kiss without being whistled or stared at."

"I hadn't thought of that," Valour said, beaming.

Petrichor ran a hand over his face. This would be a long and tedious journey.

CARRIAGE RIDE FINALLY over, Petrichor leapt out and read the street sign on the nearest house gable. The tavern was meant to be at the end of this road. He strode down it, hearing his ridiculous companions whispering behind him, trying to make each other giggle and to impress one another. He left them to it, gratified that he had been right about them ending up fornicating at the first opportunity.

He rubbed his eyes, which were as tired as he was. He was thinking that the headache and fatigue might be due to the barely averted fit when it hit him. Had he eaten today? He looked up at the afternoon sun and staggered. He hadn't attended the gloriam prayers! He had never missed them before. His heart thrashed. Careless. Undisciplined. Useless. What would Halcyon think of this failure? He forced himself to slow his breathing, warding off another fit. It would be all right. He'd make it all right. When he walked into the sanctum with Brandquist's heartsblood on his knife, it would make amends.

Right now, he had a more immediate problem. He smelled smoke. He nearly tripped on something: an old tavern sign, with one side charred, that lay in front of a scorched ruin. The smoke and odour of burned wood was overpowering and embers still glowed on scraps of blackened timber, half-melted bottle glass, and the only thing left standing—the singed stone hearth. This fire had only died out a short while ago.

"Shit," Valour said on a sigh. "Looks like word reached Brandquist about us coming here."

"Or at least Brandquist's subordinates. Unless it was merely a strangely timed coincidence," Ingrid said, seeming lost in thought. "It might also have been an accident. Plenty of these dilapidated old buildings have squatters. They light a pipe, spill some akvavit, fall asleep, and the place goes up like a Valborg bonfire."

"Could be," Valour said. "I doubt it, though."

In Petrichor's stomach, disappointment and shame writhed around one another like eels in cold water. Had those students warned Brandquist? Or this Johan fellow? He wanted to kick himself. Why on earth had he tarried? "Valour, if we had come straight here, without you delaying and wanting to take your amorous plaything with you, we might have caught the culprit."

Valour's eyes burned like the embers on the ground. "*Me* delaying? Oxen-shit. Amorous plaything? Godsdamned rude and disrespectful. Might've been on time? Only if the arsonist stood for hours next to the blaze, you pustule."

Vexingly, she was right. This large building would have taken hours to incinerate. She should've insulted him worse. Or shoved him into the red-hot embers. If she could control herself, so could he. He took a breath, and through a painfully tight jaw said, "Perhaps this setback made me speak somewhat out of turn. Nevertheless, had I been working alone, I would've come here faster. You cannot argue that."

"Speaking somewhat out of turn?" Valour lurched towards him. "You were speaking somewhat out of your arse."

"Tempers seem about to overflow," Ingrid said, stepping in between them. "And no wonder, since you've had disappointments and little to eat or drink today. Perhaps you ought to have some refreshments and a rest as you plan your next move?"

Valour and Petrichor shared a glance. He wasn't going to be the first to admit to needing a break.

Ingrid shook her head and then shaded her eyes with her hand while squinting down the road. "Do what you wish. I must check that the Kronovall's day manager is handling everything satisfactorily," she said before waving to a carriage for hire in the distance. "I can fetch some refreshments while at the hotel and meet you at the hideout in a little over an hour."

"Yes. Thank you," Valour said. "Could some of those refreshments be—"

"Fika?" Ingrid cut in. "Naturally there will be some sweet treats for the sweet treat."

"That sentence was unequivocally the worst thing my ears have ever been subjected to," Petrichor muttered.

Valour ignored him, as usual. "Great." She gave Ingrid a kiss. "Oh, and get yourself some of your rose milk. So I can try it."

"Roses are plants. Rather hard to milk," Petrichor said, putting his spectacles on to protect his eyes from the worst of the smoke.

"Was that meant to be funny?" Valour asked. "Because it wasn't. Ingrid has this drink of hot milk with rose petals and cream that sounds interesting."

"Interesting? Try sickly sweet. Or no, try *vile*."

"You two do know I'm still here and can hear you, yes?" Ingrid said, mostly focused on the carriage driver who had signalled that she'd seen Ingrid and was coming to a halt.

"Yes," Valour said. "Pay him no heed."

"Water off a swan's back, darling. I shall see you back at that basement, then." She gave the coachman, or rather coachwoman, the address for the hotel before gathering up the skirts of her dress and stepping inside.

As the carriage rattled through the slush, Valour waved. Like some lovesick buffoon.

Then… it was only the two of them.

Valour huffed out a long breath. "Right, let's start the fun walk back to the hideout."

Petrichor considered suggesting a carriage but knew that they should avoid people, including coachmen, and that they both needed to walk to clear out the frustration. He hated that he knew her so well.

He adjusted his coat, worried the smoke was infusing it, and started walking with a muttered, "No dawdling."

"You know I don't dawdle."

That was true so he didn't reply. They marched on, side by side, not speaking, keeping to the shadows or the cloaking crowds as they had been raised to.

CHAPTER 27

COMMOTION

PETRICHOR HAD RELIT the basement's fireplace and sat by it reading one of Ingrid's censored books. Valour—again only in stockings, breeches, stays, and her ridiculously cumbersome knife belt—was doing calisthenics in a corner. They were ignoring each other like it was an art form they had long ago mastered. The logical thing to do would have been to discuss how to proceed now that Brandquist seemed to know their movements. Petrichor couldn't bear it, though. Couldn't make himself speak to Valour like the professionals, and adults, they were.

He put the book down, realising he cared not one whit if the killer was the courtesan or the gardener. (Although, he was quite sure it was the latter since his alibi was having intercourse with several wood nymphs during the entire six hours the murder might've taken place. No one had that sort of stamina, certainly not after pulling weeds all day.) Valour was doing push-ups and he scrutinised her. Why did she vex him so? Was it her personality? How she had treated him? Or just that even the merest sight of her yanked away the veil between childhood and adulthood? He had worked hard for that veil.

A sound from outside made them both pivot to the door, hands going to knives, bodies into the proper fighting stance, like two identical clockwork toys. No one was trying to get in, though. In fact, Petrichor diagnosed the ruckus as coming from the street outside the house. In quiet tones, he said as much to Valour.

She nodded. "I'll go investigate."

"You will do nothing of the sort. You would only draw attention to us. Besides, you're in your stays and perspiring. I shall go."

"I am not sweating," Valour snapped back, indeed looking quite dry. "But fine. If you don't mind going, I'll stay. Shout if you need me."

Her confidence in him surprised him beyond measure, but he made sure not to show it. Petrichor threw his coat on, not having time for gloves and such, and exited through the door leading to the garden. He then took a roundabout route to the street to further mask where he came from. The commotion carried on, banging, neighing of horses, and human shouts, all so much clearer when he was outside. A fight? Here? This street was meant to be empty. Petrichor found a spot under a snow-laden tree where he was in deep shadow but had a good view.

In the middle of the slushy street, a couple of houses away from Ingrid's hideout, two big men fought outside a carriage. Judging by his outfit, one of the men was a carriage driver. He was the one shouting, currently about not getting his full payment. The other combatant was quiet, collected, only fighting as much as he had to in order to avoid the coachman's sloppily thrown punches. The calm man had a pockmarked, craggy face and wore a continental riding hat, fine boots, and a silk coat in powder blue with yellow lapels. Petrichor sniffed. That outfit was thoroughly impractical in this weather and the colours were far too foppish.

The argument carried on, the coachman bellowing about not having wanted to drive the long way out to this abandoned area in the first place, finishing with, "I'll never get any passengers for the drive back, will I?"

In a heavy accent, the man in the silk coat replied that he didn't see how that was his problem and so why should he pay extra?

In clear shock, the driver lowered his fists. "Huh? I told you when I picked you up that it would cost you extra if we went out here, you daft foreigner!"

"And I assumed you meant a small fee on top of the normal one, yes? I will not pay this extraordinary cost you ask for. This is not even the street I wished to travel to. So: no, I shall not overpay."

Petrichor saw the blue-coated man's point of view. Vinterstock's population was known to charge any foreigners double if they could, aware that travellers from the continent often came here with heavy purses. Nevertheless, seeing as this was a common squabble over owed riksdaler and not of interest to him, Petrichor made to head back inside. The horses neighed in his direction. He might've avoided human eyes, but not equine ones.

The coachman followed his horses' gaze. "Oi, you."

Petrichor took a step deeper into the shadow of the tree, then masked his voice by making it smokier. "What?"

"You a Vinterstockian?"

The driver had squinted blearily and slurred his words. Was he a 'ness drinker? No, none of the signs were there so far. Probably just one of Vinterstock's many drunkards.

"I am."

"Then you know that a fee's got to be added for journeys to a place like, uh, this place. Right, chum?"

"I am not getting involved in your dispute. I saw, heard, and know nothing." Petrichor made again to leave.

"Like shit you don't," the drunken driver bellowed. "I'm owed this coin. It's mine, and you're my bloody witness. You've got to stand with your fellow countrymen."

"I, in fact, do not. Good day to you both."

The driver bounded over to Petrichor, aiming his sloppy fists at him this time.

Bored and disgusted, Petrichor ducked the first two blows, making sure his face was as hidden or turned away as possible. Not that he thought someone this inebriated would be able to identify him at a later date, but best not to take chances. It soon became clear that the coachman wasn't going to tire himself out and leave Petrichor alone—he simply kept swinging his big hairy fists and cursing.

Thus, in one rapid movement, Petrichor measured a hard jab at the man's jaw. As expected, it knocked the drunkard out. Aware that he could not leave the driver here in case someone came looking for him, Petrichor caught the man as he fell. Trying to keep the physical contact at a minimum, especially since the coachman stunk of old sweat and ale, Petrichor carried him bridal style until he could fold the dead-weight man into his carriage. Then, not turning as he spoke, Petrichor asked the foreigner if he wanted a carriage ride back to the driver's stables and that if he did, he should get in now.

"Thank you, but no. That is… How do you say? In the wrong direction for me."

Grinding his teeth in disappointment, Petrichor didn't reply. He merely slapped the lead horse on the rump and ordered it to return home. The carriage rattled off, the horses all too happy to leave the commotion and the cold to go back to their cosy stables.

"Thank you for your aid," the foreign man said. "You carried him easily considering he was bigger than you. And what an effective blow to the face. Most impressive. And unusual."

There was a question in the man's tone. Petrichor ignored it, furious at himself for not faking being a worse fighter. Halcyon would be disappointed. The whole order would be disappointed. He wished he could hope that they would never find out, but such luck only existed in fairy stories. Petrichor moved back into the tree's shadow, making it look like he was merely returning to the place where he'd been walking before the interruption. He had to get rid of this man without making himself stand out in the man's mind. In short, he'd have to be generically polite. "Did I hear you say this was not the street you wanted? Can I give you directions to your actual destination?"

"Thank you. Most gallant," the foreigner said, avoiding eye contact. "I gave the driver the mistaken, no, the *wrong* address. I am certain I can find my own way, though."

Petrichor regarded him. This man, with his averted gaze and uneasy twitching of scarred hands, was hiding something. Petrichor's mind raced through the possible reasons and landed on an obvious one: there was a street with a similar name to this one that led to a brothel, one that catered to more perverse tastes. Or so Valour had once told him. Petrichor had avoided that entire street ever since.

"I see," Petrichor finally said. "Well, follow the road from whence you came. Soon, you will arrive at bigger streets where you can either catch another carriage in the right direction or walk into the city centre."

With that, Petrichor left, heading down the street in the opposite direction of the hideout. Only when he had seen, in the reflection of a window, that the blue-coated man had left did he turn back.

CHAPTER 28

SUGAR SHARDS

PETRICHOR RETURNED INSIDE and explained that a drunk coachman and a lost foreigner had been in a fistfight over a carriage ride fee and had both now left.

"Just another day in merry Vinterstock," Valour mumbled in reply.

They settled back into their previous activities: Valour doing her calisthenics and him trying to read, despite his treacherous brain wanting to think about Halcyon—as well as that bizarre woman he bedded. Halcyon was a man of great mind, heart, and soul. He could do so much better. The question of why that woman had claimed to know the sanctum came back to him, as well as the possibility that she knew his name. Had Halcyon mentioned him to her? If so, what had he said? Petrichor slumped, his perfect posture for once failing him. He had few good qualities, and they weren't things that Halcyon would appreciate in a person. Cursing himself, he went back to the book. The gardener was definitely the killer.

A high, clear voice called from the door, "It's only me. I'm coming in, pray do not assassinate me."

Valour all but ran over to help Ingrid with what she carried: a large, embroidered valise and a pewter mug of something... floral? Valour placed the valise on the small table for her and soon Ingrid was unpacking its contents.

"I brought some sandwiches, honey on barley and wheat bread," she said, holding up packets wrapped in wax paper. "I couldn't carry any coffee or tea, but I did get your favourite cardamom sweet rolls, Valour. The chefs were about to place sugar shards on them to make them more extravagant for the hotel guests but I told them regular ones would do for us."

"Where's the actual food?" Petrichor asked.

"Ah." Ingrid winced. "My apologies. Luncheon was nigh sold out so I'm afraid the only savoury food is some salted beef. I hoped that would suffice. As I said before, food is not my forte."

Petrichor stood back in disgust. "It is late afternoon. I haven't eaten all day. I require long-lasting nutrition, not merely sugar that will rot my brain, teeth, and innards."

Ingrid fastened him with a look. "As I said, I apologise. Since I was to hurry back here, I was working with limited time and choices."

"Just scrape the honey off the bread and put the meat on that," Valour said, waving his grievance away as if it was a mere trifle.

"And have the beef taste honeyed? I think not."

"Oh, stop complaining. You loved sweet rolls when we were kids, have one of them. I mean, look at these beauties." Valour stabbed a finger into a roll. The dough quickly bounced back up, releasing scents of sugar and cardamom. "Tor's goats, my mouth is already watering."

Petrichor glanced at the honeyed bread while his stomach stung with hunger. Perhaps he must make do? When exactly had he last eaten? He couldn't remember. That was odd.

Ingrid laughed. "Tor's goats?"

"Mm. The best food since they're re-edible. Tor's two goats can be eaten at night and next morning brought back to life again so they can pull his chariot and be dinner later on."

Petrichor huffed out, "Superstition and fairytales." But no one listened.

Ingrid picked up her drink. How typical that she could not choose a normal hot beverage like everyone else. "The goats are from mythology, then, not folklore? I know little about Nordic myth creatures, other than they all seem quite lethal."

"It's a shame you were raised here but never told of them." Valour shook her head sadly. "Not all of them kill. Some just play mischief," she said, picking up the very sandwich Petrichor had been eyeing. "But most are dangerous. Especially if you seek them out and then don't play by their rules. They don't want obedience or worship, though, only to have their basic needs met and to be left alone." She unwrapped the sandwich. "Oh, and your death if the fancy strikes them. Very straightforward."

"I see. Most fascinating. Do they ever want anything… sexual?"

He couldn't hear himself think for long enough to make a decision. Was there no way to block out their prattle?

"Both the female Skogsrået and the male Näcken are naked and use different techniques to seduce people," Valour replied around a mouthful of sandwich. "I'm not sure they lie with them, though. They only use humans' arousal to lure them to their death. I think that's meant to teach us not to be, you know, slutty."

Ingrid gave that annoying, glass-tinkling giggle of hers. "Has that ever worked?"

"It certainly never did on me," Valour said with a grin and a wink.

That was the final straw. Petrichor put his boots on. "As stimulating as it is to stand here listening to you two flirt over sugary abominations, I shall go find some actual food."

"Oh, we were ignoring you," Ingrid said. "My apologies."

"Don't apologise to him. He doesn't deserve it." Valour frowned at him. "Wandering alone with Brandquist's minions and gods knows what out there? You really think that's a good idea, snooty-arse?"

"Might you stop questioning me for one whole minute? I need food."

"And you call me a food-obsessed pig?" she snapped. "Stop being ungrateful. Ingrid is feeding you for free, even though you treat her like she's dirt. You don't deserve any bloody food! You never have."

Something snapped. He pushed past the table to shove Valour right into next year. The table wobbled and, in keeping with how this day was going, the mug of rose milk was spilled over the sandwiches and snacks.

"That's it," Valour growled at him. "Get your rude arse out of here. I don't give a troll-turd if you get caught by Brandquist, just don't lead anyone back here."

"I'm not you. As a true assassin, I can remain unseen." He put Halcyon's outercoat on over his own, pulling the deep hood so far down that he had to move his head quite far to see.

Ingrid called something about being careful but he paid her no heed.

He headed for a coffee-house not too far from the sanctum. It would be worth the walk since, at this point of the day, Halcyon was likely to be there to pick up his rye roll with venison. The trek there dragged, though, since he drew back at every sudden sound or lingering gaze. He had the feeling he was being followed but saw no one suspicious. He had not been this unnerved when he went to the sanctum's archive. Valour's worry must've gotten to him. Or perhaps it was his childhood ghosts coming back that gnawed at him? It was a dark and damp day, not so unlike that cell. He put his hand to his nearest knife and reminded himself who he was: Pre-eminent Brother Petrichor, Tenth Assassin of Axsten. He might struggle to remember things today, for some reason, but he knew that much. As long as he had the order, he was someone. Although… A thought stopped him by one of the Opera House's stained pillars. Without their aid, without attending the prayers, who was he?

He filed that away for another time and hurried to the coffee-house. He studied its smudged windows, trying to spot Halcyon. No luck. Not risking going inside, he tugged his hood deep over his face and sat against a low brick wall, trying to look like the other beggars in oversized coats.

The half light dimmed to dusk with torturous slowness. Petrichor counted every minute he was out here in the open until, finally, Halcyon appeared. Mercifully without his lover. Halcyon walked with confidence but still managed to merge with the crowd, a wide tricorne hat pulled low over his face. He had once told Petrichor he'd needed to teach himself to blend in and deflect gazes. Someone with foreign features stood out too much for an assassin otherwise.

Petrichor got up. He knew better than to grab or tap the shoulder of a passing assassin, so instead he whispered Halcyon's name.

The other man stopped, either recognising the coat or the voice as he quietly said, "Petrichor. I'm glad to see you hale and whole."

"And I you. New hat?"

"A gift from… someone," Halcyon said, suddenly ill at ease.

Did he know that Petrichor could guess who he meant? Had the woman told Halcyon of their encounter? No doubt. That would explain why Halcyon looked uneasy. His unpermitted trysts in the sanctum were revealed.

"Never mind that." The worry painted on Halcyon's face intensified. "You missed gloriam. I know you are being stalked. Nevertheless, you *must* come by the sanctum tonight. I can set up some sort of variation of gloriam after dinner but before vesper."

"I'll try," Petrichor said, unsure if he would.

He was surprised at his own reluctance to go back there. It wasn't just that when he had turned to the order for help, it had spurned him. It was seeing himself away from the sanctum and how life continued just fine outside of its strict framework. It was seeing that Valour wasn't... what? There was very little he was certain of anymore.

Taking Petrichor by the elbow, Halcyon moved them away from a group of passing sailors. "Are you making progress with finding Brandquist?"

"Yes, some." He wouldn't admit how slowly it was going. Especially not to Halcyon.

"Good." Halcyon let go of his arm. "Was he the reason you sought me out?"

Petrichor shifted his weight. He couldn't say that talking to Halcyon would make him feel better. That it already had. He felt the phantom of that warm hand on his elbow, but it was soon overwritten by a stab of headache. There was something he was going to ask Halcyon for. What was it? How could he have forgotten?

"I... sought you out to show that I was all right. Despite not attending gloriam. Not that I thought you worried about me, I merely wanted you to know that I was still working on the task and fulfilling my duties."

"I am heartened to hear it. And Valour?"

"She is still working on it too. In her own haphazard, clumsy way."

Something that might have been a smile tugged at the corners of Halcyon's mouth. "I meant if she was all right."

"Pardon? Oh. Right. She's probably got bruises after fighting Brandquist's henchmen, much like myself. Otherwise, she's fine. As Valour always is."

"Good to hear."

Halcyon's face was so familiar, yet ever changing. Today, he wore rouge, but despite it managed not to appear as foppish as most modern men did. A true beau ideal. Petrichor wanted to tell Halcyon that while Valour was all right, *he* wasn't. About the fits and the haunting memories and the headaches and recent lapses of memory. That would be weakness, though.

Petrichor hunted for other things to say. "Are… you well?"

"Yes. Worked off my feet, but well."

"Ah. Good."

"Indeed."

Why was it like this between them? Did Halcyon dislike him, or was it simply the edict of being cold and aloof that the order drilled into them? No, he must stop questioning the order in this shameful way. It must be personal. After all, Halcyon easily chatted and laughed with Valour. And they had plenty of companiable touching.

What he meant to say came to Petrichor in a rush. "I also sought you out for a favour." He pointed to the coffee-house. "When you go in, could you please purchase something for me?"

Halcyon didn't look excited. "Sure. I'm getting my regular. I am afraid I do not know quite what you like. Healthy food, right?"

"I like lean meats and wholegrain bread just as you do." Would Halcyon find it strange that Petrichor knew what food he preferred? "Also, I should like mushrooms and vegetables. If there are any."

"Consider it done. Wait here."

Something suspiciously similar to guilt grew, like mould, in him. "Can you also get cakes or buns or something of that ilk? There was an accident with spilled milk and as always, Valour wants her accursed fika."

Halcyon laughed. "Sensible woman."

"Only compared to a donkey."

Halcyon's expression went utterly serious. "Petrichor. When you next see her, take a closer look." He gave no time for replies. "I shall be right back."

Strangely bereft, Petrichor watched him enter the coffee-house. After what seemed an age, Halcyon came back out with a substantial paper bag. "Here we are. Venison rolls with pickled onions and cabbage for you and me. A whole rulltårta for Valour. Oh, and I threw in a bottle of cider for you both, too."

"Thank you," Petrichor said. "I am sorry to have taken up so much of your time. Was there a long queue in there?"

"Hm? Ah, no. I took a little longer because I was lost in thought, pondering your mission. Has... anything stood out as strange to you?"

"Strange?"

"Different than the other jobs we are given."

"Yes, of course. The target is Brandquist. That is always going to make it different from hunting a regular person."

"Naturally. Pray, pardon me. I know my statement made little sense to you." Halcyon rubbed his forehead, seeming suddenly tired and frustrated. "There are so many things happening in this city. So many orders given. So many secrets kept."

Petrichor dithered. What should one reply to that? "Are you, um, referring to anything in particular?"

"Nothing," Halcyon said, with the air of a man who had woken up from a reverie. "Pay me no heed. I may be working overmuch and not sleeping enough." He fished his own roll out and then handed the bag over to Petrichor.

Petrichor took it, asking, "How much was that?"

"My treat."

"I cannot let you do that."

"Yes, you can. Really, it's the least I can do for you and Valour."

There was something in Halcyon's voice, but for the life of him Petrichor couldn't determine what that emotion was. "You gave me your coat."

"I did. No great prize I fear, but the hood does cover your face well. Oh, speaking of clothes," Halcyon said. "I noted Valour didn't have a deuced scarf when I saw you last, and I cannot have my assassins freezing to death. Here, take this to her, would you?"

He took off his grey, woollen scarf and held it out.

Petrichor slumped. The gift of the coat was less unique now, less personal. Halcyon was merely looking after the order's two youngest members. And possibly feeling guilty for not helping them.

"I shall," Petrichor said, snatching the scarf. "Although, she has someone to buy her expensive clothes these days. She is currently swanning around in some leather battle coat."

Halcyon didn't seem bothered. "I see. Then I am glad I gave the coat to you."

"So am I."

Silence stretched out, increasing the distance between them.

"I wish the best for you, Petrichor. You know that, right? I mean, I know we do not always understand each other, but you are oft in my thoughts."

A rush of confusing warmth shot through him. "And you in mine," he mumbled.

Halcyon seemed to hesitate. "I... heard a rumour this morning. That Brandquist has taken over an old house opposite the Northgate Synagogue. Number eight Bellman Street. Don't tell anyone that I told you."

Who had told Halcyon that? Some informant? That awful lover of his? "Why not?"

The leader of the Order of Axsten conspiratorially dipped his head and smiled a little. "I am not meant to help you, remember?"

"Of course." Petrichor almost smiled back. The evening became less gloomy. "Thank you."

"Thank me by coming to the makeshift gloriam prayer tonight. Your attendance is vital. I must see that you are both all right."

A strange compunction came over Petrichor, a need to touch Halcyon, to make a connection with this paragon. Disconcerted, he merely said "Thank you" again and slunk into the shadows, with the scarf in one hand and the food bag in the other.

There was a cutting sensation in his chest. He remembered the sugar shards Ingrid had talked about. That was the feeling in his heart: sharp, lethal sweetness.

He stopped in an alley and put Halcyon's scarf on, right on top of his own more fashionable one. Two scarves. Two outercoats (and the justacorps underneath as well). He must have looked ridiculous and weak in how affected he was by the cold. For once, he didn't care.

He tucked the hand that was not carrying the bag into a coat pocket for warmth and felt something. The ripped letter. He took it out and, before he could stop himself, read it. He immediately wished he had burned this one unread as well.

CHAPTER 29
CONTROL, SEX, AND TRUST

VALOUR WASN'T SURE how long Petrichor had been gone—she had dropped her pocket watch into the trough of a pig during a stupid bet last month. Although it was darkening outside, considering that it was winter, it probably wasn't as late as it looked. Either way, the firelight suited Ingrid. She and Ingrid had talked the whole time Petrichor was out. Or Ingrid had. Valour had listened and scavenged for the few treats that Petrichor hadn't drenched. Now she watched Ingrid pull a cardamom roll apart with her fingers and eat it in dainty bites. Who had the patience to not speak until they had chewed and swallowed completely?

Probably noting Valour's growing exasperation, Ingrid quickly swallowed her last bite. "There. All done. Where were we?"

"You were telling me about that tavern Brandquist had commandeered and then torched. What did you say its name was?"

"The Hyllemor's Bosom," she said, a dreamy look in her eyes. "It was the sort of place I would sneak into when my frequent cravings for something illicit and dark got too strong. In disguise, of course, so no one could recognise me."

Hyllemor. If Valour had known Ingrid better, she might've told Ingrid how her mother would stand with her by the elderflower bushes and tell her about the mythical lady who lived in them. No. None of that. Back to the topic of Brandquist's lairs.

Valour massaged her bruised hands, cracking the knuckles. "The place was bad enough for you to need to disguise yourself?"

"Or good enough, depending on your point of view. It was deliciously wicked but had less unpleasant brawling than most other such establishments. It was scandalous due to gambling, a little 'ness use, and a lot of alcohol. Also, copious amounts of sex."

"Copious? So, more than some sneaky fondles under skirts while seated at tables?"

"Much more, darling. Nothing was 'sneaky'. There was even a stage for... special performances."

"Oh."

"Exactly." Ingrid's eyes glittered mischievously in the firelight. She should drop this line of questioning and instead ask about when Brandquist took the place over. "What, um, type of sex acts was it?"

"Valour, I do not think you want to know. It'll wreck what purity you still have."

"Pure? Me? I'm a third-generation assassin, raised with blood on my hands and death in my wake. I've fucked all sorts of women, some of them downright evil."

"And for all of that, you are purer than I."

Valour tried not to laugh. "How do you figure?"

"Your heart is pure. You want nothing more than to be a good person with clean hands and a clean conscience."

"Clean? Yes, of blood and cruelty. Sex is another matter. Filthy, forbidden sex acts—as long as everyone consents, and no one gets scarred for life—can make you feel alive." Valour had given this speech to many women who had been ashamed of asking for what they wanted. "It can be a safe release of your darker urges, so that they aren't freed in ways that can hurt you or others."

"You can be very understanding and receptive." Ingrid looked deeply sad for a moment, then her usual carefree mask was back. "The greve wasn't quite as open-minded. He had The Hyllemor's Bosom shut down, claiming ritual killings took place there."

"And did they?"

Ingrid waved that away. "Only of goats. Occasionally the owner would pause the revelries to sacrifice to the gods, usually to Freja for sex and gold. Some enjoyed that, I found it a deuced turn-off. Still, the greve overreacted and ended the fun."

"Sounds like you think there's truth in the rumours. The ones about him becoming dull and wilted with age?"

"He certainly has become *something*." Ingrid paused. "Have you ever met him?"

"Yes," Valour said without thinking. "No. Wait. I... can't remember. That's strange. He must be boring since he doesn't leave much of a memory."

It took a while before Ingrid replied. She was staring into the middle distance, a crease between her eyebrows. "I don't wish to talk about him. Let's return to The Hyllemor's Bosom. I was telling you about when the owner paused the stage shows to perform sacrifices. Such a shame. It rather ruined all that lovely wetness one had accrued."

Valour did a double take. "Did you just say what I think you did?"

"What?" Ingrid said, leaning in closer. "Does me speaking of my wetness bother you?"

"Only because it makes me want less chat and more action."

"Is that a problem?" Ingrid purred. "We are both consenting adults, Petrichor isn't here, and we know from experience that we..."

"Fuck like champions together?"

Ingrid's smile was thoroughly wild. No. It was *feral*. "Quite so."

A thrill rushed through Valour, finally settling into a persistent tug from her abdomen down to her sex.

She should resist temptation. Be in control. Contemplate how involved she wanted to get with this woman. Most of all, she should be professional and ask more questions about the beer-house.

To Hel's bloody realm with that.

She put her hand on the back of Ingrid's neck, feeling small hairs and soft skin under her palm, then kissed her open-mouthed. After a while, Ingrid halted the kiss to instead unbutton the top four buttons of Valour's shirt and pull it open. She put her mouth where Valour's shoulder met her neck and first kissed and then gently bit the muscle there. The teeth dug in and Valour moaned at the delicious pain.

Ingrid licked at where she'd bitten. "Sorry. You taste so maddeningly good."

"Don't apologise." Valour pulled her shirt more open. "Do it again."

The door slammed. "Whatever you are talking about, do please refrain from doing it again," Petrichor muttered as he marched in.

Petrichor's arrival was worse than a pail of ice water over the head. Valour wanted to scream. Instead, she buttoned her shirt back up. "Ah, stone-face. Got that stick out of your arse yet?"

It was intensely gratifying that Ingrid chuckled. No one had ever laughed at that one before.

"Comments like that make me regret bringing you your blasted fika," he said, rummaging around in a paper bag to bring out a tube-shaped thing wrapped in waxed paper. Valour could smell cake, cream, and jam. Rulltårta!

They sat down and ate. Well, Petrichor and Valour ate while Ingrid lounged on the mattress, telling them of the latest scientific discoveries she had learned from guests at the hotels. Throughout, Petrichor had a look she'd seen on his over-angled face before. She wondered now if it didn't mean that he was considering whether or not to be forthcoming?

When Petrichor had eaten his venison roll, he—with a grudging air—said, "Valour. In the name of sharing information, I have heard from… a source about another possible Brandquist lair. However, Brandquist may guess that we're going there next and perhaps set fire to *us* this time. I'm happy to go alone."

Valour swallowed a mouthful of cider, sharp apple booziness tingling on her tongue. "Why the troll-shit would you go on your own?"

"I think he was trying to make the point that he doesn't want *me* there," Ingrid said, standing up. "I should be getting back to the hotel anyway. The day manager told me of a leak on the second floor. I must see how the repairs are coming along."

Valour leaned back in her chair, trying to ooze casualness. "You, um, you'll come back soon, though?"

"Would you like me to?"

"I promised your father I'd keep an eye on you and try to convince you to mend your ways."

Ingrid put her hands on her hips. "Do *you* want me to come back?"

"I don't want to stop looking at your stunning face, so yes, I want you to come back."

The way Ingrid cocked her head and smiled made her wonder if Ingrid thought it was more than just that. Gods, it couldn't be allowed to be more than that.

"Then we shall meet up here later," Ingrid said.

As she watched her leave, Valour's bite mark throbbed. She hurried to distract herself.

"So," she said to Petrichor, "any chance you'll tell me who your source is?"

"None."

She ran a hand over her face. "Fine. Where is it?"

"Northgate."

"All right. I suppose I'll have to trust you."

It was one thing to say it, a wholly different one to do it.

CHAPTER 30
EIGHT BELLMAN STREET

VALOUR LEANED AGAINST the walls of the recently built Northgate Synagogue, a good vantage point due to it being right opposite eight Bellman Street. Petrichor stood beside her, both of them shrouded in the murk of only moonlight since the street lamp's guttering glow didn't reach this part of the pavement.

Through the falling snow and the darkness of an early evening in Swedish winter, Valour peered across the wide road at the lair. At least the street lamp over there illuminated number eight, which stood at the end of a row of neat houses in powder-pale, tasteful yellows and blues. The Brandquist lair, however, was dilapidated and a pasty, brownish green. The dead ivy covering the building like a rash didn't help. Brandquist sure could pick his hangouts. Only one door and few windows—that at least made it easy to keep an eye on exits. Valour tried to see inside, but the windowpane was covered in hoarfrost and cracks. She couldn't see any movement or hear any noises. Obviously, that would be the case if this was a trap, though. At least it hadn't been burned down.

Petrichor was keeping quiet, but not still. The normally statuelike man was ever-moving, stomping snow off his boots and flexing his fingers in his leather gloves. Valour was about to tell him to give it a rest but froze when she saw that he was breathing fast and trembling. He got out his smoke-coloured spectacles and put them on despite the darkness.

"Care to explain why you are staring at me like you've never seen a man before?" he said in the fakest casual tone she'd ever heard.

"What's wrong with you?"

"What's wrong with me? I am staring at this horrid building. In this vexing cold. With you, being your vile—and currently bizarrely sweet-smelling—self."

"Sweet-smelling?" Valour sniffed herself. Lemon, vanilla, and cinnamon. "Ingrid's perfume. Anyway, stop changing the subject and tell me what's actually wrong?"

He didn't answer for a while, only stood staring at either the house or the steam of his breath meeting the falling snow.

He cleared his throat. "The letter."

Valour followed his gaze. "What letter? I can't see any letters."

"For all the dead in Valhalla, *try* to use your brain. I obviously mean the one you stole from me and then ripped."

"Let me correct you there. You mean the one that fell out of your pocket and that we both ripped as we fought over it."

"I mean the one I'm going to insert into your nostril as you sleep tonight, *Venerated Sister Valour,*" he said with the snide tone he always used for her official title.

"Try it and we'll see how fast I end you. Back to the letter. What was in it?"

He spun towards her. "You mean you didn't read it?"

Valour quirked an eyebrow at him, trying to look as disdainful as he usually did. "Obviously I didn't bloody read it. Unlike you, I don't trample all over people's privacy."

He brushed snow off himself, putting way too much effort into it, and murmured, "I see. Never mind, then."

"What? No! You have to tell me now."

"I do not, in fact, have to tell you anything."

Valour thought hard. Petrichor had never been vulnerable in front of her. There was no way she was going to let this golden moment slip between her fingers.

"You know that spring-loaded knife of mine you've been fancying?" she said tentatively.

"The one with the fleur-de-lis on the handle?" He pursed his lips. "A weapon far too elegant for a brute like you."

Valour was about to say that it was a weapon far too slight and intricate for his oversized man-hands but stopped herself. "Tell me what was in the letter and I'll give you the blade."

He sniffed. "I don't desire the cursed thing *that* much."

"We're forced to spend a lot of time together. Shit, we might even die together. Are you going to tell me what's weighing on you like ten days' worth of snow on a brittle roof?" He was vulnerable for once, *human* even, and she wasn't going to let him wriggle out. "Or do you want me to start guessing?"

He only huffed.

"Right then," Valour said. "Guessing it is. Is it that stick up your arse? Has it left you for another man?"

He squeezed his eyes tight but said nothing.

"No? Perhaps it left you for a woman, then?" Valour asked.

Now his whole face was pinched tight. She hoped he was counting to ten.

Valour clicked her fingers as if she had an idea. "Have you found that coffee gives you hives on your private parts and you must quit the habit?"

"For the love of all things, stop," he said through gritted teeth. "I'll tell you. The letter was a reminder."

"A reminder? Like those they send out to tell people to have their chimney swept?"

"No, you ape. A second missive communicating that my application to apprentice for Master Sven Fahlcrantz has been accepted. I burned the first one."

"Who in the name of troll-shit is Master Sven Fahlcrantz?"

Petrichor lowered his hood to smooth his mud-coloured hair. Unnecessarily, as it was perfectly set and bound as ever. "Showing your ignorance once more. He is the city's foremost bookbinder, famous all over the world for his refined style and durable products."

"A bookbinder?" Valour spluttered. "You mean someone who sits at a dusty desk by candlelight, sewing pages together and then making pretty covers until their eyesight goes?"

"There is much more to it than that," he snapped. "It is an art and a science. Our population's education, and the preservation of history itself, relies on us having books that are easy to read and long-lasting."

Valour didn't hide her thrill at getting this wonderful ammunition. "But you're going to make them so pretty too, aren't you?" she said in a babyish voice. "With fancy swirls and colourful patterns?"

"Stop it."

Valour froze. She had expected him to say something along those lines, albeit more eloquently and with the usual volley of insults back. What she hadn't expected was that he'd sound so fragile. So exposed. He still wouldn't look at her and that muscle bounced in his jaw again, like a moth caught under the skin. He hadn't put his hood up, and snow gathered on his hair without him doing anything about it.

She hesitated. "Why should I stop it? You wouldn't if the roles were reversed."

"True," he said. "I'm imploring you to be the better person here. And trust me, nought has ever hurt me more, including when you drove an ice pick through my foot."

"Hey, if you try to kill my mark just to spoil my career, you get a bloody ice pick through the foot. Only fair."

He scoffed but said nothing.

Valour fidgeted and blinked snowflakes out of her eyes. "So, um, you actually want to leave the order?"

"Did you believe you were the only one with reasons to quit? How self-centred of you."

"But you love the order and its daft rituals and schedules!"

"You can love it and still need to leave."

"I suppose so. Books, though? I mean, Hel's realm, I'd get it if you wanted to go become a rifle maker or something like that. But books?"

"I rent rooms in the university. You often see me reading or carrying a book with me. Why is the idea of me being a bookbinder so strange?"

Valour stomped her feet to warm up and to give herself time to think. "I suppose because you never seem happier than when standing over a methodically executed body, bragging about your clever assassinations, and basking in the other members' praise. Seeing you sitting in a quiet room binding books, well, it feels like the opposite of that."

Petrichor tilted his head back to look up, snow peppering his face and the smoked glass of his spectacles. "It never occurred to you that I was merely taking pride in my work?"

"Bäckahäst-shit."

"Fine. Perhaps it was an act. To fit in, to be accepted."

His voice was so quiet she'd barely heard it, but it dropped even lower for the next words. Still, she heard them, and they smacked her right in the chest.

"Maybe we're both trapped, Valour. And the only way to survive is to pretend that you relish your cage."

She was about to reply when there was a drawn-out scream from an open window in a house somewhere behind them.

PETRICHOR HAD BEEN so focused on their conversation and the lair that he hadn't mapped their surroundings thoroughly enough.

He turned at the sound of the scream, pulled his spectacles off, and squinted through the thickly falling snow at the house from whence the sound had come. A window was open despite the freezing temperatures, and out through it dangled two arms with squeezed-closed fists. Petrichor followed the limbs and saw they belonged to a man who was still giving short shouts, leading to pleasured moans. Petrichor could only see the vague outline of another person behind the man, clearly doing things to him. Or were there two people touching the climaxing man?

Petrichor, wearied by his fellow humans, muttered, "Intercourse should not be performed in front of non-consenting audiences."

Valour didn't seem to hear him over her laughing. "That's the people of Vinterstock for you. They know how to keep warm by getting their hearts pounding and—"

"I will not countenance you making lewd wordplay regarding 'pounding', Valour."

"I don't need to. Clearly your imagination did it for me."

He gave her no reply. Would he have to go back to the conversation about his futile dream now? As he slowly recovered from the shock of the scream, a worse sound rang out: the eardrum-shattering sound of a nearby shot. Something whooshed past him and he grabbed Valour and pulled her fully behind the tallest snow mound.

"Shit. That came from the house we were supposed to be bloody watching," she snarled.

CHAPTER 31

THE BOOKKEEPER'S LEAD

HUNCHED BEHIND THE pile of snow, Valour used every curse word she could think of. How could they have allowed themselves to be distracted like that?

Petrichor was next to her, only now releasing the grip on her arm. He was squinting at one of the building's cracked windows. "It emanated from there. The shot must've come from a pistol. Had it been a rifle with proper range, I believe that would've hit us."

"They know we're here, then."

"As expected."

She brushed snow off herself. "Thanks. Um, for getting me out of the firing line."

"You're marginally more use to me alive than dead."

"Right back at you."

Valour regarded the mound they were hiding behind. When people cleared snow from their gardens or the street cobbles, they shovelled it into heaps like this one. It was the perfect shape for the city's children to sled down on tea-trays. Her mother had never let her do that. Or play much in general. She told herself to focus before she got her reminiscing arse shot.

Petrichor sighed. "Well, there's no point in trying to get in there now, is there?"

"None." Something moved at the corner of Valour's eye. "There is a point in nabbing that bloke, though." She pointed to a man walking along with a stack of loose papers and a pewter mug with steam rising from it. He was heading towards the building with the carefree steps of one who doesn't know anything is wrong.

Petrichor didn't answer, he only crept towards the man. Half a tick later, he had grabbed him and yanked him in behind their snow mound. Valour went one step further and shoved the bloke up against it.

He was a young, well-dressed man who gave an 'oof' as his back collided with the hardpacked snow and then blinked rapidly. "Pray, do not hurt me! Just take my purse."

"We want information about Brandquist," Valour said before Petrichor could voice his vexation at being mistaken for a thief.

"What?" The pinned bloke started quaking. "I know nothing about him. I'm merely a bookkeeper."

Valour surveyed his clothes, spectacles, and half-fallen wig. "You are, aren't you? Not just for this lot, but you're a real, legitimate bookkeeper."

The man nodded fast.

Petrichor gave a knowing sneer. "Well now, that makes it vital for you to be very forthcoming with us."

"I-it does?" the bookkeeper stammered.

"Of course," Petrichor said with chilling bonhomie. "You wouldn't want to lose your respectable career due to it coming out that you make a little extra on the side by keeping accounts for 'ness smugglers, right? Nor end up in the court of justice for aiding criminals."

When the bookkeeper didn't answer, Petrichor picked up the pewter mug, which had fallen and spilled half of its contents. Judging by the scent, and the fact that everyone but Valour was addicted to the stuff, it was coffee.

She hoped Petrichor was going to do what she thought he would.

"There's some left in this," he said, swivelling the cup and staring into it. "Mayhap I should use this steaming hot liquid to ruin something, young master bookkeeper. I could pour it over these accounts you worked so hard on for Brandquist. Or I could remove your spectacles and splash it into your eyes."

There it was, exactly what she had wanted him to say.

Valour hummed. "We might want to keep the papers. I vote for the eyes. Such a shame. What can a bookkeeper do without his sight?"

"Have mercy. I told you, I know nothing!"

Valour grabbed the bloke by the cravat and pulled it tight. "You do. You know where you're bringing the paperwork from."

He opened and closed his mouth a few times. She didn't want to punch his lights out, or let Petrichor loose on him, so she gave him a moment despite her patience running low.

"I came from the harbour office. Brandquist, or rather his minions, tell me to either work from there or here," he finally croaked. "I believe there are other locations, but I do not know of them."

"Good," Petrichor said. "It is so helpful that you're answering the questions. My associate and I have had a lot of violence lately and not having to cut you into miniscule pieces is a nice change of pace."

The bookkeeper swallowed hard against the hand around his neck. Valour wasn't gripping that tightly but he was still swaying. It was hard to tell his face colour considering how much powder, rouge, and lip tint he wore, but he seemed to be blanching. Was he about to faint?

"Where is the harbour office?" she said. "And don't say 'the harbour'. I'm neither dim-witted nor in the mood for jokes."

"It's a small shack at Southfaringway. Number seven, I think," he squawked. "You cannot miss it. It's the only blue building and more decrepit than the surrounding shipyards and fishermen's huts."

Valour didn't simply let go, like she had with the giant henchman, but glanced over at Petrichor. "I'm not asking for permission but for your opinion. Are we ready to release him?"

Petrichor was rifling through the stack of papers. "Only numbers, no useful information," he mumbled to himself. He looked up at her. "I suppose you might as well."

She did and the bookkeeper gasped in a long breath.

Valour divided her attention between him and the lair. Not only would there be armed fighters waiting for them in there, but any useful information was sure to have been removed.

Petrichor followed her gaze. "Bad idea, right?"

"Yes."

"Render this man unconscious and we can head for the harbour instead."

She was about to agree when the bookkeeper, who clearly did not want to be knocked unconscious, grabbed a discarded old snow shovel from somewhere by their feet. He swung it at Valour with a yelp. It was a clumsy, unsure blow. Nevertheless, it was a blow with a shovel and all his might, desperation, and survival instinct. It hit Valour square in the chest, knocking the air out of her lungs.

Distantly, through the pain and rage, she noted Petrichor grabbing the shovel and—just as the bookkeeper whimpered something about 'peasant brutes'—smashing him over the head.

Valour was bent over, clutching her chest and gasping in breaths.

Petrichor caught her eye. "Are you all right?"

She nodded, less bothered by the agony than by the fact that Petrichor had seen her lower her guard. She had to admit, though, she knew he'd make sure the bookkeeper didn't hurt her and that she was safely out of pistol range. This was what it could've always been like, wasn't it? If they had worked together. If they had liked each other. That thought was depressing as all troll-shit. More than that, it was pointless.

She stood up and took the rage, pain, and disappointment out on the bookkeeper, by kicking him in the face. She had no idea how much of the snob's features she had wrecked permanently and for once, she did not care. He lay unconscious, breathing noisily through the blood of his shattered nose. Valour moved to kick his head again.

Petrichor stepped between them. "If you do that, you will regret it when you've calmed. I know you well enough to guarantee it."

"Yes." She rasped in a breath since her lungs were not quite recovered. "But... he shovel-punched me in the tits!"

"Must you be so crude, Valour?"

"Must you be so lacking in pity for my lungs and my poor—"

She was about to say tits again. "For my poor *breasts*? That sort of thing hurts like all shit, you know. Especially when they're swollen like this right before my monthly bleed." She held her arms across her chest and cursed, shocked that she was willing to show weakness in front of him. A couple of days ago, she would've rather died.

Petrichor sighed resignedly. "I noted and appreciated your change of word choice and will thereby make an effort as well." With that, he dutifully went over and kicked the unconscious man's chest twice, one hard thwack around where each nipple would be. "There. I know it's not at all the same due to the physical differences and that he is unconscious, but you must accept what gesture you're given."

"Thanks."

You could have cut the sudden awkwardness with a knife.

Petrichor looked around. "We ought not linger. If you've got your breath back, we should head to the harbour."

Valour stretched her chest and grunted with pain. Thank the gods for her coat and the large amount of muscle and breast tissue taking the impact, otherwise she worried what might've happened to her lungs and top ribs. "I'll be fine. Let's go."

He was pretending not to watch her. "Shall I take the lead?"

"Mm."

They stayed in the dark, quiet parts of the street and made sure to keep the house with the shooter in their view as long as possible. And he didn't mock her when she rubbed her aching chest.

CHAPTER 32

SUPPLIES, SOUTHFARINGWAY, AND THE SEAMAN'S WARNING

As he walked, Petrichor scratched his chin. He would need a shave soon and his jaw was sore from tension. He tried to relax it, but to no avail. It would take more to get him back to his normal state of control and calm. Actually, he knew exactly what was needed. The route to the harbour would take them by the university and his rooms soon. Was it then not a moment's work to fetch his bookbinding kit? Perhaps he could use it back at the hideout while Ingrid and Valour were busy dancing around each other like courting birds? Nothing would centre him as much as being allowed to pare leather to the perfect size, sew a binding precisely right, and hammer in an embossed title. To create order and art in what had been random materials and naked papers.

They had been quiet for so long that he felt the need to clear his throat to get Valour's attention. "I should like to stop by my rooms."

"Is that a good idea?"

He appreciated that she had phrased it as a question. "Brandquist knows we have abandoned our rooms and so has no doubt relocated his minions. Nevertheless, I shall enter quickly and carefully, only fetching my pistol and some gunpowder. We are facing more and more foes. Arming ourselves further might be prudent."

"I suppose you're right. It's a Sunday so the university should be quiet." She scratched her neck, seeming unsure. "Do it. I'll keep watch outside."

He gave her a curt nod.

The timeworn, Gothic exterior of Vinterstock University loomed ahead, looking sinister and lit only by moonlight and a few guttering lamp posts. The astronomy tower was more welcoming, though, and he picked up his pace. The bookbinding kit. The pistol. Should he also pick up the riding boots Halcyon had given him? Not out of sentiment, of course, but practicality. Thinking of Halcyon inevitably brought up the question of the makeshift gloriam service.

He braced himself. "By the way, since we missed gloriam, perhaps we should visit the sanctum tonight?"

He prayed to Axsten that he wouldn't have to tell her that he had laid in wait for Halcyon and had spoken to him. He would have to if they did go to the sanctum tonight, though, since Halcyon would no doubt bring it up. Petrichor touched the scarf. Halcyon would expect to see it around Valour's neck.

"The sanctum can go burn," Valour muttered. "If the order won't help or house us when we need them, why should we follow the sacred rituals?" She shook her head. "I'm not risking my life by going there. I'm going to finish this bloody job and then hopefully use the reward to pay my way out."

Relief spread through him. "As you wish." He adjusted his hood and made for the tower entrance. "I shan't be long. Come up if you see any Brandquist henchmen coming. Or run away, whichever suits you."

She emitted a heavy sigh. "I'll come up and get you."

"Thank you," he mumbled, and hurried inside.

As he ascended the stairs, Valour stayed on his mind. Were they being kinder to each other out of necessity? Or had there always been a seed of positive feeling towards him in that oaf of a woman? Was that why she had thrown that book at him back in the cell?

When up in his rooms, he lit a taper and guided by its halo placed the pistol, black powder, and a packet of lead shot in a satchel. His thoughts were still stuck on his time in that cell. It was as if an old wound, a rift right into the soft core of him, had opened with those memories and the accursed thing refused to heal back up. He made himself form the disloyal question in his mind: could the order have punished a child, only trying to fit in, too severely? He studied his austere, cold rooms. How much of his life was his and how much of it was due to what had been done to him? On the streets. In the order.

He quickly added the kit to the satchel, then gathered up the riding boots and was about to change into them when he spotted that old book on the binding of books. He could feel how it had hit him in that cell. He touched it and found his hand clammy. He was clammy all over. Trying to stem another panic attack, he busied himself by frantically washing off with a full pitcher of water and soap, then pulling clean clothes on while ignoring soreness and bruises. Pain. It had been the only constant of his life. His earliest memories were of hunger pangs, the bone-snapping cold of sleeping on the streets, and the abuse of every sordid kind. The order had not been much better. It worked on pain, physical and mental, like clocks worked on cogs.

He packed his cologne to apply when he had time, then hesitated, and grabbed the tome on bookbinding too. As he held it halfway into the satchel, he realised that pain hadn't been the only constant in his life. There had been Valour as well. When he lived on the streets, everyone had spoken of the assassin child who prowled the city and killed with her mother. After joining the order, he had not experienced a day without her, thanks to the prayer times and meals. He shook the thoughts off and put the riding boots on.

Back outside, he held his satchel up to show that he'd retrieved what he came for and was about to apologise for the delay when Valour pointed to his feet. "What are those? Riding boots? Are you going deer hunting with the aristocrats after this?"

"These boots have quieter footfalls than my other ones. Also, they're warmer. I don't know if you have noticed, but the temperature appears to be dropping."

She gazed up. "True. It looks about to storm."

"Let's make haste, then."

As if it had heard them, the wind picked up with every step they took. The gale hit his eyes and made it impossible to keep his hood up for long. Nonetheless, he wouldn't be the one who suggested they took a carriage. Neither would Valour.

"Is it me or is the wind getting saltier?" Valour called over the whooshing.

Petrichor's stinging eyes focused past the grand custom house to a road sign beyond it. "Probably, considering we're getting close to the harbour."

At least the snow wouldn't be blown up into their eyes; the salt in the air had turned it completely into slush here. Soon the houses gave way to the harbour, and he squinted through the low light of the stars and some scattered lamp-posts to see an empty ocean. No movement, no moored clippers. The main connections to the rest of the world were severed.

"There. Southfaringway," Valour said, pointing to a sign.

It didn't take long to find the salt-bleached blue shack. It was as old and unkempt as the other Brandquist lairs. He and Valour sheltered under the roof eaves of a nearby shipyard and observed. There was no light in the windows, no footsteps in the slush outside the door, and not a person in sight. To be safe, they waited, despite the blustery wet cold creeping through their clothes and into their bones. Salty winds still blew his hood down, but he didn't care. Who would see his face here? The only people around were a handful of fishermen finishing up for the day, and they moved with their heads bowed against the storm.

When Petrichor's extremities were numb, his frustration at Valour drumming her fingers against her coat peaking, and there hadn't been any movement around the shack, he checked his pocket watch. "We've been here for nigh an hour. The coast must be clear."

"Coast. Was that a pun?" Valour said, pointing to the sea.

"Valour. It is an expression."

"All right, all right, calm your overactive sphincter. I know your sense of humour is odd and wondered if you wanted me to fake a laugh or something. Just being friendly."

"If this is you being friendly, I am relieved you have kept it from me for all these years," Petrichor muttered as he edged towards the shack.

Its door was dilapidated wood and as crusted with salt as its lock. Valour pushed past him and started examining it. She listened with her ear against the door for a long time, then shook her head at him. No noise from inside, then. They drew their weapons and Petrichor brushed the snow off the door-handle. As slowly and quietly as possible, he pushed it down. To no avail.

He whispered, "I might be able to pick the lock since—" but got no further. Valour kicked the door until the rotten wood around the lock buckled, then shoved her way in.

"Marvellous. Just splendid," he hissed. "Now everyone knows we're here, you reckless buffoon."

She stopped on the other side of the door, perusing the shack. "Petrichor. Have I asked you about the stick up your arse today?"

"No. And if you do, I shall ensure you regret it. Now cease talking and focus."

"I was just wondering if it was splintering. Or maybe sprouting twigs."

He joined her inside the dark room. "What are you prattling on about?"

"I mean that you seem in a worse mood than ever. Did someone piss in your coffee?"

"I am vexed, Valour, because I must work with you. And you refuse to keep quiet even for the merest moment, risking both our lives as well as being a nuisance."

"Calm your haemorrhoids. It wasn't that big a risk," she said as she lit a foul-smelling oil lamp. "I kicked down the door because the building looked abandoned, there wasn't a peep inside or out, and the handle was covered in snow. And now"—she indicated the space with a sweeping gesture—"I've inspected the place. It's emptier than Brother Encumbrance's head and has no hiding places."

Annoyingly, she was right. And she had gotten the job done.

"One day, Valour, I shall snap and simply bludgeon you."

"If I have to stay in your company, I might be so bloody fed up that I let you," she said while lighting another oil lamp and handing it to him.

The insults lacked their usual bite, more like a reassuring routine now.

He held up his lamp, revealing a room with no windows and only the door they had entered through. The walls were bare but for stacks of crates lining them. In the centre of the room was a table. He shivered. The space was cold due to the lack of a fire but escaping the wind was bliss. Valour went for the crates, and he approached the table. It was covered in folders, loose stacks of paper, empty ink-wells, an abacus, and three tin cups of stale coffee, explaining the room's bitter smell. He took his glove off and touched one of the cups. "Stone cold, but the coffee hasn't evaporated or frozen. Someone was here not too long ago."

"Seems so." Valour picked up an unlabelled bottle from the table. She sniffed it and then took a sip. "Akvavit. Good quality, too. Well spiced, crisp as ice, and strong as fire." She held it towards him and the powerful alcohol hit his nose. "Fancy a swig, Prince of Prissiness? It'll yank the cold right out of your bones."

Petrichor shook his head. "You know full well that I rarely drink. I like to keep my mind as sharp as my knives."

"I do indeed know that." She took a demonstrative gulp from the bottle before putting it back. Then she began opening a crate with a crowbar. He waited, but no mockery or further questioning came. A miracle, to be sure.

Petrichor joined her by the crates. The one Valour had opened held small bottles of 'ness, filled and sealed. He picked one up and noted its label with only the letter S, for 'shrewdness' he assumed. There were two kinds of bottles. Most of them were plain, brown glass ones stoppered with a cork. A set, however, were decorated pipette bottles in cobalt blue. One type for the common folk and more exclusive ones for the rich. Brandquist knew what he was doing when it came to selling.

Valour was holding one of the brown bottles with a look of... was that temptation or curiosity? She shoved it back in the crate and rifled through the paperwork on the table instead. "None of this makes sense," she said after a while. "It's nought but numbers and abbreviations. Or maybe it's a code."

"Move over," he said with a tired sigh. "I'll have a look."

"I bloody well shan't. I'm perfectly able to—" She stopped, concentrating on one of the sheets of paper.

"What is it?"

"This one has a few legible sentences. It talks about moving large quantities of 'the product' to a warehouse."

"That's what Halcyon said. That there were rumours Brandquist had appropriated some old warehouse in the city." Petrichor read over her shoulder, spotting road names that rang a faint bell. "Hm. I'm quite sure that's right on the outskirts of the city, just before the fields start." His speech slowed as it came to him. "It's in the Pestilence District."

"Ah. That would explain why no one's come across it."

The solemness in her tone was echoed in his as he said, "Exactly."

He had been a member of the order during Vinterstock's last big wave of plague. If he had still lived on the streets, he'd most likely have been one of those quarantined to the Pestilence District and ultimately buried in its shallow graves. Yet another reason to be loyal to the order.

Valour furrowed her brow. "Isn't that still quarantined until the, um, bad air clears?"

"You mean the miasma. And I'm not certain it is. I don't believe there was an official time limit. The greve knows no one will venture there due to fear and respect for the dead anyway."

He read on until Valour interrupted him by diving forward to inspect something at the bottom of the page. "Look at that."

When her annoying head was out of the way, he leaned in too. It was a signature in clear handwriting—*Brandquist*—and below that, a date. Two days ago.

Petrichor straightened back up. "Right, we know where we have to go next."

"About bloody time! I just wish it wasn't the Pestilence District. Come on."

She extinguished the oil lamps and left. He followed and nearly lost his balance as he came out. A pain like an ice pick stabbed into the top of his head hit so fast he missed a step.

"You all right?" Valour asked, flicking the hood of her coat up.

"Yes. Merely a beast of a headache."

"I've one brewing as well. The pressure of the hunt and the lack of proper food and sleep, I guess?"

He hummed in agreement. "Squinting against the wind is surely not helping." Neither was their constant arguing nor him keeping the fits of panic at bay, but he didn't say that.

"True. My eyes sting worse than when Brother Encumbrance takes his boots off," she said. "Why *do* his feet smell like that? Do you think he sticks fish heads on his toes every night and uses them as a puppet theatre?"

Petrichor didn't answer.

They moved on and nearly collided with a grizzled fisherman scrambling past. "Rattle my timbers," he roared. "Don't dally here. None should. I only came to check for urchins in my boat."

A picture of confusion, Valour frowned. "Is 'urchins' sailor-speak for something like barnacles? Or do you have children in your boat?"

"Orphans, lass. They sleep in there in droves when the boat's covered. Tonight, though, they'd be sure to die. It'll be a night like we've not seen in years."

Petrichor's breath hitched. Droves of urchins? He had been seeing greater numbers. How did Vinterstock now have even more starving, deserted children than when he was young?

"It's going to be that bad?" Valour asked.

The seaman returned to his scurrying, calling, "Anyone outside will be dead long 'fore morning. Heed this, get thee to a fire and some beef stew!"

Petrichor couldn't remember ever hearing a seasoned fisherman this frightened by the cold. How far away were he and Valour from safe shelter?

"Shit," Valour said after the fisherman was gone. "Better rush back."

Petrichor fought through the stabbing in his head and took the lead. "Agreed."

"If there's a carriage on the way," Valour said, matching his walking pace, "we'll take it, right?"

"Absolutely. We should hurry indoors, even if we must admit to weakness and take a carriage."

"You grim little martyr. You have to stop seeing help, joy, and comfort as signs of weakness."

He didn't reply, only walked faster.

CHAPTER 33

NEAR-DEATH TRUTHS

PETRICHOR GAVE UP on the coat's hood. He yearned for his hat, although that would no doubt have blown off. He wrapped one of his scarves around his head to protect his ears from frostbite. They should've marked the storm and plummeting temperature and called off the hunt for the night when they were back in the city. They had, however, been so eager to get this done. Both of them wanting to win and neither wanting to be the first to say they needed to stop. Now they had little choice but to retrace their steps, back toward the university—whose old wooden doors were always bolted shut in bad storms—and then into the city where their hideout was. It was a long walk but not a terrible one in acceptable weather. In this storm, however, it would feel twice as long while snow, slush, and ice would make hurrying harder, especially for people who were hunted and so could not shelter just anywhere.

After a short period of trudging through the slush of the harbour's dirt path, Valour said, "Well, I don't know about you but I'm tenser than a bloody icicle. Mind if we talk to take my mind off it?"

"Not if you can find something that you and I could converse about?"

"Hm. What about the fact that we both want to leave the order? I didn't think we had anything like that in common."

"We have very different reasons, Valour. You want to defect because you have no devotion to the order. I wish to one day leave to pursue another occupation."

She picked up her pace so she was a little in front of him. She kept wriggling her back in the strangest way. "I wonder how many of the other members also want out. I can imagine a few of them do. Not Encumbrance the Piss-Ant or Mire the Violent Arsehole, of course, but some of the others."

Evidently, she was fine with being disloyal to the organisation that fed, trained, housed, and saved them.

Her fidgeting was distracting. "Must you keep jostling your upper body so?"

She turned and glowered and after a beat, he understood. Her back was branded with the Order of Axsten's crest, burned into her skin over and over throughout the years. Partly as punishment and partly to instil loyalty in her. It wasn't only himself he was torturing with old memories.

She returned to walking without a word.

Petrichor cleared his throat and picked up the old conversation. "Some might wish to leave. 'Tis a lot of riksdaler to repay, though."

Valour snorted. "Hel's realm, yes. And when it comes down to it..." She seemed to hesitate over whether to carry on. "There's the thing they told us about what an assassin is good for."

She went quiet for a long time. He scratched his cheeks and nose, which were prickling with frostnip, until he tired of waiting for a response. "Are you indicating that all we can do is kill, Valour?"

"Not *only* that. We were also taught how to sneak about and to obey orders." She huffed out a long, steaming breath. "As far as I can see that only makes us qualified for the king's army and maybe the overseers, if we lean on the fact that we were taught some investigation skills."

"And neither of those reputable professions tempt you?"

She laughed as if he had said something unbelievably witless. "Shit, no."

"Perhaps you cannot do other jobs. I can. The skills we learn are transferable if you have the intelligence and will to apply them to other professions. For example, following instructions to the letter, doing our job with precision and pride, using our own initiative and having iron discipline? Those are desirable traits in a worker."

"Fine. I'm wrong and you're right. As always," Valour said in sulking tones.

But she wasn't all wrong. It was true that other members had on a weekly basis told them to stay in the order, claiming they were not suited for any other life.

Was that the university in the distance? Squinting was indeed worsening his headache. He put his spectacles on to shield his eyes from the wind, finding that it made everything so dark he could barely make out where to put his ice-numbed feet. "From what I recall, the other members continuously claim that you are right and I am wrong. Although perhaps that is due to them being unable to countenance even my very presence."

She stopped in the middle of the snow-covered street. "See, that right there is a big part of your problem."

He demonstratively walked on. "Keep moving, we must get out of the cold."

"You assume everyone hates you as much as you hate yourself," she said, catching up to him.

"Everyone does. You never miss a chance to tell me so yourself."

"I do that because you act like an arse-flute and I want to get back at you."

Petrichor didn't reply but only trembled, wishing that he'd worn a shirt of the same sensible wool as his stockings.

"I think I'm learning to read you a little." She kicked a lump of frozen slush, which shattered against a lamp-post. "For example, I bet you act like a shitbag because you think you've nought to lose by being horrible. I mean, no one liked you even back when you were trying to be nice and…"

"And what?" Petrichor slowed and took the spectacles off, placing them back in his pocket with nonchalance. "Please, do not stop tearing my personality apart now. And what?"

"It'll sound stupid."

"Everything you say sounds stupid to me. Do favour me with your awe-inspiring insights."

He kept his voice disinterested. Not letting on the obvious facts: one, she was known for being able to read people, and two, he had come to a stage where it was vital for him to understand himself.

Otherwise, those fits may never stop.

Not that any of that mattered if they died out here tonight.

"I bet a lot of why you are the way you are is because you were damaged as a child," she said, barely loud enough to be heard over the wind. "The other assassins talked about the things you had to do to survive on the streets, before the order took you in, and that'd wreck anyone."

Petrichor was trying hard not to chatter his teeth. "Is that all?"

"Keep your bloody cravat on, I'm getting there. This cold is distracting." She jumped a few times on the spot before walking on. "Anyway, after the streets you were in the order. And they beat any joy and humanity out of children, with weapons, with words, and with mind games. There's a reason why we both stay away from other people, right?"

There was silence as he warred with himself about whether to be honest.

"Yes." Petrichor looked up at the icy stars. "Still, you didn't become... like me."

"Well," Valour said pensively, "I had a parent for the first ten years. She was a coldblooded assassin, but still a steadfast mother. She loved me."

Her voice wavered ever so slightly on the last words. Was it worse to have been loved and lost it, than to never know what it felt like?

Valour sniffled. No doubt due to the cold. Tears would probably freeze. "People handle being broken in different ways. Some try to look for the light in the world and in themselves. Some lean into the dark." She wiped her nose with her glove. "Anything to keep from being hurt again."

He hummed but the wind whipped it away.

Valour stabbed a finger into his shoulder. "Don't for an instant think I'm saying you'd be a good person if you had a less shitty life. You'd still be pompous, judgemental, and arrogant." She rubbed her hands together, blowing on her gloves. "But you'd interact more with people and thereby make more of an effort. And you'd be working in a bank or something, not killing like it was nought more than a regular work task to be ticked off your to-do list."

"I would not be a bank clerk. I'd be a bookbinder. A real job, with a real home, and a real name. Not a *designation*," he said, spitting out the last word as if it was rancid. Would it have been so hard for the order to present them with names? All humans ought to be given at least a real name.

"Fine, whatever. My point was that I think you would have learned not to push everyone away and try so bloody hard to be cold."

"I do not push everyone away."

"You do."

Petrichor stepped onto a bigger road, happy that the houses now shielded them from some of the wind. There was no saving them from the freezing cold, though. It had clawed its way into his very bones. "Not Halcyon."

"Even him. You try to impress him but you try too hard and in the wrong way. You're cold and professional in front of him. That makes him uncomfortable and pushes him away."

"Who in damnation died and made you a brain-specialist?"

"No one, snooty-arse. When you're an assassin, you learn to read people, right?" Her voice was half confrontation and half held back, teeth chattering. "When you're a child afraid of every adult, you learn to read people to avoid their wrath. When you're quiet and listen, then you learn to read people too."

He squinted up the street. They were back in the city proper, there would surely be a carriage soon. "I am all of those."

"No. You don't try to please people to avoid their wrath, you just aim to be scarier than them. Also, you don't listen."

"Pardon me if I do not lend my ear to every feather-brain with a mouth."

Valour groaned. "If you shut your rude porridge-hole for a few minutes, you could read people like I can. And, as I figured out tonight, if you hated yourself a little less... well, Hel's realm, you might hate other people less."

He wanted to dismiss everything she said. As they trudged through snow and slush, puzzle pieces shifted and settled in his mind, though. It hurt worse than the cold.

"The order really brought out the worst in us, didn't it?"

Valour did a double take. "Us? What did it bring out in me? Other than my keeping people at a distance. I know about that one."

Petrichor fixed his gaze on some icicles under a roof eave. "Every time you spoke or sang as a child, they laughed at you. Every time you found a friend or lover, they mocked them or tried to turn them against you. Like with that harlo—" He stopped and corrected himself. "That *doxy* you were in love with. Not to mention your adored watchmaker."

"Aha! I've wondered for so long if they were the ones spreading shitty rumours about—"

"Stop. Let me finish or I'll never tell you any of this."

"Sorry. Go on," she muttered while shivering.

"Every time you showed mercy to a mark, they hurt you. Every time you talked about leaving, they tore your confidence down." He took a deep breath. The air was as sharp and clear as glass, and it stung his throat and lungs. "Every time you showed joy, love, or trust... they punished you. They made you hate the parts of you that, well, that you probably shouldn't hate."

Keeping doubts at bay made his head throb harder. Was the order to be esteemed when it treated its children like that? Wait. Had he already decided that it shouldn't be? Memory loss was a sign of freezing to death, wasn't it? Why were there no accursed carriages around?

"Wow," Valour breathed. "It must've hurt you all the way into the depth of your balls to say that. You really must think we're going to die out here for you to force out something nice about me."

"Just because I have never wanted to, it does not mean I am not perfectly capable of saying nice things about you."

"Ha."

"Do you doubt my word?"

She stopped the arm swinging she had been doing to keep warm. "Absolutely, you cruel arsehole. Say something nice about me without tagging on something bad afterwards to counteract the nice. I bloody well dare you."

CHAPTER 34
BREAKING THE ICE

ICE-CRUSTED TENSION CRACKLED and embarrassment coursed through Valour in sickening waves. Why in the name of troll-shit had she dared him to say something nice about her? The fear of death? Some sort of freezing of brain functions? Well, maybe the mortification would keep her warm. She was barely shivering, and it was a bad sign when your body stopped trying to keep your temperature up. Well, even if her body was giving up, her mind sure as all troll-shit wasn't.

This road hadn't been cleared, giving it a heavy layer of snow on top of frozen slush, just waiting to make you slip. A terrible combination for someone clumsy from freezing to death and hurrying. She looked to the houses. Should they knock on a door and beg for sanctuary? No point. This was one of the few times when Vinterstockians didn't help one another. Unlike people in the countryside, they didn't let vagrants and foreigners—those being the only ones out in this weather—into their homes on nights like these. You had to keep doors and windows bolted and save the warmth from the fire and the hot drinks for your family and friends. Strangers were on their own. Especially hunted assassins.

"Right. Something nice." Petrichor flexed his fingers and spoke in a voice shuddering with cold and reluctance.

"You give to others, you care about others, you… love with the might of a bonfire on Valborg's Night. Despite having had a life of people trying to beat and shame that out of you."

Unsure of what to say, Valour busied herself with trying to walk while also rubbing her frozen, stiff knees. Thank the gods the coat at least protected most of her thighs. She had pins and needles in every limb now, though. And it was getting worse. "I'm, uh, I'm surprised that you of all people think that's a good thing."

He seemed to not have heard her. Possibly due to the howling of the wind. More likely because he still had the bad habit of not listening. "You stayed a good person even with what the order did to you, what your parents' deaths did to you, what this city did to you." He fixed her with a glare. "See, *I* can say good things about *you*."

The unspoken continuation of that hung in the air. *But you cannot do the same about me.*

Taking that challenge, Valour tensed her jaw so her teeth wouldn't chatter and said, "And you're intelligent, disciplined, and hard-working. More importantly, you're not the cold-hearted monster you try so hard to be."

He said something about no one being what they display to the world, but it was hard to make out. He'd reached the stage of garbled speech, then? Shit.

She had to get them home. Fast. She strained her hearing, listening for hoofbeats and carriage wheels but heard nought but the sound of their boots crunching in the snow. Maybe it was too cold for the horses. Or anything living at all.

Her heart leapt when she spotted a house she recognised, soon followed by another one. "Hey, I know where we are! We don't have too much further to go."

Petrichor didn't seem to react. Instead, he murmured something about Halcyon giving her a scarf but it being taken and something about it making a coat not unique. Maybe his mind wouldn't recover even if they did survive.

She had to keep him talking, keep him awake. "Oi, rude-prude. When we get back, perhaps it's time to pause our hunt? I reckon we need to warm up, eat some of the leftover fika, and sleep."

"Agreed," he said. "I'm dreaming of sitting in front of the hideout's little fire, pitiful as it is."

Valour noted that his teeth were not chattering anymore, nor was he shivering.

"At dawn, we should, um..." She forced her mind to clear and her mouth to work. "We'll go to the warehouse mentioned in that paperwork. Ingrid is sure to be back by then. If she isn't already, that is."

Petrichor stared at her. "Surely you're not entering, ensuring... I mean, *entertaining*, the notion of taking her along?"

"No. Yes. No." She groaned, out of energy to defend herself. "Look, I just need to check on her and let her know approximately where I'll be before we go tomorrow. It won't take long."

"I care little about how long it takes, Valour. I care about the fact that you appear to be making decisions not with your head, or even your heart, but with your... you know..."

Looking down at her crotch, Valour tried to think of an expression that wouldn't make him uncomfortable. "Treasure trove? Honey pot? My dewy rose?" The last one would have made her laugh if she had the energy. She shook her head to clear it, but found that it barely moved. What step on the way to freezing to death was that?

"Your genitalia," he slurred, disregarding her completely. "And since my fate is currently tied to yours, I should like you to at least attempt to make decisions with your head."

They made a narrow left into an alleyway and Valour nearly missed a step, partly because she couldn't feel her legs and partly because she was glaring at the arsehole walking next to her. "What in Heimdal's bloody horn is that supposed to mean?"

"I, uh... What was I saying? Cursed cold. Right, yes, this woman has you under her spell. You share far too much information with her and allow yourself to be distracted."

"I promised her father I'd look after her," Valour said, trying to sound in control of her speech. "Then I got her into shit-heaps of danger so now she is my responsibility. Also, I don't get under women's spells."

"Firstly, no she's not. Secondly, yes you do."

She had to think that through as she had already forgotten what he was replying to. "You're talking bäckahäst-shit."

"Nay. Do not fool yourself, you are falling for this woman."

"Am not. I'm keeping it purely sexual."

They were both walking sluggishly, dragging themselves forward.

"I see the way you watch her and how you speak to her. You are falling for her, despite the danger of it."

"Again, a full heap of bäckahäst-shit." She wanted to stop talking but was pretty sure that all this quarrelling was keeping the blood pumping in her frozen veins. "But, let's for argument's sake say you're right. Why would it be dangerous?"

Valour thought she could feel the teeth marks where Ingrid had bitten her, but it was probably the cold creeping past her clothes and into her skin.

"She clouds your judgement and makes you drop your guard," Petrichor answered. "And even if she turns out to be trustworthy, she makes you dependent on her and will try to control you. That gives her a lot of power to hurt you."

Valour snorted, focusing on his daft assumptions and not on the fact that she couldn't fully feel where she placed her feet. "Like you know anything about this stuff. You *hate* people and relationships. Didn't you say they were poison at one of the vespers last week?"

"I did, and I freely admit to having no experience here. Yet, I have been around you most of my life, whether I wanted to be or not, and I can see when you have your heart set on someone."

"That's drivel. Ingrid was someone I fancied from afar. Now, I'm protecting her a bit as a favour to the owner of my living space and fucking her. That's all." She was shouting. Even worse, her numb mouth made it sound like an elk being strangled. "I mean, Ingrid can be bloody exasperating, and she lives in another world."

Petrichor tottered along, utterly hunched up. "I wager one of the reasons she exasperates you is that you know you could fall for her. And the clue is in the word 'fall'." His voice had its frequent academic research air, but not the usual patronising know-it-all tone. He could *almost* pass for concerned. "You might tumble without control and end up at the bottom of an emotional ravine, broken and without anything but the memories of the thrill of the plunge to show for it."

"What the shit are you on about?" She snapped. "Your brain is past being affected by the cold, it's full-on got frostbite. I might have to amputate it."

He coughed and she understood why; the cold ached in her throat and lungs too. "You know I'm right. You must ask yourself if this shallow socialite is worth all that?"

"Stop calling her 'the socialite' and such. You like names better than our designations, right? Well, she has a name. And how many ways can I tell you that I'm not bloody falling in love with her?"

They turned onto a main road. They should be back soon. Only a little longer. They just had to keep moving, had to keep their brains ticking over.

Petrichor pressed his purple lips together. "I am not saying that you're ready to settle down with her or anything of that ilk. I'm merely suggesting that if we survive tonight, you ought to tread carefully with that pleasure-seeker, lest she use you up and throw you away. Or worse, betray us as we search for Brandquist."

"Pleasure-seeker? I've told you; she has a godsdamned name."

"Yes, and the fact that you so ardently insist on me using it proves how infact— infat— infatuated you are with her. You never told me the watchmaker's name."

His speech kept slurring, and he walked like he was drunk. Valour couldn't blame him. Her field of vision was blackening at the edges. She blinked a few times and looked around for anywhere warm that they could break into. It was sad that the sanctum was so far away. Somehow it didn't surprise her though. Of course the order would be no help to them, even when they were dying.

"Kajsa. The watchmaker's name was Kajsa," she mumbled after a while. "Now, she *did* use me up and throw me away. But only after I royally demolished the whole relationship."

"I thought you said she left you because the order kept telling her that you were bedding other women? And due to you not wanting marriage and children?"

Valour pushed herself, they had been candid with each other thus far and if ever there was a time to open up, this was it. "Those were some of the reasons. The rest was... me. I, um, kept coming up with reasons to end it, and she'd have to convince me to stay."

"Ah. Then perhaps you're not afraid to fall for someone, you are afraid to let someone get under your skin."

Well, yes, Ingrid was certainly good at that. Valour felt that bite on her shoulder again and searched her feelings, trying to understand why she wasn't running far away from Ingrid Rytterdahl. It didn't matter. Valour's mind couldn't focus and her body wasn't obeying her anymore. Only a few streets more and they'd arrive. It was cruel that they would get this close to the hideout and not make it, but that was life for you. Or perhaps that was death for you.

"Anyway," Petrichor said, his breathing sounding shallow and slow. "My advice is purely academical. Do with it as you wish."

Valour made to reply but found no energy. She was getting that strange fatigue you were meant to get before the cold shut your mind down. The next step was going mad and ripping one's clothes off, she had heard. Or was that a myth?

Tiny flakes fell from the stars and tumbled about her face, belying the idea that it couldn't snow when it was freezing out.

Petrichor slumped against a lamp-post. She righted him and helped him back onto the street as best she could. They were near the hideout, but not close enough. She didn't have many more steps in her and Petrichor was dragging his feet even worse than she was.

Every step was like climbing a mountain. What was the point of fighting? She could simply lay down and rest. The snow would cover them and no one would miss two lonely, pitiful, young assassins who didn't understand their own emotions. The snowfall was heavy now, lashing against their faces like a fusillade of pine needles. She could barely see.

From beside her, Petrichor made an utterly bizarre snorting noise.

"What in all bäckahäst-shit was that?"

"Nothing."

"No, not nothing," she prompted. "That was some sort of snorting little laugh, wasn't it?" He was actually able to laugh without it being one of his callous sniggers? This was a night for revelations.

"I suppose you could call it that," he slurred. "I was thinking about what you said, about being a cold-hearted monster, and it turned my thoughts to an amusing play on words."

Valour tried to wriggle her toes in her boots but couldn't feel them. At least that meant she didn't feel the pain in her feet as she kept trudging along. "Really? Go on, tell me."

"We were raised to be coldblooded, right? But the way things are going, we're going to freeze to death in a snowdrift and then we shall be snowblooded."

Valour looked at him incredulously. "That isn't funny."

"Yes. It is."

"No, Petrichor. It really isn't." She made sure to not look at the snowdrifts on either side of them. "Your sense of humour must've been dropped on its head as a baby."

He gave no answer but merely turned from her.

She bit her tongue. Would it have killed her to be nicer? Especially tonight, since it might be their last one alive. "It, um, was a good attempt at a joke, though."

He didn't answer.

"And I like the word 'snowblooded'. I like snow in general." Still no reply, so she pressed on. "I used to hate snow. It shows up blood, you have to shovel it away, it ends up as slush and ice—not to mention that it's bloody hard to walk in. Still, even tonight when it might kill me, there's something nice about snow."

"Like what?" Petrichor said, clumsily trying to rub his hands together.

"Well, it turns the city lighter in the dark months."

"I suppose it does." His now bluish face looked pensive. "Fresh snow also has a certain beauty when it glitters in the sun. Like a coating of sugar crystals over everything. It changes how everything looks."

Surprise pushed past her pain and worries about frostbite. Petrichor thought of things like that? "I guess it does. Also, it softens the ground if you take a fall."

"The snow can be melted into drinking water. Or used to build structures." He tottered on and mumbled fast, like he was talking to himself. "Being coldblooded never gave me anything but difficulties. Snowblooded means you can be useful. That you can thaw. I shall be snowblooded."

Valour studied him. The cold was getting to his mind. He sounded like the vagrants she'd seen on the streets rambling to themselves before they succumbed. Her own mind was feeling fuzzy too, come to think of it.

"I will too. Snowblooded it is," she said, wondering if she would have to carry him. Wondering if they would both die even if they did make it back.

Petrichor lurched to a halt, staring ahead. "It can't be? A carriage!"

It was, and they both fell in their hurry to wave it down. Luckily the driver heard their cries and stopped, shouting at them to hurry up.

All Valour's thoughts about giving in had blown away and she forced her body to take her to the carriage and get both herself and Petrichor inside. On the seats lay two sheepskins. They dragged them over their laps and Petrichor shouted their address to the driver. Valour leaned her head back, willing herself not to fall asleep for the risk of never waking. Her head swam from the freeze as well as all the unspoken things finally spoken. None of it mattered as much as the one, vital thing. She and Petrichor hadn't died tonight.

CHAPTER 35
THE THINGS YOU DO TO SURVIVE

PETRICHOR NIGH FELL into the hideout. Without having to think about it, he and Valour went through the frostbite recovery procedures they had been taught as children, starting with removing any of their clothing that had gotten snow-wet. Next came adding energy and the gradual building of heat. Valour lit the fire while Petrichor set a kettle to boil over it. They sat huddled under their covers and blankets, forcing themselves to eat the leftover rulltårta and drink hot water. Not a word had been said since they were out of the cold, not even to remark that Ingrid wasn't back yet or how much it hurt when a frozen body thawed. Soon they dragged themselves over to their bedding.

Petrichor took the mattress and lay on his side watching the fire, dreading when it would burn out. Still, he could feel all his body parts again and relished it despite the pain and chattering of teeth. Sadly, this also meant he felt that he needed to empty his bladder. He squirmed. There was no way he was going to the outhouse.

Slowly, time ached on, giving no reprieve by letting him sleep—despite his exhaustion. Valour, on the other hand, gave whimpering little snores.

Icy winds howled and crept through the walls and floor, showing that this night would stay grim. Petrichor shivered. The thin mattress seemed to leech all the cold from the frozen floor and infuse it up into his body. He remembered a night when he was very small and had slept on the streets next to a girl of about eighteen. She had told him that there was no point in putting every rag and blanket over himself if he was to sleep on the cold ground, and showed him how to steal hay from the city's stables to lay down as a mattress. He wished he had some hay now.

What had been her name? Elsa? Eva? Ebba. That was it. She didn't mind that he was an awkward little child and took him under her wing for a few weeks. He had worshipped her. She used to make some coin at the palace. Did she perform something? Oh yes, she gave private dances for the greve. Petrichor recalled her talking about how the greve had been so chatty and charming, even to a dancing girl of ill repute. He had sounded a lot like his cousin the king, brimming with culture and charm. Now the head of their city was known to be quiet, dull, and aloof. Was that what power and responsibility did to you? Many a night, Ebba had described the palace. Mostly Petrichor remembered the tales of the lavish room meant only for theatre, opera, and ballet. Ebba said it had the softest red velvet curtains, and he had wondered what velvet was.

Petrichor moved to lay on his back to not compress his bladder so much.

He had only been in the palace once. His memory shifted, making his head hurt with the speed of it. Wait. No. He had never been inside the palace. And the wonderful Ebba had died, of course. The pox. Or perhaps just the cold. Wrapping his arms around himself to keep more of his body heat, Petrichor tried to stop reminiscing and sleep. After all, silly childhood memories were not to be believed or cared about. His memories were not to be cared about, nor was he himself. He had been nothing before the order. What would he be if they did catch Brandquist, got the reward, and he could leave the Assassins of Axsten?

Valour made a new sound in her sleep, a low moan of agony. She was curled up against the cold too and didn't have her hotel heiress to warm her tonight. By the dying embers of the fire, he could see her wince. The confidence and strength she normally exuded was gone. She looked younger, like a child in pain.

He dithered, then stumbled up and over to her. He took off Halcyon's scarf. He wrapped it as a blanket on top of her as best he could.

She stirred and drowsily mumbled, "What're you doing?"

"This scarf is yours. Halcyon wanted you to have it."

"Hm? Oh? All right." Her eyes closed again.

"I'm sorry I took it," he whispered when he was sure she was asleep enough not to remember. "I'm sorry for anything I took from you and any pain I caused you."

CHAPTER 36

TO BE ALIVE

AFTER A MOMENT of not having a bloody clue where and when she was, it came to Valour. She was at the hideout, and judging by the reddish light through her eyelids, it was dawn. Of what day? The third day of their hunt for Brandquist? The fourth? Never mind. What mattered was that she'd survived last night. Although a bit of her wished she hadn't when she felt the pain and stiffness of her every body part. This makeshift bed didn't help, being so godsdamned hard and cold. The direct opposite of Ingrid.

Her eyes shot open, a fluttering in her stomach as she realised that *Ingrid* was what had awoken her. She could smell her perfume and hear her humming while lighting the fire. Valour recognised the grim ballad. Its lyrics spoke of how sex and booze were the only ways to fend off the cold and death, like so many Nordic songs. She watched the fire crackle and spark into life, waiting until Ingrid hummed the part about death sharpening its sword before breaking in to sing the subsequent words about 'draining thine last glass and seeing death upon thee waiting'.

Ingrid spun around and trilled, "You're awake!"

"You're right! I am!"

Ingrid put her hands on her hips. "Oh, keep your droll sarcasm to yourself. Last night was a frightful freeze, was it not? I had to stay at the hotel. Did you manage to get any sleep?"

Valour couldn't remember ever being this keenly aware of being alive. She got up as fast as she could and clutched Ingrid's waist. "Some. You are a better refreshment, though, tasty little cloudberry."

"Cloudberry?" Ingrid said with a laugh. "Sounds like a

nickname that might get me *eaten*."

Valour kissed her, trying to put all her joy at surviving and her appreciation of Ingrid into it.

Groaning, Petrichor sat up. "I'm getting the both of you spayed."

"Try it and you'll find yourself castrated before you can blink," Valour replied.

He got up and pulled on his extra coat that had been drying by the fire. "Blazes, it is growing light out there. We've slept for too long." He placed a hand on where his bladder was. "I shall go make use of the privy. And, I suppose, have a perfunctory wash with some snow." He sounded petulant, like it was their fault that he couldn't have a full bath.

"On a related note," Ingrid said, producing a large paper-wrapped package. "I brought you both clean outfits. I knew not your exact measurements or preferences and so was put upon to make some guesses."

Petrichor went to the garments first so Valour waited, instead pulling her coat on.

"I see. Well. Thank you," Petrichor said. "However, I really must go see to my ablutions." He rushed through the door to the garden and the outhouse.

Valour inspected the clothes and found them nigh identical to her and Petrichor's current outfits, but of better quality. She was certain hers would be the right sizes. Ingrid was an observant woman and had, after all, studied Valour's every curve and plane. "Thank you for these," she said. "I'll get some more wear out of these and then wash in the snow and put the new ones on. We'll obviously repay you."

"Oh, we can discuss such things later." She stood on tiptoe so she could wrap her arms around Valour's neck. "Brr. You're as cold as an icicle."

Valour kissed her and then stepped out of the embrace, trying to get a better view out of the windows. "Speaking of, is the snowstorm still in full force?"

Ingrid shook her head, setting a lock that had escaped her piled-up hair dancing. "The bone-freezing cold remains, but the wind has died down and the snow clouds vanished."

"Good," Valour said with a yawn.

She was going to ask about breakfast when the risen sun streamed in and haloed Ingrid, who blinked at the sharp rays. For the first time, Valour noted just how deep-brown her eyes were. Why did this woman always find the brightest light to stand in, and then somehow manage to outshine it? The sun glinted off the glossy black of Ingrid's hair and Valour couldn't stop staring. Didn't want to. Didn't have to. It couldn't last, of course, but for right now, this wonder of a woman was hers to watch.

Ingrid took her hands in her own. "Considering the perilous cold out there, perhaps you could stay in here today? With me?"

"Can't, I'm afraid. We have another lead and must follow it."

"I see." Ingrid chewed her lower lip. "Well, I wanted to wait with this conversation but I suppose we can have it now. Before Petrichor returns."

Valour's heart drummed against her ribs. This was why Ingrid vexed her. Not her know-it-all tendency, her chattiness, nor her shallow socialite act. Not even how out of Valour's league she was. It was the serious conversation and prying questions.

"I suppose we can do that," Valour said, letting her fingers toy with Ingrid's to have something calming to do. "What did you want to talk about?"

"You, actually. And how you should run far away from someone like me."

"Sounds like complete bäckahäst-shit. What do you mean?"

"Direct as always." Ingrid tilted her head and smiled. "As clear and clean as a Scandinavian landscape with its lakes, pine trees, and snow."

"Huh?"

"Sorry. I'm getting rather poetic again, aren't I? I meant that there are no games, no pretence, no lies with you. As I say, clear and clean."

"I like to wash on occasion."

"You know that is not what I meant," Ingrid said, playfully swatting Valour's braid against her shoulder. Her expression grew sombre. "During my life, particularly the last few years, I've hurt people.

Lied. Kept secrets. Done things I regret. As I say, you should be with someone better." She looked as if the world weighed on her shoulders. "When I look into your eyes, though, and can sense how you see me. I feel somehow… cleaner. I know that sounds preposterous." She laughed a little. "But the truth is that I wish to atone for what I've done and be the person you seem to see. You make me want to be a better person. Is that not the vilest cliché?"

"Utterly terrible," Valour said, hearing the smile in her own voice. Unable to resist any longer, she kissed Ingrid again, hard and deep.

Breathless, Ingrid pulled away after a while. Then, she ran her hands over the chest portion of the coffee-coloured coat in a way that made Valour think she had twigged the effect the sight of those hands had on her.

"You know," Ingrid said, her fingers tiptoeing their way across the buttons. "There are times when you don't make me feel clean."

"Is that so?"

Ingrid unbuttoned the coat with movements slow enough that Valour could stop her if she wished. "Mm-hmm. Like right now. Well, I could imagine you making me a smidgeon dirty right about now."

Pleasure pulsed through Valour. "I could imagine bypassing 'a smidgeon dirty' and going straight to downright filthy." She reminded herself to stay disciplined but couldn't release her grip on Ingrid's waist. "But as I said, Petrichor and I have to explore that lead. The sooner we find Brandquist, the sooner I can stop working with the pus-sucker who's currently haunting the outhouse and we can be safe."

"We? As in Petrichor and you? Or as in Vinterstock? Or as in…?"

Valour didn't answer, because of course she had meant her and Ingrid. What about it? Wanting to keep Ingrid safe didn't mean anything more than that she didn't want her lover dead in a gutter. In place of an answer, she kissed Ingrid for a third time. It didn't take long until Ingrid's hands began wandering under the coat and the kiss turned feverish.

"Sorry. We should talk more," Ingrid breathed into Valour's

open mouth. "But I'm struggling to let you go."

"I am too." Valour kissed along the graceful column of Ingrid's throat, finally dipping her tongue into the hollow between those exquisite collarbones. She stopped herself, drawing back with a volley of curse words. "No. We can't do this. I have to wash, eat, and then leave."

"Oh, 'have to' are such foul words," Ingrid whispered, her eyes lidded and her lips parted. "Please, just one more kiss. One more taste."

Valour's resolve melted like ice on skin.

A clicking of the door told her Petrichor was back. He was frenziedly rubbing his hands. "Blasted winter."

Ingrid's mouth closed and Valour cursed and stepped away. "And this from the bloke who repeats that 'the cold builds character', huh?"

"It does," he snipped. "However, I have precisely the character I need and could now do with recollecting the sensation of not having my very marrow be frozen."

He stood by the fireplace, warming his hands.

Valour looked back to Ingrid, feeling a warmth in her chest that did not come from the flames. It wasn't only arousal either. She pulled herself together. "I'll quickly use the outhouse too. Then we'll head out, Petrichor. I can eat something on the way."

With that, she hurried out before she could change her mind.

CHAPTER 37
CLEANING AND CONCEALING

PETRICHOR PRETENDED NOT to watch Ingrid. She was unpacking food supplies in a surprisingly well-ordered and efficient way. Now this he could credit to her being the woman who aided her father in running the city's foremost hotels.

She caught him looking and to avoid the awkwardness, he turned to stoke the fire. "If Valour plans to eat on the way, I gather you are making her some form of breakfast?"

"That is the idea," Ingrid said, shelving the last items. "I shall make you some too. Oh, and this time I ensured that there are plenty of savoury items."

Had she been this polite to him the entire time? "Thank you."

"You're most welcome. May I prevail upon you to fetch some snow to melt for the tea and coffee?"

He quickly acquiesced and together they readied not only pewter cups of hot drinks, but food stuffs that could be imbibed while walking.

As they worked, Ingrid said, "I noted that Valour is wearing a new scarf."

"Is that so?"

"Mm. One that you wore before."

Petrichor picked up the kettle from the fire and started making his coffee. "Perchance woollen scarves simply sprout from the necks of us assassins?"

Ingrid gave him a long look. "A curious notion, to be sure."

He pretended not to hear and breathed in the scent of coffee. He could've sworn it fired his brain up. Would this warehouse be the final location? Would this be where he at last got to kill

239

Brandquist and have this whole affair done with?

"By the way," Ingrid said as she poured herself some tea. "The roads are frightfully icy out there. Best to take care when heading for the next clue, wherever it is."

"The warehouse? It's in the Pestilence District," he said absent-mindedly. Valour would no doubt spill all the details, so what was the point in him staying secretive? This woman hadn't gotten them killed so far. He checked where his satchel was. He had to remember to ready his pistol.

"The Pestilence District?" Ingrid said. "An ominous location to say the least."

"Indeed."

"Do be careful," she said. "Brandquist might not be trying to kill you and Valour, but I still fear you may get hurt."

"I am always careful." He tied his cravat in the reflection of one of the candlesticks. The result resembled wilted cabbage. He pulled the cravat off and shoved it in a pocket. "I cannot stay civilised in these circumstances. I shall find Brandquist this very day so I can wash and dress like a decent human again."

"Mm. 'Tis a shame that this place has no bathing facilities."

"Indeed. I shall have to get by scrubbing with snow and applying cologne."

"Would you like to borrow mine? I have my usual perfume but also a bottle of something smoky imported from the Far East. It should suit you."

"I have a bottle of scent, thank you. Vinterstock made."

He took it out and applied it. Discomfort stole upon him and after a heartbeat he figured out why: this was the cologne Halcyon's vile lover wore. How could he have forgotten about that?

"A nice crisp fragrance." Ingrid studied the tiny bottle. "I believe I have never smelled it on you."

"You haven't noticed it because any space you enter soon reeks of *your* perfume. I know it's all the rage to bathe in scent, but good lord woman, I can tell if you have been in a room a week after you vacated it."

She gave a graceful shrug. "My perfume cheers my mood. Moreover, it overpowers the foul stenches of this city."

A deafening crash rang out. Petrichor was at the ready in an instant but Ingrid waved him down. "It was only the house above. It falls apart more every day. We shall soon have to quit this place and find somewhere else to hide."

Wonderful. It was now a race to see what would happen first: them catching Brandquist or the hideout collapsing and trapping them down here. "We should not need to hide here much longer. Valour and I are both eager to take action."

"Of course. That is one of the things you have in common."

He was about to ask what else when a red-cheeked Valour stormed in, cursing about the cold.

Was she ready for what might await them in that warehouse? Was he?

He fetched his pistol, preparing to find out.

Chapter 38

THE PESTILENCE DISTRICT

As SHE CAME back in, Valour found Petrichor and Ingrid in what looked like an awkward conversation.

Petrichor tucked his pistol into a coat pocket and said, "I shall be outside, Valour. Do not dally."

"I told you I don't dawdle and that goes for dallying too. And drivelling," she replied.

"Drivelling isn't a synonym—" He stopped, realising she was yanking his chain, and sniffed. "Oh, you drivel constantly. And you're not funny." Then he left.

"Let me braid your hair," Ingrid said. "I'll be quick."

Valour let Ingrid comb her fingers through her snow-scrubbed tresses, making sure not to wince when those treasured fingers snagged in wet tangles.

"You feel so cold, darling," Ingrid said with a shiver.

"It's freezing out there. Another reason for you to stay here in the safe warmth. We shouldn't be long."

Ingrid finished the braid and tied it with the leather ribbon. "No. I wish to be there with you. Even if all I can do is call for the overseers if things go awry."

Valour regarded her.

"Don't look at me like I have gone mad," Ingrid said. "Maybe I'm curious? Or worried? Mayhap I simply enjoy being with you. Either way, there is nought you can say or do that'll make me stay here."

"I could tie you to a chair."

A flirty smirk crept onto Ingrid's face. "Only if you stay with me and do delicious things to me after you've tied me up. That is my favourite erotic game, by the way."

Joy warmed Valour's chilled limbs. How did this woman make her so bloody happy? "I'll keep that in mind. Come on, let's go. Doing delicious things to each other will have to wait."

They joined Petrichor who, at the sight of Ingrid, looked exhausted. "She's coming?"

The words had been little more than a resigned sigh.

"Not the whole way. She'll wait at a safe distance from the warehouse." Valour bumped the other woman with her hip. "Right?"

Ingrid gave a soldier's salute. "Out of sight and quiet as a mouse."

Petrichor gave a long-suffering grimace and marched west, towards the Pestilence District.

THEY ATE WHILE walking. Cheese and pickled beetroot sandwiches for the assassins and cinnamon buns for Ingrid.

"I have yet to see an unoccupied carriage," Ingrid said when she had swallowed her last bite. Then she snapped her fingers. "Why don't we save time by taking the tunnels?"

"No," Valour and Petrichor said in unison.

Valour threw him a glance. He could not have the same reason as her for not going down into the tunnels needlessly. In front of her, Ingrid checked her piled-up hair. Those hairpins suddenly appeared murderously sharp and far too many to Valour. The black cat crossing the road, the heimcrow cawing from a spindly tree branch, it all made Valour's skin crawl now.

"Perhaps you two are right. We should take in the sunlight while there is some." Ingrid carefully placed her hood over the hair. "By the way, did you know that the mushrooms grown in Vinterstock usually come from the tunnels?"

Valour couldn't answer, her throat too restricted.

Luckily, Petrichor replied. "No."

"They do. Do you realise that means the corpses you deposit down there are nutrients for the mushrooms?"

"I thought all growing things took their sustenance from the dirt?" Petrichor said, sounding reluctantly interested.

"A professor of nature studies stayed at the hotel last month," Ingrid said. "His theory is that fungi have invisible webs that they spread around them, drawing nutrients from anything they find. In the case of the tunnels, the decaying bodies you have gifted the city. Fascinating!"

"Not the word I'd choose," Valour croaked. She was desperate for... something, anything, to make her go back to normal.

Ingrid slowed until she could take Valour's hand.

Valour twitched at the touch.

"Are you all right?" Ingrid whispered. Her voice had gone from carefree to worried in an instant.

Valour weighed how much to admit. "Those shitty tunnels. I only go into them when I have to."

Ingrid searched her face. "All right. We shall avoid them."

Unaware of their conversation, Petrichor picked up the pace while saying, "Using the tunnels will not save any time. Furthermore, I will permit no more distractions or diversions. Step lively."

For once, Valour appreciated his dictatorial streak.

THE COLD HAD left the whole city quite empty, but it was nothing compared to the Pestilence District. When they passed through the high gates, they saw only cats, rats, and stray dogs scurrying through the husks of cut-rate houses that had been left as lifeless as the quarantined people who had once been forced to live in them.

"I have heard about how other cities handled the plague," Ingrid whispered. "None locked this many families up so they could infect each other without any hope of leaving. This is heart-rending."

"Valour and I are children of this city," Petrichor said. "We know very well what this is, thank you very much."

"As a child of a woman who died before the overseers could force us all to live here, I know quite well myself," Ingrid replied with iron in her voice.

That shut him up. He busied himself with retrieving a handkerchief and holding it over his mouth.

Valour wrapped an arm around Ingrid's shoulders and, in silence, they passed by house after house. A toy horse spattered with dried blood lay in front of a door. No wonder that, even in a housing shortage, no one had claimed these buildings. Too much pain, too many ghosts, too many people that could not be saved or helped. Beyond the houses was a hill, on which loomed a large building with an area of trees on either side.

"I'm assuming that's the warehouse?" Valour said, letting Ingrid go.

"Mm. Let us make haste." Petrichor sped up, then stopped dead.

She followed his gaze to the mound of dirt and rocks at his feet. The sick people here had buried each other as best they could. This grave was too shallow, though. What looked like the hem of a semi-decayed dress stuck up from the dirt. Without a word, Petrichor fetched stones from the closest garden and laid them so the dress was covered. He gave the grave a curt bow, then walked around it and towards the warehouse.

Ingrid murmured, "So he *is* human," as they followed.

They stopped behind a grouping of birch trees at the bottom of the hill. Valour had always thought their black-and-white bark and reediness made them eerie and sad, quite like the rest of the Pestilence District.

"How do you want to play this?" she asked Petrichor.

"Obviously we shall circle the building, examining for exits and any windows."

She craned her head to the left and spotted telltale glinting in the sun. "There are windows on the nearest side of the building."

"Excellent." He put on his shaded spectacles and stared at the ground. "The snow has been shovelled on the path up to the entrance." He nodded towards the large doors. "So I cannot discern how many footprints there are going in or out. Still, the shovelling tells us there has been at least one custodian present of late."

Valour watched the sunlight shimmer off the pristine snow. Petrichor had been right, it did look like sugar crystals. "So, two options: lie in wait to scope it out. Or find a way to have a gander inside."

Rubbing his unshaven chin, he replied, "Once more, you state the obvious."

"Once more, you're a rotting arsehole."

Ingrid coughed to hide a giggle, infusing a sensation of light and warmth in Valour's chest.

"We both know my method is waiting and yours is acting," Petrichor said with an air of someone thinking out loud.

"Mm-hmm. So, you're suggesting that we stay here and scope it out for as long as we can before frostbite sets in?"

"No, actually," he said, sounding amazed. "Considering the cold and how long this hunt has taken, I shall allow you to take the lead. We'll try this *The Valour Way*."

"That's the spirit." She clapped him on the back, instantly regretting it when she saw his expression.

Next, she turned to Ingrid but had no chance to say anything as the other woman held her hands up. "I know, I know. I shall stay here, out of sight, out of danger, and out of your way. You're lucky I have such a thick cloak and a diverting book to read."

Petrichor's upper lip curled but he said nought.

Retrieving a slim volume from a pocket within that yellow and sable cloak of hers, Ingrid leaned against a birch. Valour watched her, finding something she hadn't seen before: little lines by Ingrid's mouth, exactly where that frequent smile of hers would stop. That warmth returned to Valour's chest.

Ingrid made a shooing gesture towards the two assassins and then opened her book.

Pulling her collar up against a sudden gust of wind, Valour asked Petrichor, "Want to start with circling the building to see if there are any doors to the back? And if not, check out those windows?"

He rubbed his temples. Did he have another headache?

"Fine. Lead the way."

And so she did, carefully traversing the hill's untouched snow and cursing the loud crunch of it under her boots. The back of the building held nothing at all, and the right side had the same sort of windows as the left. They were high up and by them grew more trees, pines this time, their needle-covered branches obscuring part of the view inside. Probably intentional.

Valour brushed the snow off a branch of one of the pines and tested it. "I'm going to climb this tree and try to see in."

"All right. Do not attract any attention. Or fall."

"If I do fall, I'll make sure to do it on top of you."

"Bold of you to assume I plan to be anywhere near your landing area," Petrichor said, taking a demonstrative step back.

"Aww, and here I was thinking you'd catch me."

"Only children need to be caught or carried. But then, you were always extraordinarily childish."

Childish. She had loved climbing trees as a child but had only been allowed to scale buildings. She took a firm grip of the branch, trying not to remember her mother's words: *Assassins don't play, Valour. They train.*

She pulled herself up to the next branch. Perhaps she and Petrichor were childish? Their arguing certainly was. How could you be anything else when you hadn't been allowed to be a child when you were little, though?

When she had climbed to the right height, she peeped inside through the slight fog of the windows, spotting about a dozen people. Like the henchmen they had so far encountered, they more resembled farmers angered due to starvation than seasoned criminals. However, they held something she would expect from the city's largest smuggling gang—shiny new rifles. These were nothing like the brass knuckles and relic pistols they'd seen in the hands of Brandquist's henchmen so far, but the longer and more advanced flintlock rifles imported from overseas, made for war and long-distance kills.

For a moment her mind muddled again, making her light-headed. Headaches, memory loss, and dizzy spells? Was there something poisonous in the hideout? She wobbled on her branch, but her mind refocused, and she counterbalanced. She was congratulating herself on her success when she noticed her movement had caught one of the underlings' attention. He stared right up at her. Valour's heart halted. There was nought she could do but watch as he shouted a warning to the others.

Shit.

Valour examined her footing to find snow-free branches to climb down, but the swaying caused by the wind made it a slow process. She heard clicks from inside and hoped she was wrong in assuming that it was the cocking of rifles.

Double shit.

There was no more time. She climbed without caution. A shot rang out as she jumped to a lower branch. Judging by the deafening sound and the splinter of wood and snow flying past her head, it had nearly hit her. Thank Heimdal for the henchmen being shoddy shots and those fogged windows blocking some of the view. Not that there was much left of the windows now; shattering glass had accompanied the bullets, and pain alerted her to the fact that a long sliver had embedded itself in the meat of her hand.

She grunted with pain and heard Petrichor hissing something from below, but she couldn't make out what. She kept descending and shots kept hitting the tree or flying past into the air around her. She had to stay in motion to make herself a trickier target. The hand that had been pierced by the glass sliver was weak and its hold slipped on a snowy branch. She might've caught herself with her other hand and the grip of her thighs, but a scatter of buck-shot hit above her head and her ducking was one movement too many for her body to track. Valour fell. Tumbling, she scrambled for another branch while trying to avoid the shots, but her hands found nothing. The tree was out of reach and the ground was so close now. She shut her eyes and waited for either pain or death.

Her landing was impeded. Instead of her back thumping against the ground and the air being knocked out of her lungs, strong hands caught her and got her to her feet.

Petrichor let go of her to fire his pistol at their foes and shouted,

"Start running, Valour!"

She immediately scrambled through the snow, away from the never-ending bullets, which now came from the building's opened doors. These people reloaded fast. Just as she thought they were out of range of the weapons, Petrichor shouted and grabbed his shoulder.

"Did they get you?"

He croaked, "Just keep running."

They scurried towards where they had left Ingrid. She wasn't there. Frantically, Valour checked their surroundings. Could she have hidden when the shooting started?

"Over here," Ingrid called from the middle of the district. "I ran out to hail that."

Every god in Asgård must have been showing mercy because she was pointing to a carriage waiting outside the gates. Valour pulled the shard of glass out, regretting it when blood spurted from her hand, and tried to help Petrichor.

"Get away from me! I can run!" the stubborn arse bellowed.

And run they did, hearing voices behind them. At the carriage Ingrid was placating the coachman, who was complaining about shots, the area they were in, and saying that he should leave without them his since horses didn't like this sort of commotion.

"I know. I am frightfully sorry," Ingrid said sweetly. "We were a little worse for wear from drink last night and didn't realise our morning stroll had brought us into the Pestilence District." She put a hand to her brow. "Gadzooks, suddenly strangers were shooting at us. Thank goodness I found you."

The 'strangers' couldn't be heard chasing them anymore. Whether that was because they had given up or run out of gunpowder, Valour didn't know.

When the time came to get Petrichor into the carriage, he actually accepted Valour's help. Safely seated, he held his shoulder and blood poured between his fingers. Valour got in after him, aware that her own hand was dripping blood everywhere.

From outside, she heard Ingrid clink coins and say, "As promised, here is a substantial payment on top of your normal fee. For your trouble, discretion, and for you to make extra haste."

"Mm-hmm. Hopefully it'll cover the costs of cleaning up that blood," the driver said, while Ingrid got in and sat opposite the assassins.

As they drove away, Ingrid got out a snow-white handkerchief and tied it around Valour's hand. The shard had pierced right next to her Assassins of Axsten brand.

Valour panted, "Thank you. And thanks too for finding a carriage willing to come here."

"Papa has drilled two things into me since childhood. Firstly, when danger appears, run the other way. Secondly, when in doubt, pay your way out."

"I'm glad you listened," Valour said, peering back towards the warehouse.

"I haven't always. Today, I am relieved that I did."

Panic over, regret hit Valour like a punch. How could she have let that henchman spot her? She swore and slammed her head against the back of the seat.

"Do stop lurching like that," Petrichor said through gritted teeth. "Some of us were shot."

"Of course. Sorry."

Valour moved closer to examine his shoulder. His hand over the wound was drenched in blood and even with his many layers of clothing, the seat behind him was sodden too. This was more blood than she'd seen from shot wounds in the past.

"Try to slow your heartbeat," she said to him, aware that was nigh impossible for someone who had just run for their life.

He gave no reply but just stared wide-eyed at her.

She took off her scarf—the one that he, for some reason she couldn't recall, had given to her—and used it as a tourniquet. Petrichor was clenching his jaw, but muffled screams still escaped until the scarf was tied in place. The carriage bumped along a road made uneven by badly shovelled snow frozen to ice. Every jolt made more blood seep through the scarf, which was turning from its original grey to deep crimson.

She wished she could make the ride smoother. How much blood

loss was too much to recover from? She tied the tourniquet tighter, deciding that if Petrichor died, she would ensure Brandquist's death was drawn-out and excruciating.

CHAPTER 39

COLD FROM WITHIN AND WITHOUT

BACK AT THE hiding place, Petrichor swore as the pain really set in. Shock and the energy surge had kept the pain to a thrumming, cold thing while in the carriage. Now, however, he was acutely aware that hurtling metal had torn through his flesh, shattering things inside his shoulder that he could only hope would mend.

"He needs a physician," Ingrid said breathlessly.

"He won't want that," Valour said. "We're in hiding. And besides, the order does not put much stock in the city's butchers. We're taught to handle our own wounds."

Petrichor sighed with relief. The last thing he wanted now was bloodletting or purging. Thank Axsten that Valour knew his preferences. Distantly he heard Ingrid say something about running to the apothecary for supplies. He was preoccupied with staring at the soaked clothing around his shoulder. He tried to breathe through the pain as Valour opened the door for him and told him to strip down to his breeches and sit on the chair so she could have a look. Painful as it was to get undressed, he didn't question her orders. She was better at the medical side of things, mainly because she got hurt more often than he did. Sitting in only his breeches was freezing, but the pain and the blood from the now uncovered wound distracted him. That and the rage. How dare those second-rate thugs shoot him? He was going to find every last one of them and make them swallow broken glass... If he didn't bleed out in this accursed basement.

Valour came in with a bowl of tightly packed and surprisingly clean snow. She put some against both sides of his shoulder, mumbling, "Looks like it went straight through."

The cold stung but would soon numb him and halt the gush of blood. Why hadn't he thought of that?

"Yes," he said, keeping his voice steady. "I saw a blooded lead ball hit the snow after the impact."

"Good." She pushed harder with the snow. "Soon the bleeding should've reduced enough for me to have a look and see what can be done."

"The shot going through is a good thing, right?"

"Oden's gouged eye, yes! I don't want to hear you bleating as I pull something out of you, whinge-pot."

Petrichor watched the melting snow trickle down his chest and arm, mixing with all the blood. "I lack the energy to quarrel with you."

"Right. I'll give you a break. Especially as you got injured while following my plan," Valour said with some reluctance.

"I was the one to suggest we did it your way. I was aware of the risks."

Valour slumped with what he assumed was relief before removing her hand and inspecting the wound. "It's still gushing. I'm going to get more snow. I could bind it again, this time with your scarf, but I think it best to wait until Ingrid comes back with the supplies."

"I... should like some snow. It lessened the pain."

He was expecting her to call him weak. Instead, she opened the door out to the garden, saying, "Mm, being shot hurts worse than piss in the eyes. Remember when I took that pistol shot to the leg three years ago?"

"I do." Regret soured his stomach as he also remembered mocking her for complaining about it.

She returned and pulled up a chair next to him, squeezing handfuls of snow against his shoulder and wincing apologetically when he groaned. Needing something else to concentrate on, he noted that her hands were pink with blood and meltwater and probably the cold from holding the snow. It must be hurting her hands.

"You know," she said, "some still swear by a good bloodletting. I suppose you can say you're taking a cure here. You'll come out fitter than a fiddle."

"Sure." He was starting to feel tired. "I'm... sorry."

"For what? For bleeding? For being shot? I don't think you meant to do it. Not even you would go this bloody far to be an imposition on me."

The kindness in her voice took him by surprise.

He barely felt the pain, nor the snow, anymore. He was frozen all over, but it was an unnatural cold that seemed to start from within him and numb him, bit by bit. He was shivering so hard that Valour had to grip his shoulder with full force.

She examined the basement. "Can you see another bottle of Ingrid's wine anywhere?"

"Y-you're thinking of g-getting drunk-k-k?" Petrichor asked. His teeth were chattering harder now than when they had nearly died walking back from the harbour.

"Sure, sounds like fun. But mainly it was for you. For the shock, and because I don't like how cold you're getting. Hang on," she said and got up to grab his two coats and drape them over the unharmed side of his body. "There. Hopefully the coats will help some."

She took more snow from the bowl and applied it, frowning.

He guessed what she was thinking and voiced it. "W-why am I t-t-this cold?"

"The shock, the snow, the fact that there's no fire in here, and that you're topless." She grunted. "It... could also be that you've lost too much blood."

"If it is b-blood loss, what c-can you do about-t-t it?"

"Not a godsdamned thing. I'm already stopping the blood flow, and asking you to eat plenty of red meat isn't going to help in the short run." She surveyed the room again. "I should get you something sweet to drink. It won't do anything for your blood but it could help with the shock." She fetched Ingrid's half-drunk tea. "This should be mainly honey."

She held the mug so he could drink. He swallowed some, but the rest spilled down his chin due to his teeth chattering. Without a word, she put away the mug, got the last snow from the bowl, and applied it.

"If I d-don't bleed out, will I b-be all right?"

They both knew that some who were shot got a sort of poisoning of the blood. He didn't want her to say that out loud, though. She didn't.

"Sure. You're too shitty for them to want you in either Valhalla or Hel's realm. You'll have to stay alive."

She kept looking at the door. No doubt she hoped Ingrid would come crashing through it with some sort of wonder-working supplies. He doubted whatever she brought would help. He hadn't believed in wonders since he was around four years old.

Ringing filled his ears. His breathing hastened and his heart hammered so fast he dizzied. No. Not now. This was a terrible time to have one of his fits.

She sought his gaze. "Oi, are you all right?"

"I… will be."

She scrunched her nose up. "What does that mean? And why in all troll-shit have your teeth stopped chattering?"

Damnation. He would have to tell her.

"This will pass soon. I've been having… attacks."

"People have been attacking you?"

The room spun, he couldn't breathe, and he fought hard to get his words out. "Nay, you fool. My mind has. Caused by certain old memories, I think."

Valour watched him for an uncomfortably long time. "Old memories? From when you were a child?"

"Mm."

She looked like she wanted to be anywhere but here. Talking about anything but this. He knew the feeling.

She cleared her throat. "From the year you were locked in the cell?"

His pulse thudded in his ears and the weight on his chest was back. "A year? Was it a full year?"

"Maybe not," she said quietly. "I don't remember and none of the others ever talked about it."

Minutes dragged by until the lack of conversation was uncomfortable. His ears were busy with the thud of his pulse.

Beat by beat, it slowed until it went beyond that to the point of weakening.

"They only mentioned it when they used it to frighten or shame me," he admitted.

"What was that?" Valour said. "You're slurring your words."

"Never mind."

The weight on his chest had vanished, but so had every last drop of his energy. He closed his eyes but had to open them again as she shook him and shouted, "Hey, stay with me!"

"Why?"

"I don't think you should lose consciousness. Keep talking. About the order. Or these fits of yours. *Anything* as long as you stay awake."

"Do you want me to talk about the weather? The state of the roads? Fashionable garments?"

She didn't note his sarcasm. "Clothes, sure. Let's talk about the ones Ingrid brought before we went to the warehouse. Your old clothes are bloodied and shot-punched so fresh ones will come in handy. You'll have to stick with your punctured coats for now, though."

"Your lover did pick rather fine garments," he said through new shivers, making an effort to talk. "And she has a good hiding place here. Despite it collapsing. Too quiet for my taste, though. I prefer it when you can hear people about."

He just managed to keep himself from chattering his teeth by enunciating every word.

Valour tensed and watched him for what seemed an eternity. "Have you spoken to Halcyon about me?"

"Pardon? No. Why would I waste my precious time with Halcyon speaking about *you*?"

Her shoulders lowered. "Never mind. I just... Well, I thought you'd found out a detail about me and were laying some sort of trap where I'd confess to something and then you'd mock me." She surveyed his face. "But then I guess you're not really in any state for that. Ignore me."

"No. You wanted to talk. Tell me." Keeping the chattering at bay was getting harder. So was staying awake.

Valour got up and went to his pile of discarded clothes. "Something seems to be holding Ingrid up. This time *your* scarf will have to be the temporary tourniquet." She tied it around his shoulder, avoiding his gaze.

"Tell me what you thought I had talked to Halcyon about."

She slumped back down on the chair and rubbed her eyebrow. "It's, um, just that I can't stand silence in a room either. In conversations, yes, but in my living space I like noise around me. Human noise, preferably."

"Well, you were always the sociable one," he said. He swallowed down bitterness. "Venerated Sister Valour, who likes people and whom everyone likes."

"I do not like people. That's bloody slander, that is. I don't want to talk to people, it makes me exhausted. I want them to live their lives around me."

He gave up on hiding the teeth chattering. She would see him weak today. "So y-you like t-to know they're p-present, b-but not-t have them b-bother you?"

"Suppose so, yes."

"Well b-blow me down with a f-feather. We have something-g in c-common."

"Maybe it's not the only thing."

"What d-do you m-mean?" He shivered enough to nigh fall off the chair.

Valour took off the two cold coats she had draped him in and exchanged them for her own. Her body heat was still in the garment and it seeped into his skin like bliss. She put the other two coats over his lap like a blanket before going to the fireplace.

She added tinder and logs while saying, "If I tell you, you won't mock me? Dispute bloody everything? Belittle my ideas?"

"It's hard-d for me to p-promise not-t to do any of that, but you can b-be assured that-t I agree with your initial-l idea. R-reluctantly."

"See. That right there!" She pointed at him with a tinderbox. "Where did that come from? Why is our default to argue and loathe one another?"

"It's how w-we were r-raised," he said. "The order never-r made a secret of the fact that they w-wanted us fighting-g each other."

She hummed pensively while lighting the fire. "There had to be other ways to get us to compete and bring out the fighting spirit in each other, though. Without making us hate one another and think the other took what was ours? I mean, that only left us…"

"L-lonely."

"Mm." Valour slowly and quietly put the tinderbox back, staring unseeingly into the flames. "I could have had a… I don't know. Something other than a godsdamned arch-enemy."

The firewood hissed and popped when dried sap caught the flames.

Petrichor felt the impact of the book she had thrown at him as if it had just happened.

"The order t-teaches us to be hard. Having someone to c-care about and rely on-n would make us s-soft," he said. It stung to think how true that was. Only orphans without siblings were chosen. And as adults, the order came before any family or friends. Love was a weakness, and so not for Assassins of Axsten.

He watched her poking the fire and couldn't help but add, "Nevertheless, being t-told to be cruel to one another d-doesn't excuse the worst-t insults you threw at me."

Valour faced him. "Which ones?"

He was warming up, but the cold pit in his stomach froze him from within. How could he say those words out loud? He should forget all about this and just sleep. Fall into darkness and never wake, never hurt or be cold again.

"Tell me which ones you mean." Valour's voice was quiet and imploring rather than commanding. "If you don't, how can I keep from saying them again?"

"Like 'What d-did your p-parents die of-f anyway? B-boredom from-m talking to you?' Or the l-lovely, 'I bet your p-parents died from the pox. Or were too b-boneheaded to find jobs so they starved-d on the streets like newborn puppies.' R-remember those?"

Discreetly, he burrowed deeper into the warmth of her coat.

He wanted to sit closer to the fire but wouldn't change topic. Not now. He had long wondered how she'd react when he threw those words back at her.

Valour's face reddened. "Oh, right. That was all bäckahäst-shit. Only things I heard the others say. I liked to make jokes to make the adults laugh and pay attention to me. And I liked to hurt you. Repeating that drivel fit both categories."

"I'm glad to have been of use to you."

His teeth chattered little enough now that he could speak properly. Good. Even better that Valour looked like she had taken a hard blow to the stomach.

She scrubbed a hand over her face. "It may not be an excuse but you were constantly mocking me, correcting me, insulting me, and making me look bad. So, I said what I thought would shut you up. To fight back. To hit you back."

"Not that first day. The first day I came to the sanctum. You insulted me right away and threw a rock at me."

She fixed her gaze on his. "My mother, who was my world, had just been hanged. The other assassins made me watch, so I could be hardened." Her throat bobbed. "Then they said a new child would be accepted into the order, one who was colder and tougher than me. Ten minutes later, you walked up like you bloody well owned the place."

He grabbed the edge of the seat, exhaustion dizzying him. "Does any of that make what you did to me right?"

"No. I was trying to get air by stealing yours." She swallowed visibly again. "I'm sorry."

The only sound in the room was the crackling of the fire.

"So am I," he finally croaked. "Well, except for the things you deserved."

"Right back at you."

Time dragged on. What was keeping Ingrid? Petrichor watched more red seep into the scarf. Almost as disconcertingly, there was a pool around his chair of meltwater and blood. What would happen if he fell asleep? He would be wholly at Valour's mercy.

She was drumming her fingers against the top of the fireplace. "Do you remember the crystallised sugar sticks?"

"Pardon?"

"The sugar sticks we got. Back when Sister Glass ran the order. She used to give us those when we made each other cry, bleed, or run away."

He had forgotten that. It wasn't only sugary treats either, but praise and attention.

"I remember."

"Arseholes. Still," Valour murmured, "I should have baited you about your faults, like your lack of empathy or your arrogance. Not things you couldn't help. Or things that aren't actually flaws."

Was his heart beating too slow? "Like?"

"You know…" She squirmed. "Like being an orphan, wanting everything clean, and—when we got older—not having sex. Those aren't flaws and I'd never mock anyone else for them. With you, however, I can't stop myself."

"The fault does not only lay with you. I stabbed into your sore points too, seeking out what would hurt the most."

"You… never mocked me about my mother," Valour said quietly, her gaze locked on the fire. "And that meant a lot to me."

"Don't thank me. It was a close thing many times. To be honest, I would have used that ammunition if I didn't know how much it hurt when you taunted me about my dead parents. And I did not even remember mine."

He cursed inwardly. Fatigue and pain, it was making him too honest.

"If you had used it, you'd have gotten praise from the other members. Bloody monsters," Valour said while violently poking the fire. "Some because it's in their nature and some because the order raised them to be that way. Except Halcyon, he's obviously not a monster."

Halcyon. Just thinking about him made Petrichor somewhat warmer and energised, like he had a belly full of coffee.

"Halcyon rarely pitted us against each other or hit us," he said.

"The few times he did, it was because he was equally afeared of, and beholden to, the adults as we were."

Petrichor could see the black-haired, gangly, adolescent in his mind's eye. Could see how he winced whenever he had to mistreat them.

"True," she said. "In fact, I remember him taking a lot of beatings that were meant for me."

"He did that for me too."

Moreover, things had improved when Halcyon became leader. But by then, the damage to him and Valour had been done.

Valour scrubbed her face with her hands. "No children should grow up like we did."

Petrichor thought about the orphans he'd seen in the city over the last few days. "If I survive and get that reward, I plan to do something about that."

"I thought you'd use the reward to pay your leaving fee?"

The leaving fee. A repayment, that was how the order framed it. Repaying them for the coin they wasted on keeping him alive. Wasted. How had he never realised that everyone deserved to be kept alive?

He swayed in his seat and blinked a few times to clear spots in his vision. "I doubt the reward will be enough. Even if I did add it to my savings to repay the debt later, it would not feel right. Something must be done about the children of Vinterstock."

"It must."

He worried Valour would add something sugary or pitying. But no, she merely watched him with those eyes that always looked sad. Even when she laughed or joked, sadness always brimmed underneath. Except for when...

He made himself voice what he was thinking. "You should not push her away. She's not like the watchmaker. Let her in, because she makes your eyes less sad," he mumbled before he could stop himself.

"Huh?"

"Nothing. My mind is not my own. Fetch, um, more snow. I can feel my shoulder completely again and the throbbing is making me want to tear my eyes out."

She didn't argue or ask him to say please, only got up and went out for snow.

Petrichor thought about the order. About the letter he had burned, and the one he had not. Of futures he could've had and how he might not have one at all anymore. He did not believe in an afterworld but if there was one, what would he say to those he had killed?

When Valour came back, she wasn't alone. Ingrid was with her, carrying a basket full of objects.

"A thousand apologies for my tardiness," she panted. "I couldn't find a carriage and so had to walk the entire way. When I at last arrived, the apothecary was slow and bursting with questions. I had a hard time to convince her not to call the overseers."

Valour replied but Petrichor couldn't make the words out. She sounded as if she spoke from far away. The edges of his vision were blackening and the room spun. He opened his mouth to say something but found his muscles turning to melting wax and his mind shutting down. Unconsciousness swallowed him whole before he knew if it was death or sleep.

CHAPTER 40
TAKE THIS WALTZ

VALOUR RUBBED HER forehead, glad that her headache was finally letting up a little. She paced around the mattress where she had placed the unconscious Petrichor yesterday. Since then, he'd slept like the dead. The depth of sleep was nothing new for him. The length of the sleep? That was another matter.

"Oh, by the way," Ingrid said while turning a page of her book. "Did I tell you that Papa is coming home early from his trip?"

"No," Valour said, still circling Petrichor.

"The Kronovall manager passed on a missive from him when last I was there. Papa turned poorly and decided to return early."

"Sorry to hear he's unwell."

"He employs the best physicians, he'll soon recover. Nevertheless, I shall go see him when he's back."

"Of course."

Valour crouched down by Petrichor, noting his ashen and clammy face. "Maybe we should wake the arse-wipe and give him something to eat or drink?"

"Leave him be. You said yourself it's good that he sleeps."

"I suppose so. Maybe we should've taken him to a physician after all?"

"You have already said that. Thrice."

She stood. "Have I?"

"Yes." Ingrid put the book down next to her bottle of elderberry wine. "Come here."

Valour strode over and Ingrid took her hands, saying, "Your worry does you credit, but he'll be fine."

Not wanting to talk about him, Valour gave a half shrug. She didn't want to talk at all, since that was what they'd been doing the entire day. Well, that, sleep, eat, read, and share kisses. Her headache had prevented the kisses from turning into something more intense.

"I should do something," Valour said. Her hands, still resting in Ingrid's, were the only part of her that didn't buzz with restlessness. "Perhaps some of my exercises, or shadowboxing, or… I don't know. I need to do something physical, though."

Ingrid looked at Valour's hand in her own and slid their fingers against each other over and over again until they were so snugly interlaced that only a fool would miss the suggestiveness. "Your headache allowing, I can think of something physical we can do."

Just like that, Valour's blood sang. "How much wine have you had? Are you suggesting we fuck behind a shelf with Petrichor mere steps away, sweet cloudberry? Or out in the stinky outhouse?"

Ingrid grimaced and squeezed Valour's hand in reproach. "Do not be absurd, not the outhouse. We could, however, slip out into the garden and lean against a wall."

"It's freezing."

"Oh, come. Do not tell me you haven't had amorous refreshments in the open air before. Even in winter," Ingrid said. "We'd stay dressed but open buttons and tug up skirts. We would be quick about it. Petrichor would not know. Or even notice we were gone."

The temptation was heady and bonfire-hot. "Sure, but he's also as annoying as a shitty rash and will wake and shout for someone to mop his brow right in time to ruin my climax."

"Oh, it's all about your climax, huh?" Ingrid said. The laughter in her voice was godsdamned delicious.

"Not when you sound so amazing when you hit yours," Valour said. "Come to think of it, I think giving you yours is my favourite thing."

Ingrid leaned in for a kiss, her mouth tasting of booze and elderberry, before saying, "I appreciate the plural possibilities of 'yours' there."

"And I appreciate your ability to give so many repeat

performances." Valour's whole body pulsed with heat. Hel's realm, she could normally control her urges better than this. "If we do brave the cold and you let me run my hand up your thigh, I think today we should aim for at least thr—"

She was cut off by Petrichor groaning behind her. The annoying troll didn't look awake but stirred and grumbled. For a beat, Valour considered pulling Ingrid outside anyway.

"It seems," Ingrid said, kissing Valour's hand and then raking her teeth over the knuckles, "that we must table this conversation."

"True, my beautiful, bitey beast."

She gave Ingrid a wink, then grabbed the bowl of candied ginger and pulled up a chair next to her annoying patient. She sat there cross-legged and munched on the sweet-spicy treats, staring at him until his long eyelashes fluttered.

"Confirmed. He *is* waking up. All fun is over," she called to Ingrid, who had returned to her book.

Petrichor opened his eyes fully and moaned like a dying man. "What... Where...?"

"Let me guess. What day is it? It's Thursday, named after good old Tor." She popped another piece of ginger into her mouth. "Where are you? The basement of a crumbling house. And if you're wondering who you are, you are a pus-filled boil on the face of mankind, with a stick up your arse. How is the stick today, by the way? Suitably lodged?"

"Monstrous churl," he croaked.

"Charming as ever. Want some water?"

"No. How long was I unconscious?"

"You've been out like a blown candle since yesterday. Right now, it's..." She turned to Ingrid. "What time is it exactly?"

"Precisely four minutes past seven in the evening," Ingrid said after consulting the timepiece in her necklace.

"There you go. You've missed some really cracking meals. Still, my mother used to say the body heals best while sleeping, so there's that. How do you feel?"

He rubbed his eyes. "Vexed to have wasted so much time. Did you...?"

"Carry on hunting Brandquist without you? Nay, I spent my time doing useful things here. With someone who, unlike you, is interesting." She thumbed towards Ingrid.

"One of those useful things being caring for your wound, Master Assassin," Ingrid said, wetting her finger to turn a page. Was it necessary to lick her finger that slowly and with so much perfect pink tongue?

"Right, yes," Valour said, gaze back to Petrichor. "Before you conked out, I cleaned, sewed, and bandaged your wound. Then I dressed you in your new clothes, which was a pig of a job since you weigh more than expected. Have you been swallowing bricks?"

He touched his shoulder. "I should heal with time, then?"

"If you're lucky." She ate another piece of ginger, not surprised that he hadn't thanked her. "If not, the stitches might rip. The wound can become infected. The lead can get into your blood." She shrugged. "Oh, and something deep inside you could have ruptured and that was why there was so much blood."

"Unsympathetic brute," he said with a groan. "You could not be less helpful if you were a snow shovel made of dust."

A part of her had truly believed they would be kinder to each other after what they'd been through. Still, their tones of voice were at least less hostile. "I thought you'd want an honest answer and to be given every scrap of information."

"I would," he said. He closed his eyes. "And I appreciate that you did not sugar-coat anything."

"Oden's gouged eye, did you just admit to appreciating something I did?"

"You caught me in a diminished state." He scratched his bristly chin. "I need to wash up and try to shave."

"What, with your knife? No chance, you overgrown hibernating hedgehog. You'd probably slit your throat. You need food and drink first."

He glared at her but didn't argue. "Coffee would restore me, but I suppose I must make do with water and whatever sugary nonsense you have to eat."

Valour crossed her arms over her chest. "Ask nicely and I'll make you coffee."

"Shan't. I am too fatigued for your ridiculo—"

Ingrid shut her book with a slam. "Is that how long you could make it before quibbling like children again? Ye gads, you two are exhausting." She faced Petrichor. "There's some cold meats, slices of root-vegetable pie, and a bottle of fresh milk on the table. I shall make you coffee while Valour gets some snow to melt for you to wash with."

"Anything to make you stink less," Valour agreed.

Petrichor pulled himself up to sitting. "And some privacy too, please."

"Obviously," she replied. "Do you think I want to have to watch your pasty, naked man-bum?"

WHEN PETRICHOR HAD been given everything he needed, Valour and Ingrid went out into the garden to give him privacy. She wondered if they were still about to have sex, surprised to realise that she would be equally happy just doing nothing together.

"The skies are so clear tonight," Ingrid said as she leaned her back against Valour's chest.

Valour enveloped the shorter woman in an embrace, searching for topics that might interest her. After a while, faint dancing shimmers of green crept onto the horizon.

"Oh! I love the northern lights," Ingrid said with reverence.

"If they have any sense, I'm sure they love you back."

Valour bit her tongue. Too much.

"What a sweet notion," Ingrid said.

Valour concentrated on the lights as purples joined the greens and the streams spread across the sky. The northern lights were rare at this latitude and Valour didn't often stop to watch them anyway. They had an inexplicable quality to them, like they weren't of this earth but part of the olden magic, the Norse gods decorating the sky for some feast.

Ingrid glanced towards the house. "Do you think his shoulder will be all right?"

"I do. He heals annoyingly well. I should know, I stabbed him once."

Ingrid studied her. "Sometimes I'm not sure if you are joking or not."

"Good. You read me far too well far too soon in our acquaintance. It's about bloody time I kept you guessing."

"Fair enough." Ingrid rubbed her nose, making it pinker than even her rouged cheeks. "Argh, I hate how cold my vexing nose gets."

"Why is it vexing?"

"Nothing specific. It's one of the few things I inherited from Mama, but I prefer Papa's longer, more regal nose. I wish I would have gotten that."

"Your nose is fine." Valour realised she should say something more. "The way it's sort of upturned like that? Adorable."

"Thank you. This sort of nose suited Mama better, though. I miss how she used to scrunch it up when she laughed."

They kept looking up and Valour tightened her hold on Ingrid. The stars that could be seen were unusually bright. The moon didn't want to be outdone, though. It was full and butter-yellow. The purples and greens swirled around it all, like cream being poured into tea. Hel's realm, Valour had never seen the dark this almost magically luminated. Or so colourful. And... shit... she'd never felt this comfortable in someone's presence.

She shut her lips tight so the words in her mind didn't spill out. But something about this night, about the earlier sharing concerning dead parents, about this bewildering woman, made her open her mouth. "My father. I've mentioned him before, right?"

"Yes," Ingrid said, voice thick with empathy. "You said he was addicted to alcohol and drowned himself."

"Right." She shuffled her feet, more from unease than the cold. "I don't remember much about him other than that he was a foreign sailor who drank because he was sad all the time. My mother always said I had his eyes, though." She quickly added, "And don't give me that 'Oh, did he not want them anymore?' joke."

"Of course not." Ingrid jolted. "Especially not as I know how hard it is for you to open up."

No. Right. She wasn't in one of her usual inns with drunk doxies and dockworkers. Or with the spiteful assassins. Or talking to herself.

She cleared her throat. "This is ridiculous but whenever someone mentions that it's unusual to see a Vinterstockian with a year-round tan and such dark brown eyes, I feel... shit, I don't know... connected to a man who died before I could know him. Like a—" She cut off and rubbed her face.

"Please don't stop."

"I feel... like a part of him is neither dead nor forgotten, as long as I carry him with me in my eyes."

"That doesn't sound ridiculous to me," Ingrid said, taking on a far-away expression. "In my teens, my voice started sounding like Mama's. Saying my own name became soothing, sounding like when she did it." Her breathing became shaky on the last words.

Valour tensed. What if Ingrid cried? That would twist her heart like a godsdamned rag.

"My fondest memories of Mama are of her dancing," Ingrid said quietly. "She used to love to waltz. She taught me, you know. Both how to lead and to follow, so I could take on either role." She laughed under her breath. "I wonder if she guessed I'd need that in my love life."

"I can't dance to save my life," Valour said. "Halcyon tried to teach me the minuet and the gigue back when I was courting my first girlfriend. He ended up with a sprained big toe and refused to dance with me ever again."

It did Ingrid credit that she was neither smiling nor sniggering but looked genuinely surprised. "I would have thought you'd be well served by the training in balance and careful foot placement I assume assassins receive?"

"We're trained in that, yes. I think my problem isn't so much the footing but the rhythm. I get impatient and move too fast."

"Ah, the waltz should work well for you, then. It cannot be rushed, and you hold onto someone the entire time, allowing you to feel the rhythm through their body. Want to try?"

Valour gave a one-shouldered shrug.

"Don't look like I am suggesting we chop off our heads, darling. 'Tis only dancing. I shall lead so you can focus on your footing and the rhythm."

Ingrid stood in the middle of the garden, bathed in the various lights of the sky, and held her arms out. That kind smile. Those clever eyes. That understanding woman. Before she knew what she was doing, Valour had stepped into her embrace.

"We'll have a go," Valour said. "Don't blame me if I try your patience, though."

"I can be exceedingly patient."

"That makes one of us," Valour said, wondering how waltzing in snow would work.

"I know. No matter, I am content to be patient for both of us."

"Right. So, um, where do I put my feet?"

"About hip distance apart," Ingrid replied. "Good. Now, I'll place my hands here." She put one hand on Valour's back and wrapped her other one around Valour's right hand.

Ingrid's closeness brought a waft of her perfume and Valour had to fight not to burrow her face into the crook of Ingrid's neck and sniff and kiss and whisper affections. Would this woman ever stop making Valour feel so... She searched her feelings. Weak? No, that sounded like a bad thing. Submissive? No, that was too drastic. She settled on reverent. Petrichor was wrong, though. It didn't mean she was falling for Ingrid. She could put a stop to this whenever and however she wished. She just didn't want to.

She squeezed Ingrid's hand. "You know, it's bloody hard not to kiss you when you're this close."

With a reproaching quirk of the eyebrow, Ingrid gave her a quick peck. "There. One kiss is all you get. Now concentrate and put your left hand at the top of my shoulder." She watched as Valour obeyed and said, "Perfect."

"Thank you. I'm good with where to put my hands."

Ingrid laughed. "If you start that naughtiness, I shan't be able to teach you."

Valour opened her mouth to sling out a cocky flirtation but

what came out was a heartfelt, "Sorry. Dancing your mother's favourite dance must mean a lot to you."

"No need to apologise," Ingrid said, clearly taken aback. "Um. Right. Back to the waltz. You are aiming for an elegant and taut frame. Keep your elbow sticking out and straighten your back, leaning a little away from me."

Stiffly, awkwardly, Valour manoeuvred herself into what she assumed was the correct position.

"Excellent," Ingrid said. "Now, I shall step forward with my left foot and at the same time, you stride back with your right foot. Try to bend your right leg slightly and step on the ball of your foot."

"Like this?"

"Yes, precisely. Now," Ingrid said, "I shall lead you as we move to the sides, back and forth, and then close our feet together. I'll count to three so you get the rhythm of the non-existent music."

"All right. What do I do?"

"You simply keep close to my body so you can follow and mimic my movements."

Valour nodded. She had to get this right.

After a few stumbles, luckily without anything being sprained, she got the basics of it. They waltzed on, shuffling the snow away from their makeshift dance floor with every step. After a while, Ingrid's counting to three quieted, and a little later Valour noted that her frame had softened and her gaze was in the middle distance.

"Hey, where are you?" Valour asked.

Ingrid's eyes refocused. "I'm right here."

"Your body is, but your mind's elsewhere."

"Right. My apologies, I was thinking about... you. And things I want to tell you."

"Well," Valour said, checking her foot placement before looking back up, "we're alone. Go ahead and tell me."

"I fear it is not that easy. I'm... worried. About you."

"Why? Because of the hunt for Brandquist?"

Ingrid's eyes widened. "Yes."

"No need. Brandquist is a challenge but nothing I can't handle. In fact, so far he's been less dangerous than I thought he'd be."

"I know you can look after yourself. Nevertheless, I worry about you."

"What you should be worrying about is how long we can dance without me causing any incidents," Valour said, nodding at their feet.

Ingrid didn't laugh or even smile. In fact, her mouth drew downwards. "Please do not change the topic. We must discuss how much I... I worry about you being around me."

Valour stopped halfway into a backwards step. "Why? Is it because of that bäckahäst-shit you said before? About not deserving me?"

Ingrid stopped too. "Yes." Her gaze was fathoms away again and excruciatingly sad. "There are things I have yet to tell you. But I cannot. It's complicated and I ought to stay quiet, for others' sakes as well as mine."

Thinking hard, Valour picked up the steps again. There must be a way she could take the pain off that beautiful face. "What if you try saying some of it? Even just a bit? Then you can unburden yourself but without spilling the whole thing." Valour hurried to add, "I mean, if you want to. We hardly know each other; you don't owe me any truths."

"I disagree with your last point. That's another matter, though. Let us just leave it at..." Ingrid squeezed her eyes shut. "I wish I could change my life. Start over and make better decisions. Be the daughter and heir that Papa expects. Be better for everyone. Be better for you."

"I'm sure we all wish we could be better people."

"No." Ingrid's eyes shot open. "Not everyone does. But you do and I love that about you."

Love. Valour stumbled. What were they doing, dancing and talking like they were in love? This wasn't just too much, this was too fast, too... everything. "My point was that you don't have to tell me any secrets." Valour looked away. "In fact, it's better if you don't. If you did I'd be expected to tell you mine, and mine... are full of childhood abuse, shitty behaviour, and corpses."

A heimcrow cawed from a tree behind Valour. It sounded like a warning.

Ingrid stepped out of the embrace. "No telling of secrets?" She wrung her hands over and over. "All right. Another time? I cannot, but still must, tell you something."

Her tone was pleading, exposed even, and a part of Valour regretted her decision to shut the discussion down. All the other parts, however, screamed for these serious conversations to stop. For everything to stop so she could get control again.

And so, Valour's only reply was a vague hum.

With hands that weren't quite stable, Ingrid fiddled with the many layers of snow-white lace at her sleeves. "I think I'll go commandeer some food supplies from the hotel. I may be a while, since I should also like to spend some time with Papa. If he has returned, that is."

"Naturally. As long as you avoid Brandquist's underlings, stay as long as you need."

Ingrid still fretted with the lace. "Hopefully it is just some mild ague from which he'll recover swiftly."

"I'm sure he will."

Valour put her hands in her pockets to keep from either drawing Ingrid in or pushing her away. Ingrid, meanwhile, still looked like she wanted to talk about something serious.

For a spell, the distant noises of the city and that solitary heimcrow's cawing were the only sounds.

"I should get going, then." Ingrid stole a kiss, her lips cold and insistent against Valour's, and then she went inside.

Valour stayed in the garden, despite being freezing, swaying on the spot and wondering what in Hel's realm was wrong with her.

CHAPTER 41

THE GIVEN GIFT

PETRICHOR WAS WRUNG out like a washerwoman's rags and on top of the pain in his shoulder, his head throbbed. His weakness and helplessness shamed him to the core. Was that shame normal? Was it right? He thought of his long sleep and recalled something like dreams, or hallucinations, at one point. He had been followed through the streets by a man he could not see. Then, somehow, he had been back in the archive with Halcyon's lover. And this time he had asked her if she *did* know his name, if she knew the sanctum, and if she knew what Halcyon needed and deserved. In response, she had laughed with the voice of a dozen people and sliced his shoulder open with her razor. Now, in the cold but blissfully real light of wakefulness, a chill ran down his spine. He was glad that he normally never dreamed.

Valour lifted his bandages. "There's a little bleeding but no sign of infection."

"Thank Axsten for that."

She replaced them. "Considering the blood loss and your hindered mobility, we'll need to wait quite a while before we carry on the hunt."

"We? Are you certain you do not mean 'I'?"

"We, you paranoid pus-sucker. I told I would do this with you and I will. Unless you want me to go without you?"

"I shall countenance nothing of the sort." He caught himself and shook the tyrant out of his tone. "I mean, I… would appreciate it if you didn't."

"Then I won't. I'm a woman of my word."

He slumped. Of course she was. Valorous Valour, ever to be

admired, ever better than him. She did look disappointed to not be able to go, though. He couldn't blame her. The order was unlikely to let them share the bonus; only the one who killed got rewarded.

She blew out the burned-down candles and replaced them with fresh ones. "We should discuss next moves, anyway. Make some sort of a plan."

Petrichor shifted his arm, seeing how much movement he had, and shots of scorching pain went through him. "Planning would be good. It has not been our strong suit so far."

"Mm. I'm assuming Brandquist and his underlings will have cleared out of the not-so-abandoned warehouse, since he knows we're aware of it now."

"Not necessarily. Not if he believes the shot to scare us off worked," Petrichor said while putting his shirt on, shrugging off Valour's hand when she tried to help. "Or if he has fortified the warehouse even further so that anyone approaching is shot or steps into a bear trap."

Slowly and agonisingly, he pulled on his clothes. Tying a cravat was out of the question, though. Meanwhile, Valour tapped her fingers in a waltz rhythm against the table, clearly lost in thought.

Utter fatigue struck, causing Petrichor to sway in his chair. How long did it take for blood to replenish? He made himself sound strong and coherent as he said, "I need an hour or so of rest. We can discuss how to approach the warehouse after that. Then we must act. It makes sense to do so during the cover of night."

"An hour?" Valour spluttered. "You've nearly frozen to death, bled out, and not eaten or drunk enough. Your wound is still leaking *and* we don't know if lead got into your blood."

Petrichor sniffed. "Are you implying that two hours would be wiser?"

"TWO HOURS? Tell me you're jesting," she groaned at him. "Take at least another night to sleep and heal. Otherwise, you'll be of no use to me. We'll head out tomorrow morning."

"That is a long time."

"I need to recuperate as well," Valour said. "Hel's realm, Ingrid keeps finding bruises on me and my cut hand is still throbbing."

She blinked a few times. "The godsdamned dizziness and headache aren't helping."

She wasn't fooling him, though normally she would've worked through any pain to finish the job and claim the bounty. She was giving him a gift.

He rubbed the back of his head. "I have quite a headache myself."

"Seems to be a trend with us lately. Probably the stress and lack of rest. Let's allow our bodies to heal a smidge. We'll discuss the plan when we wake tomorrow morning."

Why was he suddenly feeling like a child? "All right."

He watched her blow out the candles and get on her back on the makeshift bed, hands under her head. Only then did he lay down on the mattress and curl up in the least uncomfortable position. Was Valour going to get up as soon as he was unconscious? The room spun. He cursed and shut his eyes against the sensation, falling headfirst into sleep so dark and thick it could've been a vat of black treacle, and knew no more.

CHAPTER 42

ATTACK

VALOUR WAS UP long before sunrise. Petrichor was deep asleep. Quietly, she lit a candle and ate some rye bread and cheese. She snuck out into the moonlit garden, breathing in the ice-crisp air and wishing she was working this case alone. She would've been in that warehouse days ago.

To pass the time she went to the trees at the bottom of the garden, placed her candle in a safe spot, and found a solid branch at a good height. She took off her coat, then began doing an exercise invented by Axsten himself after he was pushed off a bell-tower and realised he had to be strong and agile enough to always be able to haul himself back up—hence the name, 'haul-ups'. She paused occasionally to run laps, then went back to the branch. Soon after sunrise found her tree, Valour paused mid haul-up. She'd spotted something in the neighbouring garden. She hung still, squinting to see in the overgrowth and layers of snow.

Movement. Something light blue by a set of pine trees.

In a flash, it was gone. It had reminded her of something, but what? Could stress really mess up her memory like this? Light blue. Silky. With powder-yellow details. Oh yes, the bloke in the ridiculous silk coat who'd followed her. She dropped down and crept closer. She stared between the trunks of the trees that separated the two plots, but all she saw were tiny blue-and-yellow birds scrambling for pine cones. Was that what she'd seen?

Whump.

A mass of blue jumped down from the tree right in front of her. She leapt back, grateful for her trained reflexes as she dodged the first blow. The man in the blue coat stared down at her, his right fist

277

still raised. He was as tall as she remembered and held one of those foreign military sabres in his other hand.

Thank the gods she'd strapped on her knife belt before coming out here.

"You were not to see me there, wench," he said with a thick accent. "There are times I have wanted you to see me, this was not one. You are not meant to be hanging from trees."

"I'm sorry that my exercise ruined your skulking, but you really shouldn't wear that inane coat if you don't want to be spotted," Valour replied, drawing both her knives. "Who in all troll-shit are you?"

"I suppose there is no way I can leave and we can discuss this next time our paths cross? Perhaps sitting in those gold-dripping chairs in your room at the Hotel Kronovall, yes?"

He had been to her home.

"None whatso-bloody-ever," she said, moving her knives so they'd glint in the morning light.

He jabbed again and Valour ducked while noting his posture and methods, planning her counter-attack. His moves were quick but measured, so her usual style of fighting hard and dirty wouldn't work well here. This man would've struggled more with a controlled combatant. Shit. Petrichor would have been perfect for this.

"Why are you following us?" she asked, dodging another blow.

He returned to his precise stance, ready for another punch. Why wasn't he attacking with the sabre?

"Because if I desire my payment, I must know where you little assassins are."

Knives in both hands, she resorted to kicks and swore as he moved, resulting in her hobnailed boot missing his kneecap by a fraction and only hitting his thigh. He screamed but wasn't incapacitated.

"Why?" She evaded his right hook. "To spy on us for Brandquist?"

"Do not be ridiculous," he spat. "Do I look like the wretches that your *Brandquist* hires these days?"

He didn't. He was well dressed, even if oddly so, and an experienced fighter. He carried himself like a soldier and that sabre told her the rest. This was a former military man who'd turned to mercenary work up here in the hidden-away North. She'd seen enough of them to recognise the type. They were vicious, as crime or violent offences were often why they'd been forced to leave the military.

"I am not spying on you either," he said, his gaze on her knives. "I am waiting."

"For what? An invitation to play cards?"

She kicked at his middle, but he moved so it only grazed him. This was a fight of near misses. Bloody infuriating.

"Very droll. Nay. Waiting to kill you."

He punched her arm and this blow connected, nearly making her drop the longest of her knives. She was godsdamned lucky he hadn't aimed for her injured hand. This time.

"That makes no sense," she said through gritted teeth. "If you've been following us, why haven't you gone for the kill?"

He grinned. "I must wait for the situation. It must be right."

That grin made her decide that cutting him a smidge wouldn't be a problem. He only had to be able to talk. She slashed with her knife at his exposed side. But he blocked the blow and she cut the back of his wrist instead.

"What are you babbling about?" she asked.

He lowered his sliced arm, dripping blood onto the trampled snow, and instead raised the one holding the sabre. The weapon was sharpened to perfection but scratched from use, making her heart pound against her ribcage in exhilaration as well as fear. No, this wasn't one of the sad underlings she'd fought lately. This was the real thing.

"Nothing is simple or rational in this absurd city of yours. It's all—how do you say?—convoluted mystery. And bizarre magic rituals. No logic. That I must wait until all the players are in the right place before doing my job proves that," he said conversationally.

Magic rituals? What in the troll-shit? She held on to the facts. "So, you can't kill me now?"

He feinted with the sabre, making her move to the right. Then, the cunning arsehole used her dodge to kick his boot up into her exposed side, just between her ribs and her hip.

"I cannot," he agreed. "I can chop off an arm or stab your foot, though."

She breathed past the pain that radiated through her. "Care to tell me when the players will be in the right spot or whatever poetic shit you said?"

"Nay. You shall know when it happens. My employer, who I admit might be quite mad, wants you to die in a very specific way. I believe a scryer saw it happen that way."

She didn't answer, busy trying to guess what move Petrichor would've made next. She had to be meticulous and precise.

The mercenary lunged to the side, changing his footing, as he kept talking. "And I will not question it. For the fee I'm receiving, I will gladly move you and your friends into a certain scenario, like chess pieces on a board, and then slaughter you. 'Tis child's play, yes?"

"As a child, my play was beating up ugly bullies like you," she said, having decided on her next move.

"You are the ugly one, peasant."

She waited until the tall man lunged down at her with his sabre again, jerked back a mere whisker from the blade, and when his head came closer on his downward swing, she lifted her arm and swiped the blade over his scalp. The knife sliced at the top of his forehead, taking less hair than she would've liked, but causing plenty of blood flow that would impair his vision in the fight.

Tossing his head to get the blood out of his eyes, he roared, "Enough of this!" He pulled out a long-barrelled pistol from a holster inside his coat and aimed it at her thigh.

"Ugh. A pistol? You're ruining the fun," Valour said.

Yet, she was delighted that he'd felt cornered enough to abandon the fair fight.

"Have a care, wench. I know where to shoot to ensure you can never use this limb again. A problem for someone who, like you, uses her legs to run around like a headless chicken and wrap them around other women."

He'd watched her do laps around the garden then. And gods knew what else.

As she considered her options, she answered, "Meanwhile, you seem like a creep of an arsehole who I'll enjoy beating boneless with a meat mallet one day."

He smirked, using his free hand to wipe away the blood and only making a worse mess since the hand was bleeding too. "Such confidence, such righteousness. You believe you have all the answers, do you not?" He spat when the blood dripped onto his lips. "Tell me, Valour the Assassin. Do you have headaches? Dizziness? Memory loss? Confusion?"

That hit her harder than his blows had. How in Hel's bloody realm did he know that?

A clatter made them both jolt. Someone was coming down the road and shouting. Valour cocked her head in their direction to listen. They were night soil men, offering their services. What were they doing on a street where no one was meant to live? Were they lost? Or just drunk as usual?

When she looked back to her foe, the shitbag was running off. She had never known anyone outside of the order move so soundlessly. She sprinted after him but he was fast, had a head start and much longer legs, and she was knackered after her workout. Two streets away, he must've run into one of the many identical gardens, not even leaving tracks in the snow. Had he swung from the bloody trees? Valour stayed and searched a little longer, cursed up a storm, and lumbered back to the hideout.

She tossed her clothes inside and rolled around naked in a snowdrift right outside the door. She did it to wash and to calm her aching muscles, but mostly because the pain of the cold distracted her from how godsdamned furious she was.

CHAPTER 43
ANOTHER BLOODY
(AND DEADLY) MYSTERY

PETRICHOR WOKE TO Valour slamming the door leading out to the garden. She was stark naked, dripping with melting snow, and in one of her rages.

He groaned under his breath. So, it was to be one of those days.

She shook the worst of the snow off like a dog and pulled on the clothes Ingrid had brought, a process slowed by her pausing to curse, kick the wall, or toss about items of clothing.

He pulled himself up into sitting position, wishing he could at least have some coffee before asking the obvious question. "Did someone steal your garments?"

She stared at him as if she had forgotten he existed. "What? No."

"I see. Care to inform me of what has happened?"

In terse sentences, she explained that she'd just fought a man who'd been following them and detailed what he had said about killing them at a certain time and in a specific way, neither of which he would divulge. Obviously. Her every paragraph was punctuated by her using her britches as a whip to hit a chair with headache-inducing thwacks. He wanted to take the garment away from her but was preoccupied by her story. Something sparked in his fogged mind, but he couldn't pin it down.

"Also," she finished, finally yanking the britches on, "he asked if I had been having headaches and memory loss. Which you know I have."

Petrichor grasped what had sparked. "Did you say a man in a blue coat? Powder-blue silk with yellow lapels? With one of those continental riding hats in the same blue?"

"That's him. Tall bloke with a rough face. I'm guessing he's a foreign mercenary."

Petrichor nodded. "I've seen him too. Remember that scuffle out on the street? Between the drunk coachman and his passenger? At the time I thought him only a lost foreigner in search of a brothel for… particular tastes."

"Not lost. Or with an itch to scratch. Sent to godsdamned kill us," Valour said.

Petrichor cursed inwardly for not examining the man further. "And he is not working for Brandquist?"

"No. For some other person he described as 'quite mad'. Must be someone with plenty of riksdaler. Those mercenaries don't come cheap."

"So," Petrichor said, "Brandquist's underlings are all strangely inept and yet Brandquist is impossible to find. To make things worse, we have a mercenary wanting to kill us in a specific situation, sent by some mystery person who wants us dead for reasons unknown?"

Valour clenched her hands into fists. One of them still had the wound from the warehouse, its dressing wet and pink. "That bloody mercenary was even sent to our homes by whoever bathes him in riksdaler. The rich can't seem to stop making life harder for everyone else."

He watched her grimace at the injustice and for the first time realised why she gave every coin she could to the poor of this city. She had noted things getting worse in Vinterstock too, but much longer ago. And, unlike him, she had acted upon it. There would be fewer orphans if parents were not starving on the streets unaided, or dying for the king and the rich nobility out on foreign battlefields.

He flexed his hands and his unused leg muscles. "We shall find answers. No matter what we must do to get them."

Valour lit a fire while darkly muttering, "For once, we're in agreement."

*   *   *

VALOUR WAS CLEANING her teeth with Ingrid's swanky tooth powder when their hostess herself returned, carrying a crate overspilling with various food supplies. She took one look at Valour and said, "Is all well, darling? You appear uneasy."

Valour helped her with the crate. "We had a visitor." She told Ingrid about the blue-coated man.

"Ye gads," Ingrid breathed. "Do we need a fresh hideout?"

Petrichor rose. "Probably, yes. Especially as the house above is collapsing."

"We can discuss that later," Valour said. "How's your father?"

"Not too bad. He's fevered but resting and attended by his physicians."

Petrichor groaned as he, for some boneheaded reason, tried to roll his shoulder. "While you discuss people's health, I shall take the opportunity to go outside for my ablutions."

"Maybe you were right about trying to shave with your knife," Valour said. "Stubble doesn't suit you. You look like a mossy rock."

Petrichor headed towards the outhouse, muttering, "Still better than looking like you."

Meanwhile, she and Ingrid unpacked the food. Valour was thrilled to see it all, mainly because she'd eaten nigh everything edible in the basement yesterday. Including half the jar of honey. Terrible idea. She felt like a beehive.

"I'm glad your father is doing all right," Valour said.

"As am I."

Despite Ingrid's back being turned, Valour noted tenseness in her body language. Was she worried about her father? Or the terminated conversation about secrets? A hard knot formed in Valour's stomach. She shouldn't have lost her nerve and pushed Ingrid away.

Ingrid unpacked the final items. "Guess what I bought?" She held something slim above her head.

"A stick?"

"Nay," Ingrid said with a laugh. "A pencil—graphite in a stick of wood. I met a set of lovely orphans selling these new writing tools and had to buy one."

Her suddenly excited tone cheered Valour, despite the fact that she was pretty sure Ingrid had bought stolen goods, probably at a rip-off price. "I'll have to give it a try."

"We both will. Oh, and…" Back still turned, Ingrid held a small paper bag up above her head. "I got you some candied lemon peel, since you ate all the sugared ginger."

Valour moved to stand behind her, circled her arms around the other woman's waist, kissed her below the ear, and said, "You've learned how much I crave my sweet treats, then?"

"Mm-hmm," Ingrid purred. "And I chose lemon peel because I've gathered you like your sweetness with a little bite."

"Right as ever." The knot in Valour's stomach untied a little. She kissed Ingrid's neck, the skin there so unbearably soft.

The picture of impatience, Petrichor banged the door shut. "Cease being repugnant. We should eat and I need some coffee. Otherwise I shall never recover and we'll never be free of each other."

Ingrid seemed genuinely abashed. "I am sorry that our affection, or rather our carnality, bothers you. And we will find you some sustenance, Master Assassin."

"Don't be nice to him," Valour muttered. "He's unable to return the favour."

As she said it, she knew she was wrong. She had learned that wasn't true.

The three of them breakfasted. It was clear that Petrichor was forcing himself to eat and it didn't take long until he returned to his bed, mumbling that as soon as he had rested, they had to get moving.

Valour checked his bandages and the moment her hands were off him, he fell asleep as if clubbed over the head.

Finished with clearing the table, Ingrid came over. "Is he all right?"

"Other than being a very strange little man, yes."

Ingrid laughed. "He's not little."

"True," Valour said, making sure to keep her voice down. "Sometimes, though, I look at him and I see him as I saw him first. A scrawny, slumping urchin with a scowl. I couldn't understand him then and I can't now."

"Do you need to? Understand him, I mean."

Ingrid took Valour's hand and, like she herself had done for Petrichor, checked the bandages. She frowned at the state of them and gently unwound each strip of fabric.

Valour watched her work. "I like to figure people out."

Ingrid caught her eye. "Have you figured me out?"

"Some parts."

"I see." Ingrid looked away. "One day, we shall have that discussion about secrets," she said, her voice strained like a fiddle string pulled so taut it could snap at any moment. "Then you can decide if you have figured me out. And if you wish to run far away from me."

Unsure of what to say, Valour pressed her lips to Ingrid's. She tried to put comfort and acceptance in the kiss, knowing it wasn't enough.

After the kiss, Ingrid checked the hand she still held. "It's healing well. Try to keep the scab undisturbed and I do not think you shall require a bandage."

"Agreed."

Ingrid was tracing the scars and callouses on Valour's hands, then, out of the blue, she giggled. "Did I tell you about the time a drunk hatter shoved a hat pin too far in and pricked my head? He did it four times and then offered to get me a bandage. How he meant to apply it, I have no idea."

Laughing, they sat back down and spoke of wounds. As Valour shared a tale of one of her own many scars, she realised this was the most intense socialising she'd ever done. Her other relationships had been based on doing things together, everything from volunteering at almshouses to sex. Not on talking. Was this what it was like for couples who lived together? It should have scared the marrow out of her bones. Instead, she sat there feeling her cheeks ache with wide smiles as Ingrid told funny tales from her childhood.

After a while, Ingrid kissed her and stood up. "I ought to check on Papa."

"Again?" Valour heard the whinge in her own voice. "It wasn't that long since you were with him."

"He's fevered and wretched. He wants me to stay with him as much as I can."

Ingrid wasn't looking at her. Was she upset at Valour's possessiveness? Was it such a bad thing that she wanted ever more of Ingrid's company? No. Maybe not bad, but it was selfish when her father was ill. She jumped up and fetched Ingrid's scarf and gloves. "Yes, of course. Go sit with your father. Tell him I said hello."

"I shall."

Ingrid scurried off, with little eye contact and no goodbye kiss. Valour found herself doubting how much she had figured Ingrid out after all. But then, wasn't that part of the appeal?

She read one of Ingrid's books until noon. Petrichor still slept, so Valour ate her midday meal without him while staring into space. When she noticed that she was sitting there mooning for Ingrid like some kid, she went out to the tree, checking in vain for a flash of a blue silk coat. She grabbed the branch, counting haul-up sets in her head and pushing herself through the pain.

PETRICHOR APPEARED AT Valour's side after a while—she guessed it was late afternoon considering the waning light. Bleary-eyed, flushed, and with a fraught expression, he looked like he'd been hunted by wolves for days. He panted, "I cannot lay about any longer."

Had he sprinted out here? Petrichor didn't run unless chased, and barely even then. Did he have a fever? He wasn't wearing any outerwear, only his boots, which were badly pulled up.

Valour dropped down. "Because it hurts too bad or because you're getting impatient?"

"Both. My skin prickles and I feel—" He interrupted himself and scowled. "Our hideout is both compromised and collapsing, why would I stay? I'm going to go stake out the warehouse."

She scratched the back of her head. "Look, I see why. I'd want to act too, in your position. However, it can't be that far off dinner and you missed lunch. Besides, standing still watching a building when its colder than Näcken's anus in midwinter isn't—"

"Näcken?" he interrupted. "Do stop going on about your blasted folklore. It's nought but absurd little fairytales."

Taking a breath, she decided not to give him the fight he was angling for. "No offence, but you haven't recovered enough. Also, you know this is out of character for me, but we need a detailed plan or we'll end up dead."

"We are sure to die anyway," he said, gesticulating. "People like us do not live to an old age."

"Maybe not, but we don't have to throw our lives away like they're fireplace ash. Let's try to live a little longer. I hear turning thirty is quite exciting." She did another haul-up, mainly to keep warm. "I need to wait for Ingrid anyway."

"No, you do not. She's not coming along."

"Firstly, you don't dictate the rules. Secondly, whether I bring her along or not, I have to tell her where we've gone so that she doesn't return to an empty place."

Petrichor grimaced and it looked like pure desperation. "What in the blazes does that matter?"

"If you cared about anyone else than yourself, you'd know that she might worry, thinking we've been kidnapped or killed." She kept doing haul-ups. It kept her from losing her temper. "People with hearts and consciences don't like others to worry about them."

"Valour, I cannot…" He scrubbed his hands over his face with the air of someone trying to explain something to a child who'd been dropped on their head. "I mean… This is the height of folly. No, worse, it is utter poppycock." He shivered but seemed too busy to notice. "I don't know why I spoke to you about this. We have seen so far that trying to work together only leads to dead-ends and shootings. I shall go on my own."

Valour landed again. He was serious?

"What is wrong with you? You'll get yourself killed."

"If I do, I'm sure you shall be glad of it. You can finally be the finest assassin." He pointed at her. "You pretend to be a good person, but you've wanted me dead since the first time you saw me, you intolerable swine."

He marched inside. By the time she had calmed down and followed him, he had rushed out, leaving the door up to the cold, dusty house open.

She gaped after him.

Such a boneheaded arsehole. An arrogant, rude, bloody fop, happy to waste his own and anyone else's life. He always had been, just as he'd always been able to make her feel shit about herself. Or rather, just feel shit in general. She had really believed they'd become kinder to one another. And that she had figured him out, but now he was making no sense. How bloody dare he?

Valour kicked a shelf with such force that the pencil Ingrid had bought rolled off it, across the floor, and stopped against her boot.

Chapter 44
REINDEER WiTH HATS

Petrichor stumbled along street after street, as cold as he was miserable. He had been hurrying but now his body wouldn't let him move faster than an insect drowning in mud. Everything was wrong, pain and frustration throbbing through him. Why? He was never rash like this! He considered the symptoms that the blue-coated mercenary had mentioned, but shook it off. The fact was that he needed to act. All of this had to come to an end with him doing *something*, not merely lying there waiting to see if his own body killed him or if the mercenary did. Or Brandquist. Or the house collapsing. Or the fits of panic. Or his doubts about the order and his whole life. Or that accursed, dark emptiness deep inside him.

The afternoon's last light faded, and in the abyssal blackness, ice-white stars came out to gleefully watch him walk into what was probably a trap. Or freeze to death on the way. His end would be as futile and lonely as his whole life had been. How fitting. His steps slowed, hopelessness weighing him down, down, down.

"Oi, snooty-arse. Stop so I can put these coats on you."

The blunt voice of Venerated Sister Valour, Ninth Assassin of the Order of Axsten, had never sounded so good.

She snorted as she caught up to him. "Not that two coats, or ten, will keep you—a wreck missing about half his blood—from dying a death that's dafter than a wax cooking pot."

He couldn't say why, but he laughed. It sounded like the noise of someone hanging off a cliff reacting to an unexpected, nay impossible, rope appearing next to them.

Valour stopped the peal of laugher by grabbing his good

shoulder. "Whoa. Have you lost the plot?" She helped him into his two coats. "If you start babbling about reindeer with hats or whispering trees, I'm sticking you in an asylum."

"Reindeer could not wear hats. The antlers would be in the way."

"And I'm sure they're very sad about that, Mister Know-It-All. Stand still so I can help you get your gloves on. Obviously neither of us will have a scarf, since someone bled all over both of them."

Having his coat back did not only mean warmth; it held most of his knives, the poisoned needle, two handkerchiefs, and hard-wearing twine. In short, the tools of his trade. He could not be an assassin without it. It also contained his letter. Did Valour know all that?

"Why are you here?" His voice had come out as little more than a whisper.

"Because I don't want you dead." She bored her gaze into his. "I never have. Also, I said we'd do this together and I'll be damned if you get all the glory for killing Brandquist. Or if I get blamed by Halcyon for letting you die in this truly boneheaded way."

When he was dressed, Valour rubbed her gloved hands for warmth. "There. Now, can we discuss a plan, or are you too distracted by that stick up your arse?"

The emotions that had foisted themselves upon Petrichor were hard to swallow down, so it took him a while to reply. "I assumed that I, *we*, would go back to observe the warehouse for movement. I wager Brandquist's minions have abandoned it. If I'm wrong, we retreat and concoct a plan of action."

"All right," Valour said, waving her arms in oversized, stiff-armed hugging motions to ward off the cold. Making åkarbrasor, that's what they called it, wasn't it? His memory was failing him again. "Let's do some good old Petrichor-style observation."

"All right?" he queried. "What? No arguments?"

"It sounds sensible enough. Obviously, at the first sign of Brandquist's horde hiding in there, I'm throwing you over my shoulder and leaving. Or leaving without you, depending on how nice you can force yourself to be to me."

He almost opened his mouth to say he'd be nice, but it tasted too much like saying 'I'll be good' and after his time in that cell, he had sworn he would never say that again. Instead, he looked back in the direction of the hideout. "What about Ingrid?"

"I left her a note with her fancy new pencil. Now, let's go finish our kill before he finishes us. Or the bloke in blue does." She pulled her hood up. "I want that reward."

Neither of them needed to say that this had become about more than rewards or assassinations. They had to see this through. Especially now that Brandquist's crew had armed themselves with proper weapons and shot on sight. Either something had changed within the 'ness-smuggling ring or they were getting close to Brandquist.

They walked side by side silently and soon it started to snow. Quietness was such a key component to snowfall that their lack of conversation felt normal. No, the silence had been comfortable even before that.

"I nearly forgot." Valour took her hand out of her pocket and held it out to him. A rye roll lay in her palm, slightly squished. "Take it. You haven't eaten."

He was going to argue on principle but found no appetite for quarrel, only plenty of appetite for bread. He would even overlook any pocket lint.

"Thank you," he mumbled, and ate it.

They passed hawkers closing up their stalls for the night and Valour took the opportunity to buy some lingonberry juice for them both. The seller resembled Halcyon a little. Petrichor blinked away snowflakes and wondered where Halcyon was tonight. Was he with that woman?

Soon they would be halfway back to the Pestilence District and the warehouse that awaited them there.

"Valour?"

"Mm."

"When you were up in that pine by the warehouse, how many people did you see?"

She sucked her teeth. "Around a dozen? Not huge numbers."

"Good."

Valour signalled to a passing carriage, but it was occupied.

"What do you think you're doing?" Petrichor asked.

"We're taking a carriage."

"You prefer to walk."

"So do you, but you're doing a brilliant impression of a dead baby mole, and so I'm getting us a carriage."

The similes that came out of her mind were truly worrying.

"Also," she said, "I'm freezing my tits off, and quite frankly the world could not stand the loss of such a cracking pair of—"

"All right! That's quite enough of that. I see a carriage coming."

Valour laughed and hailed it.

THE PESTILENCE DISTRICT was quiet as ever, and the warehouse looked deserted by the moonlight reflecting off the snow. They hid by the birches, this time without a sarcastic socialite, and stood there for long enough that Petrichor couldn't feel his extremities. He was as cold as the thick snowflakes slowly, silently dusting down around them.

Valour hugged her arms around herself. "So. Much. Waiting. Honestly, we should have been given this hit when it wasn't bloody winter."

Petrichor took his pocket watch out but had no time to check it before Valour said, "Don't bother. I can tell you the time. It's a quarter past 'We've stood here watching an empty building for too long.' Brandquist and his pathetic dogsbodies are long gone."

He checked the timepiece. "It's a few minutes to six."

"So…?"

"So…" He braced himself to say it. "You're right."

He didn't wait for a reply but crept up the hill. Out of the corner of his eye, he saw a flash of yellow and blue, making him search for the blue-coated man. He found only a flock of birds in those colours heading for the pines. Their name came to him—blue tits. He wouldn't tell Valour that. The jokes would never cease.

At the warehouse's entrance, a careful touch of the door-handle confirmed that it was locked. He brought his lockpicks out, wondering how hard this would be with frozen-stiff fingers and the pain radiating from his shoulder. Fortunately, the lock was as shoddy as most of Brandquist's belongings, and the massive doors opened after only a little work. Right after they slunk in, the doors slammed shut behind them with the click of a lock. No matter. He'd broken in and so could surely break out if required. He was more interested in the space they had finally entered.

Valour lit two brass lanterns she found on the table, handing one to Petrichor and taking one for herself.

He spun on the spot with the lantern held high, taking in the quiet warehouse. In the centre of the space were scuffed worktables, and on the back wall stood rows of boxes and crates. Something on the left wall caught his attention—a large corkboard with notes pinned with old nails. Most of the missives were in code but there were enough words he could decipher for him to spot locations where they could sell 'ness and the names of clippers which could bring it in.

One scrap of paper merely said: *V and P to remain unscathed*.

"Hey, look. More of these," Valour called.

She was inspecting some papers on a worktable. She held them up to him; they were letters signed 'Brandquist'. Right as he was about to examine the papers more closely, she dropped them.

He tried to read her expression but failed. "What's wrong?"

"The ink." She frowned at her fingers, which had cobalt stains. "It's still wet."

He looked at the top sheet and found a line that had been crossed out with thick strokes of now-smudged ink. Unless someone had forged his signature, Brandquist had been here and written this within the last hour.

"Can you smell that?" Valour asked.

He sniffed the air. There was a spicy, familiar scent but hard as he tried, he could not place it. By the look on Valour's face, she could.

CHAPTER 45

SCENT

VALOUR'S HEART RACED even faster than her thoughts. Her nose must have been misleading her. Or it was a coincidence? No, no one else drank that. Valour bent over the cup that stood next to the pile of papers and her fears were confirmed. Rose and cream.

What would Ingrid be doing here? She couldn't have been here to see them; she didn't know they'd come. Valour's stomach clenched. Could Ingrid be working for him? She'd known quite a bit about Brandquist, but then she knew so much about all manner of things. She certainly knew Johan, Brandquist's high-ranking smuggler. Oh, gods. Were those meaningful looks between Ingrid and Johan something worse than glances between former lovers?

Petrichor snapped his fingers in front of her. "Valour? Did you hear me?"

"Huh?"

"I said I can smell something familiar but I'm not sure what it is."

"The cup. It has Ingrid's hot rose drink in it," she said weakly.

Blanching, Petrichor took it from the table. "You're right. And it's still warm."

She picked up the smudged missive and stepped away from the fragrant cup. She hadn't only dropped those papers because of the ink smudge. There had been a scent other than cream and rose. She sniffed at the place where someone would rest their wrist if they were signing their name. Godsdamned lemon, vanilla, and cinnamon.

"Someone wearing Ingrid's perfume signed that," Valour said.

She crumbled up the letter and threw it.

Shit. Shit. Shit.

The rose smell was turning putrid in her nose, and she wanted to vomit, to expel everything and anything. Sadly, that would have worked as badly for feelings as it would for smells. The cup, the perfume... Shit, it was like Ingrid wanted Valour to catch her out.

Valour's hands shook and she watched them as she again voiced her thoughts. "I think there are two options. Either Ingrid is entangled with Brandquist's organisation and forges his signature, or..."

"Or what? Ingrid cannot be Brandquist. Everyone says Brandquist is a man. You even got a physical description." Petrichor sighed defeatedly. "Obfuscations. Of course. We should have known."

Valour shrugged, barely listening. She was thinking about all the times Ingrid had snuck away. And her statements about having dark secrets and decisions she regretted making. About her cravings for excitement, darkness, and the forbidden.

"We were never badly hurt," she croaked. "I mean they shot you, but only a clean wound to the shoulder and only at this late stage when we were getting very close. I was spared anything more than cuts and bruises."

"We discussed that. They wanted us alive," Petrichor said, now distracted. He squinted at something behind Valour. "Besides, I've just noticed another one of these." He went to the cork-board and fetched one of its scribbled notes. He held it up to her. It had lines of instructions and at the bottom said: *Remember - leave V and P unscathed.*

It was so much like the one in the harbour shack. And it had the same handwriting as the smudged letter. Shit.

"Brandquist was always one step ahead of us," Petrichor said.

"One? Hel's realm, sometimes ten steps. Obviously because we, or rather I, kept telling Brandquist what we were doing and thinking."

"Slow down. Let us make certain by sifting the evidence. What do we know about Brandquist?"

"Not much. Not if we discount what Johan told me, which is

probably lies."

Petrichor rubbed his chin. "We do know something that came from reliable sources: the peculiar, raised tattoo. Did Ingrid have such a mark on her wrist?"

She observed him, stunned that he wasn't using this to mock her, to torment her, or at the very least to say that he told her so.

"Well?" he prompted. "Does she have a raised tattoo on her inner wrist?"

Valour made herself stopper the emotions that flooded her long enough to reason this out. Her mouth was so dry and her heart pounded like a hammer. "Um, no tattoos." She remembered that rush of passion against the wall, remembered grabbing Ingrid's wrist. "She does have a mass of scars there, though."

"Only scars?"

"There's no ink or dyes, Petrichor! She's the same light-brown smoothness all over. Shit, I would know if she had a bloody tattoo."

"I did not mean to question you. It's just that we should keep calm and root out the facts of the case—"

"Calm? Facts of the case? We're godsdamned talking about my Ingrid here!" she screamed, loud enough for the words to echo.

When they died down, a voice quietly said, "Oh, Valour."

There was no doubt who it was. She didn't want to turn. Didn't want to look at Ingrid.

Petrichor's expression turned colder than usual. "Ah, kind of you to drop by, Miss Heiress. We have questions for you, and I'd advise against running or drawing a weapon."

"I wasn't going to," Ingrid whispered.

Valour could hear that she'd gotten closer, could even feel the warmth of her body. She still didn't turn, only clenched her hands into fists painfully tight.

There was the faintest touch on her shoulder. "May I speak to you in private, darling?"

Darling. Now Valour did turn. Ingrid was wearing Brandquist's large, woollen, black cloak with a hood. It was the scruffiest garment she had ever seen on Ingrid. Valour grabbed the hand that had deigned to touch her and pulled the sleeves of the cloak and dress up. There was the mass of scars she had felt, but now lines were drawn on top of them, forming a large, ornate *B*.

CHAPTER 46

ANSWERS

"WHAT IS THIS, huh?" Valour bellowed. "It wouldn't happen to be a godsdamned tattoo you have criminals kiss to swear fealty to you and your drug-smuggling battalion?"

"Valour, I can explain."

She dropped Ingrid's wrist. "Yes, you bloody well better." Petrichor squirmed at how much this felt like eavesdropping. He wasn't, though. He had been given the task of finding Brandquist and, after a long and confusing hunt, he had. It was only natural that he wanted answers, right? No. That wasn't it.

Valour trembled and he didn't know if shock or rage was the cause. She wouldn't stand alone. Not tonight. Not like this.

"Answer me," Valour snarled. She was still gripping onto the wrist with the painted scars.

"I am Brandquist, yes," Ingrid said in a quiet voice. "Or I'm the current one, to be exact."

"Current one?"

"You've heard different descriptions of Brandquist because 'tis not a person but a title. A new Brandquist is chosen every three years." She gazed at her wrist in Valour's hand. "The raised tattoo, unpainted when we're not working, is taken off the retiring Brandquist using the olden magic and placed on the new candidate as soon as they've been voted in."

Valour dropped her arm. "Voted in?"

"Yes, by the organisation's inner circle. I was suggested for the role by Kristina. You've met her. She was the older woman in Petrichor's rooms. I sent her to intimidate you into standing down while I and the others in the inner circle came up with a plan."

Petrichor thought back. It was only days ago but felt like months. "The white-haired woman with the pistol?"

"Precisely," she replied, keeping her gaze on Valour. "Kristina is one of the second in commands and one of the few respectable citizens of Vinterstock still in the 'ness trade."

Valour snorted. "A good friend of yours, then?"

"Not quite. She was the first one to sell me 'ness after she caught me crying outside the university years ago." Ingrid looked down before carrying on. "I was struggling with my grades, which were adequate but not good enough for me. I wanted to please and impress Papa so badly."

"So you drugged yourself to perform better," Petrichor said, unsurprised.

"I didn't know what else to do," she said, turning to him. "I studied throughout the night and worked in the hotels or attended lectures all day. Lack of food, sleep, and leisure made my work suffer. Kristina offered me shrewdness tonics and wakefulness tonics. I was only going to take one or two, but then they helped so. Have you ever taken them?"

"No," Petrichor said with disgust, pretending there weren't times when he had wanted to drink enough tonic to have the edge over every academic and aristocrat in Vinterstock.

"They warm your body from the inside, like a glass of brandy on a freezing night," Ingrid said. "For a golden moment, everything feels right and good, then the effect kicks in and bubbles seem to fizz in the part of you that is affected: your mind as it grows shrewder or your body as it grows brawnier, and so on."

Valour crossed her arms over her chest. "Move on with how in Hel's realm you can be Brandquist, before I lose what little patience you've left me with."

"Of course," Ingrid said, sounding dry-mouthed. "Soon I was addicted. Papa despises 'ness."

The insidious thing about these tonics was not merely that they would kill you in the long-term, Petrichor realised. It was that they made people feel they weren't good enough as they were, that they required the tonics to be a better version of themselves. It didn't take a genius to see how that would lure someone like this woman in. And then trap her.

"Let me skip ahead to the obvious here," Petrichor said. "They blackmailed you."

Ingrid glared at him, but the ire faded fast. "They did. I had shown interest in the organisation. Partly because I was curious, as I am of most things, and partly because I… had a need for something darker and more daring than my dry life of work and responsibility."

"It never occurred to you to fuck a group of strangers or start bloody sword-fighting or something?" Valour bellowed.

Petrichor stepped closer to her. "Let her finish. Then you can scream at her. After that, you and I shall decide what we are going to do." He didn't mention killing Ingrid. He didn't need to. It hung in the air like a miasma.

"Fine," Valour growled. "Talk."

Ingrid rubbed at the wrinkle between her brows. "Where was I?"

"You said you took an interest in the 'ness trade," Petrichor said.

"Right. That was my first mistake. The other was taking 'ness in the first place, especially openly, while being the daughter of one of the most influential people in Vinterstock." Her hand dropped from her forehead. "Kristina decided that I would be a perfect Brandquist. I was well-connected, able to get into the grandest places as well as the common ones, and so unlike those before me in the post I would never be suspected."

Valour slammed her palm against the wall. "And you godsdamned agreed?"

"I could not upset Papa. He has no other family or friends. He's frail too, prone to ailments and never rests enough to fully recover. Too much work, too many sleepless nights, too much stress."

"When he asked me to get you on the right path," Valour said through tight jaws, "he sounded like *you* were causing him plenty of upset and stress."

Petrichor watched Ingrid slump and wondered if it was due to shame or dejection. Hopefully it was both.

"Papa could survive thinking I was out at balls and taverns every night, but knowing I was Brandquist? It would kill him. I could not live with myself knowing I had let him down so."

Valour huffed out a hollow laugh. "You mean it's better living as a blackmailed peddler of lethal drugs?"

"Nay, of course not. It was, however, the choice I could live with for the interim, knowing I had a long-term plan."

"When we first said we were going to the warehouse," Valour said, jolting forward with realisation, "you kept trying to make me stay by any means, even sex. Was that to keep me away from a lair you were using?"

"Not *only* that," Ingrid said weakly.

Valour roared with rage so loud and scorching that Petrichor flinched.

"I wanted to keep you away to ensure you were safe, as well," Ingrid said. "I didn't want to have to hurt one of you to keep you from pursuing me. I didn't handle any of this well. I was too panicked and unsure of what to do."

Valour didn't answer, too busy looking like a coiled spring.

Clearly, he was going to have to ask. "You mentioned a plan?"

"I did. You have both commented on my underlings seeming inadequate? There's a reason. From the start, I decided to sabotage Vinterstock's 'ness trade from the inside. I could not be too obvious about it, though."

Petrichor shuddered at the vulnerability on her face as she watched Valour. It made him want to leave. Instead, he planted his feet. "So, you decided to... what? Only hire unsuitable people?"

"I inherited an organisation of killers and clever criminals. I sent the most violent and skilled 'ness smugglers and dealers onto the clippers. Or gave them coin to move away, as rewards."

"You didn't kill them?" Petrichor asked, harking back to the conversation in the observatory.

"Nay, I have never killed anyone or ordered anyone to be hurt. Those students of yours were wrong. Anyway, when I had sent the proficient dealers and thugs away, I put those I knew to be of kinder hearts, or more addicted to 'ness, in their places."

He sniffed. "That was your meticulously planned sabotage?"

"It was all I could do without it being noticed. Well, that and secreting away the riksdaler earned in the trade, to then donate that money to the hospice where most 'ness addicts end up."

Petrichor didn't try to hide his scepticism. "And no one enquired about that? How long did you think this would work? How long before you had to answer questions or order someone's death?"

With an almighty bang, Valour hit her fist on the table. "What does all this matter?"

"Stop striking things," Petrichor said. "Control yourself." He might have sympathised with Valour's rage but he'd be damned if he was going to jump at every clatter this violent woman caused. She could smash things when no one else was there to be startled by it.

When she glared at him, he regretted his words. He pointed to the hand she was nursing, realising it was the injured one and that it was bleeding. "You will hurt yourself." He took great effort to soften his voice. "Try to stay calm. Would you like me to handle this?"

Valour held his gaze for a moment, then gave a terse nod.

He turned back to Ingrid. "Answer my question."

"Right," Ingrid said, eyeing the cut on Valour's hand. "The inner circle did ask questions. I told them I was using the coin to bribe overseers, harbour-masters, and kammarherrar to look the other way. In short, the organisation's savings dipped and so did the quality of the weapons used, and the amounts of 'ness bought from the clippers."

He squinted at her, gauging her truthfulness. "Do you think that achieved anything?"

"It did," she said with vehemence. "I got both the level of violence and the 'ness sales down. I would have reduced both further if the greve hadn't given you two the task of assassinating me and interrupted my plans."

"Why did he?" Petrichor asked.

"The denizens of the palace are some of Brandquist's best customers."

"Y*our* best customers," Petrichor said. If he was going to speak for Valour, he would make this woman writhe and take accountability.

Ingrid looked away. "They fund a lot of the trade and since I was trying to put a furtive stranglehold on the riksdaler coming into the organisation, I told them that I was struggling to source tonics. They were not enthused by the idea of having to reduce their intake and wanted a new leader in charge."

"I am not surprised," Petrichor said. "I am however surprised they thought any of the pathetic wretches in your employ could be a replacement."

Ingrid's nostrils flared. "Call me names if you wish, I've earned it. But I will not countenance you calling these loyal, hard-working people pathetic wretches."

He was about to ask about more pertinent things when she blurted, "One thing this shameful affair taught me was to think of others. I took on the Brandquist mantle to protect Papa and his image of me. Now I wish to protect everyone who sees me as their leader."

He raised his eyebrows.

"I do," she said firmly. "That's why I take an interest in their lives and have upped their wages with coin from my own pocket." She cast a beseeching glance at Valour. "You know they're regular people who ended up in this situation due to what life did to them. It made me less selfish to see their trust in me and how the 'ness use has hurt them."

Valour snorted behind him.

"Feeble as my attempts may be, I *am* trying to help," Ingrid wailed. "To stop their 'ness use and give them work as a reason to get up in the morning. I mean, having a purpose seems to help. Even if that purpose is—" She had been wringing her hands but stopped at the same time as her words died away. "Even if it's merely selling 'ness to others. I know, it does not make much sense. I'm in over my head."

"Back to you ending up on our hit list..." Petrichor said, wearied of this maudlin nonsense.

"The decrease in tonics did make me unwanted. However, the main reason for my death sentence was that I uncovered a secret." Ingrid was still facing Valour. "Do you remember that I asked you about the greve? If you had met him and if something about him seemed awry?"

Petrichor stood between the two women. "Stop trying to draw Valour into conversation. You are speaking to me. What secret was it that made the greve take out a hit on you?"

"I'm trying to tell you."

"Then do so faster, drug peddler."

That broke her pleading expression into one of annoyance. "Perhaps you should be more concerned with why the greve wants to kill the both of you."

Petrichor stepped closer to her. "Us?"

"The mercenary in the blue coat? He's not in my employ. My sources know not who he is, only that he has a strange accent, a tendency to violence, and a tendency to show up where you two are."

Petrichor was about to ask why they should believe any of her claims when there was a heavy rap on the door and a shout of, "Come out in the name of the Greve of Vinterstock!"

"Overseers," Valour hissed.

The knocking grew louder. "Assassins Valour and Petrichor of the Order of Axsten, we have been informed that you are harbouring the criminal known as Brandquist in there. We have the doors and windows covered. Come out unarmed and with your hands above your heads."

Valour ducked her head and whispered, "We're *hiding* Brandquist in here? What in the name of Oden's gory eyehole?"

Ingrid looked as shocked as he felt, but she shook it off. "No time to discuss. Come with me, I know another way out of here that they're not aware of."

Petrichor flinched as fists hammered on the door once more. "How can you be sure?"

"Because I ordered its creation and ensured only my most loyal workers know of it." She went to a woven rug and pulled it up to reveal a hatch. "I had a tunnel dug that connects to a less used part of the city's tunnels. 'Tis how I arrive and depart."

On the table stood Valour's abandoned brass lantern, which Ingrid seized, then she descended through the hatch.

Valour caught Petrichor's gaze. "Do you think she's leading us into a trap?"

"She hasn't had much time to plan for that."

The knocking stopped to be replaced by the clicking of lockpicks.

"Moreover," he said, "what is our alternative?"

"Shit and double shit! You're right." Valour stomped after Ingrid.

Petrichor held his lantern up high and followed them, shutting the trapdoor quietly and hoping the carpet was attached to the accursed thing, so it would remain hidden from the overseers.

CHAPTER 47
THE TUNNELS AND THE BLOOD-RED HAZE

When down in the tunnel, Valour reminded herself to breathe and not start throwing things. They had to get away from the overseers—everything else could wait.

This tunnel truly was new. There was nought but fresh dirt around them and the smell of it finally blocked out Ingrid's perfume.

A few steps in, Ingrid stopped with a sombre expression. "If you plan to assassinate me, this would be a good location. We are near some of the order's mass graves."

Gods in Asgård, this woman would be the end of her. Valour got close to her and hissed, "Be quiet."

With that, she walked off, barely catching Petrichor whisper, "Do you want the overseers to hear you? She is obviously not going to kill you."

"What about you, Master Assassin?" Ingrid said, her voice tremulous.

Valour didn't hear his reply. A week ago, he would've cut Ingrid down where she stood without any hesitation. Now, she knew he wouldn't go through with the assassination.

"Am I walking in the right bloody direction?" Valour called back to them, as loud as she dared.

Hurrying forward, Ingrid took the lead. "This way."

"As we make our escape, perhaps you can *finally* tell us this secret that made the greve want you dead?" Petrichor asked.

And why he wants us dead, Valour thought, but didn't say it. She couldn't talk to Ingrid without wanting to swear, hit something, or... wail.

"Of course." Ingrid ducked under a large cobweb. "One night I was in the greve's palace, lowering my voice and wearing this all-concealing cloak. Although, they did not seem to want to know who I was, to have deniability, I suppose."

"Cease your eternal babbling and get to the point," Petrichor said.

"I was in the palace," Ingrid said curtly, "to supply some of the kammarherrar with tonics, since they dislike interacting with underlings. Afterwards, I went to leave but came upon a strange scene."

They stopped at the sound of heavy footfalls, but they seemed to be coming from above them, not in the tunnel. Yet.

She carried on. "In a room lay a well-dressed man on a medical cot, at the foot of which stood a woman with her hands over the prone man. Another man stood beside her, this one old, dressed in rags, and ashen-faced." Ingrid wrapped her arms around herself. "The old man convulsed, frothed at the mouth, and then collapsed. As his breaths stopped, some sort of blood-red haze flowed betwixt the woman's hands and the man on the cot. I snuck closer."

"Cease the dramatic pauses, 'ness dealer," Petrichor snapped.

"As I came closer, I recognised the man as the greve. He had changed, though. His chest did not stir with any breath and his eyes were, I don't know, empty?" She began walking again, but beside them now. "I could hear the woman informing him of what he was going to do in his meetings the next day. As if she was giving him orders, but more comprehensive."

"In what way more comprehensive?" Petrichor asked.

"Instead of 'Speak to the people on the town square', it was like 'You shall get dressed, and follow a kammarherre, taking one step after the other, until you reach the square. There you will speak of these things in this manner, looking like this, and sounding like that.' It was exceedingly detailed."

"Like he was a child?" Valour asked, too curious to stay silent.

With slowing steps, Ingrid seemed to consider that. "More like he wasn't human. I mean, even a three-year-old comprehends that to walk you put one foot in front of another. This odd behaviour in combination with the red haze made me investigate further."

"How?" Petrichor asked. He was affecting a nonchalant tone, but Valour heard his interest.

"I placed spies in the palace and made them shadow the greve and the woman I saw by his bed. She has a first name that I have forgotten. Something royal? The surname was Pound, anyway. My spies brought back some palace gossip that seems to ring true."

Pound... Where had Valour heard that before?

"Which was?" Petrichor asked as the tunnel snaked to the left.

"It is my belief, and I feel I have enough evidence to stand by it, that the greve somehow entered a state where his body could be brought back from death but not his mind, rendering him controllable by another."

A shot of pain went through Valour's mind and for a moment she could smell blood and hear herself call for help. It passed just before Petrichor gave a dismissive wave of his hand and said, "That's impossible."

But Valour knew it wasn't. "Not for the witches who worshipped Hel."

Petrichor wrinkled his nose. "The Norse goddess of the underworld?"

"The goddess of the death kingdom for those who die from anything other than in battle," Valour said. "My mother used to tell me stories about those witches. They sacrificed to Hel and in return got death-themed gifts—for example, speaking to the dead or controlling those whose minds had died."

"Exactly," said Ingrid. "My investigation led me to the North's old magic. It's meant to have disappeared, right? Only remnants like Gjöll remaining?" She halted at the bend into another tunnel and looked at them both. "That is untrue."

"Stop talking such absolute rot," Petrichor said.

Was he serious? How little imagination and belief could one person have? Valour pulled his ponytail. "You'll accept that volcanoes, magnetic pulls, gunpowder, heimcrows, and the magical water of Gjöll exist, but not that deeper parts of the old magic could be real? Or that powerful?"

Thinking about it, Gjöll was obviously part of the olden magic. He pulled away from her, adjusting his gloves. "Those things are facts."

"I assure you, so is this," Ingrid said. "No one is allowed to spend much time with the greve, but when they do, they note how quiet he is. How emotionless. How eerie. If you met him for more than a few minutes you'd accept what I have, that the leader of our city is a mere puppet."

He bored his ice-eyed stare into her. "Say I believe you. Why is this woman controlling him? Do you have a neat little theory for that?"

Ingrid stiffened. "I do. Although, it's not my theory. It's what my second in command and good friend, Johan, heard from this woman Pound's own lips."

"Good friend? Second in command?" Valour bit out. "That was what the staring between you and him was about when we went to the jeweller's shop, then? He was getting unspoken orders to lie to me?"

Petrichor cleared his throat. "We should resume walking."

They did, but Ingrid's gaze was still on her. "Valour, I am so sorry for deceiving you. Truly. And I am sorry Johan was threatening when we interviewed him. He went too far with playing his role."

"So did you, lying scum. Just tell us Johan's theory," Valour said, glowering at the tunnel they had entered. It was one of the city's old ones. She was back on familiar terrain but also back in a place where she really didn't want to be. She flexed her muscles, reminding herself of her strength and how it could protect her, aware of the pitifulness of the thought. No one could fight something like *this* with muscle power.

"Johan," Ingrid said quietly, "has been a courtesan for several kammarherrar, including this Pound. In that time, he's gleaned a lot of information."

Huh. She'd finally met a doxy that she didn't feel kinship with. Although, maybe she would've liked Johan if he hadn't been ordered to make a bloody fool out of her.

Ingrid spoke on. "He believes that Pound and her associates want to keep the power and not let it go to the greve's niece, the Baroness of Kallborg, as it would if it came out that the greve was dead. Nor do they want to anger the king by admitting that they slayed his liegeman and cousin. Thus, they pretended the greve was alive and ran the city in his stead."

"Poorly," Petrichor said, almost to himself.

"Precisely," Ingrid replied, now fired up. "They leave us all to fend for ourselves. You've seen how the city has deteriorated lately. People starve and lose loved ones, and meanwhile all the riksdaler pour into the palace never to be seen again."

Neither Valour nor Petrichor answered.

With a groan of despair, Ingrid said, "Do you see now why I didn't focus much on stopping you and Petrichor, other than trying to make you lay low and cease hunting me?" She slowed so they were closer to each other. "I was focusing on who sent you, Valour. Only the greve calling off the assassination would get the Order of Axsten off my back and allow me to focus on what matters: dismantling the 'ness trade and examining what is happening with the leadership of our city."

"Care to enlighten me as to why you had me shot then?" Petrichor said.

"Believe me, I didn't," Ingrid entreated. She stopped and faced them. "I had been with you two far too much and neglected my role as leader. Kristina, who had been confused as to why our organisation was deteriorating, stepped in. *She* purchased the new rifles and gave the command to incapacitate you if you got too close."

"Yes." Valour halted too, words spattering out. "You sure did spend a shit-heap of time with us. Why was that, huh? To show how you could fool the clueless assassins? To make a fool out of me?"

Ingrid's black-lashed eyes blinked fast, clipping away tears. "No! I did want to know what the order knew, yes, but I *had* been admiring you and talking about you for so long that Papa noticed. Which was why he asked you to spend time with me. I agreed to the plan the day before he actually asked you."

The day before? She and Petrichor hadn't even been given the hit on Brandquist then. So, Ingrid had agreed because she wanted to spend time with her. Unless... she was lying again.

"When I found out that you had been set to kill Brandquist, I realised that I could safeguard you and Petrichor by keeping tabs on what you found out and trying to steer you away from the danger that my organisation posed, the damage it—"

"It?" Petrichor broke in.

"The damage that *I*," Ingrid dutifully altered, "might be forced to cause you to keep myself and my underlings safe." Her throat bobbed as she swallowed. "I hated every minute of lying to you, Valour. It was somewhat hard at first when all that was between us was fascination and sex, but a few days in... I knew I cared so much more for you, and then it was pure agony."

Petrichor scowled. "And yet you lied so smoothly."

Valour was glad he had spoken, glad he sounded so furious. She was struggling with what to do with her emotions and hearing his rage helped somewhat.

"Putting on an act is what I must do all the time," Ingrid said in a shaky voice. "As I said, I am keenly aware that I have handled this wretchedly. It is a great sorrow to me that I cannot go back and change it."

"Your woe does us little good," Petrichor said. "Valour and I are drawn deep into this, and considering what the overseers said back there, I am not sure how we get out."

To punctuate his words, he strode on. Valour caught up and stayed by his side.

Ingrid's heeled steps soon rapped behind them. "You bring up a salient point. I know why the city governance wants me dead. Why did they set you up with the overseers, though? Not to mention sending the blue-coated mercenary after you?"

"You're convinced the palace sent him?" Valour said, refusing to turn and see that dishonest, deceiving, perfect face.

"Who else has that sort of coin?"

Annoyingly, she made a good point.

"I could be wrong, of course," Ingrid continued. "Perhaps

someone else wants you framed for conspiring with me? Or simply wants you dead?"

She felt Petrichor's breath against her ear as he whispered, "I spotted a flash of blue and yellow when we entered the warehouse. I thought it only birds."

"The mercenary?" she hissed back, glad to exclude Ingrid from the conversation.

"Could be. If so, he must've tipped off the overseers. Why would he do that?"

Valour shrugged. For every answer she got, another question took its place.

"Are you whispering about how wrong I am? And who it is that is actually hunting you?" Ingrid said. "Or am I right in that the palace wants its favourite assassins dead?"

MULLING OVER EVERY complex facet of their situation as he was, Petrichor jumped as Valour kicked the tunnel wall and shouted, "I don't know! What I do know is that I don't trust you to be telling us the truth. Perhaps this is all a godsdamned diversion to shift our anger and mistrust from you to someone else."

"It is not," Ingrid said in desperate tones. Her shoulders sagged. "However, I see why you would struggle to take my word for it."

They came to the westernmost fork in the tunnels. Petrichor knew, as well as Valour did, what lay in either direction. Did the tonic-peddler? He faced her. "To the right are the tunnels that lead further into the underground system and up into the city. To the left are the tunnels we do not go in."

"Yes. I know what those tunnels are," Ingrid said, with what probably would have been an eye-roll if she wasn't so upset. "They are the ones that were used to sneak people into the palace to pleasure the greve for coin. And there is another piece of evidence for what I say."

"What do you mean?"

"The greve has not summoned any pleasure-sellers. He sits alone and barely eats. He doesn't attend the theatre or opera, nor call for those performers to come play at the palace. Does that sound like the carnal man who used to run this city?"

Petrichor found disagreeing with Ingrid sweeter than Sister Glass's crystallised sugar sticks. "He has obviously calmed with age. Many greying men find themselves one day preferring to sit by the fire and read a good book."

"Yes, but it happens gradually," Ingrid insisted. "You have to believe me when I say that this occurred overnight. Oh, they covered that up by saying he had consumption for a while and that he recovered and was more tired after that—"

"A very plausible explanation," Petrichor interrupted.

"Too plausible. Too convenient," Ingrid said. "Come now, you must've heard people be baffled by how quiet and absent the greve is these days?"

This was growing wearisome, but he was not one to give up when he was right. "Yes, because he is older and more inclined to catch up on his sleep and his plans for the city. I do not think that—"

"Enough." This time it was Valour who interrupted. "Will you two know-it-alls stop quibbling before you ramp up my headache? Or before I tear the walls of these shit-stained, godsforsaken tunnels down with my bare hands?"

Ingrid regarded Valour. "Are you all right?" Her voice was soft and fretful, like she was addressing a rabid wolf. "Do you... need to talk? About the information I'm giving you, about what I have done, or... about how being down here seems to be affecting your equilibrium?"

"Stop examining me. And do not bloody dare tell me what I do or do not need," Valour growled with the air of someone holding in a scream.

The hairs on Petrichor's neck stood up with discomfort.

"I will." Ingrid jutted her chin out. "Because I care. You already loathe me for lying, for being the person you were trying to kill, for breaching your defences. Thus, I have nothing to lose by being the one to say what you don't want to hear. You must face this."

Now Valour let her scream out, and it was a sound that plainly came from the deepest core of her.

Petrichor wanted to scold her for drawing attention to them, but something stopped him. He kept an eye and an ear on the passage behind them. Not a footfall was heard.

"What? Now?" Valour hissed. "You're just trying to change the topic."

"Nay. By you getting this off your chest, you might be able to listen to my information and trust in it."

Ingrid was silently crying now, Petrichor realised. Big tears rushing down her cheeks, trailing powder and rouge.

Valour threw her hands out. "What is wrong with you? Huh? You want me to forgive you? You wish me to solve your little problem of being the pus-boil of a drug dealer I am meant to kill?" Her face drew into a snarl. "You want everyone to listen to you because you're Ingrid Rytterdahl and you know everything and you know best? Well, you know *nothing*."

"Perhaps not. I do know that you cannot move forward without this, though," Ingrid replied, the sobs in her voice mingled with defiance. "And right now, we must move forward with what I am trying to tell you and get to what is happening in this city. Especially you, Valour."

Petrichor was certain he was intruding. He had that feeling again, though. The same one as when his targets—no, his *victims*—died. That he owed it to them to bear witness. To not leave someone alone, no matter how wretched staying made him feel. Also, there was something to be learned here. Something about how people were with each other, how they hated, how they loved, and how they talked about it. He found himself, for the first time, wanting to learn.

Valour kicked the wall. "You couldn't even stomach hearing about these shit-curdling tunnels, you spoiled brat." The words blasted out of her like buck-shot, every word meant to maim. "These tunnels are a part of me. All the foulest parts of me. The killing part of my job. The killing part of my childhood. They are in my every godsdamned nightmare. Can you imagine having constant, vivid visions of the people you killed, huh? Faces that you forget every day but remember every night?" Valour groaned like a wounded animal. "Can you imagine what they smell like when they have been rotting for years? Or the pain when they look at you with eyes so full of bloody sorrow and their withered hands clutch at you while they ask, over and over again, why you had the right to kill them?" She rubbed her face. "When they ask you if you can look their family in the eye and explain why you, waste of space that you are, had the right to take their loved one away?"

Something in Petrichor's chest was punctured, and he took a step back. His heartbeat was hastening, and he felt overheated and ice-cold simultaneously. No. She couldn't say these things. He looked to the next tunnel. They had to go, had to keep moving, get to safety and to answers.

Valour whipped her head to him and he jerked back at her expression. "Do you smell it too? When you kill someone and drop them into those crowded holes we deign to call graves? The rotting flesh, spilled bowels, dirt, and corpse maggots? The constant, godsdamned soured blood?"

"Yes." He hadn't expected his own voice to sound so strangled. The mass graves were part of their work. Nothing more.

It felt like it was just the two of them down here now. Just the two of them in the whole world.

Valour shut her eyes. "That godsdamned stink. It takes me back to the first time I smelled it. I must have been four or five." Unseeing, she held her hand out. "My mother put a knife in my palm and with her calloused hand over mine, drove the blade into a man who she'd already half killed. She said the words and made me repeat them."

There was a beat of silence and before Petrichor knew it, he had filled it by mumbling the words. "On the command of the Assassins of Axsten and the Greve of Vinterstock, you are hereby axed." With eyes still closed, Valour said the last part with him. "May your offences be atoned for in the arms of death."

Silence again.

Mutedly, Ingrid sobbed. He had almost forgotten about her. She whispered, "Valour. That is dreadful. I mean, that's—"

"Life," Valour replied in a hard voice. "At least for our kind. We don't get childhoods and, as my mother taught me, we either kill and get food on the table, or we starve."

Petrichor's hands quivered with memories. It had been hard to hold and wield those heavy knives with a child's small, soft, weak hands.

Valour's eyes stayed squeezed shut and her voice hard. "The next time, Mother told me to lay hidden on the ground in the biggest tunnel and cut the heel tendon of a fleeing mark. It was impossible with my lack of muscle power and his big leg. I failed and wasn't allowed food for two days. She wanted to cure me of my dependency on her, show me that the only person I could trust to look after me was me."

"Oh, Valour," Ingrid said with so much, too much, emotion in her voice. "I don't wish to speak ill of your mother but—"

Valour's eyes shot open. "Then don't."

How many years had Petrichor spent envying her for her happy childhood with a mother? He busied himself with checking his lantern. He didn't know what to say. More than that, he didn't know what he was feeling. For a moment, he wasn't even sure who he and Valour had been made into by the order. Or what they were becoming. Was twenty-four too old to change?

He shook that off. He wanted to leave the tunnels. They had a job to do.

Valour's gaze was unfocused but her eyes were dry. Ingrid was the one crying. He and Valour had been beaten for crying too many times to do so easily.

"Can you imagine your nightmares never changing?" Valour said. "You know each thing that will happen and be said? And yet each time you have a drop of hope that you can escape by waking?" She shook her head slowly. "But I don't. Not until dozens of them have asked their godsdamned questions and when they do, I feel the well-deserved guilt of each death. Then the smell of soured blood suffocates me, but I don't get the release of dying."

Panic crept into Petrichor's chest, his heart thrashing yet faster and harder. A fit was now definitely coming. He tried to breathe through it, focusing on Valour, who finished her tirade with, "I feel the regret of what I've done and what I'll continue to do. It's bloody inevitable."

"Inevitable?" Ingrid asked gently.

Valour banged her fist against the wall so hard that the other two jolted. "There's no way out of the order alive and there is nothing I can do when I've left. So, this won't stop until I'm dead." She got right into Ingrid's space and screamed, "Was that what you wanted to know? Huh?"

There was no fear on Ingrid's face, only sadness, as she met Valour's gaze and said, "I am so sorry."

Maybe she said something more. He didn't hear, too busy trying to calm his hammering heart and gasping breaths. It worked. Not because of him, though, but due to the shock of Valour screaming curses and punching her fist into her own shoulder over and over again. When she finally stopped, she stared right at Ingrid. "Are you happy now? Did it give you a thrill that I spilled my guts to someone who has stabbed me in the back? Get out of my sight!"

Her last words sounded as much of an order as a plea. She drew back from Ingrid, into the parts of the tunnel that neither his nor Ingrid's lantern illuminated.

Ingrid gasped in a sob-shaken breath. "No, that wasn't what I wanted, I—"

She would make it worse. She couldn't be allowed to. He cut her off. "Miss Rytterdahl, you will do as she says. Immediately."

He kept any emotion out of his voice. A fact filled the hollowness of the tunnel: there was nought more to be said or done here.

After one last, long look at Valour, Ingrid left, slumped as if the entire sky pressed down on her.

The two assassins stood there, listening to Ingrid's footfalls fading.

CHAPTER 48

NOTHING LEFT TO LOSE

A FEW PAINFUL heartbeats later, Ingrid was gone from view.

Petrichor's chest still ached with barely subdued panic and his mind whirred with the new information, discounting idea after idea of what to say. They were all as wrong for this moment as he was.

Valour cursed, under her breath this time, then once more wrapped her arms around herself. It was cold down here, but he knew from personal experience that wasn't the reason for the gesture. A rat ran by and partly ducked behind some dirt-covered fungi to watch him.

Following Petrichor's gaze, Valour asked, "What are you staring at?"

"A rat. Have you ever noticed that they have little hands? Like humans."

"No." She dropped her arms down to her sides. "I guess they can use them to pick out parts of the corpses we leave down here. Shit. Such tainted food for innocent creatures."

They both watched the rat cowering and darting its small head around to search for a way out, affrighted and alone. Its claws made him think of his and Valour's hidden knives.

Petrichor heard himself say, "You ought not be ashamed of your nightmares."

Valour kept watching the rat, like he did, but gave an incredulous little snort. "Easier said than done. You should know."

"Pardon?"

"Well, you shouldn't be ashamed of your fits. You still are, though. Right?"

He twitched. "That is not the same. When you have the nightmares, you are unconscious. You cannot control it. My bouts of panic…" He composed himself. "The order teaches us to control our waking mind."

"The order says a lot of ludicrous things."

Petrichor pulled his hair tie tighter, stingingly tight. "That is your opinion."

She sighed. "Whenever mother was… harsh, I realised that she was echoing what the order had taught her. Now, I think I've figured out the look so often on her face on those occasions—utter bloody misery." Valour rolled her neck until it popped. "Weakness is human. Guilt is human. Pain and fear are too. The order saying that we should be punished whenever we feel any of those things and that'll somehow magically make us stronger? Bäckahäst-shit."

His palms were still clammy from the barely averted fit and he had the odd delusion that the Axsten crest burned into his hand stung with the unallowed filth of his sweat. Meanwhile, Valour's cheeks were still violently red after her screaming fit. He and Valour were broken. Alone. Failing.

What had the doctrines that had been beaten into them achieved?

He checked their surroundings to make sure they had not been followed, then let out a long breath. "Perhaps the order is somewhat… fallible."

"Fallible? Shit, more like cruel and senseless," Valour said. "It's warped by its insular nature and pointless little rituals. It's bloody lost in loving itself and hating its members. Generation after generation, we all obey its boneheaded rules without question."

"Not quite true. Brother Winnow and Sister Keeper questioned the order. They even left."

She gave a hollow laugh. "And do you remember what their tortured bodies looked like afterwards?"

He did. He also remembered being the one given the command to slit their throats to end it all. If the order was wrong, what did that make his actions?

Valour held his gaze. "We could be the last generation, though."

"You mean by leaving?"

That wasn't a solution for anyone else but *them*, though. The order would be unchanged. Another set of orphans would be brought in for training and take their places. There were always ten Assassins of Axsten.

"I don't bloody well know! I think, though, that if we wanted to end the order, we could. Others might not be able to, but you and I, as pig-stubborn and unbending as we've become? We could end it."

"Pig-stubborn? Would it not be more appropriate to say we are tenacious?"

Valour seemed to consider that, then spat on the ground. "No."

"Perhaps not," he said, curbing a smile. "Either way, as much as it pains me to say this, I am glad to be as stubborn as you." She looked confused at the compliment, so he added, "A sidenote, expectorating like that is vile and uncivilised even for you."

Valour looked down at her spit. "Yes. That was disgusting. Why did I do that?"

"You're having, well, a somewhat bad day."

With a glance back in the direction Ingrid had gone, Valour only nodded.

He watched her. What would he need if he were her? Simple. Distraction and answers. Fortunately, that was what he required too.

"Valour, this will sound like a terrible idea…"

In fact, it probably was. Considering nothing ever ended well, how could something like this be anything but a disaster?

Her posture straightened a little. "Go on, snooty-arse."

"I think we should follow the forbidden tunnels. Right up into the heart of the palace."

WHAT IN HEL'S realm? Valour stared at the man she had hated, disparaged, wondered about, but always seen as the paragon of sensibleness. "You think we should sneak up to the godsdamned *palace*? This time you really have lost the plot. Like, every syllable of the plot."

He balked. "I have not. Think about it, we risk being killed up in the city. The mercenary and his employer plan our death. Meanwhile, now that assassinating Brandquist isn't happening, we're under threat from the city governance as well as the order." He grimaced and Valour realised how much easier his life would be if he killed Ingrid.

"Oh. Um, I guess you're right."

"I am. No one will help us. Our homes have been compromised, the sanctuary is off-limits, and the hideout is…" He glanced in the direction where Ingrid had gone. "Not an option. So, when all other roads are cut off, you carry on forward."

"You do know we're sure to be captured or killed?"

"Did you not hear me? We are likely to be captured or killed everywhere." He pressed his lips together, oozing exasperation as well as desperation. "We cannot even leave the city without the order hunting us like prey and dragging us back to torture us to death, like Keeper and Winnow."

"True."

"I want answers. I want to know if my city's leader can be trusted." He paused. "If my order can be trusted. I am done with being kept in the dark."

"Answers would be good," she murmured.

The forbidden tunnel lay before her. Could they find out if Ingrid had been telling the truth, both about the greve's state and that the mercenary was sent from the palace? Maybe they could even find a way out of this that didn't end up with them dead or one of them killing Brandq… Ingrid. Ought she help Ingrid retire? Or let Ingrid try to run the 'ness trade into the ground? Both of those included talking to Ingrid. No. Going into the palace was better.

She flexed her muscles. "Let's do it. We have little left to lose and I want bloody answers."

"Good." He brushed down his coat. "So, in true assassin style, we shall creep into the heart of the matter with knives drawn. I want to find every morsel of the truth."

"Sure, but how?" Valour asked. "Bribe a kitchen maid to tell us what she knows? Beat up a palace guard until he talks? Or merely stride into the greve's parlour and say, 'Good evening, Your

Worshipfulness, is your mind your own? Oh, and by the way, did you send a mercenary in a silly coat after us?' Something like that?"

"I was thinking along the lines of sneaking through corridors to overhear conversations, rifling through paperwork, seeing with our own eyes what the greve is like." He massaged his brow with an exasperated air. "However, if the occasion calls for it, we can certainly interrogate someone. Do you wish to sit down and draw up an exact plan?"

She looked back from whence they had come. No one had found them. Yet.

"You're the cautious one. If you don't have the need for a plan, I don't." She opened her coat and felt for her knives. "We'll stick with your suggestion, sneak in and try to overhear and overlook. No, um, oversee... overwatch? Hang on, what's the visual version of overhearing?"

"For crying out loud, Valour, does that matter at this junction?"

"Suppose not. I mean, you're the one who likes to get details right and has a hard-on for words."

"I do not have—" He winced. "Let's go. If things go awry, we shall dart back down here." He nodded to where the rat had been. "Like the other unwanted pests of this city."

Valour took the first step into the off-limit tunnels. There was no fence or warning signs. There didn't need to be. No one would wander in here by mistake. The rest of Vinterstock's tunnel system was all stone covered in moss, mould, and mushrooms. The palace tunnels, however, were clad in foreign ceramic tiles which were a dark green and gleamed in the light of Petrichor's lantern. Valour ran her fingers over one; it was cold and smooth like glass. Like the gemstone Ingrid had given her. No. She wouldn't godsdamned think about her.

"They say these tunnels are sometimes patrolled," Valour whispered while pulling out the knife from her boot sheath. "And trespassers are killed on sight."

"I have heard the same. I wish I had been of sound mind when I left for the warehouse, then I would've brought my pistol."

"The patrols could be a rumour the kammarherrar spread to

keep commoners from dirtying up their posh tiles."

"It could." He held up the lantern. The light travelled far, since it bounced between the glassy tiles. "There is no one around tonight at least. Have a care, though. We shan't have such luck with the door into the palace. Expect at least one guard with a rifle or pistol."

They crept forward. It didn't appear to be a long tunnel but traversing it was taking an age.

"What time is it?" Valour whispered.

Petrichor consulted his pocket watch. "A quarter past eight."

"All right. From what I've heard, the greve takes his supper at six-thirty and eats at a snail's pace." Valour dredged up every detail she'd heard from drunkards crowing in alehouses about their time working at the palace, sifting what was true. "I'd wager that at this stage, he's digesting in a chair in front of a fire. Probably on the top floor of the palace and to the west. It has the best views of the city and, from what I've seen from the outside, his most favoured rooms."

He hummed. "Surprisingly knowledgeable and perceptive."

"It's only a surprise to you because of the way I talk and that I don't read much." She gave him a glare. "I listen to people, observe, and reason things out on my own, though. There are other ways to be intelligent than the reading that you and... Ingrid hold so bloody sacred."

Petrichor stayed silent, no doubt making up some clever insult to snap back with.

Valour moved aside as a cluster of rats ran past. They were moving away from the palace entrance. Probably a clever move.

"You could not have managed otherwise," Petrichor muttered.

"What?"

He gave her one quick glance. Just one. "You have challenged the order and done things your way—meaning very hazardously—and been allowed to do so, because you are remarkably successful. You've survived and flourished against the odds, while keeping to your moral code, in *Vinterstock*. That takes a high degree of intelligence."

She struggled with what in Valhalla one should say to that and so silence reigned until the lantern's halo of light showed a door ahead. She wasn't sure why she needed to say it, but she was in no state to fight the impulse, and so murmured, "Humbly, we ask."

Petrichor chanted the rest of the prayer with her. "Our predecessors' spirits to guide our blades. Fate to help us on our path to obeying our orders. Luck to make us as hidden as our targets are unhidden. And death to take our marks, but never us."

The gloriam prayer. Why had it been that one that came to her? She met Petrichor's gaze. Those ice-blue eyes looked more human in the dark down here.

"Right then. Lead the way," she said. "If we're going to go get ourselves flogged or hanged, let's be quick about it."

Chapter 49
The Servants' Corridors

Petrichor held the lantern higher. The rounded door ahead of them was sturdy and painted the same emerald green as the tiles. On the ground next to it lay an unlit lantern, a packet of gunpowder with the city crest on it, and two empty 'ness vials of the upper-class type, but no guard could be seen. They had been in luck tonight.

So far.

"What now?" Valour whispered.

"I am assuming it's locked."

She put her knife away long enough to crack her knuckles. "And I'm assuming that, as we said, the other side will be manned."

"What say you to me picking the lock and opening the door, after which you knock out the guard?"

"You think it'll be that easy?"

"Unequivocally not. Nevertheless, my head is splitting with a headache, my shoulder aches, I feel like I have scarce eaten for a month, and I grow weary of wondering what the sensible method is."

"Fair enough. Open her up, I'll deal with whoever is on the other side." She waved the knife in her non-dominant hand. "This is only a deterrent. No lethal force unless necessary."

"Why? You're the one with principles," Petrichor said as he put the lantern down by his feet.

"You have them too. You've just ignored them since you were little."

Petrichor quashed the urge to get rid of Valour and do this alone, concentrating on his lockpicks. "Shush."

"You only shush me when I'm right."

He stopped mid-pick. "Will you be quiet so I can open this door?"

"Hm. Yes. I think I will, actually. You're welcome."

The click of the lock was nigh inaudible and so was the pressing of the door-handle thanks to the treacle-slow pace with which he proceeded. The door opened in their direction and without a single creak. Only a couple of steps beyond the doorway was the straight back of what appeared to be a youngish man. A glossy blond ponytail tied with a silk ribbon peeked out from under the palace guard's uniform cap. He was shuffling his feet and humming, more interested in practising some sort of jig than being watchful.

Then the guard stopped.

Perchance he felt watched, maybe a breeze came from the tunnels, or perhaps he could smell them. Petrichor inwardly cursed that he had put cologne on. Whatever it was that caused it, the guard spun on his heels. He looked right at them. After a beat, he appeared to be about to call out, so Petrichor hit him in the mouth.

While the guard was busy staggering back, Valour said, "Hey, that was my task!"

"Oh, I'm frightfully sorry." He faced her. "Should I unpunch him so you may do the honours?"

"What you should do is go shrivel up like a salted snail."

Bickering when they had a foe to beat was a terrible idea. However, Petrichor's aches were torturous and he had been forced to put up with Valour for days on end. Moreover, they could beat a jigging adolescent dandy with their eyes closed.

The sound of a blade being unsheathed made Petrichor question that last thought.

A palace guard's sabre touched his throat and a long, uniformed arm wrapped around him, locking his limbs at his sides and making him drop the lantern. The guard was stronger than expected and he was pinning Petrichor's arm in a way that made his injured shoulder scream with pain.

Instantly serious, Valour snarled, "Release him."

Petrichor turned his head to see the popinjay of a guard grin. "Shan't. I've long awaited some action, someone to bed or someone to thrash, and had nought. Then you appear."

"The only one getting thrashed tonight is you, lad," Valour said, performing her usual trick of letting her knife glint in the candlelight. "Unless you let us tie you up and leave you here. In such case, no one need be hurt."

"Hurt?" The guard giggled with malicious glee. "Threatening me, eh? Good. Ordinarily, I am to take intruders to the kammarherre, but if I'm in lethal peril I'm allowed to simply execute you. Let's see if riff-raff like you bleed as the rest of us or if only dirt comes out."

Petrichor was about to dispute being called riff-raff but felt the sabre cut into the column of his throat and decided against it. For now.

"Put your knife down, pitiful vittra, or I'll carve him open like a dinner ham," the guard sing-songed.

With reluctance and a muttered, "Vittror are not pitiful, respect your folklore," Valour obeyed.

It mattered little, Petrichor supposed. She had other knives. Not to mention the damage she could do with only her body.

"Ah, that's better." The guard, stinking of snuff and wine, sniggered again. "Do you want to say farewell to your lover before I kill him? I can turn my back so you can straddle him one last time. That is if he can get hard when his death looms."

"Wow. You misread this in so many ways that I don't even know where to start." Valour tilted her head as if examining the guard. "You know, you sound like a very violence-obsessed and sexually frustrated little pup," she said conversationally. She took one measured step closer with her arms clasped behind her back. "Although, you won't have to worry about your urges tonight."

The guard snorted while raking his gaze over Valour's curves. "Whyever not? You planning to satisfy my needs, big she-bear?"

"Shit, no," she said as she moved her hand out from behind her back to show that it held a thick, bronze statuette. "I'm planning to punch your lights out."

During the last word, she smacked him on the side of the head with the figurine. He dropped back like a felled tree, and Petrichor barely caught him and lowered him soundlessly to the ground.

"I suppose I should be grateful that you didn't miss and hit me." He shook himself off, rolling his poor shoulder, and grudgingly said, "Nice blow."

"First of all, I don't miss," Valour said, pointing at him with the statuette. "Secondly, I paid attention when Sister Sequential taught us the anatomy of the head. The trick is to aim the bash just right—you want full unconsciousness but little permanent damage." She studied the bronze figurine. "Some old king, right?"

"Possibly," Petrichor replied, ashamed of his knowledge gap and still nursing his shoulder.

With the look of someone having swallowed vinegar, Valour said, "Ingrid would've known." She replaced the statuette on a shelf and picked up her dropped knife.

Together they used the twine from Petrichor's coat to tie up the guard and in a nice flourish, Valour stuffed his cap in his mouth and tied it in place with the silk ribbon from his hair. When finished, she picked up Petrichor's dropped lantern and handed it to him. "Ready?"

Relighting its extinguished candle with aid of a wall sconce, he muttered, "Raring to get this over with."

He closed the door out to the tunnels and blinked to get used to the well-illuminated hallway ahead of them. "This is less adorned than I had expected."

"We're in the servants' corridors. They're here for easy passage between vital parts of the house. And so that the rich folks don't have to see their staff."

"Yes, of course." Why hadn't he thought of that?

The long hallway's walls were dotted with sconces, their candles long and made of beeswax which left the air heavy with the scent of honey. Valour took one and held it up in front of her.

She noticed him staring at her and said, "What? Some of us don't have a lantern."

"Have a care. Wax will drip onto your glove and ruin the leather."

"Better the glove than my hand," Valour replied. "Stop fretting over my appearance and come on."

They kept close to the wall, Petrichor doubting this decision with every step. But what else should they do?

"Look," Valour whispered.

A young woman in footman's—footwoman's?—garb came out of a room. She carried a silver tray with small, high-stemmed glasses and a bottle of what must have been port. The woman strode ahead and when the hallway split into two, went left.

Valour, massaging her forehead as if she also still had a headache, quietly said, "Do we avoid her or follow her?"

"Follow her. The other route might be a dead end or lead to servants' areas, but she is taking those glasses up to the heart of the palace. There you and I can find either clues or someone in the know to interrogate."

"All right." They crept after the woman and Valour whispered, "Although, if we don't find anything up there, we should come back here. Servants hear, see, and guess more than the rich think."

"Yes. However, making them divulge their masters' secrets will put them in a dangerous situation."

She gaped. "Bloody Ragnarök, did getting shot give you the ability to think of someone else? Nice. And you're right, our quarrel is with the leaders of this city—we'll take our knives and questions to them."

He didn't tell her that he had meant the servants would take longer to interrogate due to their fears, and that he wasn't actually worried about their discomfiture. Let her think him a better person. Perhaps that was a start to him becoming one.

The footman—footwoman?—with the tray had slowed, occasionally stomping as if her foot itched or something was lodged in her shoe. If she stopped to remedy the problem, he and Valour had to be ready to hide. But where? There were occasional alcoves to shelter in, but would fate smile on them enough that the servant would stop right as they were near one of those? The woman walked on, the glasses clinking against one another every time she stamped her foot.

Ahead of them was an arch and when Petrichor squinted, he could see stairs beyond it. They were so near getting up into the palace proper. If only this servant could keep from stopping, they might make it. They kept their distance and Petrichor tried to not dwell too much on the fact that once they were on those stairs, there would be no alcoves to dive into if the servant were to stop or turn around. Also—it could not be avoided—he worried about Valour's actions. She might trip. Or sneeze. Or cough. Or simply go over and flirt with the servant. Actually, that last concept might work. He had seen countless women melt like the Vinterstock canal in spring when Valour showered them with attention.

The stairs creaked under the servant's boots. Therefore, when Petrichor put his foot on the first one, he was as careful as if walking on cracked glass. Over his shoulder, he noted Valour stepping with care. She was looking around like a regular visitor, though, hands in pockets. Vexing, overconfident woman.

One step at a time, they closed in on their goal. Petrichor watched the woman with the tray, his heart pounding out the words 'Don't turn around' with each beat. After what felt like an age, they were up the stairs. The footman took a hard right and sat down on a statue's plinth. Petrichor halted out of her line of sight, holding his arm out to stop Valour. He could hear a shoe being unbuckled and what sounded like a pebble rolling out and across the floor. Then the click of the shoe buckle and the woman's steps again, going further down the hall.

Petrichor spun to face Valour and pointed to the left with a questioning expression. Valour took the hint and turned left, leading them down dark wood-panelled passageways. This was the palace proper, and here a footman was the least of their worries. They might run afoul of kammarherrar, more guards and servants, not to mention the greve himself. And, if Ingrid had been truthful, the woman who—with the use of unknown dark magic—controlled not only the city's leader but the *actual city*.

Why had he suggested this? His head wasn't right. And it still hurt like blazes.

After checking he had easy access to his blades, Petrichor followed Valour, his nerves taut as bowstrings. Was this the night when death would finally claim him?

CHAPTER 50

LIES

WITH AN IMPATIENT sigh, Valour rolled her bunched-up shoulders. So far, they'd headed down two different hallways that had led only to stairs back down to the servants' corridors. She was dizzy, confused, and headachy. She couldn't stop thinking about Ingrid. And she wanted to bloody well get this over with. Although, what would her life look like when they were done?

Petrichor stopped, pointing to their right with an unsure expression.

"No. We tried that way last time," Valour whispered.

"Are you certain? I do not think we did."

"We did, snooty-arse. I'm confused too, but I remember that painting." She pointed with her candle to the wall next to them, making the flame flicker.

He squinted hard at the image of a Viking longboat cleaving through a vast sea. She wasn't sure if it was due to his eyesight, which she was starting to think was as shitty as his manners, or if he still had the same confusion and raging headache as her.

The palace was nicer than expected. She had worried it would be all gold and fancy silks. But it was Scandinavian to the extreme: clean and unpretentious, in various shades of wood and whatever that local greenish marble was called. The place smelled of soft pine soap, and the wood-panelled walls were decorated with animal heads and paintings of animals, nature scenes, or the old gods. Any metal was aged silver or copper.

She jumped at what sounded like a child's shout, finding that it was only a large black cat meowing. It had the long fur and ear tufts of forest cats, and a good set of lungs.

Valour quickly crouched down to it. "Shh, pussycat. Be a poppet and don't give us away."

"From whence did it come?" Petrichor asked.

When Valour indicated the direction, he went to investigate. Meanwhile, she petted the cat to keep it quiet. It sniffed her candle and she decided to blow it out. Up here, there were wall-mounted candelabras everywhere; relighting it would be easy.

"There's a narrow passage next to that statue," Petrichor hissed. "How in the name of Axsten did we miss that?"

"Due to our fun new symptoms, I guess." She watched him slip past the statue and addressed the cat. "You can come with us if you'd like, Master Palace Mouser. Be quiet about it, though, or the Archduke of Arrogance over there might make you into a hat."

As she and the cat followed said Archduke of Arrogance down the little passage, she thought of the tales of people entering this palace but never leaving. And of the greve being... What had that foreign mark said? Right, 'eerily changed'. Now and here, it was hard to dismiss such accounts—especially the ones from Ingrid—as only rumours.

"I must say, 'tis a shame that Ingrid could not be trusted," Petrichor whispered, showing that he had probably been thinking something similar. "We could've used a guide who has spent time in the palace."

Valour tried to compose her features, glad this passageway was less well lit and that he had his back to her.

"That impossible woman," she muttered, more to herself than to Petrichor. "I can normally read people. Why in Hel's realm did I fail to see what she was like?"

"Pardon?"

He sounded as shocked as she was to be talking about this, to him of all people, without either of them currently dying in a blizzard or from being shot, as had been the case over the last few days.

"Sorry. The day and this headache must've gotten the better of me." She shouldn't have blathered on about the tunnels earlier. Now it had apparently become a habit to spill her head's contents.

"Ignore me."

The cat tried to rub around her legs as they walked, but she kept her gaze on the stiff back and tight ponytail of the Tenth Assassin of Axsten.

"No, no. Dull as your pitiful love affairs are, I should welcome a break in the tension. And in my vexing pain." He touched his shoulder. "This socialite of yours seems the type who has plenty of experience with hiding her feelings, actions, and thoughts," Petrichor said, ever happy to inform people.

She forced herself to skim over Petrichor's reference to Ingrid as *her* socialite. The image of Mahadev Rytterdahl came to Valour's mind. He had scrutinised and inserted himself into every facet of his daughter's life, leaving her with nothing of her own. Unless she kept secrets. "True. But the fact remains, I shouldn't have godsdamned trusted her."

"So, you are angrier with yourself than with her?"

She stomped a little harder than she needed to on the wooden floor that was so well oiled it gleamed in the candlelight. "Oh, trust me, that lying temptress is the one I'm bloody angry with."

Petrichor sighed and took on what Valour thought of as his annoying 'Professor Know-It-All' air. "Valour, I enjoy my solitary life and it comes naturally to me not to trust anyone. You, however, wish to be part of society and to belong. You do better when you have someone by your side."

"What's your point?" she said, trying to sound forceful despite being preoccupied by the cat nuzzling her ankles.

"That you ought not write the sociali— I mean, Ingrid, off so soon."

His words reminded her of something. What? Right. What he had said after he was shot. Something about not shutting Ingrid out because she made Valour's eyes less sad? "Why? Why her? If all I need is someone to lean on, would I not be better off finding someone I can trust? Someone who isn't a drug lord?"

Petrichor stopped by one of the beautiful candelabras and turned. That condescending and judgemental expression of his was back. "Yes, Ingrid sold dangerous, addictive preparations.

She's a reproachable person. Meanwhile, *we* take people's lives and glory in the act. Are you truly the right person to judge others, Valorous Valour?"

Every word hit her like a brick. "I know, you arse-wipe," she hissed, thereby making the cat meow. "Just as I godsdamned know she had understandable reasons for becoming the Brandquist. And that she risked everything to dismantle the 'ness trade. That wasn't the problem."

He didn't need to know how it hurt her pride that she'd been running around with the actual Brandquist right under her nose—*under her hands*—while chasing shadows. She had to admit that she was grateful he'd said nothing about that, at least to herself.

"Her bloody lying was the problem. I was... open with her. And in return, she lied right to my face. Over and over," Valour continued, keeping her voice under control with great effort. "She took me to people who would help me find Brandquist. Listened to me work our theories on how to find him. How am I expected to forgive that?"

"So, you want to forgive her, then?"

That Professor Know-It-All tone was going to get him clobbered one day. "What do you mean?"

"Well, if you did not, you could either punish her or try to forget about her. Then move on with your ridiculous little life. The fact that you're this hurt and bleating that you cannot forgive her makes it obvious, even to me, that you want her in your life."

She huffed.

He started walking again, skulking close to the panelled walls of dark-stained wood that was polished to the sheen of a still lake in moonlight. Even in this dimly lit passageway, it was obvious that this palace really was the pride of the city's woodworkers. The ceiling beams even had ornate carvings of flowers, curlicues, and the greve's crest. She had heard that the wood in here was only ash and elm, the types of wood that Oden and his siblings used to create humans. That could have been a tavern tale, though. She wished she could take in more of this place, but her energy and focus were on the discussion and her headache.

Petrichor looked back at her over his shoulder. "This does not concern me, and the topic is growing quite tedious, so I shall merely impart one last thought. You are upset because she didn't tell you?"

"Yes."

"Well, you only became acquainted enough to speak to one another less than a week ago. Perchance she was working up to it? Maybe she would've told you when she knew she could trust you?"

With no reply to that, Valour vaguely hummed and then changed the topic. "Hey, since you know these things, why does this palace look so old-fashioned Scandinavian? I thought the blue-bloods wanted their homes to look continental."

He peered about him, right as they passed a wooden window showing the starry sky through warped glass and lead latticework.

"True," he said. "No Italian stucco, English clean-white walls, or French gold décor, as is the growing fashion. Quite the surprise that the greve has not kept up to date with what other Swedish nobility are doing."

The conversation was stopped by Valour tripping over the cat. In her defence, the adorable furball was nigh invisible in this dark and devoted to its hobby of getting underfoot.

Petrichor stopped. "Careful, you clumsy churl. If that thing yowls when you step on it, dozens of palace denizens will flock to us."

"Speaking of, haven't we seen surprisingly few people? I mean, we know loads of people are employed here and these spotlessly clean hallways show it. Why is the place so empty?"

"I do not know," he mumbled, picking up his pace.

The passageway led to a small atrium. It was flooded with light from a giant copper chandelier and boasted four new corridors.

As they stopped and examined the different paths, Valour murmured, "She tried to tell me."

"Pardon?"

"Ingrid. She tried to tell me she was Brandquist."

"Oh?" He sounded uninterested, his focus on examining the hallways.

Valour swallowed repeatedly. Ingrid's face, lit by the northern lights, haunted her. "I told her that I didn't want to reveal secrets. That it was too early for us to share confidences, and that she wasn't ready for the sort of tales I would tell."

"It was foolish of her to want to tell you," Petrichor said, squinting down the nearest passage. "I would not have shared such a precarious secret with someone I barely knew."

Valour chewed the inside of her cheek until she tasted blood. "That still doesn't excuse her running around hunting Brandquist with me. Or with us, I mean."

There had been no need for Ingrid to gain as much of her trust as she had, not if she was just going to tear it apart.

Petrichor sighed. "Look, let her explain or do not. I am more interested in what route we shall take next in this accursed palace." He indicated a passageway with his lantern. "I think that one has the most places to supply cover. Agreed?"

"Yes, those thick pillars would be perfect to hide behind." Valour was glad for the change of topic. And grew even gladder when her new fluffy friend entered the corridor in question and sat to wash by one of the greenish pillars. "The cat likes it. Since cats are Freja's sacred animals, perhaps that's a sign from her that we should go that way."

"Gods do not provide house tours," Petrichor muttered, and crept past the feline.

Valour paused by the cat, bending to give it a quick stroke. It was a pretty thing—all healthy muscle and long, glossy fur—nothing like the ragged strays that lived around the sanctum. When she was little, her mother had sometimes let her feed them fish-heads. A hazier recollection came to her, a foreign-speaking man in a sailor's shirt so old and torn that his brown skin showed through it in numerous places. He had a length of ship's twine and used it to play with a litter of kittens. He let her try but she kept dropping the twine. It was the only memory she had of her father sober and happy.

The palace's mouser ran away from her, chasing down something skittering across the opposite passageway. She watched it go while thinking about her parents. Would it be easier to forgive and trust

Ingrid again if everyone she cared for hadn't left her?

She growled at this bout of what she worried might be self-pity and hurried after Petrichor.

CHAPTER 51

THE MAZE OF HALLWAYS

THE STUFFED HEAD of a moose scowled down at Petrichor as he traversed this latest hallway. He stopped. The animal looked familiar. Had they passed it back when they ducked away from that set of guards? Or when they thought they heard footsteps but it turned out to be echoes from the floor above?

Valour followed his gaze. "That moose must've been sprinting at some speed to run straight through the wall and get its head stuck like that."

He didn't even acknowledge the inane joke. Why was the palace so empty, and why was he so lost? The wooden walls, ceilings, and floors, the unadorned silver candelabras and chandeliers, the pillars in the green-grey Kolmårds marble—it all looked the same. Only the paintings and stuffed animal heads changed, and now he could no longer keep them separate. He normally had such a reliable inner compass; how could he be *lost*? At least Valour was equally disorientated.

The hallway ran out, finishing with a gigantic painting of well-dressed hunters skiing after a herd of reindeer in an oversnowed forest.

"Dead end," Valour said. "Time to start opening doors? We might find some incriminating paperwork, signs of magic use, or a sign that says *Ingrid R lied about everything*. If all else fails, we could nab some lone kammarherre to question."

"Good grief. 'Tis not that easy, you rash fool. How do we know that the door we open will not reveal a whole cluster of kammarherrar and palace guards?"

Where was everyone? They had wandered these halls for who

knew how long and had only needed to dodge one small group of guards, not counting that popinjay they tied up down by the tunnel door.

"We don't," Valour said, and opened a door.

He leapt back, cursing inwardly. Where was the 'On the count of three…' or the careful glimpse inside the room before the door opened fully?

With her knife drawn, Valour crept in. She looked left, then right, and nodded to him that it was clear.

"Has it occurred to you that what you just did could have been done with caution?"

She fished around in her pocket and pulled out her half-burned candle, lighting it from the one in his lantern. "Mm-hmm. Things like this are like winter sea-bathing, though. Hesitate too long and you may lose your nerve. You have to just jump in and try to stay calm when you've done it, enjoying the rush."

"If you get me killed tonight, I shall haunt you until it drives you mad."

She snorted out a little laugh.

The room was an antechamber with a smaller door ahead.

She whispered, "I'll take the other room, you check this one?"

"Agreed."

His room contained a side table laden with ornamental snuff boxes, above which hung a tapestry of a sun-drenched, buxom goddess in a carriage drawn by giant cats. Was this Valour's beloved Freja, then? Damask-cushioned chairs stood on either side of the table. On the opposite wall was a bookshelf with drawers at the bottom. The shelf held books on hunting, peerage directories, and a few old religious tomes in Latin and Persian. Beautifully bound, but not clues. The drawers were empty. Petrichor rubbed at the shooting pain between his eyebrows until the light from his lantern fell upon the re-emerging Valour.

"A vacant guest bedroom," she said. "The beds were unused, the dressers and wardrobes empty. The fireplace had fresh firewood but the grate was clean."

He considered double-checking her work. No. She was reckless, impulsive, vulgar, and loud, but she was a better investigating assassin than he had given her credit for.

"There's nothing in here either."

"Let's move on, then," Valour said.

They returned to the hallway, checking another few rooms and finding much of the same—unused guest rooms and empty parlours. No letters, no signs of the old magic, and not a soul in sight. This whole endeavour seemed suddenly so rash and hopeless. What were they doing? Why would they find answers here?

Outside a powder room, Valour put her hand against the wall. "I'm so dizzy. What in all the pig shit in Alfhem is wrong with us?"

"I don't know," he said. "Some sort of miasma?"

"No. That can't be it. I started to feel like this before we came here."

He had to agree. "Poison then?"

"We haven't eaten the same things, silly arse."

He bristled. "Fine, feel free to put forth a better suggestion."

She tapped her fist against her lips as they crept into yet another hallway.

He glared at her. "No? No brilliant ideas? Nothing I can shoot down like you did my suggestions?"

"It does remind me of something I've heard about, but it can't be that."

"Be what?"

She ducked to avoid a stuffed boar's head. "It sounds like what people get after quitting—"

A clacking ahead made her quiet. The wall curved and beyond it walked someone with resounding footfalls—a palace guard with their heavy boots? Luckily, they went in the opposite direction and entered a room, judging by the sounds of an opened door.

Time trickled far too slowly as, step by agonising step, they crept out of sight of that door. As soon as they were at a good distance, Petrichor said, "I want us to have a plan for what to do when we encounter someone."

"And I want fika," she said, hurrying her steps. "We don't have time for either."

He was about to argue when she stopped dead below a painting of what he thought was Loke and Sigyn. What was she doing? He prodded her arm. "Yes. Norse gods. I know you like them. Can we move on now?"

"It's not that. Sigyn's hair reminded me of something. You know that main conspirator Ingrid mentioned?"

Petrichor searched his memories. "Pond?"

"Pound."

"Right," he said, annoyed at his currently unreliable memory. "What about her?"

"I thought I recognised that name when she said it and I just figured out where from."

He threw a glance down the hallway. Still empty. "Well, do not keep me in suspense. Where?"

"The sanctum."

"What? Don't spout nonsense."

"I'm not." Her expression was stricken. "One of the copperplates on the wall says *Pound* and shows a menacing but beautiful woman with great hair."

At last Valour's obsession with beautiful women came in handy. What did it mean, though? Could Ingrid have seen it when they were in the sanctum and said that name to confuse them?

Moving again, Valour added, "I assumed this Pound was dead, though. Aren't all the etchings in the sanctum of assassins long gone?"

"Gone being the operative word. They put up an etching of you when you are no longer an Assassin of Axsten, not necessarily due to death."

"You mean she managed to leave?"

"Or she's one of the rare members to ever be banished."

Valour just clicked her tongue in response.

They moved down another hallway. Or was it one they had already traversed but going the other way? It terrified him that he could not trust his mind. He rubbed his eyes, where the headache had moved to, as he and Valour turned to go up a staircase.

"Do you think the order might be connected to this mess somehow?" Valour asked from a few steps above him.

He nigh missed a step. "Most certainly not."

"Oh, don't start thinking the best of them again," she said with a groan. "We've made such good strides with getting you to see the order for what it is."

"Do not be absurd. I am merely showing respect and loyalty."

"It doesn't deserve that, Petrichor."

They left the staircase and entered an atrium, that he guessed was on the second floor, in weighty silence. How did you stop believing in something that had been your lodestar since you were a child? A child. Alone, starving, crying in a cell. The sigh that escaped his lips came from the depth of his soul. "Yes. Fine. Perchance they are somehow involved."

"Do you think that's connected to why the two of us were given this hit?"

Valour led them down a corridor of more Kolmårds marble, and he peered into any open rooms. Still no people around, still the haunting stillness. And no clues to suggest anything untoward. Well, except for the lack of people.

"I don't know," he said, his voice shakier than he would have liked. He blamed it on all the whispering they had to do.

"Or that the people who are after us aren't just Brandquist minions, like Ingrid said? Perhaps the man in blue was sent by the order."

Now that was truly absurd. Her dizziness must have been affecting her thinking. "Obviously, they do not want to kill us. Firstly, they could simply slit our throats over supper if they wished. Secondly, we *are* the order. Why would the others want to get rid of us?"

"Because we've become better than them?" Valour said. "Or perhaps they know that we both want to leave?"

The corridor snaked to the right and narrowed.

"You forget about Halcyon," he said. "He would not do that to us."

"I wouldn't have thought so either." She pushed a door that had been ajar to reveal an empty parlour. "I love Halcyon, but he isn't the saint or hero you think him to be. He's human. Someone broken by the order. A killer. Just like us."

"Nevertheless, if the Order of Axsten wanted us dead, they wouldn't have sent us to hunt Brandquist, they would have assassinated us."

"Mm, I suppose."

He wasn't surprised that her struggles with trust had increased today.

They checked another room. This one was grander than the others, with an oversized crimson velvet bed. There was exquisitely carved furniture in exotic woods and lavish paintings of the royal family, including one of the greve as a young man. The room's smell was less opulent, though. It was stale and mildewy.

"The greve's bedroom?" Valour asked.

"I suppose so."

While he went through the drawers, finding nothing but clothes, she examined some books on the bedside table. She blew layers of dust off them. "I guess he doesn't read much anymore."

There was dust on quite a few things in the room—the full decanter of brandy, the brim-full snuff box, the bed. The other rooms, empty as they were, had been cleaned meticulously. Did the maids not come to this room? Did no one come in here at all?

They shared a look and left the eerie room without a word.

A few steps away, Valour said, "So, changing the topic so I can get the hairs on the back of my neck to lay back down, I've been wondering, why did you apply to be a bookbinder's apprentice when you couldn't afford to pay your way out of the order?"

He was going to tell her to mind her own business, but he was too tired, too achy, too confused to argue. "If I answer, and you mock me, heed me when I say I *will* slice your ears off with your own knife."

"Fair enough."

"I wanted to know, to prove, that my bookbinding was good enough."

"Was that it?"

He stalled while avoiding a massive taxidermised bear. She had been open with him, hadn't she? "Perhaps there was also a wish for some form of... hope. To feel that the dream was neither dead nor impossible. That good things can happen."

Hope. It was such a foreign thing to him and such a cruel mistress when he did indulge in it.

Instead of answering, Valour doubled over so fast she nearly extinguished her candle.

"Are you injured?" he said, checking for enemies.

She waved him off. "Only my godsdamned monthlies coming early and with stellar timing. I'm not bleeding yet, but the cramps just hit and they're bad this time."

Petrichor stepped back. "I see."

Valour straightened and scoffed. "It's not catching. You don't even have a womb. Those of us who do should be used to this shit." She continued walking, her hand still on her lower stomach. "Childbirth hurts. Monthlies hurt. Growing breasts hurts, and even fucking can hurt."

Surprised at the last fact, Petrichor couldn't think of an answer. He looked around. They were still alone. "Do you, um"—he cleared his throat—"need to rest?"

"No. Thanks, though. When the chance arises, I'll punch someone until they're in more pain than me. I find that helps."

"Remind me to duck if you get close."

She smiled sadly. "Mate... you never let anyone get close to you," she said with what he feared was pity but hoped was some breed of empathy.

Petrichor's pondering dissolved at the faint sounds of strings.

CHAPTER 52
SPLENDOUR AND PERIL

VALOUR HALTED. MUSIC. Haunting, melancholy, and familiar. A high-pitched female voice singing about death looming and how it reminds us to savour the day we've been given. Valour's heart sank. Of course it would be the ballad she and Ingrid had sung together.

She collected herself. "Should we follow the music?"

"If we are to find anything out, I suppose merely roaming empty corridors is pointless."

"I'll take that as a yes," Valour said, heading that way.

They followed the singing and the strings that accompanied it, until it quieted, replaced with raucous applause. A *lot* of applause. It sounded like more people than the palace's usual inhabitants.

Petrichor stopped in a recess, and she ducked in with him. Ahead of them was a vast space with open doors, and from within another song started up. The halls they'd travelled so far had been fully Nordic. Natural, clean, and understated. This room, however, was decked out in gold, mirrors, and colourful paintings of naked, beautiful people lounging on unnaturally green grass or chasing each other between exotic trees. The gilded ceiling was festooned with giant crystalline chandeliers with sugar-white candles that blinded her, especially if she caught sight of them in the many mirrors. The greve—or whoever was controlling him, if you believed Ingrid—was clearly trying to hide the rugged, dark, old-fashioned nature of Vinterstock and make this ballroom more continental. It looked like an imposing bear had put on rouge and a golden wig.

The many looking-glasses gave her a good view of the guests.

Besides seeming drunk and lustful, they were also dressed oddly and wore masks. A masked ball. Typical.

Petrichor crept closer. When she followed him, she was hit by the room's air, all stale heat, wine, and perfume, as heady as it was overwhelming. At the furthest end of the ballroom was a raised dais with a string quartet and a woman. She wore a fawn mask and a wig so high it appeared ready to reach for the chandeliers and catch fire. Behind them was a tapestry with wood nymphs and the words *The Hunt* in swirling letters. The high-wigged singer curtsied and started up again, this time a jauntier piece in a different language. Most of the crowd cheered in languages as varied as their appearances. Foreign dignitaries? She should've listened when Ingrid prattled on about masquerades.

"No wonder the hallways were so empty," Valour whispered. "Everyone's here."

Petrichor only nodded with a disapproving frown.

Valour, however, was curious to understand the appeal, despite this being a bloody waste of riksdaler that could go to feeding whole families. These guests certainly ate well, though. Servants crowded around the guests, offering trays of what must have been shucked oysters and some sort of tiny eggs served in nests of purple leaves. Some servants were waving fans at the wooziest attendees in the stuffy hall. Valour swallowed a groan as another wave of cramps hit.

"Should we leave? Or try to pass ourselves off as guests and investigate further?" Petrichor said by her ear.

Everyone in there was dressed-up and sloshed. Most were foreign and focused on watching the musicians, taking too many pinches of snuff, or secretly fondling each other. If ever there was a place they could sneak in undetected and overhear some conversations, this was it.

"Let's go in."

On a table by the doors stood a mass of fluted glasses filled with white wine. Over two of the glasses an abandoned wolf mask was draped, probably because it had a stain of something red in one corner. Valour put the mask on and grabbed some wine, handing a glass to Petrichor as well.

He took it and sneered at a couple giggling and groping each other in the nearest corner. "No decorum. Not only dressed as animals but behaving like them." He indicated the full crowd and added, "Well, not only animals, since 'The Hunt' is the motif."

He was right. There was a theme to the masks and the extravagant dresses and silk suits. Most were embroidered with flora or fauna, but some had bows and arrows. Most masks covered only the tops of the faces, leaving mouths free for food, drink, and tasting the other guests.

Then, for a moment brief as the brush of a moth wing, Valour thought she saw a familiar face in the crowd. She blinked and it was gone. *She* was gone. A passing similarity? Wishful thinking? Hallucinations? Valour gripped her glass so tight she worried it might shatter.

Petrichor began sauntering between the groups of revellers and she followed. All they overheard was either in foreign languages or small talk about the music and food. She picked up some gossip about the royals but nothing about the greve. Some bloke wearing a lynx-themed outfit lay slumped against the orchestra's dais. The costumed man was fast asleep, stinking of wine and stale 'ness. She carefully pulled his mask off to give it to Petrichor, who grimaced but put it on.

They passed two burly kammarherrar whispering to each other in a corner. They wore their usual palace outfits but had added animal masks and overly powdered wigs. She and Petrichor hid behind tall statues of the king and queen, close enough to overhear and see a little through the gap between the nearest statue's arm and body.

The taller kammarherre drunkenly slurred, "All I'm saying is that I wish I knew who"—his voice lowered—"Brandquist is."

This was more like it. What did the palace know about Ingrid? Valour wanted to celebrate that here at last was something relevant, but stayed quiet and leaned back.

"I know you're new and curious, pretty thing," said the other kammarherre, equally slurry. "Nevertheless, there's a sound and longstanding palace tradition to not learn anything about Brandquist or their excuse for an organisation."

The larger man smiled coquettishly below his half-face musk ox mask. "Of course."

For a moment they only shared eye contact and leers as if they planned to wank each other off right here in this crowded room. And considering what was going on, as long as they stayed discreet, they could probably have gotten away with it.

"But you know, do you not? Grant me a clue?" the taller kammarherre insisted, now toying with the shorter man's lapel.

"I don't," came the suddenly stern and sobering reply. "We do not give the drug-peddlers any credence by acknowledging them or questioning them when they are here. It is not only tradition but a firm rule. 'Tis wise to have deniability if the overseers come asking questions."

"Ah, of course," the man in the musk ox mask said, chastened. "Anyway, let's not ruin such a delicious night with conversation, handsome." With that, he hungrily fondled the other's crotch. Then they were kissing, fervently and with the sloppiness of drunkenness.

Valour and Petrichor moved on, him mumbling, "the affluent and their love for plausible deniability."

She thought she knew what that meant. Shit, was this why they'd needed her and Petrichor to figure out who Brandquist was? The people in this palace had made sure to never dirty their own hands by simply asking? The rest of the conversations they overheard were of no interest, and even when Valour noted doors leading to other rooms they all, annoyingly, had a servant with a tray of food or drinks by them.

"This is pointless," she mumbled after a few turns around the room.

Petrichor seemed like he wanted to argue for arguing's sake, but instead groaned and said, "Perhaps we ought to carry on checking the other rooms and hallways. Somewhere there must be paperwork to examine, and this is a good time for it since everyone is busy in here."

"True," Valour said. "From what I've heard, the writing rooms and the library are on the same floor as the ballroom."

He fixed her with an incredulous glare. "Why did you not mention that before?"

"I only remembered now," she answered truthfully. "You wouldn't believe how much former, or current, palace servants say after a few ales. But you must sieve through gibberish and exaggerations, meaning I don't have the full information at my godsdamned fingertips."

He spun on his heels and headed for the door. When they got to it, she saw him glance at the stage and, as if speaking to himself, murmur, "So that's why the students enthuse about trained opera sopranos. Art and science combined. Like a perfectly bound book."

Recognising that their kind weren't allowed music like this, Valour listened while she put her glass down. She didn't like it, but Petrichor looked spellbound. And unusually human. There was no time for that, though. She grabbed his sleeve. "Come on, she's so bloody loud that you'll hear her in the neighbouring rooms."

Still masked, and so able to claim to be lost guests if discovered somewhere unexpected, they re-entered the hall and carefully opened the nearest door. The room was an empty library with nothing but bookshelves and chairs. There was however an archway leading to another room which, thank the gods, contained a writing desk with a tall stack of letters. They both rushed to it but halted when there was a cough for attention behind them. A side door had opened and in came a woman in an extravagant dress and an arctic fox mask that covered her entire face, both only a shade whiter than her pasty skin. Her movements were deft and quiet as an assassin's. She went to the desk to retrieve a piece of paper and a quill.

"A thousand pardons," Petrichor said. He was probably going to launch into the excuse of being lost guests but was stopped by the woman in white holding up a hand.

Valour went to speak, and if necessary to attack, but Petrichor grabbed her arm, mouthing the word "Wait."

The woman wrote with precise movements. Valour was more fascinated than worried about being found out. Strange. Perhaps Petrichor had been right and they had little left to lose. Or the confusion had finally broken their minds. Either way, Valour found herself drawn to the milky-white jewel hanging at the woman's throat. Ingrid would've known what that stone was called. Valour cursed to herself and tried to divert her mind, but that itrine still in her coat pocket seemed to weigh enough that she could feel it.

Done writing, the arctic fox woman handed Petrichor the note while opening another desk drawer and pulling out an iron ball the size of a child's fist. She held it close to a candlestick on the desk and Valour noticed something sticking up on the ball's top. That couldn't be what it looked like?

The note, in neat letters, read:

> *Valour & Petrichor,*
> *Welcome.*
> *I suggest we all quietly enter a room further away from the masquerade. If you refuse, I shall light this bomb and toss it your way. If the festivities are to be interrupted, I would have it be due to something outrageous. The guests will prefer that.*

So, the thing on top of the ball was a fuse after all. Valour studied the bomb, held too bloody close to that candle. It was small enough to cause an explosion that would take out nothing but this room, maybe only the half that she and Petrichor were in. It all depended on how much black powder it contained and how willing the arctic fox lady was to sacrifice the library. Through the holes in her mask, the determined set of her mouth and her frenzied eyes made her look willing to sacrifice a lot of things to get her way.

She was right about the guests. They'd enjoy going home and gossiping about the unhinged Swedish ball where a bomb was set off, but would scorn any palace where commoners could amble in, capture guards, and steal rich folk's masks. Valour measured the distance to the side door. The woman in white might have time to escape out of it. They wouldn't.

Valour tried to sound fearless as she asked, "Who are you?"

The woman shook her white-wigged head and pointed to the note. With that, she beckoned to them, then left through the library with the lit candle in one hand and the bomb in the other.

Petrichor got close enough to Valour to whisper, "This is a splendid opportunity to get information. Thus, let's do her bidding for now. She can be no match for us in the long run."

Valour relaxed a little. She and Petrichor might be damaged, but broken glass was more dangerous than the intact kind.

When they had trailed after the woman into a room further away from the festivities, their hostess took them in with a snicker. "Hark, I have caught myself a wild wolf and a lethal lynx. Or, should I say, a little bitch and a castrated house cat?"

It took Valour a while to realise she was talking about their masks. "Have a care or this bitch will bite your face clean off. Who the shit are you?"

Petrichor gave his usual haughty sniff. "She is nothing but some ill-mannered kammarherre with delusions of grandeur and a flair for dramatics, and obviously she has a death wish too."

"What I am, you insolent fool," the woman snapped, "is the true leader of this city." She paused to take her mask off and smile at them, much in the way an arctic fox probably did at cornered prey. "The palace denizens call me Ulrika Eleonora. It has been some time since I have given my last name. Yet, when I speak it, it will be the one you know me by."

Next to Valour, a blanching Petrichor staggered back as if he had seen a ghost. Did he know who this was? Valour was pretty sure *she* did and while Petrichor seemed frozen in disgusted shock, she was bloody thrilled to speak up.

"Allow me to piss all over your theatrical monologue," Valour said. "You're Pound. I recognise you from your copperplate in the sanctum."

This Ulrika Eleonora Pound scowled like someone had stolen all her coin. The way she wrote, the way she moved, the way she needed to decide where and how they conversed... This woman liked control and having things the way she planned. Valour could use that.

Pound's full, painted lips pressed together in irritation. "I am indeed Ulrika Eleonora Pound. It is a blessing to have a full, real name. Not just a designation, like I was a thing or a concept."

Petrichor squirmed. Valour didn't blame him. Imagine finding out that you share a pet peeve with a snake like this. She took a deep breath, and as she did, she realised the two people shared something else: they both had that liquorice and pine scented cologne. Yuck.

"Now that introductions are over," Pound said in an aristocratic drawl so exaggerated it was plainly fake. "Perhaps we can decide what to do with you two. Or rather, you listen while I figure it out. You have made quite the mess by walking in here. As much as I love the order, its assassins do often create messes."

"Is that what you used to do when you were an assassin?" Valour asked.

She got only a scoff for a reply and decided to chance her arm.

"I read in the sanctum's archive about your expulsion. Was what they said about your behaviour true?"

She kept a close eye on Pound's pallid, painted face. Would she know that Valour had never bothered with those books?

"My behaviour?" Pound snapped, looking to the door when laughter was heard from the hallway. "There was nothing wrong with my behaviour. It is obvious for anyone with insight that the Order of Axsten should not be a lapdog, but a leader."

Valour thought hard, piecing those words together with Pound's current scheme of being at the forefront of the city's governance. "So, you really thought the order should rule Vinterstock? How would that even work?"

"Is that all the records showed? I cannot believe Sister Glass noted only that, nor that she banned me. That short-sighted, jealous vittra." Pound's nostrils flared. "I had a detailed, perfect plan for how the order should control Vinterstock and how it should metamorphose into a governing force while still maintaining its time-honoured, deific traditions. *That* should have been in the books."

Valour couldn't believe that had worked! This woman was defensive and liked the sound of her own voice. Or... perhaps Pound had missed the company of her own kind and wanted them to witness and understand? Either way, this all boded well for getting answers. And, Valour hoped, for keeping her talking so she didn't light that bloody fuse.

"So, you came to work as a kammarherre after your expulsion?" Valour tried.

"Do not be absurd, child. You cannot just become a kammarherre. Not unless you are an aristocrat. I started as a palace guard and clawed my way up." Pound's indignation waned, replaced by another predatory smile. "You two do not remember the first time we met, do you?"

The vixen's voice had been plummy and sniggering. It shouldn't have made Valour feel like an icy steel spear had just been shafted down her spine.

"This is the first time, isn't it?" Valour queried.

"No," Petrichor breathed.

"That night during the Valborg festivities was our first meeting. Then I truly *was* a regular kammarherre, rising in the ranks at too slow a pace. And you were gawky youths with blemishes. Remember?"

"Valborg Night? Wait. We were in this palace..." Ashen-faced, Petrichor was rubbing his forehead and frowning as if in extreme pain.

"What's wrong?" Valour asked him quietly. This would be a terrible time for him to have one of his panic fits.

"There's something... I can see scenes in my head, like blurry memories that are not quite mine."

Valour's skin goose-pimpled. "I don't think this is the time—"

He rubbed harder at his forehead, leaving red marks. "We'd been to the yearly bonfire and as a reward for our hard work that spring, we were to see the palace and meet the greve. No, that never happened. What in all blazes is this?"

"Ah. There you go," Pound said with smug satisfaction. "I always said that his drug scheme was not tenable."

"What the shit are you on about?" Valour asked.

"I knew that when you stopped receiving your dose of forgetfulness tonic at gloriam, the memories would seep back in after the merest suggestion. I told my dearest Halcyon as much."

Petrichor balked. "What?"

Pound laughed as she put her mask back on. "Are you shocked

that Halcyon has been drugging you for years to hide memories from you? Or that I term him 'my dearest'? You, little boy, should at least not be surprised at the latter."

Petrichor's mouth opened but nothing came out.

"Both, you arse-boil," Valour answered in his stead.

Pound eyed the door. "Look, I have a masquerade to host, I cannot stand here and explain every little thing to you insolent urchins."

"Explain? You mean to tell us unhinged lies," Petrichor said through gritted teeth.

Pound's calm, superior air vanished and her nostrils flared. "Unhinged? How dare you? The plain truth is that your sainted Halcyon lied and tricked you to make you forget that he took you here the night the greve died."

"Died?" Valour and Petrichor said in unison.

"Not a full death, obviously. Only one of the mind. Fortunately, my family kept to the runes, incantations, and blot of the olden magic." She searched their faces. "I have told you this before. It is curious that you do not recall even one whit. That is useful information."

She still studied people like an assassin, then? Valour gave exactly one rat's arse what Pound found useful, though. She wanted her own information. "Blot? Like the sacrifices to the gods? Olden magic?"

Her thoughts went to what Ingrid said about the red haze and the man who frothed at the mouth and collapsed.

"How else would I have controlled the greve? Moreover, without olden magic, would *your* forgetfulness tonic have operated as it has?"

Pound's body language was softening down from the rage. Valour couldn't afford for her to stop talking and start lighting fuses. "Everyone knows how 'ness works. Addicts use forgetfulness tonics to forget their whole pasts, living only in the present. It has nothing to do with you or your alleged magic skills."

"Nothing to do with me?" Pound's eyes flashed. "I planned it meticulously. I used certain magical runes to blank your mind of that very night and then forgetfulness tonic did the rest, taken in full right afterwards and in smaller daily increments ever since. 'Tis deuced brilliant work, I'll have you know."

A sting of grief hit Valour. Her mother had so many times told her the old tales of Oden, the All-father, giving humans some of the magic runes that could control the elements and even bring back the dead.

The very picture of disbelief, Petrichor said, "Lies and nonsense. Are you actually claiming you can use magic from the Norse gods to alter the function of 'ness tonics? Counteracting the complete erasure of the past that forgetfulness tonics usually bring?"

"The tonics are made from products of the olden magic. Of course they can be altered and specified with more olden magic." Pound gave a half snigger, half snort. "It never ceases to amaze me how people get used to something extraordinary to the point of it becoming ordinary, like the 'ness potions, but then cannot grasp something new that is equally extraordinary. Even when it is kin to the first extraordinary thing."

"Such an expert," Petrichor muttered.

"Indeed I am," Pound stated. "I have sacrificed enough to the gods to be in their favour and thus be granted certain magics. Such a thing takes years of hard work and study, and must be done in this city, where we still keep the gods alive in our souls. I have achieved what no one has done for hundreds of years."

"To completely rid yourself of humility?" Valour asked.

She regretted it right away. Maybe angering Pound would be what made her light that fuse. Still, it ate at Valour. The gods so rarely concerned themselves with human affairs. Why did they fall for this arse-wart's blots of innocent humans?

"To wield the power of the gods. Or at least a morsel of it, which is more than any human has done since the days of our Viking ancestors," Pound said, seeming drunk on proving herself. "The magic of the gods burns within me, yet more with every blot I sacrifice, so much so that I get glimpses of the future. 'Twas how I knew there would be a dramatic death scene taking out several enemies in one blow. Meaning you two and Brandquist, I believe. The glimpses were also how I knew to work the tonics and the runes to make you forget."

Valour tasted bile. She'd taken 'ness every day for years? Would her body ever recover from that damage? She wanted her memories back.

Her skin was still goose-bumping and prickling and then… Shit. A white-hot stab of pain at the top of her head and scattered memories piercing her mind. A Valborg Night. Cold? Yes, it had been a cold spring that year and she'd worn her least raggedy cloak. They'd sung and drunk akvavit by the city's biggest bonfire. Then Halcyon said something important—she fought to remember it through the unbearable headache. He'd said that bringing the two most promising new members, showing how vibrant, youthful, and flexible the order was, would convince the greve to stop—Stop what?

She groaned and considered banging her head with her hand to dislodge the memories, but she was in enough pain. Instead, she tried the memory technique her mother had taught her: focus on the details in the memories and build from there. Details. A grand room. Far away from everyone else in the palace, for privacy. Halcyon, Petrichor, Pound, and herself standing by an impressive fireplace. There was a tart alcohol taste on her tongue… The greve had been drinking lingonberry liqueur, and he'd given her and Petrichor a glass of it too. Neither of them had known to sip it but downed it like it was a shot of akvavit. Yes, that recalled berry booziness coated her mouth now, and she could remember the greve and a younger Pound arguing.

Here and now, the older Pound was boasting on and on how, after many experiments, she had managed to alter the effects of the 'ness. Valour tried not to listen but it was something about scorching the right runes into the skin of the person whose blood went into the tonic and then adding the rune-burned skin into the tonic to infuse. Could Pound not shut up? Valour had to focus on her memories!

Petrichor croaked out some follow-up question, as ever overfilled with godsdamned academic interest.

"No, that is not all," Pound said. "You do not merely syphon the bleeder a little, like when normal 'ness is created. You exsanguinate them fully, sacrificing them to the gods."

Valour finally blocked Pound and Petrichor out. She continued to put the puzzle pieces of her memories together, detail by detail. That chilly spring night. The fireplace with a roaring fire. The lingonberry liqueur.

The greve had taken the last sip from his tiny, delicate glass. "Say what you wish, bring me whatever star acolytes you have, you shall not convince me. The facts are that the Order of Axsten is costly and archaic. I shall disband it and train my overseers and hangmen to assassinate."

Pound's expression had gone from charming persuasion to murderous rage in a heartbeat. "Assassination is not just murder. 'Tis an artform with sacred rituals and techniques."

"My dear, you can be such a diverting companion and I am certain you shall have a wonderful career as a kammarherre," the greve said with his characteristic charming, carefree laugh. "However, the moment the subject veers to your beloved order, you become so het up. You need to calm down and let all that go. I know what is best. The order will be disbanded, starting at daylight."

Valour could recall how Pound's hands became white-knuckled fists at her sides. "This is not only about costs, is it? You resent the order for being older and more feared than you."

"Nonsense. Who needs fear when you have admiration? The order is nothing but faux-religious poppycock. It is pointless. And"—he gave her a pitying smile that had a hint of spitefulness—"it is dead. You and your companions have wasted your trip, I shall not be swayed."

Pound's white-knuckled hands had changed somehow then. Yes. They had the dull metal of knuckle irons on them now. "You will not be swayed? Would you have been swayed yesterday or the night before, when I refused to enter your bed? If I had lain with you, would my order be safe?"

The greve gave another untroubled laugh. "No. It would still be disbanded. I fear you really do not matter as much as you think you do. You, *my tamed beast*, are but the lowliest of my kammarherrar since the organisation you love so much threw you out," he said in a voice so full of jolly breeziness that he might've been discussing a comic play he'd seen. "I cannot imagine being banned from something as wretched as that timeworn, dismal, useless excuse for an organisation. The shame must be giving you heartburn. Still, it offers a lesson that you need to learn: you are not in control, my darling doll."

That had been when the first blow struck. Pound had used her powerful fists with those knuckle irons to hit his long, aristocratic nose. The greve had tried to call for the palace guards but she had struck his mouth. As the greve protected his face—silly man, he should have protected his whole head—she jabbed over and over again. At the side of his head, the top of it, the back of it—pounding on, like Tor with his hammer, until Halcyon yanked her back.

Valour could see it so clearly in her memories now, the greve lying with blood pooling around his head like a gory halo. Valour had started calling for a physician but Pound broke free from Halcyon and punched her in the stomach.

"Keep quiet, child," Pound then snarled, blood spatter and spit on her lips. "I shall fix this."

Now, in the current time and place, Petrichor and Pound had continued discussing his memories of that night.

Pound said, "I should have ignored Halcyon's pleas and killed you the moment you were away from prying eyes. He begged so prettily for us to try the forgetfulness tonic route, though." She sighed. "Well, my curiosity regarding your memories is satisfied. It is time to decide what to do with yo—"

Petrichor sniffed and ran a hand over his hair. "You know what? It really, absolutely, definitely is not."

With that, he took off running like a scolded cat, with a grip on Valour's coat sleeve.

CHAPTER 53

LOSE YOURSELF IN THE MASQUERADE

POUND'S PERFUME LINGERED in Petrichor's nostrils as he ran. Or perhaps it was coming from himself. Did Halcyon like their shared cologne?

Halcyon.

He had saved their lives, but he had done it by drugging them and stealing their memories, by lying for years and years. And he had been bedding and obeying the woman who had wanted to kill them. Petrichor ran faster.

"What in Freja's damn cats are you doing?" Valour screamed from behind him.

He called back to her, "Are you telling me you wished to stay?"

Inwardly, he cursed. He was out of breath already. An Assassin of Axsten should be able to run for hours. Blood loss and pain must have sapped all his energy, or maybe it was withdrawal.

"Stay? With the murderous go-getter and her dainty death orb?" Valour shouted back. "Shit, no. But I'd like more bloody answers. Or at least to not be escaping right into a crowded room where her kammarherrar wait for us."

Ah. Yes. He was leading them into the ballroom, wasn't he? He hadn't planned anything but merely sprinted away from the memories, from that woman, from what Halcyon had done to them. Still, Valour didn't need to know that. "There's safety in a crowd. Pound would not dare blow us up in there for fear of hurting some viscount or baroness."

"She can have us collared and thrown out, though," Valour retorted. "She wanted to avoid that, but you're not giving her much of a choice."

"She will not shout orders to her kammarherrar and draw attention to our presence unless she has to. She'll come for us herself and she's older, out of practice as an assassin, and encumbered by that robe à la française. Did you see the panniers on that gown? Too wide, and no doubt metal. She shan't catch us."

"All right. If you're sure."

If he wasn't rather busy at the moment, he might have appreciated her faith in him.

He threw himself into the ballroom and its throngs of people. The nearest group turned to gape at him. Damnation, he should've slowed earlier and sauntered in. He stood still and awkward like a statue under their gazes until Valour said, "Pardon the hasty entrance, everyone. He was worried he'd miss the minuet. It's his favourite dance."

The crowd appeared sceptical but turned away. No doubt they had seen odder things tonight.

The two of them strode deep into the crowd with forced composure. Valour grabbed a wine glass and over the rim of it murmured, "So. Bloody forgetfulness tonics, huh?"

"Quite," he whispered back, a knot in his stomach. "No wonder there was so much pressure to attend gloriam. Even if we missed dinner and vesper, we had to make it to gloriam."

Valour had taken her mask off and was looking behind them for Pound. "Mm, it wasn't for the reading of the targets after all, huh? I bet our drinks were always so over-brewed to mask the 'ness taste."

Right as they jostled deeper into the crowd, Petrichor heard thudding footsteps and called-out orders. Pound must've arrived and was liaising with her kammarherrar to find them. Yet, they weren't ordering the guests to clear out, meaning Pound was still trying to keep a low profile. Good.

He realised Valour wasn't by his side and turned. She had been stopped by a handsome blond in a gold lamé three-piece suit and an elaborate cravat fixed with a stag's head pin, which matched his mask. His outfit screamed foreign aristocrat, probably English. The fop eyed Valour with admiration. Why did things always happen to her? Could she not aim for one discreet, mundane moment for once in her life?

The gold-clad lord gave Valour a charming smile as he removed his mask. "Sink me, m'dear, I cannot tell if your costume is that of an explorer or an outlaw?" She stared at him blankly, so he spoke on, punctuating his words by waving the elegant stag mask in his hand. "No, that would not follow the theme. A woodsman, then? Either way, ye gads, but 'tis marvellously peculiar."

"I don't have time for your aristo-nonsense. Move. Or I'll have to shove you," Valour said in neutral tones.

The aristocrat sniggered, but there was something beneath the inane facade, an intelligence in those twinkling eyes. "Such rudeness for the stranger who plans to detain the two kammarherrar who hound you."

Petrichor looked behind Valour and yes, two kammarherrar were coming this way with thunderous expressions.

"We're leaving. Right now," Petrichor hissed to her.

Valour didn't answer but, while looking the fop right in the eye, reattached her mask.

"Ah, a wolf in assassin's clothing?" he said. "Excellent. Faith, madam, but I believe I like you best of all the attendees at this soiree. Godspeed."

With that he bowed, gestured for her to move on with his ring-studded hand, and then headed straight for the kammarherrar while acting drunk and shouting about needing directions to the powder room.

"I think I see a door free from guards or servants over there," Valour said, leading the way.

True enough, there it was. Petrichor followed her towards it. Blocking the way, however, was a group of young men. Like moths to a flame, they were buzzing around an older woman with lidded eyes, plump lips, and no mask. They all reeked of 'ness and kept moving about, making it hard to go around them. A younger woman in a wolverine mask joined them. She was flapping her fan across her face and the lace at her bosom heaved with heavy, excited breaths as she said, "Gentlemen, Mama, I have just this minute heard that there are menacing intruders at the ball! A man and a woman in low-born clothing. If you see them, you are to inform any of the servants or kammarherrar. Is this not exciting?"

Petrichor and Valour instantly but subtly turned and headed the other way.

"Low-born clothing. Balderdash," Petrichor hissed, smoothing the lapels of Halcyon's coat and wishing he had been able to change.

"Never mind that. We need to get out of here bloody fast."

"I know," he groaned. "We should not have come to the palace. Once more, I begin to think that we are not half as clever as we think."

"Speak for yourself, huffy breeches. I never thought I was clever."

She grinned and the familiarity of it nearly calmed him. The reprieve in his fretting was brief though, as a big hand grabbed his arm and yanked. Before he knew what was happening, he was pulled in through a trapdoor behind a tapestry. Valour was drawn in a heartbeat after him.

Petrichor quickly examined his surroundings. He knew from books what this space was, a retiring room—a smaller chamber connected to ballrooms, made to let the wearied rest on divans before returning to the festivities. Or to copulate, in pairs or groups. The room, made to fit no more than two dozen people, was lit only by the small fireplace and an oversized chandelier filled with beeswax candles. That, in combination with an opened bay window, meant the small room smelled of night air and honey, not the ballroom's odour of powder, competing perfumes, sweat, and an undertone of sex. Petrichor took a deep breath, only to be punched in the left side of his stomach and lose his air completely. Pound stepped into his immediate view. Since it was only her in here, she must've been the one to yank him in. That, and the power of her jab, showed her physical strength.

Valour leapt between them with fists raised. "Get away from him and fight someone who's ready for—" She stopped as Pound picked up her little bomb and waved it.

Petrichor made himself stand as if the blow hadn't hurt like damnation. He glanced at the trapdoor.

"I have kammarherrar on the other side of that door. Even if you could escape, it would do you no good," Ulrika Eleonora Pound said, wiping her brow. The powder on her face had dissolved during their chase and the shadows under her eyes, in combination with her scars, crow's feet, and that cruel but full mouth, made this stunning woman look daunting beyond compare. If he had still wanted to be a cold-blooded killer, Petrichor would have tried emulating her. Now he worried that there were far too many things they had in common. And he loathed her.

Pound held the bomb to the fire. "Lay your weapons on the floor and stand in that corner."

"I won't. It's an empty threat. You risk blowing yourself up if you light that in here," Valour said.

"At this point, I am enraged enough to take that risk." Pound held the bomb close enough that the fuse nearly touched a flame.

They both dropped a knife each.

"*All* of your knives."

Reluctantly, they obeyed.

Pound picked up Petrichor's longest blade, brandishing it in her free hand. "I simply cannot decide whether to kill you, which would bring the risk of someone hearing screams as well as me having to handle the notable fight the order trained you to provide…" Here she bowed a little in a perverse mockery of respect. "Or stick to my well-ordered plan. I do so hate changes in my plans after I have made them."

"Your plan?" Valour asked.

Pound tutted, bomb in one hand and knife in the other. "Do not feign ignorance. That is beneath followers of Axsten. I know my mercenary told you of the scenario in which you are meant to die. Although we require Brandquist here for that. I thought you three were meant to be together?"

Ingrid was in their death scenario, then. It was astounding how the socialite wormed her way into everything.

"Not anymore," Valour said. "Let's strike a deal. I'll tell you how

111111111111

to find and capture Brandquist in return for a certain answer."

The sudden coldness in her voice made him cast a glance over at her. She wouldn't really give Ingrid up?

His stomach was less agonising now. Would it be possible to leap over to Pound and grab the bomb before she had time to light it? It didn't matter. She would use that knife, either throwing it or stabbing him.

"Since I require some time to decide how and when you are going to perish," Pound said, "I suppose I can answer one question. You have as long as it takes for me to make my mind up."

Pound walked over to a bowl. She gripped the knife differently to free two fingers to pick something else up. A fresh, black cherry? The last of the year's imports were plainly earmarked for the palace. Pound must've gotten spoiled; she wouldn't last a day back at the sanctum. And to think she had stood in the archive and complained about the assassins going to seed.

Still holding the bomb near the fireplace, Pound chewed the fruit while making direct eye contact with Valour. "Ask."

"What is Halcyon's connection to you?" Valour said.

Perplexed, Petrichor gave her a look. He thought he was the only one spending possibly their last moments in life thinking about Halcyon. He should have told Valour about meeting this woman in the archive. They should have trusted each other sooner.

With nonchalance, Pound spat the cherry stone into the fireplace, making it hiss. "I was his mentor when he was a fledgling assassin. When I was ousted, I needed a connection to the Order of Axsten and so took him to bed."

"Took? You mean *lured* him to bed," Petrichor said.

Pound frowned, showing Petrichor that he had figured out something she didn't want him to. Grudgingly, he could see it now. How he could've fallen for someone like this fiend—confident, strong-minded, powerful, and a classic coldblooded Assassin of Axsten—if he was a young, lost, and lonely Halcyon.

She put another plump cherry in her mouth, biting into it so they could see the blood-red juice spreading over her teeth, then drawled, "My, you are upset, aren't you, little killjoy? Halcyon owes me a great deal. I was the one who prepared him to be the next leader when Sister Glass perished."

"And in return?" he said through tight jaws.

She again spat the cherry pit into the fire, then gave him the sort of pleasure-in-hurting-others look that Encumbrance usually wore. "In return, I ensured he would need me, that he would love me more than his own life and give me whatever I desire. Information, assistance, indirect control of the order, and of course... that delectable body of his."

Petrichor had to clench his hands to keep them from strangling her.

"You slept with another assassin?" Valour said in nauseated tones.

"Oh, we did not sleep much," Pound said with a smirk. "Still don't."

His stomach lurched. In his mind, he saw it once more—that day when he had opened Halcyon's door at the sound of moaning and seen a woman riding the order's leader to the bed's breaking point.

A much older memory sparked and with his voice barely controlled, Petrichor said, "On that Valborg Night, when you had beaten the greve into an unconscious mess... Halcyon agreed with us that a physician should be called."

Pound gave a hollow laugh, looking up at the chandelier above. "Oh, poor Halcyon still wants us to come clean. Every year I must convince him not to, reminding him that we would hang for our crime and of how utterly lost he should be without the order." She pinned her gaze back on them with the air of a cat enjoying the panic of the mouse. "Furthermore, he often points out that if he left, the order would be led by Brother Encumbrance or Sister Mire. Something that would mean more frequent and bone-crushing punishments for you two, which sounds perfectly acceptable, nay lovely, to me."

Halcyon did care for him, then? Or was it just for Valour's sake?

"That night," Pound continued, sounding distracted as she clearly still pondered their death scenario, "it took ages before he saw reason and left with you. Anyway, I stayed here, getting ready to control the greve and through him, this city."

"And how you fail at it. The city's citizens starve and often see no other way to survive than turning to crime and taking 'ness," Valour said. "You couldn't lead ants to spilled sugar."

"How dare you, insolent bloody bitch?" Pound roared, her fake accent now replaced with a normal lower-class one. "Spending our riksdaler on the city's defences, upgrading the palace, and planning to extend Vinterstock's borders is more important than feeding inbred peasants who'd die from the pox anyway. They are a drain on resources and so are you." Pound swished her knife through the air in front of them. "Time for *my* answer. Where is Brandquist?"

CHAPTER 54

MAKE SOMEONE PAY

VALOUR HAD BEEN trying to figure out a way to make Pound drop both her weapons but found none. Now her patience was gone and her anger boiling over. She threw herself at Pound without any thought. When she was a hair's breadth away from that knife and bomb, a voice behind her said, "Stop moving or I shall shoot you right in your empty head."

Slowly, Valour turned to see about eight kammarherrar behind them. She hadn't even heard them come in over the rush of blood in her ears, the revelries in the ballroom, and the godsdamned droning on of this power-hungry monster. The kammarherrar had swords or pistols drawn. The one who had spoken was the milky-blond man she'd seen on the square the day she was told to assassinate Brandquist. He pointed a duelling pistol right at her head, as he had warned, and grinned.

"Tut-tut. I did warn you that I had kammarherrar on standby. Someone like me always has followers," Pound said. "I have had years to gather up my own temporary version of the order. Soon, I will be ready to elevate the real thing, and Vinterstock, to a gloried future."

Controlling the order with Halcyon as a figurehead, and Vinterstock with the greve as a figurehead, until she did away with the men and stepped into the light. A shrewd plan. *If* Ingrid hadn't gotten in the way and pulled her and Petrichor into it.

"A gloried future? You mean one where only the godsdamned rich survive?" Valour asked. How many poor and unmissed commoners had died as sacrifices for this woman to use her magic?

"Not the spoiled aristocrats, if that is what you mean. Only those strong and coldblooded enough to take power and coin shall prosper," Pound said as if stating the obvious. "We shall rid the city of the weak, creating a stronger population with plenty of provisions since Vinterstock will no longer be overpopulated."

Valour was about to say how boneheaded that was, since those Pound thought of as weak could have strengths that she was too bloody narrow-minded to see. But to Valour's indescribable shock, Petrichor, of all people, got there first.

"A misguided scheme. Any ecosystem needs variety. Remove one group completely and the system will suffer. And a group of individuals with different strengths will succeed better than a homogenised one," he said with his most condescending sniff. "Furthermore, your reasoning is inhumane. Empathy may not be my strong suit, but I've seen how it can be an asset."

Valour gawped at him. He hadn't just changed. Fenrir's shitballs, he had blown her mind at how much a person even *could* change.

"I need not listen to you," Pound said. She turned her attentions to her followers. "Search them for additional weapons, then tie them up. We will keep to the original death scenario. It is cleaner and will work better for our future plans. Besides, my scrying showed me this is how it will happen."

About to put up a fight, Valour stopped when she felt that pistol pushed against the back of her head. She couldn't reveal the truth about Pound's atrocities if she died tonight. She sighed. She was really starting to hate pistols.

"You're not only inhumane, you know," she said to Pound. "You're a predictable, pathetic arsehole."

Pound got closer. "Insulting me is bad for your health. Besides, Axsten bade us to keep clean language."

"He did. Wonder what he would think of you calling me a 'bloody bitch' a while ago, huh?"

Pound's right eye twitched. Ah. A chink in the armour. Pound loved the order and Valour had seen how hazardous that was. In Halcyon, in Petrichor, in her mother.

"I shall search this one myself," Pound said, roughly frisking Valour and, after finding no extra weapons, taking her coat and the stolen mask. When finished, she pushed Valour onto a chair with enough force that the wood creaked. Then, for good measure, Pound punched her. Blood as hot as her rage poured from Valour's nose as she screamed curses. Two kammarherrar tied her up so tight that it was hard to breathe.

She thought of her momentary vision in the ballroom. No. That was nought but desperate hope and hallucinations playing tricks on her.

Next to her, Petrichor was unmasked, searched, and relieved of some sort of long needle before being bound to a second chair. He'd been clever enough not to fight and get himself beaten up, but bore the procedure with dignity and disdain, like it couldn't really touch him. She should have done that too, as judging by Pound's glares, that enraged her even more. Petrichor won again. He was an arsehole too. Everyone was, and Valour wanted to scream until they stopped it. She struggled against her ropes, making her period cramps and headache worse. Valour would make someone pay for all of this.

THIS TIME WHEN Petrichor faced the likelihood of dying, he wasn't even frightened. Only resolute to understand things before he died. He casually sat back, as much as the ropes allowed, and asked Pound, "When did you decide that the forgetfulness dosing wasn't enough, that you would kill us after all?"

Ulrika Eleonora Pound was adjusting her many-layered dress as if it chafed. "Do be quiet. I am deliberating how to get you into the staged scenario. We require Brandquist in situ and we need to sneak you out of the palace."

Valour laughed, facing Petrichor. "I bet it was when she realised that we were racking up more assassinations than she ever did."

Slam. This time it wasn't a punch but a hard slap that Pound gave her. The blood from Valour's already punched nose sprayed across the wall.

"Or maybe," Valour slurred through the blood dripping into her mouth, "it was when Brandquist saw too much one evening and you decided that loose ends must be tied up." She spat blood in Pound's direction, missing her.

Petrichor saw Valour's scheme. Buying time by ensuring Pound kept talking and simultaneously making her divulge more than she wanted to by provoking her? Not a bad tactic.

He pretended not to understand that a staunch member of the Order of Axsten followed rules, even if it was to their detriment. "Palace traditions or no, I am stunned you did not a whit of research into who Brandquist was? Tsk. Axsten taught us to be meticulous in our reconnaissance."

Her upper lip twitched. It really was too easy to make her lose her composure. "I did enough research, you foul annoyance. I found out that the Brandquist changes, and that judging by the cloaked figure who came, it was a woman. One who sounded young, affluent, and uncomfortable in her role."

Confidence trickled into him. Pound not knowing Brandquist's identity, and surely kicking herself for not finding out earlier, was why their death scenario hadn't been arranged yet. It made sense, they themselves had only figured out Brandquist's identity on the way here and had told no one. He was about to push her further when his head swam and, before he could stop himself, he swayed as much as the ropes allowed.

Pound chortled. "Dizzy? No doubt the withdrawal. I shall have to tell Halcyon. These past weeks, he has badgered me about stopping the dosing since you were getting side effects from the tonics." She rolled her eyes. "One of you having unnatural sleep patterns and the other extreme nightmares, apparently? Both early signs of 'ness addiction and clear warnings of permanent damage starting. But—"

"Hang on," Valour interrupted. "My monthly came early. Is that a 'ness side effect?"

Pound and Petrichor both stared at her.

"No?" She sighed. "Shit. Well, I had to ask. I'm usually so regular. Probably the stress bringing it on, then."

"Gods in Asgård, why am I wasting my breath on you?" Pound said, still distracted by planning their death.

"Because we're the rare breed of people you feel there's any point in talking to," Valour said with scorn. "And you've missed that ever since you were kicked out of the order."

Wide-eyed, Pound stared at her. Had Halcyon not told her about Valour's infuriating skill at reading people? He had to say something. To keep Pound answering questions and to keep Valour from being beaten insentient. "So Halcyon wanted to stop dosing us?"

Pound gave a dismissive hand gesture, back in her own thoughts. "Mm. The soft-hearted man blathered on about being responsible for you and no longer caring what happened to him, or the order, if it saved you from permanent damage. Such a disappointment."

Valour sniffled through her bloody nose. "So instead of letting him stop drugging us, you… what? Decided to give us a high-profile job as a treat and then kill us?"

"Not a treat, you bird brain," Pound snapped. "It was an ingenious way for me to get rid of Brandquist and you two at the same time, without me risking being charged by the overseers or having Halcyon blame me." She put on a theatrically worried expression. "After all, you were hunting the dangerous Brandquist. So easy to be killed in a pistol fight. Two dead assassins and a drug lord having slaughtered each other. Who would question it? Moreover, who would care?"

Halcyon would. And Petrichor was sure he'd see through Pound's ruse.

Valour lit up. "The mercenary! To keep yourself completely out of this, you hired a weirdly dressed foreigner to do the dirty work."

Still wriggling to find a way this tied-up position wouldn't hurt his shoulder, Petrichor took a moment to appreciate that he figured out the mercenary's role long before Valour.

"Oberleutnant Schneider is certainly better robed than you," Pound said, glaring at Valour's clothes.

"What? That silk coat is pointless. It—" She halted, and after a beat started giggling.

He stopped wriggling to regard her instead. Valour had been gazing into the empty part of the room but now she looked back at him, the very picture of elation. Was she hallucinating? Or losing what little wits she had once had? Why couldn't he have been captured with Halcyon instead?

Halcyon. Petrichor would have given anything to speak to him. Yes, he could see how Halcyon would foolishly fall for this woman. He even partly understood the drugging. The lies, however, he could not forgive. Like Valour, he was sick to death of lies. Thus, he would at least get the truth out of Pound.

"This mercenary of yours," Petrichor said. "I assume he was the one who told the overseers that we were hiding Brandquist in that warehouse? Why did he not simply come in and kill us?"

"The inept man sent a messenger boy to me saying that he could not pick the lock," she said, only half focusing on the conversation. "I replied that I was alerting the overseers, who would make quick work of that door. Then it was up to him to make sure you escaped their clutches and got somewhere he could set up the death scene."

There was a rap on the door and a drink-slurred voice asked if whoever was in there would not come out and play the parlour games that were starting.

"Return to the ballroom and act normal," Pound said to her kammarherrar. "Keep everyone out of here, ensure our dignitaries are contented and occupied, and ensure no one speaks overlong to the greve."

One of the kammarherrar, a tall woman, glowered at Valour and Petrichor. "Are you quite certain we ought to leave you alone with them?"

Pound's eyes flashed. "Do you truly imagine that, even without this bomb, I could not handle two tied-up, unarmed children?"

Children? Petrichor balked. They were well over twenty.

"Of course not. Pray pardon me," the tall kammarherre squeaked. "We shall return to attend on you when suitable, Ulrika Eleonora."

The kammarherrar bowed or curtsied and left.

Throughout all of this, Valour kept sniggering.

"What in the name of Hel herself can be so amusing?" Pound growled.

After a shaky breath, Valour stifled her giggling fit. "Sorry. It's the fatigue mixing with relief, I suppose. I wasn't hallucinating. I can still trust my eyes and my head."

Pound sneered. "Of what are you speaking, you inane girl?"

Petrichor stiffened at the sound of a pistol being cocked.

Rising from behind one of the divans was a clear voice. "She's talking about me. Also, she's not a girl. Trust someone who's had first-hand experience, she is utterly and completely a red-blooded, full-grown woman."

The last words were said with such love and lust that any lingering question of who the voice belonged to vanished.

Petrichor's exasperation broke through his tension and he muttered, "Good evening, Miss Rytterdahl."

Keeping her pistol aimed at Pound, Ingrid playfully curtsied at him. "Well met again, Master Assassin."

CHAPTER 55

FLASH POINT

BREATHING CORRECTLY BECAME hard for Valour. Pound was giving the newcomer and the door calculating glances, no doubt wondering when Ingrid had snuck in.

Ingrid's bravado cracked, momentarily showing a face saturated with fear, but she stood assertive and firm as she told Pound, "Place that bomb on the floor, far away from any light sources. If you do not, I fear I must shoot you before you have time to light the fuse."

Valour tried hard, so godsdamned hard, not to gawp at Ingrid. Her bottle-green dress was embroidered with gilded animals and had a plunging neckline, her cheeks were as rosy as her lips, her tall wig was glossy black. But the most important thing Ingrid wore was an expression of iron determination. She was a vision of beauty and force mixed as she stood like a Valkyrie, ready to protect two wretched assassins that she hadn't known for long. Hel's realm, she had no right to look like that. Or to make Valour feel like this.

With a look of someone calculating, Pound slowly put the iron orb down at her feet.

"How?" Valour said, her joy switched back to her earlier fury at Ingrid. "I saw you in the bloody ballroom but couldn't believe it. How can you be here, dressed up, and moving around like you were invited?"

Pound had her gaze on the ornate pocket pistol in Ingrid's hand. "Miss Rytterdahl was invited but declined her invitation due to being at her father's sickbed, I believe. The only question that matters is why some vain little minuet-dancing chatterbox is pointing a weapon at me."

Valour muttered, "Pound, meet Brandquist."

Understanding dawned on Pound's features. "Ah. I did once entertain the notion that you may be the current Brandquist." She squinted at Ingrid. "However, when we spoke, you seemed such a self-centred and spiritless creature, preoccupied with sex and showing off your pointless knowledge."

"And that reveals one of your main misconceptions. It never occurred to you that I could be exactly what I seemed but also so much more," Ingrid said. There was no triumph in her voice, though. Nor was her gaze set on Pound, but on Valour.

Her heart thrashed. Ingrid wasn't here for Pound; Ingrid was here only for *her.*

"When we parted in the tunnels, I feared for your safety, my darling Valour. I ran to a friend who lives by the tunnel exit and borrowed a wig and an on-theme dress." Ingrid touched one of the embroidered animals at her waist, a wolf. "No mask, of course, but when I entered the palace I simply claimed to have dropped it."

My darling Valour. Those words hurt like salt scrubbed into a wound.

"Never mind the outfit. Did you inform anyone of where you were going?" Petrichor said.

Yes, what they needed was proper reinforcements.

Ingrid's fingers left the gilt-thread wolf. "I left a message with my friend to contact Johan, telling him to send members of our organisation. I also sent a message to someone else who might help."

"I am glad *someone* took precautions," he admitted. "Valour and I are not of sound mind. We have been drugged with small doses of forgetfulness tonics for years and recently have not received our daily dose."

Ingrid rounded on Pound. "You gave them 'ness every day for years? You know what that does to a person."

"Not as well as the individual who sold it to me does," Pound said with a cold smirk.

There was a crash outside. Some drunk guest falling over, maybe?

Ingrid's attention went to the door and that was when Pound picked up the bronze bowl of cherries and, with perfect aim, threw it at Ingrid's middle. Having thus unfocused Ingrid, Pound twisted at the waist. She kicked out her leg with whip-snap speed, right at Ingrid's hand. The pistol flew upwards, its pearlescent handle glinting in the firelight before it landed far away from the fighters.

Next, Pound drew her knife and stabbed it towards Ingrid without flourish, just a clean jab to kill. Ingrid jumped away with surprising agility. Still, that couldn't make much of a difference against a former Assassin of Axsten. Although… 'former' was the word. Gods, Valour hoped years sitting in cushy chairs and drinking sugary liqueurs had ruined Pound's fighting form. Unless, of course, that only led to Pound growing tired and so making use of that bomb? Or grabbing Ingrid's pistol? After all, Ingrid wouldn't have taken the shot, but Valour knew all too well that everyone else in this room would, especially a certain shit-awful former assassin who now killed mercilessly and gladly.

For now, Pound lunged again with the knife, nicking the hand that Ingrid held up in defence.

Valour's heart didn't beat right. She was still angry, hurt, and humiliated. Yet, she worried so for Ingrid. And she was… captivated. By Ingrid's scent, the words coming out of her mouth, and how she moved. By the way Ingrid looked at her as if assuming Valour hated her and still not asking for forgiveness. Ingrid could've skipped town, alone or with her father. Or begun covering her tracks. Or done something, anything, that would have benefitted herself and protected her *dearest papa* and his reputation. Instead, she was here. Risking her future and her life. Moreover, considering the timescale, she couldn't have given it an instant's thought. She'd believed Valour needed her and had run headfirst into danger.

Now, Ingrid nearly tripped over the bronze bowl and Valour stopped breathing, struggling even harder against her ropes. This couldn't end well. The only comfort was that Pound wanted them in her bloody scenario—it was probably easier to march them to that location than to carry their corpses out of the palace—and that she hadn't called for the kammarherrar. No doubt pride kept her from asking for help when all she was facing was an unarmed socialite without combat training. Still, Ingrid and her quick reflexes were holding up unexpectedly well. Pound slashed with that long knife, and Ingrid kept dodging. In moving around clumsily in those wide-hipped dresses, they had kicked the knife, the pistol, and several cherries somewhere out of sight. Ingrid kept dancing away from Pound and glancing down, clearly searching for her pistol. The wig slipped and she threw it on the nearest divan, seeming to care for it as little as she did her own safety.

"You cannot even keep your wig on," Pound jeered. "How do you hope to best me?"

"I probably shan't. If I do die tonight, you simply must sate my curiosity regarding your name. You got to pick from any in the world and you stole a former queen's name? How unimaginative," Ingrid said while throwing the fireplace's bellows at Pound, the only damage being soot on her ice-white dress. "I once studied the names of those who change their identities. One knave chose Baron Whaste-Land. *Barren wasteland*. That is a choice with flair."

Valour bit her lower lip to stop her chuckling at the bloody silly pun.

Pound, however, stayed grim. "What are you going on about, you prattling nouveau riche?"

Before she could answer, Petrichor shouted, "Miss Rytterdahl, for once refrain from babbling and find a weapon!"

In that beat of distraction, Pound charged again. Ingrid dodged the knife but took an elbow to the side of her head. The blow caused several small things to tumble from Ingrid's hair. Valour figured out what they were: the shoddily attached pins that had been under the wig. Now Ingrid's thick hair cascaded down over her face, obscuring her view. Valour's panic rose. She had to help. While Ingrid brushed her hair out of her face, Valour reached out a foot and just managed to trip Pound up. Now what? Her gaze flitted across the room until something on the darkest wall caught her eye.

"Ingrid."

Her former lover spun towards her, happy to take her eyes off the person who might kill her, just to answer Valour's summons. What a dim-witted thing to do. Still… Shit, there was no denying it… No one had ever trusted Valour like that before.

Valour nodded towards the wall, aware that Pound couldn't see the gesture since she had only half gotten to her feet. Ingrid turned to what Valour had indicated, a crest shield crossed with two ornate swords. Gods knew if they were sharpened or blunt as butter knives. While Ingrid approached the swords, Valour kicked towards Pound again for attention and said, "Hey, has-been. I wonder what would happen if I screamed?"

For once, Petrichor immediately helped. "What if we both screamed? Surely, you would not have time to kill us both before one of your guests came blundering in? Should we find out?"

"You infuriating pests," Pound hissed, moving towards them with her knife held out. "I think I will execute you two and this sad excuse of a drug lord in the scenario myself. Perhaps right outside the sanctum?"

"You'll never be allowed near the sanctum ever again," Valour said, trying not to look at what was happening behind Pound, thereby giving away that Ingrid had raised the bejewelled sword over Pound's head. With arms trembling under its weight, she brought it down. Valour winced. She had struck with the blunt side instead of the edge. Still, the blow hit Pound's skull square on, and she staggered back, holding her head and moaning.

How long before she gave up and called for her kammarherrar?

With a grunt of pure rage, Pound let go of her head and held the knife out towards Ingrid once more.

Ingrid arranged herself into a questionable en garde stance, holding the heavy sword out straight with her elbow locked so that the weight of it made her arm shake. She'd have no power to lunge or to jab. And to make things worse, the panicked woman stood so upright she could be knocked over with a feather. Valour wanted to scream.

Pound grinned at the sight and planted her feet wide while flicking the knife back and forth, as if debating where to stab first.

Ingrid moved her leg and a scraping noise came from the floor.

She had found and kicked her pistol towards Petrichor and Valour. They couldn't pick it up, of course, but it was a good distraction. Pound regarded the pistol and Ingrid took the chance to plunge the tip of the heavy sword down into the former assassin's silk shoe.

Ulrika Eleonora screamed as her foot was stabbed, first just noises of pain and then three words, "Kammarherrar, attend me!"

Valour's heart sank.

However, nothing happened.

After yanking the sword out and throwing it away, Pound had slumped down on the nearest divan, ripping a part of her dress off and wrapping it around her foot to stem the blood. From outside came nothing but jaunty string music, the clinking of glasses, and raucous shouts.

Valour laughed. "They can't hear you. Parlour games, remember? They're probably busy playing the one where a person is blindfolded and feels up the others to guess who they are. They'll be too busy, and too horny, to care about you."

With a start, Valour noticed that Ingrid had grabbed the sword and crept closer to Petrichor during this comment, and was now applying the blade to his ropes.

Shit, what else could she say to keep Pound's focus on her?

"Um. I mean, you might be able to trust low-level aristocrats to serve as kammarherrar and keep secrets, but give up a good party to focus on work? When there's booze and consensual groping to be enjoyed? Not bloody likely."

Ulrika Eleonora Pound didn't even bother replying. She got more settled on the divan and untied the blood-soaked tourniquet from her foot. What in Hel's realm was she doing? She'd bleed out. And why was she so calm? Had that sword blow to her head finally made her lose the last bit of sense she had?

Pound began mumbling under her breath and circling her hands around her foot. Red haze streamed from Pound's hands and Valour could make out words in old Norse, offering up three coming deaths in return for healing from the medicinal goddess, Eir. Valour shook her head. If the gods were real and had for once bothered to get involved with mortals, she could buy that the goddess of the underworld dealt with Pound. But the other gods too?

There was dull scraping as Ingrid tried to sever the ropes. She was making too much bloody noise. How did she not expect Pound to notice?

CHAPTER 56
ARMED, UNBOUND,
AND HAPPY To KILL

PETRICHOR FELT INGRID sawing at his ropes with the blunted ornate sword and gave minute squirms, to further the fraying.

Meanwhile Pound, with no more limping, rose and retrieved her bomb. Petrichor wasn't sure she had seen Ingrid and so didn't warn the socialite. He should have. Pound leapt over, grabbed a fistful of Ingrid's hair, pulled her to her feet and struck her middle with the iron ball. Ingrid collapsed with a loud yelp, covering her stomach and groaning. He hoped nothing within her had ruptured. If only he could reach the pistol that had slid under his accursed chair!

Ingrid tried to get up again and in response, Pound held the bomb near the fireplace. "Oh, do stay down, useless little heiress. If you don't, I shall light this, despite being loath to blast the room to pieces and risk not being able to escape in time. Nevertheless, you have all pushed me far enough to do it."

Ingrid stopped, crumpling into a defeated heap, clutching her stomach.

With a satisfied hum, Pound went to the door and perused the ballroom. "Some kammarherrar are making their way over here. They shall ensure you are rendered unconscious and dealt with, *after* my masked ball has ended. I spent a lot of time refurbishing that ballroom and preparing this inane frippery." No doubt to counter the rumours of the greve not keeping up with the times and the other nobles.

With a pained expression, Ingrid staggered up, one hand over her stomach and the other one grabbing the blood-tipped sword. Petrichor was impressed with her tenacity, even though her attempts to save them were beyond pitiful. She paused when singing filtered in from the ballroom. The soprano must have rejoined the string quartet.

Ingrid tilted her head, listening with a devout expression.

"Cut her bloody head off," Valour hissed.

Instead of obeying, Ingrid made eye contact with Valour and held it, some emotion between them that he could not interpret.

When Pound shut the door and spotted Ingrid, the socialite smiled dreamily and said, "This aria is one of my favourites."

Next to him, Valour started shuffling in her seat, making her chair bounce with her useless, impatient fidgeting.

He sighed, so weary of them both. "Again, Miss Rytterdahl, this is not the time for your fact-spouting."

"If we are at death's door, we might as well enjoy this wonderful aria, Petrichor. And you could return to calling me Ingrid." She closed her eyes and swayed perfectly in time with the music. "This is a woman, a mezzo-soprano to be exact, singing a song about loving every woman she sees, wanting them, and not knowing what to do with this new and urgent need and love for women."

Petrichor stiffened. *Mezzo*-soprano? There was a whole world of the finer things that he had been denied. And now he'd die without knowing them.

"Drop the sword," Pound said, sounding as tired of this nonsense as he was. "You cannot even use it."

Ingrid seemed too hypnotised by the music to hear her. "Oh, how I love it when women sing breeches roles."

"Breeches?" Valour asked, writhing even more intensely. "What are you on about?"

"It's when the role of a teenage boy, usually made for a castrato male, is played by a woman in opera. Most audiences find it quite titillating."

"Ingrid," Petrichor warned again, seeing Pound's expression darken.

She ignored him. "Such an odd choice for that aria to be played here, though. Considering the opera it came from."

"I have had enough of your prattle," Pound said, raising her bomb to use it to bludgeon Ingrid.

"Oh, I was not prattling. I was doing two things at once," Ingrid said. "Firstly, I was pointing out that said opera is loathed by the aristocracy due to its take on the social classes. Odd for the greve to want it played. However, perhaps not so odd for a low-born, social climber like you?" She tutted. "Such an embarrassing mistake, one that your guests may just pick up on. Secondly, I was buying time so Valour could reach the pistol and kick it over." She bent with a groan and swapped her unwieldly sword for the more suitable pistol. "Quite clever, if I do say so myself," Ingrid said, aiming the pistol at Pound's head. "Put the bomb down, you soulless bore."

With bared teeth and a moment's hesitation, Pound did so. How long until she realised that Ingrid, despite being the Brandquist, wasn't the killing kind?

"Quite clever?" Valour said. "Shit, it was brilliant. I would applaud it, but I'm a little tied up at the moment."

There was a code of knocks on the door and Pound called, "Enter." In came three kammarherrar, two of them with drawn pistols, creating a standoff with Ingrid.

"You took your time," Pound said.

"A thousand apologies." The unarmed one bowed low. "You bade us entertain the guests and keep them away from here and so we did."

"Dimwits," Pound grumbled. "Where are the others?"

"Some went to stop the duel between two quarrelling lovers in the rose garden as well as the betting that the onlookers set up. Others, hm, well, they are unaccounted for."

"You mean they ducked into bedrooms with guests," Pound said.

"Quite possibly, Ulrika Eleonora."

"That was not what I meant by 'entertain' them." She grimaced. "The disappointments you have brought me today are astounding. In the morning, you claim to struggle to find more unmissed sacrifices. And in the evening, you cannot even obey this sort of simple order? Unbelievable."

Sacrifices. How many people had died before their time to keep the greve's body moving?

Pound rubbed at her brow. "Never mind. Keep your pistols trained on the hotelier's daughter until she puts hers down."

Ingrid's eyebrows rose. "And what if this *hotelier*, not only one's daughter, decides not to put it down?"

"Then, alas, this becomes a messy shoot-out, with any survivors required to explain what happened here to the overseers." Pound took a step closer to Ingrid. "Note that your side contains you, not a fighter, and two tied-up people with 'ness withdrawal. My side, however"—she drew her knife from its sheath while indicating for the unarmed kammarherre to pick up the sword—"are armed, unbound, and happy to kill."

Petrichor kept trying to make those frayed ropes snap, but to no avail. A knock of two short and four long raps distracted him.

"More of my associates joining the fray," Pound said. "I suggest removing that pistol from my forehead, spoiled brat."

Ingrid's hand trembled, making the pistol wobble. But she did not lower it.

Entering their small, way-too-hot room, was a kammarherre and the foreign mercenary. Behind them trailed the greve. His eyes reminded Petrichor of those of the palace's animal heads, and his features were slack as if made of dough.

Petrichor wished they could break whatever unholy magic Pound had used to achieve this, wished that people could see what was actually behind the greve's altered state. However, he could do nought, so there the greve stood, a puppet and a symbol of Pound's power but useless to them.

"You again," Valour said to the mercenary. "And again in that flimsy, ridiculous coat that you can abso-bloody-lutely not be discreet in."

Schneider drew himself up. "This is a dress uniform coat from my country's navy. I will wear it and care nothing for the circumstances or risks. Someone like you could never understand."

Wow. Schneider and Pound were a fine pair. Both obsessed with organisations that had discarded them, to the point of making them frenzied, volatile, and unable to function in normal society.

Petrichor was not oblivious to the lesson there.

"Enough," Pound said. "Schneider, draw your weapon and run this socialite through if she does not lower her pistol."

He immediately unsheathed his sabre. "With great gladness."

Gazing down at the blade at her breast and then over to Valour, Ingrid said in a cracking voice, "I'm sorry. I tried."

Valour looked like she wouldn't answer but after a beat whispered, "It's all right." Those simple words appeared to hold a lot more meaning than they should be able to. To his amazement, Petrichor found that he was actually, truly, sad for them.

The door opened again, this time without any polite knocks from guests or coded ones from kammarherrar. Petrichor's heavy heart rose at who walked in.

CHAPTER 57
DEFENESTRATION

PETRICHOR'S HEART MIGHT have risen, but his whole body tensed against his ropes. The other person Ingrid had sent a missive to was... Halcyon? Petrichor stared unblinking at his hero and his betrayer. Halcyon closed the door behind him and then stood there, tall, broad, and solid as an oak. Several emotions coursed through Petrichor like storm clouds roaring across the sky. Fury, confusion, resentment, a thin strand of hope, and what he feared was some sort of deep-rooted affection. Petrichor couldn't parse all of these... feelings. However, he knew beyond certainty that he was unmanned by profound relief. Halcyon was here, in the flesh, armed and ready to get them out of this accursed and lethal farce. And yet, Petrichor wanted nothing so much as to revile and scream at him until his throat was raw.

Halcyon slowly lifted and aimed a rusty, old-fashioned musket at Pound and said with a low and cracking voice, "Do not move. Please."

Pound said nothing in return. She only smiled.

VALOUR DIDN'T KNOW what to do or say. She spluttered the obvious, "You're here?" at Halcyon. Then—distracted by the burly leader of the assassins wearing Sister Mire's infamous long scarlet cloak, his wet hair loose, and crumpled breeches with *his actual nightshirt* badly tucked into them—she added, "What in Oden's gory eyehole are you wearing? Whoever helped you dress for the masquerade needs to be slapped with a cold fish."

Halcyon grimaced. "I am not dressed up. I was in the bath when

388

I received a message from Miss Rytterdahl. I pulled on the nearest garments and ran to the tunnels. Valour, Petrichor, what were you thinking?"

"You dare question us?" Petrichor shouted, his usual superior calm gone. "When you have lied, drugged us, and stolen our memories?"

"And joined up with old shit-for-heart over there?" Valour added.

Halcyon had been looking at them with pleading devastation. Now, his gaze went straight to Ulrika Eleonora Pound. She smiled wider at him and her body language changed to domineering seduction.

Halcyon lowered the musket a bit, seeming ten years older in the blink of an eye. "Some things you cannot stop. Like breathing... or like loving someone that you shouldn't."

"You could carry on loving her and still refuse her commands," Petrichor said.

Pound took one step closer to Halcyon. "The assassin ovum cannot understand. You are mine," she said, stating it as a simple truth. "Have been for more years than these children know."

"Thirteen. It's been thirteen years," he whispered. "I was eighteen the first time you came into my bedchamber."

Pound's eyes gleamed in the firelight. "And I have been with you ever since, have I not? Only I can understand you and provide what you need."

Slowly, oh so slowly, Halcyon raised the musket. "There are many things I thought I needed. You, the order, the life that was hung around my neck when I came to this bloody cold country." Valour had never seen the vulnerable look that was on his face as he added, "Perhaps what I actually need is the ability to live with myself. I have gone through the motions for so long, self-loathing festering away in that hollowness in me, the one you said you'd fill."

"I do fill it." She gave him a reassuring nod that made Valour's stomach turn. "I will fill it, my dearest."

"I am weary of your lies and promises. I want to be able to see myself in a looking-glass and not look away."

"Only aiding us to make yourself feel better, then?" Petrichor said.

Valour wanted to kick him. This was not the time.

Halcyon's throat bobbed, his full attention on Petrichor. "I am sorry. I shall earn back your trust one day. And hopefully, I can get to know you then, Petrichor. I never should have let my discomfort around you stop me from that."

Petrichor didn't get a chance to reply as the door slammed open. Honestly, Valour had seen popular taverns with fewer people in them than this small room. Someone should sell tickets. She worried about shots being fired in here, though. This bloody silly side room was small enough that you could kill when you only meant to wound. Weapons could be wrestled aside and miss. If guests came running in at the sound of shots, they'd be caught in the crossfire. Shit. Valour had to get out of this chair and the ropes before the room became a slaughterhouse.

Half a dozen strangers stumbled in, the first one saying, "Apologies. We were stopped. Had to convince them that we'd come to mend a broken window. The palace guards would only let six of us in, though. Everyone else had to go home."

"Better late than never," Ingrid said with faked calm.

Halcyon indicated the new arrivals. "I came upon this group of reinforcements loitering in the tunnels, discussing what to do and where to go."

"Oi. That's not fair. We were coming up with a bloody plan of operation!" bellowed a ragged man. "Lucky we took our time. Wouldn't have thought up that window ruse otherwise."

"I am grateful that you made it at all, and for the loan of this musket," Halcyon said. "Due to my haste, I forgot that my assassin blades were still in my waistcoat."

"To quote the shitty tyrant over there, enough!" Valour said. "Get us untied so I can beat the living shit out of her."

Being a woman of only necessary words—Valour could respect that at least—Pound punched her in reply. It was a good blow. It hurt like headbutting an anvil, and it both split her lip and loosened a tooth at the back of her mouth.

Oberleutnant Schneider laughed, his sabre still prodding Ingrid's chest.

"Leave them be, Ulrika Eleonora," Halcyon said. His face was stern but there was tender familiarity in the way he said her name. "I do not want to shoot you."

"Nay, you do not. And you *will* not."

"Neither of us know what I will do tonight," Halcyon replied. "I must begin protecting those under my care, no matter what it costs me. Besides, even if I didn't shoot, you are outnumbered."

Valour assessed the room. Shit, he was right. The odds had turned in their favour. They had Halcyon, with his ancient but assumedly still serviceable musket; Ingrid, who was switching from staring at Schneider with cold defiance to glancing over at where the pistol lay; and, of course, the six Brandquist minions. Half of them carried those fancy new rifles Valour had seen in the warehouse and the rest brandished butcher's knives and clubs.

On the other side was Pound with her knife—and that bomb discarded somewhere behind her feet, Schneider with his sabre, two kammarherrar with pistols, and one with an ornamental sword. She wasn't going to count the greve, as he merely stood there like a clockwork toy missing half its cogs.

Out of action was another of those decorative swords on the wall and, of course, two furious assassins tied to godsdamned chairs. Although, Petrichor was still shifting against his frayed ropes whenever Pound was not watching.

Smiling, Pound took another step towards Halcyon. "Outnumbered, my sweetest? There is a ballroom brim-full of my guests and kammarherrar beyond that door."

"Ah, but they are not yours," Halcyon said. "The aristocrats out there believe they are here for the greve, who is one of them. If they find out that *you* invited them, *you* ran Vinterstock, *you* all but killed their friend and leader. What then?"

"Stop it," Pound said, her smile instantly vanishing.

Halcyon turned to Valour and Petrichor. "Have you found out everything?"

"I think so," Valour said, not wanting to meet his eye. How could he throw away all they had shared together on the command of someone like Pound? And yet, she was willing to bet she'd understand his reasons more than Petrichor ever could. Love and attraction could upend a world.

"Good. I, um, was considering sending you an anonymous note, you know," he said. "One that might bring back your memories of that Valborg Night."

"Why didn't you?" Petrichor said in low tones. "You helped us with clues on how to find Brandquist. So why not aid us with this too?"

"I meant to. But I was unsure of what to say, what might work. Also, I was detained. I told you we had received a multitude of targets and I had my charitable works to tend to." His frown smoothed. "I was also busy handling a new threat for Ulrika Eleonora."

For the first time, Pound looked unsure. "What threat?"

"The suspicions of the city's aristocrats and the foreign guests out there, my worshipped one," he said, with bite in the last words.

"Impossible."

Halcyon shook his head. "You've been occupied with tracking Valour and Petrichor, and your puppeteering has slipped. I overheard a nobleman say he had spoken to the greve and had the same reply about soup repeated over and over. There have been similar reports from other nobility."

"Lies," Pound growled deep in her throat.

"Nay." He stood a little straighter. "My only lie to you was one of omission, when I did not warn you about this. Valour." She jumped as Halcyon addressed her. "Do you remember the target you killed on the day you got the hit job on Brandquist?"

"The foreign murderer with the beauty mark? Sure."

"He was a suspected murderer, yes," Halcyon said. "And I thought that was why he was on the hit list. Yesterday, a kammarherre claimed she had put the foreign fop on the list herself, because said fop had been gossiping about finding the greve much changed.

Offbeat and—"

Valour recollected what she had overheard. "Taciturn. He said the greve was uncharacteristically taciturn."

"That is an understatement," Ingrid huffed, glancing at the inert greve.

Valour's womb cramped. Gods. This was turning into the worst night of her life, even counting that one where she'd suffered pneumonia, dysentery, *and* listening to Petrichor lecture her on hygiene.

"And you told me none of this?" Pound asked Halcyon. "What good are you to me if you do not provide me with pertinent information?"

Halcyon watched her a long time, his eyes dry but filled with weary sadness. "Did you ever love me? Even a little? Or did I see love in you because I needed it?"

Sparks flew out of the fireplace, some landing in one of Schneider's ridiculous sideburns. He leapt back and rubbed at it. Taking the opportunity, Ingrid grabbed the pistol and aimed it at the swearing oberleutnant. Valour couldn't help but be impressed by her quick reflexes.

Oblivious to, or disinterested in, the rest of the room, Pound held her arms out to Halcyon. "You are my dearest."

"No, the order and your ambition are. Was that why you kept me in your grasp?" he asked with a mirthless, pained smile. "To have someone inside the order so you could one day come back? Or was it so you could control the Order of Axsten through me while running the city through the greve? How much power is enough?"

"Put that ludicrous musket down and we can go somewhere private to discuss this," Pound said, voice softer.

"I wonder if you would not simply stab me if I didn't hold this weapon," he said. "And even if you did not, I shan't let you convince and confuse me again. I have reached the limit of what I will do, what I will swallow, to keep your affection and guidance."

"Is this about the two children, dearest?" Pound said. "Fine. I can use my magic to make them forget again. With some more tonics—"

"No. We are done poisoning them," Halcyon said, gripping the musket so tightly that his knuckles whitened. "Valour and Petrichor are our own kind, Ulrika Eleonora. How can we keep endangering them, or worse, kill them?"

"No one is my kind, Halcyon," Pound snapped. "You know that. I am above all those tied to sentimentality, possessions, or emotions."

Valour was about to say that superiority and disdain were emotions too but was distracted by a bead of sweat trickling down her forehead. She shook her head so as not to let it get in her eyes. This room was too small for the heat of the fire, the chandelier, and all these tense people, without causing a massive sweat. Except for Petrichor, of course, who had no doubt had his sweat glands removed. She threw a glance at him. He had wiggled enough to nearly break the ropes.

Should she ask Ingrid and her underlings to start shooting and end this?

Pound advanced on Halcyon. "One last time, put that silly antique down and let me talk to you."

Halcyon's eyes widened. "No. Stop moving."

"Should we shoot her?" one of the Brandquist minions asked Ingrid, raising their rifle.

Before Ingrid had time to answer, Pound lunged at Halcyon. A shot sounded, so loud it made Valour's ears ring. It was too noisy to have come from one of the kammarherrar's pistols or the henchmen's modern flintlock rifles.

Halcyon had lowered the musket, meaning it should've shot Pound in the left leg, blowing her kneecap to shreds. No projectile had shot out, though. Be it due to a dirty barrel or the age of the weapon, the powder had not ignited. The bloody heirloom had misfired.

Everyone stared at Halcyon, stunned that he had taken the shot. His expression painted him as more shocked than anyone else. Until his face grew stony. "Give me your rifle," he said to the henchman next to him.

Pound wasn't going to give him another chance, though. She

lunged with her knife, stabbing him in the stomach. Once. Twice. Thrice. She stood back and shook her head as if he had disappointed her. "I wish you hadn't made me do that, sweet pet."

Valour screamed, expecting Halcyon to fall to his knees. But, of course, he didn't. He raised his boxing-bruised fists and, with blood blossoms spreading across his nightshirt, hobbled towards Pound. Before he got to her, though, Pound rammed into him and pushed him towards the tall bay window. The pane broke, and as more cold air rushed into the room, Halcyon's body mercilessly tumbled out.

CHAPTER 58

THE FRAY

NO. PLEASE NO. Stuck on the chair, Valour couldn't see how Halcyon had landed. On this side of the palace there was only a slim portion of grass. Had he reached it? Or had he been impaled on the sharp fence separating the lawn from the streets of Vinterstock? There was a tiny chance that he might've survived the fall if he landed on the grass and didn't break his neck. But with his guts knifed open like that... could he have survived even the push through the window? Oh gods. Disregarding what her mother, the order, or Petrichor, would say, Valour let herself cry. She had loved him. Despite knowing that such an act always ended with her being left alone and broken.

Petrichor wasn't screaming or crying. Valour stared at him in amazement and realised it was because he was trying not to draw attention to himself. He was wet-eyed and pale as death but still fidgeting so fast he was surely ripping his shoulder wound open and tearing the skin off his wrists. However, the ropes must be nigh torn.

Gods help Pound when he got loose.

Meanwhile, Ingrid kept her pistol on Schneider but her gaze on Pound. "I think it about time that we overthrow the people who have ruined our city, fellow Vinterstockians. Aim low."

That was all she needed to say. The underlings with rifles shot at the legs of Pound, Schneider, and the kammarherrar. The room filled with smoke and the stench of black powder, despite the broken window.

Guests knocked on the door, slurring voices enquiring about the shots.

Ingrid called to her underlings, "Bar the door with one of the divans. The last thing we need is bystanders getting caught in the fray."

Someone appeared behind Valour. She couldn't see much but smelled that piney cologne that only two people she knew wore: Petrichor and Pound. She braced herself in case it was the latter, there to slit her throat. No cold metal touched her neck. Instead, deft hands worked at her ropes.

Petrichor's deep voice cut through the clamour. "Sit still."

This was his first action after getting loose? Not killing Pound or jumping after Halcyon? Not even joining the fight?

"Thank you," she said when she was free, not meeting his eye.

"Don't mention it." He leapt into the fight, heading for a kammarherre, and was lost in the hazy air and tumult.

Valour got up, coughed due to the smoke, shook blood into her numbed arms, and put her coat back on. She planned to either locate her knives or grab the remaining ornamental sword from the wall. She didn't get that far. This time, something sharp and cold actually was at her throat.

An accented voice by her side said, "Stay there, assassin filth. If I do nothing else useful this night, I shall finish my commission of killing you."

She made sure Schneider could hear her blow out a long uninterested sigh over the noise of the fight, which was mainly melee now since there was little time to reload. She pursed her lips in faked boredom. "Oh, Schneider, you silly-looking man. You will keep bothering me, then?" If she was going to die, she wouldn't go begging or defeated. She'd taunt this arsehole until her last breath, hoping it'd give him a heart attack. Or at least heartburn.

"Go on," he snarled. "I dare you to utter one more vile comment about my coat with my sabre at your throat."

A stray shot from somewhere in the room rushed past her left ear, making her momentarily lose hearing on that side. She moved, enough to get out of the firing line but not so much as to get Schneider's sabre through her neck. "I'd finished mocking the coat. I was planning to start on your bloody hilarious sideburns."

"Once more, you boorish Northerners are too unworldly to understand the fashions."

"Oh, I know side whiskers are the new fashion. Halcyon has"— she wouldn't use the past tense for him—"grown some and they are neat and handsome things. Yours look like sloshed mice passed out on your cheeks."

"Like most of your weak sex, you stick to foul chatter instead of action, yes? Well, the action of my mighty sabre will speak louder than your insults."

In the blink of an eye, he vanished from view with a yelp. Ingrid had come from the side and bull-rushed him. "Perhaps if you 'chattered' more and acted less," Ingrid said, getting her balance back and daintily brushing down her dress, "you and your 'mighty sabre' could have been told that you were standing in a puddle of slippery, smashed fruit."

Schneider gave an animal roar and went to stand up. Valour quickly gave him a set of well-placed kicks, including one to the head, and he crumbled into a heap of nose blood and cherries.

"Are you all right?" Ingrid asked her.

Valour murmured, "Yes," but avoided eye contact. "You?"

"Some bruises and cuts. I took a shot to the hip, too, but thanks to the dress it merely grazed me."

Meanwhile, Valour's kicks hadn't been as hard as she thought. Schneider regained consciousness and quickly slithered behind the remaining divan. He had one of the kammarherrar's discarded pistols with him, but Valour was sure he had no gunpowder or lead shot for it. His sabre lay at her feet and she grabbed it while checking the room for shot and powder. Instead, she found an injured Pound. She was throwing rifles, pistols, and the unused knives and clubs out the window, keeping only a rifle for herself. Shit. Pound's cohort now had all the firearms. However, despite losses and injuries, Valour's side still had more fighters since the overindulged kammarherrar lacked the stomach for combat.

"That'll do her scarce good. I've just gathered up all the powder flasks," said one of Ingrid's henchmen from her side. His leg dragged limp behind him and he was bloodied, but his arms were full of the gunpowder containers and his smile triumphant. How old was he? A few years younger than her perhaps?

Valour wanted to buy him a glass of celebratory milk and make sure he got home to his mother, but for now had to settle for saying, "Good work. Time for you to go, I think." She looked to the door. "Why don't you and your companions scuttle out the way you came, dodging any kammarherrar and telling the guests you know nothing about the shots. Keep to the lie about mending a window."

It probably wouldn't fully work but the people out there didn't want these folks. Coin-hoarders only cared about people with power.

The henchman turned to Ingrid for approval. "Go ahead," she said with a tired smile. "You've all done more than enough tonight and I thank you from the bottom of my heart. We shall stay and finish off the remaining foes."

Valour paid them only scant attention. The worst of the fight being over meant that Halcyon's fall returned to the forefront of her mind. She headed for the window to check when a scornful voice behind her said, "Do you think it is wise to turn your back to me, girl-child?"

"Probably not," Valour said, turning. "But wisdom's overrated."

Pound stood proud, despite bleeding from several injuries, and held a rifle pointed at her and Ingrid. It must've been reloaded because, with great theatricality, she cocked it and aimed it at Valour, saying, "It seems the gods are against you. Halcyon was wrong about you, by the way. You are useless and—"

Petrichor interrupted with a hard jab to Pound's head from behind, then another one to her temple before she had recovered. He kept hitting until Pound was out cold. He faced Valour and they nodded solemnly to each other. For Halcyon.

Valour kicked the unconscious Pound, whose head was bleeding. If Valour was ever to write a book about all of this, she'd call it *Head injuries—the pros and cons*. And get Petrichor to bind it.

When Ingrid's underlings were gone, Ingrid and Valour

barred the door again with one of the divans. Outside, guests still clamoured. Hopefully, they would block the route for any kammarherrar or palace guards on their way here. Valour took count of who was still in the room: one passed out Pound, two dead kammarherrar, one greve impersonating a hibernating dormouse, one oberleutnant dazedly searching for powder and shot, two dead Brandquist minions, and one Petrichor now fighting the surviving kammarherre.

"I shall locate the bomb to ensure no one else gets hold of it," Ingrid said.

Valour let her go; she had her own task. She would kill Schneider before he got his weaponry together and took her life first. She closed her eyes for a beat as doubt crept in. She was so tired of killing and how it made her feel. Still, she didn't have the luxury of saying no tonight. She stiffened her sinews. One quick stab through the heart, she could do that. She had to.

She spotted something odd out of the corner of her eye. Petrichor had subdued the kammarherre and then gotten up on the divan, where he balanced on a pile of cushions and swayed as he used a knife to pry the chain loops of the oversized chandelier open. She sucked in breath as she understood. Below the chandelier sat Pound, holding her head and looking dazed. Right next to her was Schneider. He had taken Pound's rifle and was aiming it at Ingrid, who had her hands up and her gaze locked on the oberleutnant's.

"Schneider, is it not? Please hear me out. Shoot me if you wish, but why waste your time and risk being caught by the city's overseers?" Ingrid threw a quick glance toward Valour. "At least let the two assassins go, lest you draw the anger of their order."

Schneider only snorted, one eye on the room and the remaining fighters.

Without care for her own safety, Ingrid neared until the rifle nigh touched her chest. "Please look at me. This is a messy affair, one that you are better off leaving." Her voice was calm, but her breathing was laboured. "You're a mercenary, right? I can triple your fee. Simply lower the weapon and come with me to my father's office, where I will pay you handsomely."

"We are past such options," he said, glowering at Ingrid. "You brats have put me in the maddest temper, so I want each one of you dead. And beautiful, rich girls like you? We all hate you. And so, killing you is always..." He raked his eyes over her body. "A pleasure. It stirs the loins watching you, what do you call it, bleeding out?"

Valour wanted to pounce and strangle him. Ingrid looked like she shared that urge. They both had sense enough not to, though. If anyone rushed Schneider and tried to take the rifle, he'd shoot. If that chandelier dropped, however, it would land on both the armed mercenary and on Pound. Incapacitating them both in one move would not only save Ingrid. It would, at last, end this.

Suddenly, *godsdamn it*, Schneider noticed something was going on above and behind him. He'd been distracted by Ingrid's clever words and, no doubt, her beauty. But now he began to turn towards the sound of Petrichor fiddling with the chandelier.

Valour had to act, had to bloody well distract him!

She was just about to shout something, *anything*, when she saw Ingrid rapidly search the pockets of her borrowed skirts. She retrieved a small silver tin. She opened it, called Schneider's name, and when he faced her, threw its contents into his eyes. Wig powder! The white stuff, made to stick and cover, coated the top of Schneider's face, including his eyes. He didn't drop the rifle trained on Ingrid, but with his free hand, he rubbed at his eyes while cursing in what Valour assumed was German. With any other foe, she would've shouted to Ingrid to duck and then rushed him. But everything showed that Schneider was only slightly distracted. He kept that rifle steady at exactly a hair's breadth from Ingrid's bosom, finger firm on the trigger, and his white-knuckled grip on the weapon showed that no one was taking it away from him. A trained soldier could fight and kill without his eyesight and while in pain. Maybe if it had been someone else at the end of that rifle, Valour would've taken the risk anyway? She certainly would if it was her own life at stake. But Ingrid's? No. No matter how Valour hated her, just... no.

Ingrid looked at Valour and the message in those emotive eyes was clear: *I have given you a chance. No matter what happens to me, please take it.*

Valour stuck Schneider's sabre in her empty knife sheath. The longer sabre made a hole in it, but did secure the weapon to her. She also picked up a dead henchman's club and tucked it into her breeches. There was no way she'd find herself unarmed again tonight.

Finally, she grabbed a chair and went over to Petrichor. "If it drops, will Ingrid be clear of it?" she whispered to him while climbing onto the divan.

He peered down at the placement of Pound, Schneider, and Ingrid, clearly estimating the drop zone. "Yes. There might be debris propelled towards her but nothing lethal, I believe."

"Then move."

"Pardon?"

"You had the right idea but the wrong tools. Move."

He made room and she placed the chair next to his pile of cushions and said, "Hold it still."

This time he didn't question her, despite his sceptical sneer.

Valour stepped onto the chair, still half listening to Ingrid distracting Schneider by telling him that wig powder caused blindness and he must get all of it out, and him replying that unless she shut up he would shoot her right in the mouth. She took a deep breath. Then, she clambered onto the chair-back. Petrichor held it still and stood so that her ankles could rest against his shoulders. Despite that, and her Axsten balance training, she wobbled. She was too exhausted, too achy, too fired up. Never mind. Better she fell than Ingrid be shot.

Everything seemed to take so long, even though she distantly knew it happened during mere heartbeats. She grabbed the chandelier chain and in a careful procedure that took far too long, transferred the knife from Petrichor's hand to hers. She looked at the chain's big links and found the semi-opened one. She applied the knife to it. Her hands shook. Her stance did the same. Carefully, she took the club out of her breeches, wishing she could move faster.

This chain had to give way before Schneider fired.

CHAPTER 59

THE DROP

PETRICHOR COULDN'T THINK straight. Perchance it was due to the withdrawal, dehydration, pain, or the many days of living on edge. In his ears a sound repeated, the torn gasp of a man falling out of a window. Petrichor ground his teeth until his mouth ached. This night must be a punishment for his life's wickedness. He shouldn't think about that now. He could only focus on one thing: this chandelier and the vengeance it could bring. Valour was wobbling perilously on that chair-back, like an accursed poodle on a ball in one of those travelling circuses. Halcyon was… No, he couldn't think of that either. The floor was strewn with bodies. However, the two people he most wanted dead were still alive— Pound and Schneider. And they were right under this chandelier.

He could not stop recalling what Pound had seen in a vision: *'Twas how I knew there would be a dramatic death scene taking out several enemies in one blow*. Perhaps it was the gods conversing with him, perhaps it was some sort of guardian angel, or perhaps it was just himself, but something in Petrichor knew that the 'blow' was this chandelier crashing down upon his enemies.

Yes, the chandelier must fall. Before Halcyon's murderers moved away. Or Ingrid moved into its trajectory.

Sweat prickled on his brow. "Valour, make haste."

She had produced some sort of crude club from her breeches and replied with only a hum. Then, she whacked away at the knife she used as a lever in the circlet he'd partly opened. She rocked on the chair with every blow, and he struggled to keep it still. What was worse, she had attracted Schneider's attention. And the blasted man now aimed the rifle up at them.

Vexingly, unbelievably, *typically*… the Valour Way worked. The chain loop began opening, but the hammering motion proved too much for the precariously balanced Valour, who just managed to save herself by clinging onto the top part of the chain. The chandelier swayed, the crystals clinking and the candles flickering. The lower part of the chain creaked, loop after loop opening there.

Schneider, who had just slammed the rifle into Ingrid to keep her from grabbing the weapon, aimed it back up at them.

Petrichor looked from him to Valour and for a moment froze. Would she survive if she fell? His eyesight unfocused. The fall… the fall would kill a person. Must have killed *him*, must've killed Halcyon, if the stabbing had not done the job. Valour's scream unfroze him, bringing him back to the present and to someone that he could still save. He took a firm hold of her and eased her down on the divan just as Schneider shot at where she had been.

While the oberleutnant reloaded, Valour panted, "That's the second time you've caught me."

"Well, 'tis the second time you have climbed something perilous to aid us both."

Valour moved her focus to Ingrid, motioning to her to leap back, which the hotel heiress did with compete trust.

Then, together, Petrichor and Valour watched as the chandelier creaked and swayed and…

Dropped.

He held his breath. There was a beat of deafening silence and then a crash that flooded the room with noise.

The chandelier fell like judgement on Pound and Schneider, scattering shards of glass, hot candle wax, and a few still-burning wicks across the room. Fire began to catch on the clothes of the dead bodies and the rugs. Both Pound and Schneider were trapped under the metal and glass. Pound had been struck on the head and neck; the latter bent in an unnatural position. Unlike her, Schneider was still alive, albeit severely injured. The oberleutnant lifted the rifle and again aimed it at Ingrid but seemed to struggle to pull the trigger. Valour jumped to the floor and unsheathed what Petrichor now saw was Schneider's own sabre. She mumbled something before stabbing him right in the heart. Petrichor wondered what she had said but had no energy to consider it for long.

He checked the room. No foes were left standing. His hands trembled and he was unbelievably tired, emotionally and physically. Was it over? Would this ever be over? He could only think of one thing he could do to make sure it was.

CHAPTER 60
BLAME AND ESCAPE

VALOUR STOOD WITH the sabre held above Schneider's prone body. Her last kill. No matter what it would cost her, she had to make this the final one. She felt it in her very marrow.

"The last time. This I vow," Valour whispered and stabbed the sabre into Schneider's heart. She twisted the blade, for good measure, and pulled it out. Schneider collapsed bleeding next to Pound. *Bleeding.* Pound was bleeding from her foot wound again. Valour thought of the gods. If you did not follow through on your sacrifice, they took back their gifts. For a moment she felt like the room contained something more than living and dead humans, like the very gods were in the smoky, blood-stinking air around her. An ancient presence that was as daunting as it was soothing. She could almost hear swords banging against shields as a drumbeat and booming god-voices saying her name.

Calm and contentment rolled over her, like mist across the icy sea. "You were wrong. The gods weren't against me," she said to the dead Pound. "And they weren't on your side. Your scrying showed you the wrong death scene. Your gift of raising the dead was second rate, considering the state of the greve. No Valkyries even came to take you to Valhalla." She allowed herself a tired smile. "Also, I was clearly far from useless. I was ten times the assassin and ten times the woman you ever were."

Her celebration evaporated as she saw Ingrid. She was crouching down at each of her dead henchmen, closing their eyes while crying and whispering, "What have I done?"

Valour hesitated but finally said, "They came voluntarily and most of them survived."

All in all, their group had been lucky. Or, more likely, protected by the gods. Shooting in such a small, crowded space meant that a lot of the firearms were jostled or pushed aside and missed. Not to mention the rush to shoot had brought about more misfiring.

Ingrid stroked the hair of what had been a middle-aged man. "Most. Not all." She gave a heartrending moan. "I should not have employed non-fighters and given them pitiful weapons. If they'd had those advanced rifles and known how to use them, everyone might have lived."

Brushing away floods of tears, Ingrid's hand left a streak of gunpowder soot over the rouged smoothness of her cheek.

Valour put her hand out to wipe it away, then stopped herself. "Your sabotage was meant to rid Vinterstock of the drug trade. You couldn't know this would happen."

A broken-looking Petrichor arrived by their side. "I suggested we come to the palace, dragging Valour with me. You came to save us, bringing these underlings, and... Halcyon. 'Tis all my fault, not yours."

Shocked at his statement, Valour said, "Bäckahäst-shit. It's no one's fault but Pound's."

She got the feeling Petrichor didn't believe her.

The three of them stood there, watching the devastation in shock, when there was a thump behind them. The greve had tumbled into a boneless heap. Of course. No more magic-wielder, no more puppet.

Valour blinked through the still gunpowder-laced air, checking one last time. It was fine. None of their foes were left standing. Her taut muscles unclenched.

Ashen-faced, Petrichor held his injured shoulder. "Where is everyone else?"

"Ingrid and I made her henchmen go home. That last kammarherre you fought, did he survive?"

"No," Petrichor said. He seemed far away, dazed even, and his eye twitched. With some hesitation, Valour gave his good shoulder a squeeze, but he pulled away.

"What are we going to do?" Ingrid asked. "That divan will not keep the door shut forever, especially not when the guards and overseers arrive and take a battering ram to it."

Valour chewed her lower lip. They couldn't leave that way. They couldn't be found in here with corpses of the city's leaders, either. "We'll jump out the window."

"Are you sure?" Ingrid said. "It is such a long way and—"

Valour held up a hand. "We have to risk it. Can you gather up the divan pillows and drop them through the window?" She trusted Ingrid to be able to judge the angle of where they would land.

"Of course."

Petrichor said nothing. He wore a devastated expression and kept glancing at the window. Had he not dared to check on Halcyon either? If they didn't look, he could still be alive.

There was a bang on the door, bringing Valour back to their urgent crisis.

"Next, um, let's see," she said. "We do what Pound was going to do: stage a death scene."

The greve's unnaturally arranged body gave a sound like a wheezing bellows and slackened. For so long, he had been only a puppet being yanked about. Valour found she could relate. Well, no more, both their puppet strings were cut. One of the candles from the chandelier lay by the greve's tall wig, which now caught fire.

"That is how we stage the death scene," Ingrid said, pointing to the flames spreading over the wig. "A fire. We can decide later what we tell people. But for now, this ensures that everyone dangerous in this room is truly dead and does not come back."

Come back? Valour hadn't even thought of that. She looked at Pound's dead eyes and broken neck. Was the corpse smiling? Slightly pointed teeth glinted white as snow, some with blood on them. Yes, a big godsdamned fire was a good idea.

"All right," Valour said, glancing at the door where there was still banging and shouts. "We need something to make the flames spread fast."

Ingrid produced a gold filigree bottle from a pocket in her

panniers and held it up. "Petrichor and I have the perfect thing for that. Perfume contains alcohol."

"Whatever works," Valour said as she grabbed a candle from the floor. She set it to every flammable thing she could find until she was halted by Ingrid at the body of one of the henchmen.

"Wait. Not him." Ingrid stoppered her perfume bottle. "I pray you help me drop the bodies of my people to the ground. Please? I owe it to their families to let them bury their loved ones."

Valour nodded, expecting Petrichor to say something about sentimentality. But no, he merely meandered around with his tin cologne bottle, splashing with a far-away expression.

Like most Vinterstockians the two henchmen were thin from undernourishment, so dragging them to the window was a quick task. Valour didn't look down as they dropped them, letting Ingrid aim the bodies' fall. That done, Ingrid poured what was left of her perfume on the curtains and the divan. Petrichor had emptied his cologne and, as if in a trance, stood staring at Pound. Valour grabbed a few half-burned logs from the fireplace and put them around Pound's body. The fire was spreading fast. The room's scent of gunpowder, blood, and sweat became overshadowed by a mix of perfumes and burning.

"Wonderful," Valour snarked. "If we don't get wrongfully accused of all this and hanged for murder, we'll die from breathing in the sweetest-smelling fire fumes ever."

"The bomb," Ingrid said with a gasp. "The fires will light it!"

Petrichor shook his head and held up his hand, in which the iron ball lay. He handed it over to her, mumbling, "No need to worry about that."

Gaping, Ingrid pulled out its fuse. "This isn't attached."

"It's fake," Petrichor said. "Like everything else Pound made and did, it was mere shadows and tricks. Halcyon's heartbreak would tell you that."

"One problem less, then. Come on," Valour said, eyeing the fires. "We have to go."

With a bang, the burning divan that had been barring the door gave way. Ingrid grabbed Valour's hand and ran for the window.

Valour took only long enough to check that Petrichor was right behind them before she leapt. The night air met her, cold and whooshing past far too fast. She squeezed Ingrid's hand and tried to aim for the cushions. Then she shut her eyes and thought two words. *Gods, please.*

Everything was pain as she impacted. No matter, that was the theme of the night anyway. What mattered was that most of her body was on the pillows, only her lower legs having hit the lawn. Ingrid had landed more on the grass but was moving and sounded coherent as she complained about pain. She had steered their jump. She'd better not have thought letting Valour take most of the pillowed landing would lead to forgiveness or something, though.

The dead henchmen lay behind the pillows, and to the left of them, close to the fence, was Halcyon. His face was turned away but even by only the light of the moon and the streetlamps, Valour could see his clothing was soaked in blood and that he lay unnaturally still. At least, unlike Sister Mire's blood-red cloak, he hadn't been impaled on the fence and pinned up there for all to see. The cloak dangled in the breeze, like a hanged creature, as dead as Halcyon.

She yanked her gaze away. Her heart ached and her eyes welled up, but before tears fell, something distracted her. Someone was missing. Petrichor still stood in the window. Shouts and the roar of burning came from behind him, but he didn't seem to notice.

"Jump, you pus-brain!" Valour screamed, her throat raw from smoke and pain.

"No." He looked back to the room where people were no doubt trying to get past the burning divan and enter. "The logical thing is for me to remain here."

"Logical? What in troll-shit are you talking about?"

"Someone should stay and explain. Take the guilt if need be. Time has come for me to stand accountable." A big flame roared up behind his shoulder but he didn't react. "You and Ingrid have people who care about you. I only had Halcyon, little as he liked me."

His voice shook with emotion, mainly guilt and grief she guessed.

"Ye gads, man! That does not mean you should stay up there," Ingrid shouted.

"It does. You two try to be better, to improve yourselves and the world around you. I have done the opposite. Until tonight, when I will finally do the right thing."

"Argh. Don't make me throw a rock up at your dramatic arse!" Valour bellowed.

"Go," he said, all emotion now gone from his voice and face. "Get to safety."

"Not without you, brain-wart." Valour planted her feet and held her arms out. "You've caught me twice. It's my turn to catch you. Jump!"

Slowly, he shook his head.

There were people in the room now. Valour could make out water being thrown at the fire.

Panicked, Ingrid said, "I cannot let him take the blame or die. What can I do?"

"Nothing. I mean, I don't know."

She guessed what Petrichor wanted, though. He wanted punishment, wanted the pain to stop, wanted this mess to end in a grand gesture to make up for all the ill he had done. Bonehead.

She engaged the muscles of her held-out arms. "Petrichor, I know you don't care about yourself, but *I* need you to jump. If you die or get captured, it'll weigh on my bloody conscience. Besides..." She made herself say the rest. "I, we, I mean Vinterstock, may yet have need of you. Please, mate, just jump."

People were crowding him. They were out of time.

Valour had expected either another decline from Petrichor or for him to be grabbed and taken out of sight. What she hadn't expected was a person about her height and weighing only a little less than her to be plummeting towards her at great speed.

How in Oden's gouged eye was she going to catch him?

The answer was... she wouldn't.

As soon as he landed in her arms, they both sort of crumpled in a heap on the cushions, with her breaking his fall.

"Ugh, get off me before you crush something valuable," she croaked, barely any air left in her lungs.

"I shall be glad to. You need a bath," he said, rolling off her. "Strike that. You need two baths. You should have moved and let me land on the cushions."

"A bath? I smell like fire and blood, just like you, barnacle-licker. And I caught you to be nice, since you've caught me twice in the past."

"That was different because it was thought through and useful." He stood and brushed himself off. "This was not."

"You know what, melodramatic arse-flute? Next time, I'll let you die."

"Next time? I—"

"I fear," Ingrid interrupted, "now is not the time for this."

She was looking at the palace. Not up, though. The people in the burning room seemed to have left when the flames could not be controlled. No, she was peering around the corner where Valour could just make out a set of guards coming out of the front gates. Heading for this lawn.

Ingrid's gaze flitted to her dead underlings. Then, with reluctance in her voice, she called, "Run!"

When they had sprinted to the fence, Petrichor stopped dead.

Valour groaned but turned to ask, "What now?" She regretted her tone when she saw his stricken face. Was he about to have one of those panic attacks? Was he more injured than she had guessed? No, he was staring at the impaled cloak.

"I must retrieve Halcyon. Keep running, I will catch up with you."

He darted back and Valour stood there dithering. Gods in Asgård, that man would be the death of her. Before she had decided what to do, he returned with Halcyon in his arms. His progress was slow. Halcyon was literally a dead weight and had been heavy enough when alive. Talk about the height of folly.

"Petrichor, I loved him too. But we can't be slowed down by carrying a dead man," Valour said.

"He is alive."

"What?"

"Valour, he's actually alive," Petrichor said in a voice so full of hope that she didn't recognise it as his. "He's breathing."

She rushed to take half of Halcyon's weight. Together they all climbed the fence with great effort and shit-heaps of pain, especially when they tried to get Halcyon over without making him bleed further. After landing on the other side, they ran off as best they could.

Valour allowed herself one glance over her shoulder. There were only five or six guards coming; the rest must have been fighting the fire. Still, neither she, Petrichor, nor Ingrid were in a state to fight anyone off. Nor to dodge rifle fire. They couldn't let themselves be caught.

With hard-booted steps and shouts of 'stop' and 'surrender or die' echoing behind them, they ran faster than their battered bodies wanted. Ingrid led them to a posh townhouse. Considering it was by a tunnel entrance, Valour guessed it was where Ingrid's dress-lending friend lived.

They were by the door when that familiar sensation overtook Valour enough to make her shout gibberish.

"What's wrong?" Ingrid asked. She was staring behind them, probably expecting to see the guards nearing. Or perhaps even the dead Pound with flames in her hair and magic streaming out of her hands.

Valour grunted. "Ignore me. It's just that, argh, my monthly started gushing and I loved these breeches. They're muslin, godsdamnit!"

Never mind that she was by now covered in Halcyon's blood too.

Clearly relieved, Ingrid laughed. "I shall buy you ten new pairs." She jerked back. "If you will let me, I mean. I am sure you no longer want anything to do with me."

Petrichor screamed, "Do not even consider having this conversation now! Halcyon needs a physician if he is to have any chance of staying alive."

He must have been panicked if he was now trusting Vinterstock physicians.

"Of course," Ingrid said, going first into the house.

Valour had never been so happy to leave the fresh air and hear a door shut behind her. In the distance, she heard the guards' shouts and footfalls disappear down some other street. Right before Ingrid asked their hostess, a plump and attractive woman, to run for a physician.

CHAPTER 61

A CLEAN START

THE NEXT MORNING, Petrichor woke from what felt like hibernation. He pulled down the heavy blankets he was under and struggled to sit up. His eyes were like sandpaper after last night's fire smoke and gunpowder, and he rubbed the debris and sleep grit out of them. To think he'd worried for so long about being too weak for the order when the weakness he should've fretted about was his eyes. Not that the rest of him wasn't feeling feeble and painful right now too. He was on a sofa in a room with soft-lilac walls. The sofa had a twin that stood opposite with blankets crumpled on it, on top of which lay Valour's coat.

"You are still alive, then?" the woman herself said, appearing at his side. "Phew. For a while I thought you'd survived the last few days' shit just for me to lose you when everything is finally settling." Her tired face was bruised, and her lip cut.

He recalled the physician coming over, sewing up Halcyon's wounds, and saying that the knife seemingly hadn't pierced any organs. The medico also informed them that if, against all odds, Halcyon survived the blood loss and didn't get an infection, he could recover. Could. Not would or even should. Just could.

Petrichor sat up straighter. "How is he?"

"Weak as under-brewed tea. He's awake and has eaten a few spoons of porridge, though."

Petrichor let out a long, shaky breath. He noticed that her loose-hanging hair was wet and that she was wearing fresh clothes. "You've been up for some time."

She put her hands in the pockets of silk breeches that were far too nice to be hers. "Mm-hmm. Ate breakfast, had a bath, and

415

borrowed rags from Ingrid's friend." She moved her hands about in the pockets. "Oh, and clothes from said friend's late father."

"I slept through all that?"

"Like a felled ox. Even when I re-did your bandages."

He touched his shoulder and made himself say, "Thank you."

"You owe me for life, snooty breeches."

He decided to say nothing about that, fearing it was true on many accounts. "How is Ingrid?"

Valour's carefree manner evaporated. "How would I know?"

"You have not spoken to her?"

"I've seen her. And avoided conversation like the godsdamned plague. Anyway, Halcyon wanted to see you when you woke up."

"I should shave, wash, and borrow some clothes first."

"I'd do that afterwards. Who knows how long Halcyon can stay awake?"

Petrichor sniffed himself. Smoke, sweat, and blood. He itched with the need to bathe.

A familiar voice rang out, but it was hoarser and frailer than usual. "Valour? Is that Petrichor you're talking to?"

She went out to the hall and called into an opposite room, "Uh-huh. His Highness wants to have a bath."

"Tell him that can wait. I must speak to you both this very moment."

Valour returned. "You heard our... trusted leader."

Her voice was heavy with sarcasm and despite himself, Petrichor couldn't blame her.

He pulled himself up from the sofa, realising he had new bruises gifted to him by Pound's kammarherrar. Valour didn't offer help and he wouldn't have accepted it if she had. Together they went into a bedroom finely decorated with watercolours of snowy landscapes. Under a window stood a bed, and on it, propped up with pillows, was Halcyon, Eighth Assassin and Leader of the Order of Axsten. Petrichor had always thought of him as the picture of strength and robustness. Now he was a paper-doll version of himself.

"Good morrow." Halcyon gave a watery smile. "I cannot stay awake for much longer and I worry that when I sleep, I will do so for some time and wake up muddled. If I wake at all. So, please let me say a few things."

Petrichor stood back, so Halcyon couldn't smell him, and clasped his hands behind his back. "I shall not stop you."

Halcyon swallowed. His mouth sounded parched, but he didn't ask for the water glass at his bedside. "First order of business: the mess left at the palace last night. I considered making up some conceivable lie for what happened and taking the full blame. However, I believe the truth must come out."

"Obviously," Valour said.

"When, or if, I recover enough, I will contact Klara af Silverblad. If I die, you must do so in my stead."

"You'll live. I've seen you in worse condition than this," Valour lied, leaning against the wall. "Who's this Klara?"

"She is, *was*, one of Ulrika Eleonora's kammarherrar, but had fallen into disfavour because she questioned the morality of what they were doing," Halcyon croaked. "She knows everything and will corroborate my story when I tell it in the court of justice. She has wanted to face her crimes for quite some time. As have I."

"Are you certain?" Petrichor said. "*Everything* will come out."

Halcyon's drawn face was set. "And so it should. This whole situation is one big, infected boil. It needs to be opened up to be cleaned and healed. No more secrets and lies." He put a hand to his stomach, feebly rubbing at his bandaged middle. "The overseers, the court of justice, and whoever the king sends, they must investigate not only all that Pound and I did, but the extent of the olden magic, the existence of the gods, and the 'ness trade too."

"That won't be popular," Valour muttered.

Halcyon sighed. "I am past caring."

"You should care," Petrichor said, fixing his gaze on his own bruised knuckles. "I have not forgiven you. However, it was not all your fault and either way, I don't wish to see you hanged for your crimes."

"I may not be executed. After all, I have useful and powerful contacts, I am coming forward with the truth at my own volition, and I have a history of doing good deeds for Vinterstock."

Petrichor digested that. He had a thousand replies, some sarcastic, some needy, some reprimanding, some comforting. When his mouth opened, he wasn't sure what words would come out. "I understand why you drugged us. I can never condone it, but I know you did it so that Pound wouldn't slit our throats." He took a step closer to the bed. "There was a third solution, though. After that night, you ought to have ceased giving us the tonics and let us in on the story. We could have pretended we had forgotten that night. You needn't have lied and deceived. You should have trusted us, sided with *us*."

His breathing picking up, the tendrils of the ice-hot panic slithered between his ribs to squeeze his lungs and heart. He couldn't have another attack now; this was too important.

Then Valour was there, not touching him, but standing by his side. Her steadiness was infectious, and he mimicked her slow breathing. Probably not even aware that she was helping, she kept her focus on Halcyon. "Or you could've just let us escape the order and Vinterstock. I don't know if you were aware that Petrichor planned to leave, but you knew I was."

"Ulrika Eleonora would somehow have known. And hunted you down and killed you," Halcyon croaked, shame marring his handsome features.

Petrichor made his voice cold. "Then you should have killed her first." Even he heard how that coldness sounded feigned, emotion crawling in. He wanted to, but could not, add, *I would have killed for you. Why did you not kill her for us?*

"He's got a point," Valour said. "You struggled to spend time with Petrichor, but I know you cared about him. And about me. We loved you, still do, even if you don't love us. Why did you pick her over us?"

Halcyon's sleep-drooping eyes shot open. "Never doubt that I loved you back. Even though the order does not allow it." He pinned Petrichor with a feverish gaze. "Yes, you unnerved me. Not merely because of your unique personality and how you socialise, though. The main reason was and remains…"

"What?" Petrichor made himself say.

"Guilt. Every time I saw how cruel, cold, and obsessive you had become, an Axsten assassin to the core, I knew it was my fault."

Petrichor scoffed. "Absolute balderdash."

"It was my fault. I should have made more of an effort to protect you," Halcyon rasped. "Because I was older and because I saw something familiar in you."

"Familiar?"

"The order noticed a sensitivity in you, a need to please, and to find a family. They had seen those same traits in me and punished me for it, trying to tear them out of me. I pretended that it had worked. Then you came along, Petrichor, and you didn't know how to pretend." His words were harder and harder to make out. He reached for his water glass and Petrichor, hesitating for only a beat, got it for him. Halcyon took it with unsteady hands and sipped. "So, they broke you and rebuilt you cold-hearted and coldblooded." He shrank back in his pillows, gripping the glass. "I should have stopped them, but I was only a teenager and deep down, I still wanted to please them. To belong. I should have saved you then." He blinked away tears. "I should have saved you then, and I should have saved you both from Ulrika Eleonora. I did not really choose her over you. It was just…"

"Just what?" Valour said, her voice unreadable.

"I was spellbound and addicted. She made me feel safe and strong. I do not know if there was magic involved or if she simply knew how to manipulate me." He sounded a heartbeat away from sleep but carried on. "Through the years, I became more obsessed with pleasing her than the order. Perhaps because *she* had been the teenager when *I* came to the order. But like I did not protect you, Petrichor, she did not protect me. Even though I believed she did."

Something jagged and hard was in Petrichor's throat and swallowing did little good. "Well, you quit your addiction last night when you took that shot at her."

"It will be a longer process than that, I fear. If I survive, that is," Halcyon said, not a trace of self-pity in his voice. "Enough about this. Merely trust me when I say that the Order of Axsten did not drag the humanity out of you, Petrichor. 'Tis still there."

Petrichor wanted to say that it should be Halcyon's job to help him find it, to make amends for the drugging and lying. That he needed Halcyon to keep him accountable when he slipped back into his old habits. Maybe Halcyon could even teach him about emotions. More than that, Halcyon could make that promised effort to allow the two of them to get to know each other. If Halcyon lived.

Instead of any of that, he said, "I'm certain we shall discuss this further."

Halcyon gave one single nod. "It would be my honour."

"You look ready to collapse, Halcyon. Should we cut to the chase?" Valour asked.

"Yes," he said. "I do not expect either of you to forgive me. I shall however say the words and mean them with everything that I am: I am sorry. I hope whatever sentence I get will give you some sense of justice being served."

Petrichor wasn't sure how to respond. He looked to Valour, who sighed and said, "I've thought about this all morning and just this minute decided that I don't have the time or energy for a grudge against you. I doubt I'll ever trust you again, but I do forgive you."

Interesting. Would she take the same tack with Ingrid? Would she trust her, or anyone, ever again? He wasn't sure he would. Or perhaps ever truly had. Except for Halcyon.

"Thank you, Valour," Halcyon rasped.

Petrichor clasped his hands behind his back. "You and I shall talk more of this later."

They both knew that meant forgiveness of some sort, and that it meant so much more than that. Halcyon nodded with what Petrichor guessed was gratitude and humility.

The room was quiet for a spell and Halcyon's head dipped. He shook himself awake, nearly spilling the water. "One more thing. I shall disband the order."

"About bloody time," Valour said with clear relief. "Even if you hadn't, I'd never take another life. I'm done with death."

"So am I." Petrichor hadn't meant to say it, but it had slipped out.

"It is a great sorrow to me that you were both, or rather that we were all, raised to kill and not allowed to choose another path," Halcyon said before taking another trembling sip.

"Is that why you're disbanding the order?" Valour asked.

"That and my long-time doubts about whether Vinterstock needs assassins killing on the whim of the city's leader." He drank the last of his water.

Petrichor took the glass and replaced it on the table. "What is the alternative?"

"I believe it ought to work better with the overseers, the court of justice, and the country's cabinets of chosen spokespeople deciding. Vinterstock is run in the wrong way: unjust and unbalanced."

"Exactly like she said," Valour mumbled.

"Pardon?" Halcyon said.

She blushed. "Oh. Um, nothing."

Halcyon's eyelids fluttered shut and his breathing deepened. This time, he did not shake himself awake.

Valour and Petrichor left the room, shutting the door gently behind them. They returned to the drawing room, sitting down on their individual sofas.

"Have you truly forgiven him?" he said quietly.

Valour blew out a long breath. "I'd say I've started the process." She eyed him. "You have to, as well. He'll need you, and you'll need him."

"Ah. Sounds familiar."

"Petrichor, don't."

"You ought to speak with Ingrid."

"Shit, no! She lied to me, she deceived me, she's an arsehole, she's the…" Valour, out of words, waved her hands.

"What? The villain of this? Nay." He looked out the window at the busy street. "Neither is Halcyon, who also lied to you. Nor you with your kills and your bullying of me. Nor I with my callousness and my kills." He rubbed his dry eyes. "Unless we're all the villain? To many in this city, we would be seen as such."

Petrichor couldn't stop wondering what made them better and more virtuous than Pound. Was it their lack of intent to hurt anyone? Or was there perhaps scarce difference at all?

He ran a hand over his hair, yearning to wash. "Either way, mark this: the only one of us who has never intentionally taken a life is your chatty socialite."

"Shut up."

"What was it you said down in those tunnels?" Petrichor queried. "Oh, yes. 'You only shush me when I'm right', was it not?"

"Go have a bath, stinky arse."

And that he did. It took hours, much scrubbing, and several pots of hot water until all that had happened could be flushed away with the bath-water. Until he was ready for a clean start.

TEN DAYS LATER, Petrichor was taking the next step in that start. Halcyon was in the middle of the hearings about his crimes—and so was Ingrid. The two kammarherrar who had colluded with Pound (but survived as they'd bedded masquerade guests instead of attending her in the antechamber) had already been given public hangings. Brandquist's organisation had been dismantled, the underlings getting floggings, impoverishing fines, or transportation to penal colonies. Ingrid's fervent plea for them to be given time in a sanatorium to get rid of their addictions was ignored.

Others were already taking up Brandquist's mantle, of course, smuggling 'ness via land and keeping better to the shadows. Petrichor did fret that the devil they had was better than the one they were about to get. Today he and Valour stood outside the court of justice, examining the contents of the purses of riksdaler they had just received as rewards for uncovering Pound's scheme and defending the city.

Valour gave a happy yelp. "I'm going to buy so many cardamom buns and sacks that I can fill with pebbles."

Petrichor looked up from his counting. "Sacks filled with pebbles?"

"To lift."

"Pardon? Oh whatever, I am in too good of a mood to worry about your never-ending witless drivel," he said before catching himself.

No more unnecessary insults, pressing on bruised memories, or mocking weaknesses between them. "Actually, that was perhaps uncalled for," he finished.

"I…" Valour coughed. "I appreciate you saying that."

They were saved the rest of the exchange as an urchin selling sugared violets approached them. Valour gave her a coin and received a small paper bag of the treats.

She popped a few violets into her mouth and around them said, "So, what will you do with your reward?"

He watched the violet-selling girl leave. She might live in *that* ramshackle cottage. Perhaps with the messenger boy who liked gryphon seals and didn't know about the colour cream. Distractedly, he answered, "I shall live off it. Thus, allowing me to give my savings, earmarked for buying my way out of the order, anonymously to…" He cursed himself inwardly.

"To what?" Valour said, and crunched down on the sugared petals.

"Have a care. The things you eat ruin your health," he said.

"Stop changing the subject, grumpy guts. What are you giving your savings to?"

He saw no other way out of this than telling her the truth *or* asking her to go throw herself in the canal. "Mrs Mariedal's Orphanage."

Valour balked, as he had expected. "An orphanage? You bloody hate children!"

"Hate is a strong word. They are annoying, dirty, gullible, emotional, and loud. Nevertheless, the world should not let more children grow up to be like me."

She grinned and leaned in, stinking of sugar and violets. "Condescending and with a stick up their arse?"

"I was referring to someone being broken until the strangest things unravel them." It was impossible not to think about the panic attacks or his extreme reactions to getting blood or filth on himself. Although, acknowledging those things had lessened their power—in fact, his control over them grew a little each day. He cleared his throat and finished with, "Only to then be rebuilt cruel and cold, with their worst traits amplified and sticking to them as their only protection."

"Right. Sorry about the, you know, unkind joke," Valour said, clearly as ill at ease with their new politeness as he was. "Children do deserve a place to grow up where people care about them. I'll spend most of my bounty on charity too. I wish we didn't need to, though. Something has to be done about the way society is."

"Be that as it may, charities are a good start."

"Mm."

She ate some more violets and watched people bustling past. He rolled his still recovering shoulder, wondering if he should leave. No, this wasn't how things should be left.

"By the way," he said, "I went to take a look at our basement hideout yesterday, merely out of curiosity."

"Oh? And?"

"The house has more or less collapsed."

"Figures. It seems many things have collapsed lately," she said, knitting her brows. "What will you do with your time now that neither of us have to kill anymore?"

He couldn't help it, he looked to the building three houses down. To his great vexation, Valour followed his gaze. She read the building's sign out loud, "Fahlcrantz and Åberg's Bookbinding and Printing." She put away her violets with a pensive look before bursting out, "Of course! You're free to sit around putting clothes on books now."

"Valour."

"Fine, fine. Sorry. I'm sure bookbinding is a very important art."

"It is." He picked non-existent lint off his sleeve. "Not that it matters. I shan't bother Master Fahlcrantz. I did not reply to any of his letters. He has doubtlessly already taken an apprentice."

Something tugged at him. A notion that it actually mattered very much. And something worse, something that could be called hope if it had lived in any breast but his.

Valour gave him an unreadable look before storming off to the bookbinders and pulling the bell chord. Petrichor hurried after to drag her away, but it was too late, the door opened and there stood a man in a crumpled blue banyan and little round spectacles.

"Master Fahlcrantz?" Valour asked.

"Aye, I'm Sven Fahlcrantz. Who is asking, please?"

"My, uh… This man… was regrettably unable to respond to the letters you sent regarding the apprenticeship but has now come to enquire if the role is still available," she said.

Petrichor had no idea she could be that eloquent.

With neutral curiosity, Fahlcrantz looked Petrichor over. "Oh, really?"

Two storms warred within Petrichor. One was familiar, the one that claimed that good outcomes only happened in sentimental stories, that he was helpless, and that his fate was to be nothing more than a useless child who became a coldblooded killer. It wanted him to say that Valour was mistaken and then leave. The other storm was new, bringing fresh air and soft snowflakes that covered the grime in him with clean brightness. That storm susurrated one simple message: not coldblooded, snowblooded. Snow thaws. Things change. And so can men.

With sudden but calm certainty, Petrichor knew that this choice was his. Not the order's. Not Valour's. His. And fine, he would try it. He would give this sugary concept of hope a chance. He adjusted his coat. "Yes, Master Fahlcrantz. I am the one who sent in a folio notebook bound in cream calf-skin with embossed gilded letters as a sample of my work."

The bookbinder yanked his spectacles off, his face all lit up. "Ah, of course. The impeccable one with a banded spine. 'Twas stellar work, the best stitching I have ever seen from a novice." He replaced the spectacles. "Pray pardon my flawed memory, what was your name again? I recall it was something odd, without even a family name. What was it? Petrus? Petri? Oh, *Petrichor*, right?"

Petrichor winced but before he had time to reply, Valour said, "It was. But that was wrong. It's Peter, um… Kårh. His name is Peter Kårh."

He stared at his former co-assassin, about to argue. On principle as well as because she had made this decision for him.

But then, people were usually given their names, were they not? And *Peter* felt... correct. More so than anything he would've chosen. If he had ever even permitted himself a name. He said the full name in his mind and liked it.

He very slowly bowed his head to her. "She's right. My name is Peter Kårh."

Petrichor the Assassin had died, in one of the many ways that he had constantly feared he would. Peter Kårh, however, was fully alive and not lingering in death's shadow.

"Well, Peter, if my working terms are acceptable to you, the apprenticeship is yours," Fahlcrantz said, smiling like he had delivered a lavish gift. Which of course he had.

Shock struck Peter breathless. It had gone right. He had managed it. Something in him, in his chest and deeper still, was cracking. And through those hairline cracks, light and warmth spilled in.

"Yes," he mumbled. "Thank you. Yes, please."

A messenger boy came running toward Peter, ruining the miraculous moment. Oh deuce take it, what now? Luckily, it was Valour he addressed. "Valour the Assassin?"

"Not anymore," she said, shoving her hands in her pockets with a friendly smile. "But your message will be for me."

The lad didn't look impressed at her unclear reply. "You're to come to Hotel Kronovall, miss. Someone there needs to speak to you in your room. And it's hasty."

Hasty? Skies above, the urchin meant urgent. Was there a way to keep children four carriage-lengths away from him at all times?

Valour gave the lad a coin and after some dithering, the bag of sugared violets too. "Righty-ho. I'll go now."

As she left, she called over her shoulder, "Snooty-arse, three weeks from now will be the eighteenth. I assume you don't care, but that's my birthday. If you fancy fika at about two-thirty in the afternoon on that day, I'll be at Anckarström's coffee-house."

He waved her off, certain of two things. One, he would keep that appointment. Two, the vexing messenger boy currently devouring violets was the same one who had delivered his letters. He should have recognised the lad before but all children, particularly if dirty, looked similar to him. The point was that the child was whole, hale, and soon to have a brighter future.

Petrichor, nay Peter, knew he must be smiling as he turned back to the esteemed master bookbinder to decide his first day of apprenticeship.

CHAPTER 62

WAITING

AS THE MESSAGE had decreed, Valour waited in her hotel room. She hadn't taken her coat and boots off. Assumedly, she was about to see Mr Rytterdahl and have to stand there like a powerless numpty as he explained that considering what happened between her and his daughter, it would be best if she left the Kronovall.

She'd miss this place. Daylight streamed in through that wonderful big window, refracting where the glass was warped, sending a column of light across the bare dresser. How long ago was it that Ingrid had pointed out the lack of decorations in the room? Valour swore under her breath and put her hands in her pockets. Her fingers met the reward purse and beneath it, something small and hard. That godsdamned gemstone.

She held it up to the light, letting it gleam with faint little pulses as she spun it. There was a moment where she almost threw it at the window, hoping against logic it would shatter the glass and fly all the way to Hel's bloody realm. Her shoulders sagged. She placed the gem on the empty dresser. It looked lonely on the big surface, making her heart hurt even more. She was about to toss the stone in a bin when there was a knock on the door. She opened it to find not Mr Rytterdahl outside, but his daughter.

"Good afternoon, Valour. May I come in?"

Valour's heart constricted. "I thought you let yourself in and left it up to the person in the room whether to throw you out or not?"

"Not anymore. There are many things I don't do anymore."

"Oh, spare me the 'I've changed' twaddle."

"I have not come to make excuses or to apologise again. You know very well how sorry and remorseful I am. I am here to give you some pertinent information for how we are to avoid each other, as well as to bring you a suggestion."

Against her better judgement, Valour stood back just enough to let Ingrid enter, that godsdamned perfume shimmering off her as she moved past.

Ingrid stopped over by the window, with her shoulders slumped and dark rings under her eyes. "From today onwards, I shall be in the hotel but shan't be in your way."

"Uh-huh. How in all troll-shit are you going to guarantee that?"

"I have been sentenced to house arrest here. The only person I am to see is the guard at my door, who will hand over my daily meals."

"That's your punishment? Being locked in your bloody room?" Valour threw her hands out. "For a crime others would be flogged to death or transported for?"

Ingrid flushed. "Yes. However, 'twas not the only punishment." She took her long gloves off, gingerly and with deep winces, and showed both sides of her hands. They'd been scorched with irons, probably three to four days ago considering the scabbing.

"Pardon their unsavoury appearance, the bandages only came off this morning," Ingrid said. "Apparently, the overseers brand thieves with a T and deserters with a D. They had no letter for what I did and so used the city crest."

Valour knew thieves or deserters only received one brand. These blistered burns were a swollen mess filling most of the backs of Ingrid's hands and one in each palm. They covered where the Brandquist tattoo had been on her wrist as well. She looked at her own hand. The one brand the Assassins of Axsten had scorched there had been smaller but still hurt like piss in an open wound, much worse than those on her back.

Valour stood firm. "So?"

"So nothing, I suppose. You asked about my punishment, and I answered." Ingrid carefully pulled the gloves back on. "Papa worries no reputable spouse will marry me looking like this," she added, rolling her eyes.

"He ought to worry more about infection and lasting damage that could make it hard to use your hands."

"Precisely what I said," Ingrid replied, showing no sign of self-pity.

"So, house arrest and… What is the official term? 'Being burned in the hand', right?" Valour said, unable to keep the unspoken out of her voice.

"It is. And I know what you're thinking. It is still more lenient than what my underlings received and thus unfair in the extreme. You're right. My riches protect me and that is beyond unjust."

Valour knew many would prefer some lashes or painless transportation to what had happened to Ingrid's hands, but said nothing. After all, Ingrid would have access to the best salves, creams, and pain-killing tonics.

"Much as our society is changing, 'tis still unequal," Ingrid continued. "My class and Papa's wealth mean I receive clemency. If I had been an aristocrat, I would have gotten an even lighter punishment."

"I'm sure the fact that you're a beautiful, charming, young woman helped your case," Valour muttered, hoping Ingrid wouldn't take it as a compliment.

"Funnily enough, my judge said I was too old to be as naïve as I have been and to fall victim to blackmail, so *he* did not consider me young." She held her hands up in pacification. "However, I know what you meant."

Valour looked at those hands she had adored, and which could now be wrecked for life.

"I hope this is an acceptable thing to say," Ingrid murmured, following Valour's gaze to her gloved hands. "I pray that when the wounds heal, they will appear similar to the ones on your back."

Similar? Yes. They, and their godsdamned scars, were and would always be similar in many ways. Such utter shit.

In reply, Valour only gave the vaguest hum she could and followed up with, "How long will you be locked up for?"

"Fifteen years."

"Unless Mahadev Rytterdahl manages to buy your freedom by

claiming that the branding was punishment enough."

Ingrid looked down. "While I doubt he will succeed, Papa will certainly try."

"And you? What will you do?"

"After the fifteen years? I don't know," she said with an air that this wasn't important. "I do know what I want to try and do during my house arrest, however."

Valour said nothing, letting the heavy silence roll over Ingrid.

The other woman squirmed but ultimately spoke on. "It is something I have been contemplating for years. And that you and I have touched on several times. The layout of Vinterstock society is not only unfair but unequivocally broken. And it's not only here that it is happening, but in the entire country."

"Mm-hmm." Valour crossed her arms over her chest. "And *you* are going to fix that? From your frilly little bedroom?"

Ingrid flushed even more crimson than last time. "No. What I do wish to do is to use my time for good, to serve the community I have injured. I may be imprisoned, but I am allowed correspondence as well as visitors who speak through the door." She paused, seeming to contemplate how to proceed. "Ever since I was old enough to understand the world around me, I have made connections with those who also see how things need to change. Mainly others in the merchant class but also people that I met while being the Brandquist."

Valour remembered Ingrid saying she 'collected' friends who wanted the injustices of Vinterstock, and the country at large, to change.

"And you are now going to send them letters asking them to… what? Rebel?" Valour couldn't keep the sarcasm or the bite out of her voice and didn't care to try.

"In a way, yes. I am going to suggest they meet and confer," she replied, sounding unusually bashful. "That they put aside their differences, their infighting, and constantly striving only for their individual gain. That they stand together, taking inspiration from how other countries on the continent are holding the upper class and royalty accountable."

"Like France? Where they're rumoured to be talking about storming the royal palace and chopping the heads off the king and queen?" Valour pointed out. "That'll never happen here. People here bloody love their king, for bringing us more culture, national pride, and what have you."

"I do not think it has to come to murder." Ingrid was animated now, eyes wide and burning with fervour. "I think we can demand that power and coin is spread more evenly by protests, withholding of labour, and yes, perhaps storming a few palaces."

"Storming palaces? You're going to orchestrate that from your bedroom?"

"Of course not. I lack any form of power or sway. What I do have is connections, ones that I can introduce to each other. And ideas. Don't forget, I have dined with *and* sold 'ness to the upper classes." Her eyes burned yet brighter. "I know their ways and their secrets, Valour. I even know a couple who would support an uprising of the people, as long as it didn't mean they themselves would be beheaded."

"And this uprising would lead to... what?"

"Many things, but mainly a fairer sharing of wealth. Instead of those of us with coin giving it to those without through charity, it could be done in a systematic way, through taxes."

"Taxes already exist, Ingrid."

"Yes. However, the taxes we—especially the merchant class and the landowners—pay in this country mainly go to wars. And the king's cabinet, even the representatives of the commonfolk we have on there, do nothing about it."

"So that's your plan? Saving the poor through *taxes*?"

"I want it to go to the poor, yes. And the sick, the elderly, and the orphans. Granted, we need an army to defend ourselves. However, we do not need any more expansions of our nation's borders, or to go to war in order to settle grievances with old enemies. That coin could be doled out to those who need it most."

Valour fully agreed but didn't want to admit it. "We already have the almshouses, orphanages, and workhouses."

"Surely we should not shut away large swathes of people who

cannot afford to pay rents or who are too sick to work in some cold, disease-laden depository? People must be helped to live in their own homes and to keep their family together. Or to find jobs if they can work. Or to get medical help." Ingrid pointed to the window. "Look at the people slumped on the streets, merchant class and commoners alike, drinking alcohol to cope with their wretched situations or imbibing 'ness to fake being good enough at something to escape it. They need help, not to be left to die." She furrowed her brow. "Look, this can all be planned by people with exceptional minds and bold hearts. Academics, politicians, neighbourhood elders. They might even find a worthy use for the magic that we are currently discovering and examining."

That last point struck a nerve. Valour had been thinking something along those lines. The magic given by the gods, the very gods her mother had loved so much, shouldn't be used to make harmful drugs. It was a wasted gift.

Ingrid finished her little speech with, "The first step is to gather those people in one place and to galvanise them. I can do that from within my confinement."

"Uh-huh."

Ingrid seemed to deflate, sitting down on the bed. "You think this to be idealistic, foolish drivel."

"I wouldn't say that. I just wondered if you were doing this for the people or to clean your soiled conscience."

Ingrid grimaced. "This would not be enough to scrub out such indelible stains. Nothing I do would be enough for the harm I have caused."

Harm was too mild a word to Valour's mind. They had both done more than just *harm*. She wished she was smarter so she could figure out good and bad. She thought of Loke, the god of mischief. He could be righteous, and he could be evil—it was all in what he was doing and why he was doing it. Perhaps there was no simple answer.

For a while, the only sound was the grandfather clock's ticking.

Ingrid rocked ever so slightly where she sat.

Valour ran a hand over her face and then sat down on the bed too, as far away from Ingrid as possible. "I have struggled with guilt most of my life and at those times turned to Halcyon. He always told me, 'All we can do in this life is try to make sure our good deeds outweigh our bad ones.' I guess that's one of the reasons why I've helped those in need."

Halcyon. He had gotten a much longer punishment than Ingrid. No wonder, considering his crimes and that he didn't have a rich father. And yet, most Vinterstockians would not blame him as hard as they did Pound, Ingrid, or even herself. Women were meant to be virtuous in every situation.

"Good deeds outweighing the bad. I would like to believe that," Ingrid said quietly. "All I know is that I must devote myself to helping others. Perhaps that is selfish. Perhaps I am doing it to make myself feel less guilty or to distract myself from my self-loathing."

Valour blew out a long breath. "You know what? I don't think a widow that can't afford firewood or an orphan who's famished gives a shit." She knew she wouldn't in their position. "I don't think they care much about you or your reasons. All most suffering people care about is the impact your actions will have on their lives. If you help them or hurt them."

The deepest of the lines on Ingrid's brow smoothed. "I like that idea. I hope my future actions make their lives better, and that they do not think of me one whit."

"Are you saying you don't want any credit for this change you are going to try to bring about?"

"The only name I want spread about is *Valour*."

"What? Why?"

"The people of Vinterstock need someone to gather around. Someone who gets things done and who cares. Someone who cannot be bribed, cowed, or affrighted. Someone who has lived among them. Perhaps a former assassin who scares the breeches off the nobility?" Ingrid said with a frail, tentative smile.

Someone whose father was a foreign, destitute sailor who got no help or comfort from society but had to search for it at the bottom of a bottle, Valour added in her mind.

"Furthermore, I can make most of those from the merchant class, and even one or two of the upper class, listen." Ingrid locked gazes with her. "But the large group, whom we need to convince to risk what little they have in order to make a change, is the common folk. For natural reasons, they won't listen to a word from some spoiled, naïve, and guilt-ridden heiress who used to sell them 'ness."

"And you think they'll listen to me? You know what I'm like. I can't shake hands and make rousing speeches."

"Yes, you can. When you speak from the heart, it is always rousing. Besides, the people don't require honeyed words or over-evaluated speech-craft. They need plain speaking and naked truths. That is why I mentioned that I had a suggestion for you."

Having said that, Ingrid watched her through the veil of those long, ink-black eyelashes.

Valour knew what she was about to ask. She refused to make it easy. "Why would any suggestion you make interest me?"

Flinching at her tone, Ingrid swallowed visibly. "If you do not want to be involved, I will do this without you. However, I do believe you would be invaluable to the cause, and I feel compelled to ask you… to please be the figurehead for this venture."

There it was. Valour stood again, beginning to pace. "Uh-huh."

"Valour. People trust you and they are right to do so. Furthermore, while I am locked up in this gilded cage, you will be out there. Out on the cold streets of Vinterstock, doing your best to help anyone who requires it. I am only asking you to take the next step in that and strive for real change."

"This isn't some ploy to get me to forgive you, then?"

"Nay," Ingrid exclaimed with wide eyes. "I swear on my mother's grave that I don't plead for your assistance in this to alleviate my guilty conscience nor to earn your forgiveness, only to attempt to right the wrongs around us."

Valour stopped pacing. Every drop of calm she'd fought to attain since that night in the warehouse drained away, and she no longer cared if she was being selfish or unreasonable.

"So bloody commendable. I wish you would've been so good-hearted with me," she snarled. "How could you spend your days with me, kiss me, share confidences with me, and godsdamned *fuck* me while lying, tricking, and betraying me?"

Crumpling until she sat with her torso slumped over her knees, Ingrid buried her face in her injured hands and mumbled into them, "As I confessed at the warehouse, I handled everything wrong. So unforgivably wrong."

"You think?"

"But, as I also told you," Ingrid said, looking up at Valour from her folded position, "I stayed near you because I was falling for you and wanted to keep you away from harm, while simultaneously searching for a way that I could stay alive, and you could finish your work. Without having to kill me."

Those last words pierced Valour's rage. She was glad she'd been spared the decision of whether to kill Ingrid. The lies had been good for that at least.

She breathed deep. "If you'd been open with me, we could've found that way together."

Ingrid straightened up. "I… did attempt to tell you."

"Shit." A hard knot formed in Valour's stomach. "You did. And I didn't let you."

"I should have pushed harder. I was frightened of your reaction and so was glad to be silenced."

Valour uttered a faint, vague hum.

Then there they were. Quiet, overwrought, despondent. Ingrid sitting destroyed on the bed. Valour standing in front of her, trying to hold on to her fury despite sorrow wanting to replace it. What a sad, bloody mess.

When the grandfather clock chimed, breaking the rock-heavy silence, Valour scrubbed her face with both hands and said, "Right, I know myself. Despite your reasons and the justifying circumstances, I'm going to struggle to get over this."

She remembered what Petrichor—*Peter*—had said about her clearly wanting to forgive Ingrid. And yes, she had been so happy when spending time with Ingrid, felt so alive, so seen, so accepted.

"I know," Ingrid whispered. "And I do not blame you or ever

expect any forgiveness."

Valour laughed mirthlessly as she accepted the truth. "Oh, I'll forgive you." Forgiveness was easier than rebuilding trust, though.

"You will?" Ingrid sputtered.

"Mm. I have to. It'll be a long process, though." She snorted and looked up at the ceiling. "I mean, I have to come to terms with the shame of having been cluelessly fucking the very person I was searching for."

"You cannot think like that," Ingrid said, her voice steady. "There was no way you could have known. I have vast experience in covering my tracks and wearing the deuced mask of a vain, seductive fool."

A mask. Yes, they had all worn masks, hadn't they? Ingrid, Halcyon, Pound. Even Peter and her. There was safety in masks, but they could also suffocate you.

"Still, I should've known," Valour said with an embarrassing crack in her voice. "And I should've let you tell me the truth."

"Do not blame yourself. It is fully my fault."

"I don't think blaming ourselves or each other does us any good," Valour countered. She faced Ingrid. "We can't try to change the way the country's run if we're busy with that. Just give me some time to get over the worst of my anger and later, via letter or by talking through your door, we'll dive into that godsforsaken mess."

Ingrid's beaming smile lit up the room. Shit, it lit up the whole world as far as Valour could tell. She would miss seeing that smile.

"You will help me try to bring about reform? A hundred, nay, a million thanks."

"Sure. But we will be equals in this. You won't be giving me orders and expecting me to bow and scrape to you."

"Of course not! My days of giving orders are happily in the past, anyway." Ingrid was blinking furiously to clear her wet eyes. "In regard to giving you time, I shall not pressure you but merely take whatever you can give me and focus on our task. I feel it will do us both some good to act, and to get out of our own heads."

"True." Valour knuckled her tense lower back. "I'm way behind with my training due to too much brooding and resting my injured body. I'll probably go do some boxing after this." That gave her an idea and after some hesitation, she voiced it. "You know, I could teach you some boxing or wrestling. Any kind of self-defence to use the next time a power-crazed former assassin, who controls the dead with help of the gods, lobs a cherry bowl at you."

Ingrid gave a croaky but heartfelt laugh. "Ye gads, I have not laughed since… well, since last time you made me laugh, I suppose." Her chuckling became a smile. Or a smirk? "And, if you would like, there is a certain type of 'wrestling' we could perform. One where you could get out some of your pent-up frustration."

Valour looked to those damaged hands. "No, we can't spar now. I might hurt you. I couldn't live with myself if I did."

"Sweet Valour, I didn't mean sparring."

Valour caught on. That had been a smirk, then. "Ha! Really? I haven't even forgiven you and you suggest we jump into bed? Also, again, what about your injured hands?"

"Well, I am to be locked up tomorrow, so if any part of you desires me, 'tis now or in fifteen years. And I am starving for you. Besides, as I said, I find that a tumble in the sheets can resolve a lot of built-up emotions," Ingrid said with a brazen expression. "When it comes to my injuries, you can tie me up to ensure I do not use my hands. I told you before, rope-play is my favourite game."

Desire was building in Valour's core, whether it made sense or not. Worries overwhelmed it, though. Was she too emotional? Would they hurt Ingrid's hands? Was this right when so much was unresolved? But gods, to go fifteen years without kissing this woman everywhere was painful.

Ingrid stood. "I know I have no right to say this but… you should trust me. At least with this one small thing." She walked to Valour, stopping where their faces were but a hair's breadth apart and their breaths mingled. "Tell me you do not want this, and I shall leave and say no more of it."

Every part of Valour roared with need now. And they had decided it was time to act more and think less. Their bond had begun with sex, too. Perhaps it could help mend it. Valour's lips parted and before she knew it, the words spilled out. "I want this."

Ingrid kissed her then, frenziedly so their teeth collided. They soon settled into the kiss, though, and did it right. With her pounding pulse making her light-headed, Valour undressed the woman she was currently feeling pretty much every emotion for.

Ingrid tried to take Valour's clothes off too but yelped at the pain in her hands.

"Careful." Valour gently gripped her arms. "Shit. We have to find a way to do this without you touching me."

"I told you," Ingrid stated, clear and simple. "There's only one way. Tie me up."

"I thought you were done giving orders?"

"Not when it's the orders we both want, treasure."

Treasure. She didn't think anyone had ever seen her as that. She couldn't stop the smile tugging at the corners of her mouth. "Fine. One last order it is."

THAT EVENING VALOUR lay sated, spent, and naked on her front with Ingrid—now untied—on top of her. They spoke of their pasts, their secrets, and the choices they had made.

While Ingrid kissed a burn scar on her back, Valour considered the fucking they had just done and how different it had been from their first time. Not only because it held so much more emotion, but because she herself had become so much more. And she wanted to grow further. Maybe even to love and trust without holding back. She wanted to give Ingrid all of her, she wanted to give Ingrid everything in the godsdamned world, and she didn't care a bloody bit if she should or not.

Ingrid stopped kissing scars and said, "You know, having given it some thought, I don't believe the blackmail and sabotaging the 'ness trade were my only reasons for being the Brandquist."

"No?"

"No. I think I also wanted to strike out at the world around me."

"Well, it can be a shitty place."

"Mm. It robbed me of my mother, picked out a life for me that I didn't want, and made my father grow up fighting those who hated him for being different. Yet, I see now that I had the incorrect approach. If the world is wrong, I should try to fix it, not strike out at it."

"Mm." Valour spun herself around, slowly so her lover slid off her gently. "Also, the world has some good things in it too." She kissed Ingrid and caressed down her slender arm until she came to where the burns at her wrist peeked out from the glove. There would be no Brandquist tattoo there anymore. Nonetheless, *someone* would still kiss it and swear loyalty and fealty. When Ingrid came out of house arrest and they had worked through their problems, Valour would place her lips to that scar and promise herself to the woman who had changed everything. And she knew Ingrid would reciprocate.

She didn't tell Ingrid that, though. They weren't at that stage yet. There were a lot more conversations to be had and getting to know each other to be done. Besides, sometimes being the silent type meant that you could wait for the perfect moment to say something. No matter how long that wait would be. Valour was learning that wonderful things were worth being patient for.

CHAPTER 63

IN IRONS IN THE BELFRY

IT WAS A week since Peter had last seen Valour, back when she'd made him speak with Master Fahlcrantz. And yet, Halcyon asked about her every time Peter came to see him in this accursed bell-tower. Today was no exception.

"I don't know how she is. I have told you before, I shan't converse with her until the eighteenth," Peter said, trying to hide his impatience. And his slight trembling.

Below the bell chamber of Vinterstock's belfry were holding cells for those awaiting hanging, flogging, or whatever other awfulness they had been sentenced to. The old stonework let in gusts of the high air and so it was as cold as it was dark. The windowless tower had scant illumination, but luckily a sconce with two tallow candles hung on the wall behind Peter, flickering with the draughts and throwing shifting shadows where he stood facing Halcyon's cell.

Seeing Halcyon behind the iron bars brought forth memories of his own imprisonment in the sanctum. On the first visit, he had fallen into one of his fits of panic, but Halcyon had helped him breathe through it. Now, only the merest palpitations and breathlessness remained. He and Halcyon had become more comfortable around each other, but a sort of distance still remained.

"Right," Halcyon said with a pained sigh. "There is yet another two weeks until you meet. Yes, of course. The days meld into one another in here."

Petrichor understood his distress. For some reason, the former leader of the assassins had been left to rot in this normally temporary hold, awaiting his punishment for much longer than anyone else. Perhaps that was an unspoken part of his punishment; someone like Halcyon loathed waiting idly.

"Both you and Valour have mentioned that." He rubbed at his forehead. "I simply cannot keep what day it is clear in my mind, often thinking it's the eighteenth already."

"Do you want it to be the eighteenth?"

"Yes," Halcyon said, immediately and with clear worry. "I want the two of you to talk, to lean on one another. You are both used to having the order tell you what to do and give you structure. Now... well, you have everyone you work with at the bookbinder's, but Valour is alone."

"Valour is never alone. Ask any female doxy or, well, *any* woman in Vinterstock."

"That is not fair. Valour makes friends with everyone, not just women she wishes to bed."

"Yet more proof that she isn't alone." Peter squirmed where he stood on the uneven flagstones, facing his Halcyon both behind bars and clapped in irons. The jailors must have feared him to feel both were needed. "Enough about Valour. How are you?"

Halcyon smiled. He had lost weight but seemed uncowed by his fate. Only when his past crimes and deceit came up did Halcyon ever look cowed.

"I am quite well, Peter. I have had an idea."

"What sort of idea?"

"You know what my punishment will be and how it limits my future."

Peter knew all too well. Weeks in the tower while awaiting a public birching, then twenty years of transportation. At least it wasn't whipping, branding, running the gauntlet, or being hung. Hanging was a common outcome in Vinterstock and Peter hadn't breathed until the judges grudgingly dismissed that option, due to Halcyon's role in stopping Pound at the eleventh hour. As well as his high-up contacts pleading his case, of course.

"I do know, yes."

"Well, they cannot stop me from thinking. Nor from passing on my ideas and my savings to you."

"Ideas and savings?"

"I have spent a lot of time thinking of you and me. About when we were children, orphans who starved and froze until the order took us in."

Halcyon thinking of him in any way warmed Peter more than a fireplace could. "I see. And what did this pondering lead to?"

"Orphanages." Halcyon neared the bars. He smelled of lavender oil and wood ash, showing that yesterday must've been the day of the week when they made prisoners scrub off so as not to spread lice. "I know you donated to an orphanage but that you, like me, fret over what the coin is being spent on and whether meagre donations will be enough for upkeep and such."

Peter inclined his head.

"Thus, we should start our own. Obviously, no one will let me do such a thing, and I cannot do it from a penal colony anyway, but you can. I can be the force behind you, teaching you what to do, advising from afar, and donating my savings."

"You need your savings where you are going."

"I cannot touch that fortune without the kammarherrar seizing it," Halcyon whispered so the overseer by the door couldn't hear. "It will come to better use in your hands. So, what say you to my idea?"

Peter considered this, taking his time. "No. It's no good. You and I would not have the merest clue who to employ as matron or what locale might be suitable."

"Right." Halcyon sagged where he stood.

Peter could not stand the sight, so hurried to voice his counter-suggestion. "We should purchase an existing one that is decrepit, as indeed they all are. I suggest the one I donated to, Mrs Mariedal's Orphanage. The matron there seems sensible enough to take our offer and caring enough to ensure the orphans are well tended."

At this, Halcyon's features shone, despite the paltry light of the candles. "Yes. With our funds pumped into the establishment, it could do more than merely limp by. It could thrive and grow, helping mayhap as many as thrice the current number of children."

"And perhaps allow the orphans to stay beyond the age of thirteen."

"Why not? Now, due to my absence, I shan't be able to have anything to do with the daily running of it. And I know you will not want to, either."

Peter winced at the thought of children. Their loudness. Their unpredictability. Their snot. Their playing with those marbles that littered every Vinterstock street lately. Good lord, what if they wanted him to play with them?

Unaware of these horrid thoughts, Halcyon spoke on. "But we do know how to organise. You are organisation personified and I, well, I ran the order for a long time." He moved his heavy manacles, scratching under the left one. "I handled the bookkeeping, the supply purchasing, and ensured that the upkeep of the building was maintained."

"And you did an excellent job of it."

"Thank you. So, I could teach you to do those things. I assess that we have a few weeks before the sea ice melts enough to allow the boats access to the penal colony. And even after that, I shall only be a letter away."

Peter ran a hand over his chin. How long would a letter take from so far abroad? It didn't matter, they could make it work. And the idea of spending these remaining weeks together, learning from Halcyon, was irresistible.

"That is," Halcyon said, "if you will have time to work on the improvement on this Mrs Mariedal's Orphanage outside of your bookbinding work?"

He considered his long evenings and early mornings of boredom. "Certainly."

Halcyon's features eased. "Can you imagine how different our childhoods could have been if we had lived in a well-heated orphanage with kind staff, toys, and plenty of food?"

"Without scraping by on the streets? Or killing for the order? No. I cannot imagine it."

"Well, you will see it reflected in the next generation of Vinterstock children. If you decide to accede to my idea?"

There was not a morsel of hesitation in him. "I do."

Halcyon stretched his hands through the bars, stopping when the manacles got in the way. Peter's hands closed the rest of the distance. He watched their clasped hands. So different in their colouring, fawn skin against the palest cream, but so alike in their protruding veins, callouses, and scars. They were nigh the same size too; he'd never noticed that. Peter wondered if he should pull away now, but recalled what Valour had said about unclasping his heart, and so braved rubbing his thumbs against the backs of Halcyon's hands. Just the once.

"Then we have an accord," Halcyon said, seizing Peter's attention. "I shall tell you where I have hidden my savings. Please contact the owner of the orphanage as soon as you can."

"I will do so as soon as I leave here. And return to you with the answer right away, so you can start instructing me immediately if we get a yes."

"Excellent." Halcyon tightened his grip, his strong fingers rough but welcome against Peter's skin, as the tower bells tolled the hour, far too loud and so close above them.

Peter wondered if he might find a bookbinder to apprentice in whatever country Halcyon would be exiled to. Perhaps it would be a land with sun, one where anyone could start anew.

When the bells quieted, Halcyon croaked, "Yes, excellent indeed. I am overjoyed to be using my life and my skills to bring about something good." He kept his gaze on their entwined hands. "I know I can never make up for the evil I have done and the evil I let flourish by averting my eyes to it. Forgiveness is out of my reach, as the priest who visits the convicts said this morning." Halcyon leaned his forehead against the bars, then lifted his face to Peter's again. "Nevertheless, as I have so many times told Valour, all we can do in this life is try to make sure our good deeds outweigh our bad ones. Do you think that's true?"

Thrilled to be asked his opinion, as if his hero was his equal, Peter said yes. He felt his face draw into a scowl. "Those Christian priests. They speak so much about good and evil, about penitence and forgiveness, heaven and hell. Things are not so black and white. If the

445

events my eyes and ears have witnessed were real, the old gods exist. And they often commit what you call evil, or allow evil to exist, but many still worship them." Peter allowed himself the indulgence of caressing those well-used hands with his thumbs one more time. "No one is morally unblemished. No one lives without making mistakes and causing hurt. It does not make you evil or only forgivable if you do what the church, or the synagogue, or the Norse shrines, or the sanctum of Axsten, or any other house of priesthood wants."

Halcyon hummed. "Perhaps all we can do is learn from it and try to be better."

"And endure our punishments," Peter said, before considering the horror of the topic.

"Indeed." Halcyon furrowed his brow. "May I prevail upon your compassion for one more thing? Will you be there when they birch me? I do not wish to face it alone."

"It's a public punishment. Most of Vinterstock will be there to jeer. Valour will no doubt be there to throw rotten turnips at the Master of Flagellation. Considering her good aim, she will hopefully knock him out."

"You know that was not what I was asking."

Halcyon's voice was a broken whisper and Peter could not meet his eye. How could he watch the rod strike against that precious back? How could he hear the cries and grunts of pain from the only person he had ever looked up to? Ever... loved.

He lifted his gaze to Halcyon's. "I will stand where you can see me. Through every blow."

"Thank you, Peter. Pain bothers me little as long as I am not alone."

"Then pain is not a problem, as you will always have me."

This time it was Halcyon who squeezed Peter's hands, and it felt like an embrace.

EPILOGUE

THE EIGHTEENTH

HE STARTLED WHEN Valour snapped her fingers in front of his face. "Are you listening to me, Petrichor?" She held her hands up in apology. "Sorry, *Peter*. I promise I'll get used to calling you that at some point."

Peter had only vaguely heard her ramblings. He was busy marvelling at the absurd idea of the two of them sitting in a coffee-house, sipping hot drinks while politely discussing the weather.

"I fear I wasn't quite listening, no. You were saying something about the temperature?"

"I said that it's been a weirdly warm and snowless set of weeks since I last saw you. If the year carries on like this, it'll be hotter than a fevered horse's arse come summer."

He shuddered at her imagery, wondering why it had to be an equine anus in particular. "That is possible. At least fewer people will freeze to death this year."

"True."

Valour drummed her fingers against her cup.

He sat still, searching for a topic. "Happy birthday."

"Thanks. Ingrid ordered me a godsdamned plumed hat."

"A practical gift. Covering one's head contains the heat in the body."

"Um, well, she meant it as a joke. But sure, that too."

"Ah. I see."

Silence hung around their table like fog. Well, except for Valour's incessant tapping against the cup. Peter blew on his coffee to take his mind off her vexing behaviour. The cup was overfilled and a little spilled on his sleeve. Panic crept in, but he fended it off with deep breaths and the technique he'd recently discovered: focusing on a practical solution and not how he was feeling. The stain was a problem. He couldn't get rid of the stain, and wiping at it would make it worse. Fine, then get rid of the whole sleeve. He took the justacorps off, folded it and put it out of sight. It was too tight anyway and these days he could simply purchase a new one. His breaths were calm and strong. Strength didn't lie in removing any weakness from one's character. It lay in looking weakness in the eye and figuring out ways to lessen it and handle it, while still living with it. Weakness was as natural as breathing.

Valour didn't comment on him ripping his justacorps off and neatly folding it, only to then tuck the mist-grey bundle under his chair. She just cleared her throat and said, "I, um, see you had your hair cut."

"Yes."

"And grew sideburns."

"Indeed."

She grimaced ever so slightly but said nothing about his choices. Instead, she tapped her teacup louder and glanced back and forth from his face to the door.

"So," she said on an outbreath, "um, are your eyes bad enough that you need those spectacles all the time now, then?"

What sort of witless question was that? He pushed them further up his nose. "No. I wear these to soothe my twisted ankle."

Valour threw her hands out to her sides. "And there it is. Rudeness and sarcasm. You can't help yourself, can you?"

"It was meant as a jest, Valour." It had been, too. Well, mainly.

"All right."

"Is that a scratch on your cheek?"

"Hm? Probably. I climbed a tree before coming here." She grinned. "I never got to do that just for fun when I was little, so I'm making up for it now. It was great!"

"I see." He didn't. "Well, to each their own."

A broadsheet lay on the table next to them and Peter picked it up. Names he knew very well stood out to him. Encumbrance. Mire.

He had confronted them, and the other crueller order members, about a week ago. He had finally vented his spleen at them, telling them how they made him suffer as a child and how he cursed them to never again know a moment of peace. And yes, there had been a couple who had responded with violence. And yes, they were repaid punch for punch and bruise for bruise. And yes, naturally he ensured they left his face unblemished. Peter Kårh would never go to his bookbindery with a blackened eye.

He pointed to the article. "Have you seen what they are saying about our fellow ex-order members?"

Valour squeezed a wedge of lemon into her tea. "That the old shit-weasels volunteered to go to war or turned criminal? Oh, yes. Didn't I tell you that assassins don't lend themselves to other jobs?"

"*They* did not suit other professions. Because all they know is death, obeying orders, and cruelty."

He considered the praise he'd started getting for his bookbinding, the comelier rooms he had moved into, and the contentment he had in both of these new environments. As shocked as he had been to realise it, he was living proof that there were good outcomes in this world. Even for assassins.

She shrugged while stirring her tea. "No matter why they got to where they did, they've earned their misery. I don't fret about them. They don't deserve my time."

Peter laid aside the broadsheet. "Halcyon says that none of them have visited. Only you and I come to see him."

She grinned. "I hear you're there every time they allow visitors. Usually staying until you're thrown out."

"I visit when work allows. I need breaks to stretch my legs and rest my eyes anyway." He thought of the orphanage, which had of course been thrilled for the riksdaler and aid from two benefactors. "As of the last fortnight, he and I are also entering into a sort of partnership."

Valour's vexing grin grew. "Of course you are."

"Pray tell, is there anything awry with that? Or with me visiting Halcyon frequently?" He sat forward. "Are you perhaps guilt-stricken since you do not visit him often enough?"

She bristled. "Some of us are making and maintaining new friendships and have a romantic partner to speak to, even if it is through a door. Not to mention planning a whole godsdamned…" She mouthed the word "revolution", then carried on speaking at her usual loud volume. "Besides, it hurts to see him there, locked up for far too long and awaiting the birching. Yet I'd say I visit Halcyon the natural amount."

"Oh, so you decide what is the natural amount of visiting? Pray, excuse me, I was unaware that you were the overseer of social interactions."

"Hey, I think it's great that you're not alone anymore," she said, sounding exasperated. "I simply wanted to see if you could admit how much he means to you and that you actually have a heart in that stony chest of yours." She dragged a hand through her hair, making some of it pull out of the braid. "Hel's realm, what will it take to make you stop bloody sneering at me?"

He may have been sneering, but she was intentionally pushing on his sore spots. "It's Helheim."

"Huh?"

"You use that curse often, but not correctly. The Norse realm of death for those who do not go to Valhalla is ruled by Hel, yes. However, it has a name. Helheim. I thought it was about time that someone did you the favour of telling you."

He shouldn't have to say out loud how much Halcyon meant to him; it was obvious to anyone who wasn't a halfwit. He shook off the vile feeling of having his chest opened, revealing naked, raw emotions to her.

She opened her mouth. Then closed it with a snap. She brought her cup up to her lips and took a long and overly loud slurp. The revolting sound went through Peter like metal carving into his bones.

"Uncivilised churl," he said, going back to the broadsheet despite having read it all.

After a while he couldn't keep pretending to read the same lines and Valour had slurped up every drop of tea.

The silence no longer hung like fog but covered them like a suffocating blanket.

She put her empty cup down and began tapping it again.

He checked his coffee. Still too hot to drink.

Her fingers tapped faster.

He squirmed in his seat.

Their gazes met, then broke apart.

He sat back and sighed. "We do not actually work as friends, do we?"

"Shit no."

"Then what do we do? Never see each other again?"

"Of course not, bonehead," Valour said, pouring herself more tea. "I'll see you here on the eighteenth of each month. Then we can sit scowling at one another while making sure that the other one is all right?"

"Yes. I suppose I can live with that."

He knew it would be more than that. He would aid her group that discussed reform and rebellion. He'd do so not only because it was a worthy cause, but because Valour might have use of his assistance. And if he told her about the orphanage, he knew she would do everything to help. Moreover, there were the books. Halcyon had informed him that Valour had, covertly, bought the first set of books he bound for Fahlcrantz and Åberg's.

That was all reason enough for him to brave asking what he needed to. "Before I finish my coffee and leave, I must ask you something. If I don't, I'll change my mind and never bring it up."

She made a face. "Please don't make me explain how babies are made."

"You are an infuriating, dim-witted sheep."

She toasted him with her teacup. "I'll take that as a compliment considering the rumour that you like being fucked by sheep. Ask your question."

For the briefest instant he worried there was such a rumour, then refocused. "When I was locked in that cell as a child, you brought me a book one day."

"Correction, I threw a book at you. And as far as I remember, it bloody well hit you like a bull's-eye. Despite it still being dark out. Impressive, huh?"

"Never mind that. Why did you give me a book?"

"Pity." She squeezed more lemon into her tea. "And wanting you to shut up."

"I see. Additionally, you choosing that particular volume interests me." He paused, thinking about the book and what it had planted in him. His dream. His path. His salvation. His future. "It came to change my life, since it was a guide to bookbinding. Why did you select it?"

Her face was blank. "It was small enough to go through the hatch but thick enough to hurt if I chucked it at you. Child logic. I actually think I found it while shooting my slingshot at stuff on a garbage heap on the outskirts of town."

He couldn't help it; he broke out in laughter. Soon she did too.

"I really cannot stand you," he said as his laughter waned.

She wiped away tears of mirth. "I know the feeling, you condescending pus-sack."

Peter raised his cup. "Again, happy birthday."

"And a happy new start to us both," she replied, toasting him as well.

He took the first sip of his surprisingly palatable coffee, watching the woman seated in front of him embarrassing them both by pleading with the staff to start selling cardamom buns. He was looking forward to not having to see her for a while. Happy to care for this... this what? He would never use the word 'sister', but he couldn't think of a more fitting one. Either way, he was happy to care for Valour from a *vast and safe distance*. They might despise each other, but they would never be wholly alone again. Even better news was that their destinies were finally their own to choose.

Gods permitting.

ACKNOWLEDGMENTS

I first have to thank everyone at Solaris Books for their commitment to *Snowblooded*. Especially the incredible Amy Borsuk who dove headfirst into this story and improved it as she swam around pointing out its depths and its shallows.

But Amy and Solaris wouldn't have seen *Snowblooded* if it wasn't for my truly lovely agent Saint Gibson, who in turn couldn't have fallen in love with it unless the story had been critiqued by the great: Aisling Wright, Carol Hutchinson, Lisa Topping, Miira Ikiviita, Penny Young, and Zohra Nabi. Also, many thanks to everyone on Patreon for their support. Finally, thanks go to my friends and family back in Sweden who don't mind that I often disappear into my books.

FIND US ONLINE!

www.rebellionpublishing.com

/solarisbooks /solarisbks /solarisbooks

SIGN UP TO OUR NEWSLETTER!

rebellionpublishing.com/newsletter

YOUR REVIEWS MATTER!

Enjoy this book? Got something to say?

Leave a review on Amazon, GoodReads or with your favourite bookseller and let the world know!